ODD GEMS

SOAKED.

Written by
SURI R. MOON

ODD GEMS – Soaked © Copyright 2020 A. Robinson

Thanks!

Special thanks to my son, you are a real rock. Thank you to my family and friends for the support, and encouragement.

-Suri

Prologue

No one ever knew why they were the way they were. Their questions eventually faded away over time, as they were convinced that they would never get the answers. They were natural human beings born into the second realm of existence, but for a short time.

The beings of Giphtem, the first realm, dwelled parallel to the second realm. Both Giphtem and the second realm, where natural humans lived, were obliged to follow the rules for interactions between the two parallels.

There were only a few gems spread throughout the earth who had seen real glimpses into Giphtem. Nevertheless, it was common for each human to encounter the first realm for themselves -at least once in their lifetime.

However, it had always been in some milder manner than the gems had ever experienced. And sadly, that common sense is not nearly as normal as it was before.

The original "gems" were those who had been attached to a task for the sake of the greater good. Sometimes they just conveyed messages to a person in power, or for the masses, depending on what was required of them. Sometimes, the task was just to show up and be seen.

The ability to receive such guidance was given to them by Giphtem, and no other way. In legend, a human who was willfully adjoined to the first realm by unconventional means became known as a "false gem."

Equally, when the human was unwilling to partake and was forced to do so, then they were called a "blameless gem." But when the unwilling human's own DNA mutations factored alongside the process itself and created physical changes within them, they were called "odd gems."

These odd gems would be considered cursed by the people of the land, and the offenders who created them could never tame them. All the same, the odd gems were too powerful for the second realm. Yet, they were too human to reside in the first.

Over time, the rulers of the earth had found that it was better to kill anyone they believed to be an odd gem than to sacrifice the safety of the people. Yet, in Giphtem they couldn't allow a living human to physically enter, not even for safety.

So, the odd gems learned how to remain living on the earth humbly, and how to keep their abilities a secret. They made certain rules of their own, careful to align themselves with the presence of both realms.

No true gem ever wished to be one. It was not desired because the burden was too heavy for most. Ultimately, the yearning to be one was the difference between a true gem and a false gem.

False gems were constantly obsessed with gaining the benefits of the first realm before their time, through eccentric practices. Only in death was an earthly inhabitant naturally designed to enter the first realm. If they did enter before their time, it would undoubtedly cause a world of confusion and corruption.

In modern times, technology had broken through many of the boundaries originally outlined by Giphtem. One man's own neuroscience research procedure crossed humans over into the realm that they were neither permitted to enter nor manipulate.

Dr. Leroi Maquiller's procedure was to strip a human's memory, program a new memory set, then upload it to their brain. To help secure a prospect's participation, he had them convinced that he would remove the thing they wished to forget while adding some attribute they wished to possess. He was giving each subject a new life, in a false sense.

Advantageously, Leroi Maquiller and his content writers were sure to include some of their own superfluous agendas to the subject's program coding. In many ways, they had rewritten the life of their unsuspecting subject.

This caused those people to commit acts that they would have never thought up on their own. They did his bidding. The first realm didn't respond with any messages other than seemingly freak accidents, and other disciplinary efforts that denied access to false gems trying to enter Giphtem.

Every subject whose memory was erased via Maquiller's method subsequently became able to see the two parallel realms, simultaneously. Granted, many of the false gems went crazy, unable to distinguish realities between the two realms. Some gems died while attempting to complete one of Maquiller's riskier preprogrammed tasks.

All subjects, true and false gems alike, could see signs in the sky. But no one subject ever noticed them all. Sometimes, the blameless gems and the odd gems saw signs that they couldn't understand, at first. But it always clicked, eventually.

For false gems, they could never translate the signs they saw. They would only be drawn into a state of confusion and chaos because the messages were simply not for them.

Those subjects who had been willing participants in Maquiller's research ultimately died never knowing the depths of the help that came through the signs from the first realm. The dwellers of Giphtem were sorrowful during those times because the beings in the first realm were just as powerless to the rules they had created as any other being, near or far. They were not willing to sustain contact with any false gem.

Nevertheless, when a new generation of odd gems eventually came about, the beings of the first realm were elated. They were glad that they could communicate with them, and they would later use them to right the wrongdoings. It was then that the gentle and uncanny realm of Giphtem decided that it was time to recompense Maquiller and Co.

While Maquiller himself was just a neuroscientist trying to get some recognition and fortune, his corrupt scientific practice had become the catalyst for fatal errors concerning life, death, and perception. Through all of the constant tampering, memory setting, clever substances, extortion, and murder, Leroi Maquiller found his wish for success.

Conversely, Leroi Maquiller had made a grave mistake from many angles. His obsession with power and money caused him to inadvertently make the two realms collide. As the earth gradually became lost in its course, he became even further indebted to Giphtem.

In 1998, Maquiller programmed thirteen small children who were in no wise willing subjects in his research. He'd unintentionally created a monstrous weapon against himself in the process that would later prove to be fatally detrimental.

Maquiller was the man behind a string of kidnappings in 1998. Through effective programming, the missing still didn't know who they were twenty years later. They'd been gone for two decades, and they hadn't a clue.

The neurologist's imperfect scientific procedure caused eight of the thirteen children whom he nicknamed, "grandies," to adopt superhuman abilities. But all thirteen children, each of whom was programmed at age four or five, were innocent and altered against their will.

Nonetheless, the formidable eight had involuntarily been made the newest generation of odd gems. They had been kept living under Leroi Maquiller, who had assumed guardianship of all thirteen grandies.

A haze was frequently in their thoughts, and sometimes they had seemed to lack self-control. It was because of the overshadowing internal program content. Just about every subject who completed the process was preprogrammed to instinctively handle Maquiller's dirty work encompassing politics and pleasures, bit by bit.

As for the dirty work, there was much of it to be done. Trying to balance their own moral compass amid their sporadic incoherent crime sprees, they had found it difficult to maintain any level of normalcy.

One day, the superhuman grandies, formed the Cr8. They all agreed it was a silly name. But they liked it because there were eight of them, and it reminded them of the many records Maquiller had once hoarded.

There were at least fifty crates of vinyl records in Maquiller's home, where they grew up. They mostly used them to *play deejay*, scratching the albums up in the name of artwork. They desperately wanted to have *a normal childhood* like other kids, but it just wasn't possible. So, they were constantly fueled by their imaginations, and they were able to find their childhood in those very imaginative moments.

On the first day of summer in 2008, when the Cr8 members were in their mid-teens, the eight of them had been led to gather in a daffodil field. The Cr8 grandies had all become bewildered by an unusual development in the sky.

As the day went on, they all testified that something bizarre was happening to them, and only them. They complained about seeing weird shadows and hearing strange noises.

As they all gradually gathered together in curiosity, they learned that they were all witnessing the same disturbingly huge flock of black birds in the sky that day. The birds created strange, elaborate patterns as they flew together in design.

While the ones who were present waited for everyone else to arrive, the birds continued the air show which only the Cr8 had perceived. Although they were able to see many signs, the other grandies couldn't sense it one bit. Even Maquiller himself had wondered over the eight teenagers, who had been staring at the sky for several hours.

They wouldn't speak about it with anyone outside of their circle. In fact, the Cr8 could never discuss those things without sounding mentally ill to the people around them. So, the youths had learned to keep the alternate world they sometimes lived in a secret amongst themselves.

Because of their secrecy, no one else witnessed what the extraordinary grandies were consumed with as they lay in the field that day. Preoccupied, they were unable to look away from the flock of black birds which had progressively become dense enough to block their view of the sun. That afternoon, the sky had become darkened –in their eyes.

One by one, they showed up. Upon arriving, each teen took a seat in the field with the ones who were already there.

At first, the oldest grandie Fowley Court had been lying with his back to the ground in the field of daffodils that was part of Maquiller's property. He'd been hiding out there by himself, knowing he felt strongly compelled to observe the birds.

His gleaming silver eyes were on the sky, and it consumed all of his attention. In fact, they had all watched the dimensions of the flock grow, massively. It really didn't matter where the grandies of the Cr8 were because the huge flock demanded their single-mindedness from wherever they stood.

Kai showed up at the field not too long after Fowley, then TJ. The three of them sat in amusement, ogling at the black birds they had already been studying since the afternoon before. Thereafter, each of the Cr8 members arrived, alone.

By the time all eight of them arrived under the deeply dusky sky at high noon, there was no time for any further speculation. The last thing any of them saw that day was the surreal flock of black birds covering the sun.

There was no physical opportunity to look further into what could cause such a phenomenon. Right where they stood, the ground was abruptly removed from beneath them, opening up a large sinkhole that instantly swallowed them all.

Upon awakening, none of them remembered the sinkhole. Their memory of any kind of first realm activity was nonexistent. This was their first *calibration*.

The calibration was a sporadic reset that commenced a whole new *decatoure*. A decatoure is a time period of exactly ten years spent in the duality of the two parallel realms. To start off the Cr8's first of three calibrations, was a big black sinkhole.

The day after the sinkhole was a very hazy one for everybody on the estate. The Cr8 had awakened in their own beds at home.

They knew that something had shifted, but didn't know what. They couldn't detect any physically tangible difference, but they all felt, "changed."

Then, just an hour later, a couple of the other five blameless grandies discovered a devastating count of dead black birds all around the property. The dead birds were numerous, and they thoroughly covered most of the ground around Maquiller's living headquarters. It was like a great plague of sorts, and it was eerie.

They had come running back into the house, screaming bloody murder. Obviously shaken to their nerves, they drew everyone's attention to the horrid sight just beyond the front door.

Supernaturally, the Cr8 had perceived that it was for them, but that was the new extent of their knowledge regarding the first realm, and black birds. They had to re-learn those otherworldly things after going through a calibration.

Post-calibration effects scared them all, and it seemed to drive Maquiller mad. Soon after, he had begun to feel like something was wrong with the Cr8, while the group of teens began to wonder about the man whom they called their guardian.

The calibration of an odd gem was, and still is, a life event that Maquiller had no control over when it came to the grandies. He couldn't interfere with whatever messages Giphtem had for the blameless gems, to their benefit.

Slowly, the grandies began to learn about their superhuman abilities, all over again. They all were destined to possess multiple powers in each ten-year cycle between calibrations.

Interestingly, each grandie had only one gift which they could actually master in each decatoure, and they were lucky if they found out what gift that was. Finding out which one was their own true superpower early on in a decatoure would give a gem a great advantage. Nonetheless, they would easily exercise different skills along the way.

Even though they wouldn't remember any of their first-realm encounters from before, the skillsets within each odd gem's power would become intensified every time a calibration occurred. They were strengthened.

Whenever there was a calibration happening, no turn of events could hinder what was meant to be. Nothing could stop it from happening, and no one could mess it up. Calibrations required a certain level of perfection that no one would ever achieve by trying.

The challenge for them was learning their own skill sets. Sometimes, it was tough for an odd gem to acknowledge that they even had superpowers at all -for that matter. Getting used to possessing such gifts was difficult because they were also forced to keep it a secret from the world, and all of the juggling therein was a burden.

It seemed as though none of them were ever truly comfortable with having the powers they harbored. Getting comfortable was difficult to do while having no memory of the first-realm events from the previous decatourial cycle to build on.

It was always a thorn in the side for all of them. One day, in the future, they would know the truth. They may finally understand why they were so different from everyone else.

While the calibration altered their memories, it had also been protecting them from Maquiller's outrageous programming timelines. Calibrations improved their strengths, yet also weakened Maquiller's influence.

The oppositional angles of the two realms created conflicting emotions, and sometimes actions. Regardless, they were all gradually becoming more mentally independent from his guardianship as time went on.

The first calibration in 2008 made Maquiller enraged. He'd noticed that the eight hyperactive teens were not completing all of their preprogrammed tasks, like the other five.

He also knew that it all had started on that day of the black birds. He'd figured that they all were spitefully keeping a secret from him, considering their nonchalant ignorance whenever he'd ask them about what they were gazing at that day. In reality, they simply couldn't remember.

He was especially angry about not having the power to interfere with the obvious disruption, which he'd concluded was a programming glitch. He also was very reluctant to take the highly unfavorable medical risks involved with programming a subject with hyperactive tendencies, multiple times.

The Cr8 were his most prized subjects, and Maquiller would go to war to retain them all. He loved them like his very own children, in his mind. But he didn't understand that the war had already been waged against him for his deeds, and they were going to use his *prizes* to win it.

One day, they decided that they were ready to learn what life would be like without Leroi Maquiller. All they ever did was help their neurotic "adoptive father" run his corrupt, soul-consuming, family practice. They wanted out.

They'd become progressively accepting toward the signs sent to them from the first realm all over again. Their relationship with the "other world" was obsessive and vital. Sometimes, the other world made more sense to them than their own, paradoxically.

Whether they wanted to or not, they were destined to one day comprehend the contrasting gravitational pull between the technology that programmed much of their character, and the uncanny parallel realm that exposed an entirely different truth. They would be odd, but they would still be gems. Maybe, they were always meant to be that way.

*******End of Prologue*******

ODD GEMS Soaked by Suri R. Moon

Chapter 1

Strange Lights in Dark Places

An injured and mentally exhausted woman sat inside of the twenty-four-hour diner somewhere around 10:30 p.m. on Wednesday, June 20th. She watched out of the window, hoping to permanently escape her trackers who had yet to give her any opportunity to rest from the woes of the day.

Although she hoped that they were all stalled somewhere in the town, she anticipated their arrival at any given time. She had been in an ongoing pursuit for at least eight hours, dragging herself from place to place to elude those who were sent after her.

Inside the diner, Pearl occupied a booth. She was aching, and she could barely endure the stinging caused by the forty-plus cuts she suffered all over her body. She was also aggrieved by the extreme side effects of a mind-blowing experiment gone wrong.

What she originally was searching for when she left home that morning wasn't half as sinister as what she had found that day. It quickly, and ironically, become the most unforgettable day of her life. Pearl Lerell wasn't dead, but her life had definitely been taken.

Yet, she possessed an inconceivable capacity for knowledge, except knowing who she really was before that day. After the experimental procedure performed on her that morning, she was subsequently coerced into bonding with an entirely different world that was blatantly parallel to her own forgotten existence.

She pulled out her file that she had grabbed from the Center on her way out, finally getting the chance to read it. She looked up at one of the TVs that were hanging on the diner walls.

The date in the lower-right corner of the screen was June 20, 2018. The news was airing live traffic-cam footage, as the reporter recapped the story on traffic congestion and how much it had changed in Seattle over the past twenty years.

Pearl looked around the diner. There were only a few other patrons and a small staff. The waitress walked up behind Pearl and approached her booth, stopping to refill her coffee. Pearl became startled and jumped in her seat.

"Oh, I'm sorry. Thank you very much," she said. Embarrassed, Pearl just nodded her head as she let the waitress pour.

"Are you sure you're okay, sweetie?" she asked Pearl for the second time. The waitress's enormous rose tattoo peaked near the top of her chest. The name, Mala, was inked inside of a waving banner that encompassed a rose and stem.

The first time the waitress had asked, Pearl just gave her a blank stare and she came off as bothered. She hadn't meant to, but her mind was everywhere all at once. However, the second time she asked, Pearl realized the waitress was genuine, and truly clueless regarding the world outside of the diner that day.

"No, I. I'm," Pearl stammered as she didn't know what she was trying to say. "I will be okay, I'm just having a very rough day," she explained.

"I can tell," the waitress concurred with one of her eyebrows raised as she spoke. "Let me know if you need anything else, okay?" she added. Pearl felt welcomed by her even though Pearl looked like she couldn't even afford the cup of coffee she was holding.

Pearl accidentally let out a sudden giggle, and the waitress began to wonder what was so funny. It was nothing really. Pearl was mixed up emotionally and capable of awkward outbursts.

"What is it?" the waitress asked, searching herself for wardrobe malfunctions or stains. Pearl noticed that

Mala was her name, as the name tag confirmed. So, Mala's name was displayed across her chest twice, and a comically unstable Pearl found it entertaining.

She had needed something, obviously anything, to help her cope with the hysteria of her own world. At that point, she was willing to settle for the simple irony in the redundancy. It made Pearl wish she would be so lucky to have a tattoo, to remind her of her own name.

Pearl shook her head and dissolved the thought, saying, "Please don't mind me. Everything has been ironic today. I promise you that I am just in my own world," she replied. Feeling bad about what she had started, she told her,

"I was just thinking about something else," she expounded as she shook her head and fanned the air with her hand to ward off any further inquiry.

"You're sure?" Mala asked then leaned in a little closer to Pearl's face, "I don't have lipstick on my teeth, do I?"

"No, not at all. Trust me, you are way more intact than you're thinking," Pearl assured the waitress who struggled with her glossy fire-engine red lipstick. Pearl herself was covered in filth and cuts, and she was hurting all over. She meant every humble word of it.

"Oh, all right," Mala laughed loudly. "I just had to make sure, 'cause you never know. And, your food will be right up shortly," she added. With a slight and sympathetic smile, she walked away to tend to the other tables.

But then again, on the backside of her uniform, there was an obvious stain. A red substance that one could only hope was ketchup had soaked in right where the thigh meets the buttock.

Pearl realized that the awkward conversations weren't over. She raised up her arm too high and provoked a sharp shoulder hurt. Painfully reminded of her fall earlier that afternoon, she held it up halfway and waved her hand at Mala.

"Excuse me," she called out for Mala's attention. Once they made eye contact, Mala nodded once at Pearl,

"I'll be right back in a minute," she said as she held up her index finger. She walked into the kitchen area too hastily for Pearl to stop her. Then Pearl really laughed, at least as hard as her pain would let her.

She knew she wouldn't get back on her right ankle unless it was totally necessary. She had turned it that afternoon when she landed oddly after jumping out of a moving car and landing in some blackberry bushes. She wasn't going to chase Mala down. She glanced down at the folder she was holding under the booth table.

She turned her arm around to see the back side of it, where she had found the last blackberry thorn. As she suspected, there was yet another. She'd been pulling thorns out of her skin all day, and she was tired of it. She was just plain tired.

Pearl pulled her hand from under the table, her bruised knuckles still clenching the manila folder. Her natural reaction was to hide the file from all eyes.

The waitress wouldn't have known what she was looking at had she caught a glimpse of the medical file, anyway. Still, Pearl was severely on edge and overprotective about the documents. In her given position, she couldn't afford to make attempts to answer any questions for anyone.

She studied the first page with diligence. Vital statistics such as her blood pressure and heart rate along with basic information like her name, height, weight, and race were listed on the form. The "program completion date," was recorded as "Wednesday, 6/20/2018" and the time was stamped, "10:10 a.m." There was also a subject number, sixteen.

The subject number was a number that had been assigned early on in the study procedure to each participant. On June 20th, Pearl was made the sixteenth subject, year-to-date. From what she could remember, she just woke up in the Center with a killer headache followed by a seizure.

She looked around the diner and out of the windows for any followers. When she looked around, there was nothing that concerned her for that moment. Then, she thought about the oceanic development in the sky.

Even though the sky wasn't visible to her right then, goosebumps still raised up on her arms and legs just from thinking of it. Outside the diner in the town of Opal Firs, the law of gravity was being defied. Pearl shuddered, then shook it off.

She noticed a well-matured man with sparkling gray hair. He was sitting at a table alone, and he wore a navy-blue sweater with tan slacks.

His face was shaven, and the expression emitting from him was an assertive one. His aura poured out confidence as he engaged with a chessboard on the table in front of him.

Pearl studied him for a short mesmerizing segment. She watched him make quick and decisive moves for both sets of pieces on the chessboard. After securing a checkmate in less than a minute, the man instantaneously began to return the pieces to their default positions.

Pearl was momentarily drawn in by it. She didn't know why, she just was. She looked away from the man to check out of the window again, like she had been doing every thirty seconds or so since her arrival. The lot was still mostly empty.

Pearl flipped the page over to find notes from the clinical observation. The *observer* was a medical assistant, nurse, or doctor who monitored the subject's post-procedure behavior and recorded everything they witnessed. If a subject responded well, they then would be released to go back out into the world.

Of course, they didn't leave the Center as the same person they were when they arrived. No one ever did. Some subjects had been programmed to keep their same name, address, family, friends, hobbies, job, etc. But in no way were they the exact same person.

Contrarily, if any subject tested ill or with negative side effects during the post-procedure-treatment window their fate became very grim -and really fast. The sensitivity of the "Hippo Project," as it was titled on the first page, had limited the amount of available information for the public eye.

The participants blindly agreed to the terms. Circa 2008, they signed the waivers out of desperation for the small monetary gain to ease their financial hardships. The Center's sleazy recruiters had made sure that they were choosing the most vulnerable people they could approach.

They were chosen carefully because the candidate's life would be in jeopardy the minute they declined the offer. While there had been a couple of fatal incidents involving the silencing of a candidate, the preplanning that was done by the recruiters played a large part in keeping that number very low.

In addition to money, the subjects also received *enhancements* to their lifestyles. It was a dream that sold itself to those candidates. However, in Pearl's case, the participant never volunteered.

Regardless, confidentiality and completion were both encouraged and enforced -in every case. Whether coerced or guided, completion was and always will be the Maquiller Research Center's end goal.

Pearl read her name out loud, "Pearl Lerell." She stared at her name with a sour face. She didn't like it, but only because she knew it wasn't her real one. Nonetheless, she feared that it might be the only name she could reference.

From what she gathered from the file, it looked as if the Hippo Project authorities had special travel arrangements in process for a private investigator named Pearl Lerell. She read it with disbelief as she flipped through the rest of the pages to get a brief summary of her review. The confusion it kindled was heavy to bear.

The Hippo Project didn't just affect the subject's memory and life, it had also aimed to master the re-creation of both in that same subject. Pearl was problematic as a subject, or "sub," as the medical staff had commonly called them. She was not programmable.

She also was fully aware of her memory loss. Ironically, Pearl knew she had forgotten something, but just couldn't recall exactly what was lost.

It was torturous for her to try to sort it out alone, but she intuitively felt that she should avoid the authorities as well. It was a wise thing to do, in the meantime.

She had also retained the ability to form new memories. Yet, the Project required that the subject be coded with new memories that were predestined and outlined by the Hippo Project's content writer. That was not possible for subject sixteen.

Not only was she still forming new memories of her own, but she was also absorbing data like a sponge. Plus, she exhibited great retention of the details.

She glanced out the window to check for trouble. She saw that she was still in the clear, for the time being. She sipped the hot coffee as she turned her attention to the news again.

She looked up at the TV, and the news anchorman was reporting a five-day weather forecast. She figured that at least one news station would have heard about her fleeing the Research Center earlier that day. Considering the few cops she had scoped around the Center as she snuck away, she was surprised that she had yet to hear any reporting on it.

"Great, more rain," she spoke bitterly under her breath and rolled her eyes away from the TV. She looked around the restaurant, and as she glossed the diner over her eye caught two men outside.

It was the security agency she had been avoiding. The two men appeared to be in-house officers from the Research Center.

They were looking around the premises outside, still hunting for her. Just when she'd thought she would've had a little while to breathe, Pearl had quickly become overwhelmed by those who had been chasing somewhere behind her all the while.

Repeatedly, she had been eluding the pursuers. She quickly learned how to navigate her surroundings in the town of Opal Firs after learning that the security team from the Center had been ordered to retrieve her, dead or alive.

Hence, there they were in the diner parking lot, relentless at work. Again, she was hurriedly forced to travel a new, unfamiliar path for which she had yet to see a map. She could only run into the woods.

"Why won't they leave me alone?" she asked herself, shaking her head. Luckily, she saw them before they saw her. She rolled the manila folder back up with her hands.

She put the file back into her trampled black leather backpack, zipped it up, and dashed out. She fled out of the side entrance of the restaurant and into the woods before she ever got the chance to eat her food or pay for the coffee.

****

Pearl snapped somewhere around 4:00 a.m. In the deeply grim dusk, she dropped to her knees. She cried in her defeat on the damp forest floor. She was lost, alone, and terrified.

After the batteries in her flashlight had died, Pearl began to panic. Nothing could calm her, and no one could help her. She was in a dark place, which she could never describe with dialogue.

It was at that time in the woods when she learned exactly how scary the dark could be. The pitch-black carried with it a slight humidity that shifted her inhalation, creating shorter breaths.

There was a faint, but continual siren-like buzz that was resonating in her ears. The darkness of her surroundings, and the fear of being alone in it, caused a consuming nyctophobic episode. Still, she blindly navigated the blackest parts of the woods that were created by sporadic patches where the tree count was extremely dense.

She cried out for about fifteen minutes, wailing from the top of her lungs as if she were suffering from ailing pains. She had an ugly breakdown, as she couldn't get a grip on herself.

She lost her voice and thousands of tears. She was just about to lose hope when she noticed that the siren-like buzzing sound had become louder while she wept in the dark. Yet, while it was still dark, she perceived a light increasingly shining behind her.

She started to tremble when she imagined turning around and seeing the guards or the police. But that idea abruptly vanished when a single, brightly lit butterfly that was about two inches wide appeared to be beckoning to her.

In the dark woods, it seemed exponentially brighter than the first time she had seen one. Nevertheless, it was still just as bizarre. There was no question that there was something vital for Pearl to gain; light to see where she was going -for a start.

Pearl was astonished and silent as she lifted her hand to welcome the colorfully luminous and mesmerizing insect. Its wings created a vivid halo of soft fuchsia light that emitted in a two-inch radius around its thorax.

It briefly rested on her index finger knuckle, fluttering its electric wings. Its abnormally enlarged face had character, and the well-lit expression on it was mildly humanistic in a way.

It was an aura that brought optimism to Pearl, who had been wallowing in her anguish just minutes before. But then, the illuminated area behind her started to brighten intensely. The butterfly flew off of her hand

and away from her, heading toward the approaching electric radiance.

When Pearl turned around to watch it go, she inhaled in bewilderment. Pearl's skin crawled with goosebumps as she gaped at the huge swarm of butterflies, and each one looked slightly different from the next. They had begun to form closer together, and their light became brighter as they did so.

There were three hundred of them. They buzzed in unison, and they moved as a unit. As they moved around one another, the fuchsia light that came from them dimmed and brightened alternately, depending on how they spaced themselves apart.

She flinched at the sight of the many animated faces, thinking that maybe she was hallucinating. But as real as the pitch black was in those woods early that morning, so were the self-illuminating butterflies.

When they spoke to her, the swarm spoke as one,

"Just head west," they caroled to her. Although the buzzing was present, the sound was beautiful to her ears. Pearl replied with tears,

"But I don't know where I am. I don't even know who I am," she cried to them. She had many reasons to cry. But right then, Pearl realized that she was no longer shedding tears because she was alone in the dark woods. She wasn't crying because she was in agitating pain, or because she couldn't remember her own identity.

She wasn't even crying at the fact that people were after her, trying to capture her. She cried because she was in the woods at four-thirty in the morning, having a full-blown conversation with three hundred chanting, fuchsia-glowing, light-bearing butterflies about which direction to go. Even she wouldn't believe her story, and she didn't expect that anyone else would.

"They need you," the butterflies harmonized the words, and it sounded almost hymn-like in its resonation. "Just head west," they reaffirmed.

Just as Pearl was about to stand to her feet, she looked around her newly lit surroundings. She paused. She screamed hysterically, looking around the small clearing that she was kneeling in the center of.

There were four corpses scattered apart around the clearing. Two appeared to have been there for a long time, while the other two appeared to be more recently deceased. One was a man who had clearly died by decapitation, and his severed head was still near his body.

Another body was a woman who appeared to be in her thirties. It seemed apparent that she had slit her own wrists with a hunting knife that was on the ground next to her body. Pearl immediately looked to the swarm,

"What happened?" she questioned. Pearl was calm and politely inquisitive, as she had no idea if the swarm had caused the demise of the four corpses in some capacity.

"They need you," the swarm repeated.

"Who?" Pearl screamed. "Who needs me? And what could they possibly need me for? What in the hell is happening?" she begged for clarity just as some animal suddenly scuttled away from the clearing.

Pearl became frightened, and she jumped back and away from its direction. She was briefly frozen while she felt the absence of her own heartbeat for a half-second. She quickly searched around with her eyes, trying to identify the beast. Whatever it was, it had disappeared into a dark corner of the clearing.

As one, the swarm glided over to the deceased woman, and the brightness moved with them. Pearl got up and followed, not to be left in the dark. They moved in tightly together and hovered over the corpse, making the body well visible.

Ruby was the name on the tag of her scrubs uniform. "Ruby? Did she work for the Center?" she inquired to them. Their light became as a soft pulsating flash, to answer affirmatively, and Pearl had no hesitation in translating their language.

Ruby's eyes were closed. Her skin was pale and ashy. Traces of her beauty still managed to show, even though it was clear that she had bled out. There was a small, open book on her lap. Pearl figured Ruby must've been reading it, or writing in it when she had decided to die.

Pearl grabbed the journal and put it in an empty compartment of the backpack. Before she had it zipped up, the butterflies had migrated to hover over the man's corpse, yards from Ruby.

His body was leaning into a tree, slightly off to the side as his back rested up against the huge stump. She noticed that his surprised eyes were still open in his detached head, which was sitting upright on the ground near the tree. A grouping of insects had been attracted to the severed head, and they had taken up residency.

At first, it wasn't as easy to identify him as it was to identify Ruby. Pearl did not want to touch the man, although she had acknowledged that her own blood was physically all over those woods from all of her scrapes in the dark. She was paranoid and careful not to touch anything more than she accidentally had already.

She stood up where she had been squatting to study him and took a few steps toward the other human remains. Notwithstanding, the butterflies stayed in place to signal that she was still missing something. When Pearl reached a darkened area in the clearing, she turned around and stepped back over to where the swarm's light remained.

They moved in even closer to the man, and his stiff body leaned. He slowly fell over, onto his side. They lit the area to make sure that Pearl saw the folded envelope barely poking out of the back pocket of his damp and dirty trousers.

Pearl looked up at the bright group of mysteriously fascinating Rhopalocera beauties and their surreal electric fuchsia light. She then repeated to herself and them,

"No one would believe this," she said, shaking her head with concern that she might be dreaming the whole thing. She also feared that she could be lying somewhere unconscious on a bad pharmaceutical trip. But deep down she knew that probably wasn't the case.

Trembling, she looked upward to the swarm. She inquired again, "Do I need to take the envelope?" she probed, pointing at his pocket.

The soft, pulsating flash returned, so she grabbed the envelope. She took a quick look at it. The letterhead stationery was from the Maquiller Research Center, and there was just a single page. The first sentence had flowed something like the first line to open a separation statement of sorts; a letter of resignation.

The handwritten letter was signed by Devan Rice, and Pearl wondered if it had ever reached its intended recipient. Whatever it was about, Pearl would have to find out later. Firstly, she needed to make it out of there alive.

For the other two corpses, nothing stood out when she looked over their bones and fragile matter that she was wise not to touch. Through Pearl's frightened and pensive eyes, it appeared that both bodies had been there for much longer than she could even wildly guess.

She searched around them as the butterflies stayed stationary about ten feet above the ground behind her. She found nothing to help identify them, and the butterflies did nothing to highlight them.

She tucked the one-page letter into the backpack compartment with Ruby's journal. She returned her attention to the exquisite insects. The swarm had begun to fly westward ahead of Pearl to light the path in front of her. Pearl followed behind them with mixed emotions.

The swarm moved forward in silence, except for the soft buzzing noise they naturally created. Out of the corner of her eye, Pearl caught something moving. She looked over to the corners of the swarm's light where it met with the darkness, and she saw a shadow in the shape of a person.

She soon learned that there were several shadows near the edges of the dark. They all seemed to be in a hurry, each traveling in their own direction. Each one moved swiftly in their quest, and Pearl was trembling when she asked the swarm,

"Who is that?" she screamed in fear. The swarm didn't give her any obvious answer, they just kept gliding as one. Pearl then grew even more scared as she continued to track in the light. As she approached a big tree, she noticed a shadow standing next to it.

It was a tall and slim presence that didn't seem to be in a hurry, and the only movement she detected was of its head. She was nervous about passing by it, as the swarm moved forward slowly.

When the butterflies reached it, the figure disappeared into the short-lived, illuminated scenery. She shook her head as if trying to retune her perception. Her heart was pounding in her chest.

Pearl kept watching the place where the shadow had been standing, and the light slowly started to fade away with the swarm as they moved forward on the path. Pearl wondered after the figure she thought she'd seen.

She stood still for a moment, waiting to see any of the shadows again, and there was nothing. Then, the swarm's light passed by just enough to make a dark edge once again. The big tree became dimmed again, and the lanky shadow figure returned.

Unlike the first sighting, Pearl tried to find the source that was casting it, but there was nothing. Knowing she only had a few seconds before it would fade into complete darkness, her brown eyes rapidly searched the surroundings.

Pearl soon grasped that it wasn't a shadow at all. It was a dark figure that was only seen wherever the light met the darkness, and it terrified her. Screaming, she ran to catch up to the swarm. Pearl decided to walk with them, and not to fall behind them again.

She began to realize the space between the treetops where the deep sea-green sky and aggressive waves of water peeked down from the treetops' background. Only then did Pearl remember that the sky was no longer blue, and hadn't been for almost a day.

She stared at it, reminded of the weird and wild waters that were still forming up above. A ferocious, yet soundless aquatic spectacle that had initialized in the afternoon sky the day before was throwing its crashing waves around in every direction.

It appeared to be closer to the ground than it originally had been. Even though the waters had begun their formation around the afternoon sun the day before, they had covered the moon during the night.

That night, the moon could not be seen by any gem. Pearl couldn't ignore the vicious, growing sea that was slowly filling up the sky for reasons not yet known to her.

She noticed that the crashing waves had drawn a little nearer as she had stopped to study it, which she tried to do as little as possible. It was too intimidating for Pearl to stare at.

She continued on forward, but slowly. With a lot of bodily pains, she took heavy steps. She anxiously marched toward a destination outside of the trees, and her breathing improved as she got a little closer to it.

The light from the butterflies slowly faded as they led her closer to her exit, and dawn. It had felt like forever before she would exit the woods, but she eventually did.

Her mind was preoccupied with the swarm of magical insects, the four unknown corpses, the two miraculous human survivors she'd encountered the day before, and her own lost identity. Pearl felt like she was still at square one, squared. But on the bright side, at least there was light.

*******End of Chapter*******

Chapter 2

Just a Little Rain

(Thursday, June 21, 2018 - 5:30 a.m.)

It was getting close to dawn when Pearl came stumbling out of the forest. She looked back into the woods for any sign of the butterflies. They were gone, and so was their light that she had watched slowly fade away, as the surroundings were becoming illuminated by natural daylight.

She had been bleeding through a few new wounds she'd collected in the woods, and she still had numerous wounds from the day before. For the worst parts of the past seven hours, she had been fumbling around in the dark.

Pearl was completely enclosed by the pitch black in many of those dim instances. At some moments she'd tried to figure out what creeping thing scuttled up her leg. At other times, it was some startling noise in the dark that tripped up her heartbeat.

It still made her recoil. In reality, what she had witnessed was a miracle and a mystery. Strangely, the things she had been able to see while in the light of the butterflies were more spine-chilling than the things she couldn't see in the dark.

She was still carrying the leather backpack. Its straps had become loosened and raggedy, and it was wildly bouncing off of the backside of her body. Had she not needed the essential contents in the backpack so badly, she would've already ditched the thing.

Despite the purely traumatizing and mind-boggling experience in the woods, Pearl was no longer lost in the deep dark. Then, near dawn, she finally made her way out of those unknown paths that she had left stained with her tears and blood.

"Where to go from here?" Pearl asked herself. She sighed loudly in a breath, still ruminating about the inexplicable experience. She limped on toward a beachfront parking lot.

The crashing waves changed formation, creating a space in their center for the rose-gold sun that would eventually occupy the opening later in the day. The waters had yet to fill up the sky completely, yet the greenish-gray sky had become less visible.

The waves were only getting larger, and every gap would eventually close up. She watched the sky that was slowly brightening in the background.

Seven hours lost in the woods was just a fraction of her bigger ordeal. Pearl's real problem was much more sinister, and most likely permanent. She was deprived of any memory of anything that had occurred before dawn on Wednesday, June 20th.

Memories of loved ones, scheduled tasks, her name and address, and any other vital daily info prior to dawn that day were erased. Woefully, Pearl's internal glitching made her fully convinced that she had lost her mind. It's why she hadn't faced the public, or the authorities, in her mental state.

Having overheard the observer's conversation with the head psychiatrist at the Center, she learned that she had gone through a procedure. It was a process in which they were supposed to strip her memory and reformat it in some way.

The reformatting step was unsuccessful, leaving her in a continual state of misunderstanding. She couldn't answer simple questions about herself, but she'd also discovered that what the Center told her was a lie as well.

After falling victim to the grimy operation, she began to suffer severe migraine headaches that could surface just from trying to think. Some extent of brain hemorrhaging is what it felt like, and the episodes sometimes felt more seizure-like. The attacks were excruciating.

For Pearl, it had been a living hell with no mist. By 5:30 a.m. on June 21st, Pearl was a 33-year-old woman with a memory of none but one day of her entire life. That, and the people who had spent that whole day trying to return her to the Center.

Pearl knew she was *missing screws*, and she had quickly become uncontrollably obsessed with that void. She was still desperate to figure out where she came from, or where she was going -for that matter.

Without so much as a flash of her past reality, Pearl was a struggling woman with an overwhelming pile of questions to be answered. The only thing she was truly aware of was the fragility of her dear life. Pearl had no clue about who to call, and she definitely had even less information on who to trust.

Pearl walked up to the beachfront parking lot with a few minutes left until dawn, wobbling in her strides. Intrigue grew in her eyes, and they widened slowly as she approached.

Yards ahead of her was a red, four-door, sports sedan which Pearl was surprised to see parked. She immediately recognized it from the Maquiller Research Center parking lot.

The car was parked, and it appeared to be abandoned. She walked up to check the license plate and confirm that it was the same car from before. The vanity plate, DOCIZN, surely established its identification.

That little stretch of sand on the Puget Sound used to be the headquarters to any and every teen who didn't want to go home, circa 2000. However, when Pearl arrived there, it had been a desolate place on a normal day for years. Pearl was standing in the yet-to-be-commercialized outskirts of some poor crying town.

It seemed as if she were the only person around for a distance, and the deep-red sedan was the only vehicle in the eerily silent parking lot. *Who parked it there?* She wondered. She groaned at the pain in her ankle, lifting it off the ground briefly.

Her ankle was still hurting, and it wasn't aided by the weight she had been putting on it all the while. Regardless, she pressed forward quickly toward the car. She noticed a little boarded-up shack, and she stopped to make sure she didn't find anyone else around.

She found nothing, so she kept heading toward the vehicle. She noticed that her breathing was less limited than it had been in the deep forest. Pearl gratefully utilized every breath that she took in the dewy morning air.

"What the hell is it doing here?" she said under her breath with a squinty expression on her dirty face. She whispered to herself to battle confusion, "*This is all wrong. This car was at the facility. That imposturous 'research clinic' that was clearly polluted with demented medical professionals,*" she ruminated.

Thinking about the wild turn of events that had occurred in the past day, her eyes began to tickle with tears as if the red car was a trigger of sorts. It made her think of Kai Paw as well. Kai was a man in his mid-twenties who was employed by the Research Center as a tech, or a medical assistant of some sort.

He is the one who had been instructed to take all of Pearl's belongings to storage. Pearl recalled the last time she saw Kai. He was driving a silver, four-door sedan that wasn't nearly as flashy as the red sports sedan there in the beachfront parking lot.

Once she'd found her way out of the facility that housed her confounding nightmare, he was ordered to help capture her and bring her back. He was driving the silver car, and a uniformed security guard was in the passenger seat.

Glad to recognize the same red sedan she'd noticed outside of the Center when she left, Pearl hoped that it contained something useful. Perhaps, some information to turn things around for her horrendous circumstances would suffice.

Pearl softly pressed her hand against her chest as she smiled exhaustedly. But before she could celebrate, paranoia made her snap.

She quickly recalculated with the possibility that she wasn't the only one around. She abruptly paused her tears and corrected her poise to accommodate the worst possible development.

She spun herself about sharply, getting a brief 360-degree view of the sand, the lot, and the woods that she had just staggered out of. She briefly dreaded that she might not be alone. But Pearl calmed herself and became more aware to listen to her surroundings.

With her eyes closed, she heard the town sirens blaring in the distance. The sound was afar and could barely be heard. Other than the bashful waves from the water that morning, there was stillness where she was.

Everything was calm and silent, except the water in the sky. Silent? Yes, it was. But there was nothing calm about it. The nerve-wrecking view was threatening at a minimum.

She looked up at the menacing, splashing waves that were pinned to the sky above her. It was much easier to just look down and try to ignore the aquatic mystery that had been hovering over Opal Firs since the afternoon before. Neither Pearl nor anyone who could see it dared to stare into it for too long.

Regardless, her excitement returned to her as she whipped her attention back to the sedan. "Everything I need to know might be in that car," she reasoned with herself. She frantically searched the pockets on the ripped, green hoodie she was wearing over her shorts jumpsuit.

Her legs displayed cuts and bruises from the hem of her shorts to the top of her filthy white socks. She pulled out a set of keys on a ring with an emblem of a rose. There were three keys and a fob.

One of the keys was small and silver. Another was copper, and it was the mid-sized key. The largest key was silver, and the ridges were two-sided.

The sedan sighting made her eager to find something that could help her remember what happened the morning before. Or, more importantly to her, something to help her remember what was forgotten. After she calmed her anxieties, she slid the car key into the driver-side door.

Pearl tried to turn the key, but it wouldn't budge. She removed the key from the lock and tried the fob on the chain, to no avail.

She knew it was possible that the keys were not to the red car, but she had to at least try it. With all of the unlikely occurrences she'd observed already, she was shameless in her curiosity.

Biting nothing but a tight jaw, Pearl was thinking aloud when she shouted to the air, "Oh hell. Well, that's that." Pearl started to check for an unlocked door. The driver-side door was locked.

Anxiety began to set in again as Pearl marched around the front of the sedan to try the passenger door. It was locked, too. She took a few deep breaths before the tears could form in her eyes, trying not to induce one of those sickening migraine attacks she had been suffering at times.

"Calm down," she coached herself. She reached out for the rear-passenger door handle, but she was stunned by what she finally saw. Startled by the sight, she immediately felt a migraine intensifying in her head.

Pearl leaned her face toward the window and gasped. Cringing, she took a few frozen steps backward. As she backed away, she looked down and saw a small puddle of blood below the door.

Her keys were right next to the puddle. Pearl was baffled, and she hadn't even felt the keychain drop from her hand. She stood there, dazed and nauseous for a moment before she fixed her sight back through the window.

The victim and his clothing were utterly soaked in blood, and the number of stab wounds was upward of twenty-something punctures. Pearl began to become more unsettled as she registered the disgustingly tragic sighting.

Pearl couldn't identify the body. The corpse was covered in blood, and a piece of paper covered the victim's face. Pearl wondered why someone would make such a gruesome scene.

Still, it was obvious that the person she saw was indeed murdered. Pearl was not inclined to conclude that the corpse was Kai Paw, the victim in the back seat had a thicker physique than him. She considered the doctor from the Center, whom she couldn't get a good look at when she saw him in the facility hallway.

The wounds on the man's torso were made by a knife blade, and the rigid slit across his throat was possibly made by one with a serrated edge. The cut was wide and messy, unlike a smoother incision. No matter the blade, it was certainly *overkill*.

"What a damned bloodbath," Pearl said to herself while she held her hand up to her own neck, empathically. "But, who is it?" she feebly whispered. She scanned the inside of the vehicle for anything that looked like it might have belonged to her.

Peering into the window, she noticed many loosely stacked papers on the front passenger seat and floor and additional files or documents of sorts that were scrappily thrown around in the back seat. She couldn't make out the words on them because they were mostly turned face down.

On the other papers, only the document titles were printed large enough for her to see. They all appeared to have the names of individual people at the top as if the documents were titled for them.

The rest were too far away or had fonts that were too small to read. She saw the top part of one particular paper that displayed her name, Pearl Lerell. She couldn't tell what the document was for, but the name was printed largely in bold font at the top.

She finally broke, and her panicking went well over the top. She was grasping the ill concept of being associated with the abandoned car, and the brutally butchered body inside of it.

There was enough cause for another attack. Somewhere between worrying and straining her eyes to read the papers, she self-induced an attack.

"But why? Why won't they just let me go?" she yelled out, fuming. She got herself worked up a bit before pulling back, fighting off the episode.

She snagged the keys off of the ground and put them back into her pocket. She fleetingly looked up at the savage waves. She then quickly lowered her shaking head, acknowledging her own stupidity for looking at it.

With no surety about what might happen, she tore off a small piece of the already ripped and dangling cloth from her hoodie to wipe her fingerprints from underneath the door handles. She knew it wouldn't be long before someone discovered the eye-catching red sedan, and the body in the back seat. She became exasperated.

Pearl put herself to the ground for fear of falling. She held herself in an upright fetal position, rocking herself back and forth. The migraine was like an increasingly painful contraction in the brain. Each attack she had before it had its own personal range of pain and symptoms.

She had endured a couple of migraine attacks with vomiting, and a couple without. A couple were like brutal seizures. No two episodes were the exact same to Pearl, and that's what made each attack so terrifying.

In the process of incapacitating her memory, the procedure performed on Pearl left her with an unusually hyperactive hippocampus. She had already noticed that she exhibited alarming physical strength that seemed to come, and go when least expected. All while she was being robbed of her own memories, she was gaining freakishly super-human skills.

She had become a sponge that could remember just about every new thing she encountered. Everything Pearl came across long enough to briefly study, she remembered. It was simply too overwhelming for the human brain to process, and it was also capable of bringing about an episode.

One may think that this could be both a blessing and a curse. But the awful headaches and seizures exposed otherwise. That, and the fact that the Research Center authorities weren't letting up in their pursuit to find her made it a curse through and through to Pearl.

What's the point in remembering everything I'll ever see if I've forgotten everything I've ever known? Where are my real memories? She thought to herself in anger. The paradox that she experienced mentally distressed her.

Pearl sighed a little as the pain subsided. She was thankful that the attack didn't last as long as some of the others. She quickly got back up on her feet and dusted herself off.

As she tried to straighten herself out, she had an epiphany. She had been given a seemingly universal message by a couple of random people, and she pondered on the message,

"Careful not to touch anything," the coffee shop cashier Pamelah said to Pearl the day before. Pearl was drawn to a hanging amethyst wand that she saw inside of Emerald Coffee and Books. The bookstore's owner Nomad Artman sold crystals, natural stones, and other miscellaneous gifts alongside books, magazines, and cappuccinos.

The message was so demanding. Even when it came from a random brown-haired preteen who approached Pearl the afternoon before, asking her to hold his backpack while he entertained his friends with a skateboard trick.

His piercing green eyes were oddly sincere. For a brief tick, there was an ancient kind of maturity in the kid's overall demeanor that made Pearl yield.

"Don't' touch anything, promise?" he'd insisted, practically shoving his red canvas backpack into her arms. Pearl had laughed lightly at the kid who was simultaneously trusting and paranoid.

"Of course not, Pearl replied with a jokingly distrustful smirk. *"Don't kill yourself, kid?"* she remembered her response, surprised at being unexpectedly delegated by the boy. She was covered in cuts and bruises, and the boy had paid it no mind. She still wondered after that kid.

Pearl abruptly pulled herself from her thoughts to focus on what she needed to do there at the red sedan. She didn't see anything that looked like a probable item of her own in the car, although she was disturbed about her brand-new identity being listed in any fashion next to a murdered corpse.

If it was a setup, she knew she needed to get any papers with her name on them out of the car, period. Pearl couldn't see how the recurring universal advice was applicable in the instance.

She examined her thoughts, searching for answers. Sadly, she lacked the knowledge she needed.

In her new state, she wouldn't understand that the Center had already been ensuing the Hippo-Project-research scheme for more than two years with no local press coverage. Sadly, the person she used to be would have known all about it.

The Center was systematically elusive from scrutiny because of nothing other than muscle, and money. Pearl Lerell would have ripped through someone's chest had she known the depths of her own current misdirection. The people of the nation would shudder in anger if they knew where some of the missing children of 1998 really were.

Unfortunately, she had no hunch that she'd already met one of them. A very nervous and paranoid Pearl decided to find something to break the car window with. She walked back to the woods entrance where she had come from, in search of something heavy.

Right near the entrance was a piece of tree that appeared to make a great walking stick. She wondered if someone had recently put it there. It would have worked just fine, but next to it was a rock that could've easily weighed around eight pounds or so.

"Perfect," Pearl exclaimed when she saw it. She was walking back toward the sedan with it when she heard sirens. They were much closer, and much louder, than they were moments before. Pearl quickly ran back into the woods.

She didn't run too far into the trees, just enough to hide and see where the sirens were heading. The sound decreased, as they were moving farther away. Only then did Pearl come creeping out of hiding to resume her attempt to get into the car.

She stopped about seven feet from the car window. Pearl threw all of her weight into it, hurling the big stone at the drivers-side window. She almost lost her balance as she let it go.

She watched with adrenaline as the big rock flew through the air and hit the window. Ineffectively, the rock shattered into gravel-like pieces on contact. It shattered like glass.

"Bizarre," Pearl thought as she stared at the car window with wonder, slightly turning her chin to the side. The window was still intact, and without a scratch.

All she did was trigger the most startling car alarm that was sounding a loud, intermittent horn. She was frozen in confusion, and it hindered her response to the noise.

She quickly kneeled down to examine the rock that had become a pile of dirt. Yet, it was changing again, and it was becoming sandy in its form. The appearance and color were also morphing before her eyes.

It became more like a finely ground, deep-purple-colored, crystallized sand and less like gravelly, cream-colored grains. She held it in both palms, letting the surprisingly bright and iridescent, opal-like, purple sand fall through her fingers for a few seconds.

This, again? Amazing, she thought to herself as she exhaled. It was the second time she had unintentionally created purple sand, and she just couldn't figure out how she did it. She incoherently ignored the alarm for a time, as she gawked over the purple grains.

She became entranced by it. She was astounded by the twinkling, suddenly colorful remains of the eight-pound rock.

She grabbed one more handful and poured it into the inside pocket of the green hoodie she was wearing. Finally, she gathered what she had done.

She covered her ears as she looked around. The disharmonizing noise of the high-pitch siren-like note and the annoying blasting horn finally alarmed Pearl, and at least one other bystander.

"Hey, what in the hell are you doing?" Goose hollered from across the lot. Goose Gary was the groundskeeper and property landscaper.

He was standing across the lot near the entrance of an old hiking trail that was in terrible need of trimming. It looked like a long while had passed since anyone hiked it. His sudden holler nearly gave Pearl a heart attack, or an episode.

She quickly covered her black hair, and as much of her face as she could, with her hood. She then stood straight up on her feet to see who was shouting at her. She saw a man running toward her and the car, so she grabbed her backpack and scurried away.

She left him in the dust, and out of breath. She had briefly looked back one last time with curiosity at the sand pile near the car. But she didn't stop her sprint for at least ten minutes, except to pause for a quick breath here and there.

At those instances, she checked on the outrageous development in the sky; bullying waves of sea-green being suspended up high by an external source of power that had yet to be identified. When she did finally stop running it was only to hide inside of a small vacant building, hoping she might straighten herself out there.

"Oh shit," Pearl cried out. "Dammit. Dammit," she screamed as she slammed her palm flat against the wall inside. She was shaking so badly she couldn't even grip the zipper of her hoodie, as she tried to take it off to cool down after running so hard. She was sure that she just made things much worse than they already were.

Just as she caught her breath, she heard the inclining sirens coming back toward her. *You've got to be freaking kidding me,* she thought in her panic that just wouldn't calm. The sirens faded away, and it quickly became apparent that they were most likely heading toward the beach front. Pearl figured that the groundskeeper had already phoned the police.

"Whatever it was in that sedan that might've helped, it won't now," Pearl carped, throwing her arms up in the air. She spoke exhaustedly with deep breathing, and dryly through her cracking vocal cords.

Wildly, the plump raindrops began to pour down heavily outside. It was violently beating upon the thin tin roof top of the small building, and Pearl listened.

At first thought, the rain furthered the devastation of her situation. But it also created an opportunity for her to think as she hid in the building, she hoped. Even if it was only for the moment, it seemed to Pearl that the rain might actually aid in delaying the pursuit.

She took off the destroyed hoodie and the jumpsuit that Nomad Artman gave to her on Wednesday. She also removed her socks and shoes. She walked out of a side door of the building and into the morning rainstorm, propping the door open with a can of paint.

She just stood there with her arms raised up and outward, finally allowing herself to embrace the sky-bound waters. For the first time, she didn't worry about gravity when she looked into it. She hoped that the rain would rinse her problems down and away, along with the dried blood around all of her cuts that she had been treating as best as she could.

A sad calamity it was. But she somehow knew that everything would be all right, although she was not. Hope was much less costly than worry to Pearl. She considered the one employee from the Center who seemed to be a bit out of place: Kai Paw.

She didn't know if Kai's intention was to help or to harm, and she tried to make heads or tails of it. She didn't know if the red-sedan fiasco was really a setup to conspire against her or not. Even if she had found something that belonged to her, would she have recognized it?

She was also saddened that she wasn't able to read the document in the car with her name at the top. In any case, those ships had already sailed, and Pearl didn't have time to cry over it anymore. The best thing she could do is get away from the scene.

She knew she could cry as hard as she wanted to and her tears would just camouflage with the rain, but she didn't. She couldn't. She was becoming cried out.

Lowly minded, she prayed blindly to the water-filled sky as she had no idea about what she really needed. The oceanic scenery was slightly obscured behind the big falling raindrops, but it was undoubtedly present and active.

She had no pre-thought of what to say or think, or if the heavens would even help. So, she let the rain say it all for her.

Pearl was unpretentious as she stood there bare, silent, and soaked. In fact, even if she did still have her memory, Pearl couldn't have remembered ever being as humble as she was just then.

*******End of Chapter*******

Chapter 3

Purple-opal Sand

On a normal Thursday morning, Goose Gary would make his rounds to a handful of properties that he liked to stay on top of. June 21st was no exception, and he arrived at work early.

He was drafting a new cost estimate and proposal for a client. He was going to be clearing an old path where the wild bushes had grown over, blocking the hiking trail. But he was also there early for one other more unconventional assignment for which the instructions had yet to become clear.

Once Pearl had bolted off, Goose Gary continued to check out the sedan. He jogged up to it then noticed the small slick of blood from a few yards away. He shrieked at the sight of it, knowing it couldn't be good.

Staying clear of the blood spill, he walked around the front of the car to the driver's side. He peered into the window, and he grabbed his chest over his heart in revulsion when he saw the slain body.

Goose stepped backward about a yard, looking around for any sign of another person or witness. He pulled out his cell phone from the top pocket of his work jumpsuit, ready to make the emergency call while he checked around the car.

He then noticed the heap of metallic, purple sand. The rich purple-opal color stood out to Goose, as it sparkled to the point of brightness. He personally hadn't seen anything like it before.

In times past, he had heard of a substance called Purple Opal Sand. It was called that because it was reported to be a vibrant milky purple. Immediately, he knew he would need to find those old notes he'd written down when he first learned of it.

It was written of in a lost journal that he had stumbled upon many years ago, and an out-of-print comic book that he randomly came across shortly after. The comic had already been pulled from circulation while still mid-agreement, for some unknown reason.

He understood that he may have come across something special, as it clearly fitted the description. The alluring purple sand became brighter and brighter right before his eyes.

He was compelled to keep some of it because if it were real Purple Opal sand, he just hit a jackpot. He stored some of it in one of the empty baggies that he would normally use at work to clean up after the occasional dog owner who didn't pick up after their pet.

The metallic-purple sand reminded him of another marvelous sign that was operating in the sky and had been since the day before. It was the most extravagant of them all, and it was still hovering over Opal Firs that morning.

The *signs*, or warnings, were clearly visible to him. There was no doubt that they were shown to him to be heeded in some urgent way. They had shown up multiple times, and in multiple forms. In every sense, each sign was extraordinary to behold.

"An elephant, a fox, and a huge turtle," Goose recollected to himself, still in awe as he remembered the order in which the animals appeared in the clouds on the previous day.

After the peculiar clouds, in the late afternoon that same day, a new development had begun. The upper waters had begun to form, and no one else around him had perceived the intense and displaced aquatic movement above them.

Subsequently, they also did not experience the horrific fear of drowning that Goose Gary had felt in that fragment. What Goose was witnessing he had thought as unimaginable, but he knew it was for him.

His fellow laborer and friend, Darrell, had only seen "normal clouds," as he had explained it, before asking if Goose felt all right. Darrell had loaded the work truck and walked over to where Goose was standing. He had just quietly observed Goose holding his head upward, gawking at nothing but a few clouds, from what he himself could see.

Normally, he would have interrupted with an inquiry as to what Goose was looking at. But on that day, he just watched Goose because he'd realized that he had never seen that look on his friend's face before in fifteen years of friendship. He knew something was going on, and he'd felt compelled to remain quiet.

After that, came the very *vibrant battle of seas in the sky,* which was still brewing over Opal Firs as Goose stood there in the parking lot. It had grown bigger and much closer than before.

The animation itself had intensified drastically since Wednesday afternoon. Goose looked up at it, fearfully attentive. He remembered speechlessly gaping upward, thunderstruck at the wild unearthing.

He had hoped that if he could see it, then others like himself could as well. Just like Pearl, he had been trying to ignore its presence because it was downright too overwhelming. It was outright intimidating to look at, but exceedingly challenging to look away from.

For all of those who had seen the shapely clouds, in addition to the colorful oceanic manifestation, it was much like a roll call for something significant, or consciously exigent. Anyone around for miles who was seeing it knew without a doubt that something unprecedented was priming that afternoon.

Goose imagined how loudly the crashing waves would roar had the sound been turned on. The muted manifestation was awkwardly threatening. It was a disturbance to the senses, and just a matter of time before its viewers confirmed that the noise was just as demanding as the sight.

Goose had survived a mild heart attack in his past, and he was known to struggle with his cholesterol level. Yet, he was only one of several witnesses who all desperately needed to keep their eyes toward the ground during the manifestation.

When it came to looking at it straight on, he feared for his heart just like Pearl feared for her headspace. In fact, no one could bear a surprise like such and feel safe or *okay*.

Goose shook his head violently to not let himself get stuck in the inexplicable, considering the unexplainable corpse in the car. He proceeded to make his phone call, but not to 911. He called Kai Paw, and Kai picked up after the first ring.

"Hey it's me," Goose said. "I'm here, I see the car. And I see the uh," his voice both shrunk and deepened as he spoke. "I've seen it. You didn't tell me there was gonna be a," he began to argue uneasily, but then he paused abruptly. He'd become mindful to protect the privacy of their call. Kai interjected,

"I know, I'm sorry, I never did get a reasonable opportunity to explain that. But, it's more helpful than hurtful, please trust me," Kai implored, calling for Goose's trust before setting the next steps. "Please listen. I need you to stall the call to 911 until we give you the word," Kai instructed him.

"All right," Goose replied, shaking his head with some dissatisfaction. Kai resumed speaking,

"I still need to find our subject. Granted, if we don't find her, then we'll have to move forward without her. But, you play by your normal schedule for as long as you can manage. Have you seen the sky?" Kai suddenly remembered to mention the spectacle, as he observed it from where he stood.

"Yes, I'm looking at it right now," Goose said with his eyes on the sky, and he was glad to confirm that he wasn't the only one he knew who could see the waters above. Kai's excitement was just as notable, but he cautioned Goose,

"Don't look at it for long, it's very consuming. I felt like I was briefly paralyzed when I glared into it for too long yesterday," Kai warned him. "It's not time. It's moving closer though."

"Yeah, man. It's much closer to us than it was yesterday. What's happening?" Goose asked, hoping Kai had an answer.

"No clue. But, what I do know is that whatever is in store, it is probably going to happen today. And, it will not happen until all the right people are gathered," Kai spoke with a confident intuition.

He occasionally had sharp premonitions or reliable hunches like so. "Let us know if anything changes," he added, pausing for Goose's agreement.

"Speaking of your subject, I found a woman trying to break the car window," Goose said with warning. On the other end, Kai's eyes widened with hope. Goose was waiting for his response when he probed, "You think that was her?" he asked.

"What was she wearing? Was she wearing scrubs or sweats?" Kai inquired anxiously.

"I don't think so," Goose recalled. "No, shorts. She was wearing shorts and a green hooded sweatshirt. She had mid-tone skin and dark hair, from what I could see," he added. "I was across the parking lot and I tried to catch up to her, but she was too fast," he expounded.

Kai sighed in wonder as the description was pretty close. But Goose then realized that the purple sand near the car might be the information to help Kai. Kai spoke with a decisive tone, saying,

"If you don't hear from us by three o'clock this afternoon, call them and report the car. Yeah. Report the *abandoned car*, and say nothing about the body. Just stall the best you can, like you haven't even seen it yet," Kai requested of him yet again.

"You want me to keep it under wraps for nine damn hours? You're kidding me," Goose snapped.

"No one goes out there, you should be okay," Kai reminded him. "Besides, I said to stall for as long as you could. Please just deter whomever you can, if you can. Otherwise, play dumb," he suggested.

"Dammit, Kai. All right, fine," Goose concluded with tension.

"I'm so sorry, but it has to go this way, I'm sure you-" Kai began to reply. But Goose jumped in abruptly to make sure that Kai knew the possible nature of the woman he had just seen.

"There's Purple Opal sand on the ground by the car," Goose revealed.

"Purple sand?" Kai exclaimed, expecting more details.

"Yes, there's a heap of sparkling metallic-purple colored sand, and it's just like it was described in the files we had talked about before," Goose elucidated.

"Considering the last twenty-four hours, there's no telling. It might really be Purple-Opal sand." He became even more thrilled as he verbalized what he was seeing while realizing how senseless it sounded. "This really could be it," he declared.

Goose realized that the past day of his life had been very eventful, and colorful. He explained with regret, "If that was your subject, I didn't know. I probably scared her off.

"So, now I'm worried that the police might get here earlier than we want them to if she was to go to them." But Kai was joyous on the other line, saying,

"No, that's it. The purple sand. It has to be her. And, she wouldn't be going to the authorities," Kai exclaimed.

"Are you sure?" Goose asked, listening for certainty.

"Yes," Kai whispered to him favorably. "In fact, please collect the sand. Try not to leave any trace of it, just in case," he added.

"Okay then, let me get on it," Goose concurred.

"Thank you. Be safe, Mr. Gary," Kai said to his friend and clandestine pen pal of several years. They had never seen each other in person until Kai arrived in Washington. However, they had already been maintaining ongoing correspondences cross country for years.

Several years ago, Kai sent an anonymous letter to Goose Gary, the Project H.E.A.D. subcontractor with the fascinating comic book collection. What had started out as anonymous grew to become mutually supportive communication over time.

Kai had been purely fascinated by the concept of the magically metallic, purplish-opal sand, ever since Goose spoke of it to him. No one seemed to know what Purple Opal sand was for. But to Kai, it was a must-see.

Although Goose had heard of it via an outdated comic book series, and internal Center knowledge dating twenty years back, he had never actually seen anything like it until the sand pile in the parking lot on June 21, 2018. He talked into the receiver with more fervor after he found that he had good cause for his optimism.

"Please, don't mess this up for me. This is my life," Goose replied in his rightful paranoia as he massaged his temple. "I know this has to happen one way or another. Let me get to work before someone else shows up," he said before he hung up.

Goose disconnected the call and moved forward to collect any evidence of Pearl's purple sand pile. He first caught another glimpse of the sky, and he quivered.

He kneeled back down to start gathering the sand. Goose noticed that his right hand, the hand he used most for daily gardening and landscaping, was completely free from scars and flaws. He then remembered that he had also used his right hand to examine and store away some of the illuminating purplish sand.

He stared at his fists, holding both of them up to compare. He opened his palms wide. His left hand was still very much scarred, calloused, and borderline arthritic. But his right hand appeared, and felt, as it did decades ago in his youth.

"What's going on?" he asked himself. He had just countersigned his third miraculous exhibition in just twenty-four hours alone. He humbly looked up to the suspended, clashing, sea-green waves, recognizing one fact which he proclaimed to himself, "Well, this is absolutely crazy."

****

Pearl was lying on the unfinished flooring in the old building, while the dim Pacific-Northwestern, green-tinted daylight peeked through the windows and door frames. The rain had let up a bit, and so had the seawater sky brightened some.

She realized she couldn't stay safe for much longer in that location. She was wondering how she could replace the dirty jumpsuit and hoodie that she had no choice but to wear again.

She also needed to read the file, the journal, and the letter. She felt she needed to get out of town, and soon. For that time, she had taken refuge in a room that was left in mid-renovation status. So, it appeared.

A menacing, frictional noise briefly blared outside of the building window. Pearl's frightened eyes jerked her head toward the sound.

Horrified and jumpy, she quickly sat up. But only to find a tree branch swaying in a gust of wind and brushing against the sill. She shook it off.

She drew the black leather backpack to her. She unzipped the largest compartment, pulled out an apple she had gotten at an outdoor fruit stand the day before. Pearl took the first bite she'd eaten in a noticeable while.

She continued to dig through the contents with one hand while she ate the apple with the other. She suddenly remembered the sand from the parking lot in her inner hoodie pocket, and she grabbed a small amount out with her fingers.

She tossed her apple down on a piece of plastic, using it for a dish. She slid back a foot or two to rest her back against the unfinished drywall with one leg knee up and heel down. The other leg was stretched straight outward, to not put pressure on her injured ankle.

She examined the grains. Still sparkling, the fascinating purple sand fell through her fingers and some of it landed on her thigh.

Then, it began to itch for several seconds. She started to dust herself off and ended up just migrating the sand from her thigh down to her leg. It was then that Pearl realized that her knuckles were no longer bruised.

Seconds later, she noticed that there was neither pain in the leg that she spilled the sand on, nor in the ankle. She saw that the cuts from the many blackberry thorns and the bruising from her fall on that same leg were all gone, vanished.

She immediately began to sprinkle the sand on herself from head to toe. As sparingly as possible, she treated every limb.

Pearl's health was soon replenished, and she became like new. She ran throughout the place, anxious to prove her own naturally athletic ability. Then, in her excitement, her laugh was abrupt and heavy at how long it had taken her to understand what the purple sand could do.

She then recalled the man in the standoff with police at the convenience store, and the kid who was hit by the car. Pearl finally understood the supernatural recoveries.

She rested with her back on the floor, using her backpack for a pillow while she contemplated the Hippo Project, Kai, and Nomad Artman. She had ditched Nomad at some point the day before, and she felt some sense of regret about it. She knew deep down that Nomad was there to help, but his means to do so were too counterintuitive to her in the instant when she ditched him.

She also continued to obsess over the unbelievable swarm of butterflies, and the unexpected dead bodies, at multiple scenes. On top of all of that, the extremely odd event in the sky demanded her attention wherever she went.

"Wait a minute," she shouted with a sudden thought. She swiftly sat straight up and turned to her backpack, remembering she had Ruby's journal and Devan's letter. She pulled them out and prepared herself to read them both.

Before she began to read, she became distracted. She began pondering over her time in the Research Center. Pearl remembered the morning before when she had quickly rummaged through a light pile of clothing. She was hoping to find some kind of self-identification before Kai caught her snooping.

There was neither a wallet nor purse. A rose keyring was on a table not too far from the pile of her items, and it was the only thing she could manage to stash before he returned to the room to gather it all. She didn't even know what they belonged to, and she kicked herself for not finding something more before he returned.

Kai came back into the post-examination room and stuffed a pair of black pants, a plum-colored sweater, a pair of black leather ankle boots, and a pair of black socks into a large clear plastic bag before he carried it all out of the room. Pearl, like all other in-patient subjects, had only been allowed to wear a gray sweatshirt and matching drawstring sweatpants. She wore them with a pair of simple white canvas shoes and white crew socks that were provided to her by the Center, while her own clothes were put aside.

The door for that room hadn't been shutting properly by itself, so Kai closed it with an intentional pull almost every time he left out. Occasionally, he'd forgotten to pull it shut completely, and it was only at those times that Pearl could hear or see anything in the clinical area.

When Kai left with the bag, he also rolled out the high-tech, project-specific EEG machine he had used to monitor her brainwaves. He rolled the machine down the hall and away, but he never turned back to close the door completely. Pearl's gut screamed, "Leave now." But she counterintuitively reasoned that staying was the best option, considering her medical ailments at that moment.

About five minutes had passed when Kai returned from the place where they had gathered the subjects' old belongings, and Pearl heard his footsteps that stopped short of the cracked room door. Once he returned to the Hippo wing, Kai was stopped by somebody in the hallway before he reached the room.

Pearl was able to hear talking but couldn't quite make out what was being said. So, she quieted herself as much as she could to listen. She overheard two distinct voices carrying on a conversation a little way down the hall.

Pearl paused her thoughts and opened a bottle of water that she had been carrying in the backpack. She took a long and much needed chug.

Her water was still on the cool side. The weather in Opal Firs was supportive of the temp. She looked at Ruby's journal with intentions to start reading it, but Al Canna and Kai Paw stuck to the forefront of her brain.

Canna had been one of a trio of doctors who all held personal stakes in advanced scientific approaches. They all shared the same opportunities to conduct research regarding neuroscience and the place for artificial intelligence in that world. Pearl had learned that while she was on her way from the procedural wing to the post-programming part of the building.

When she'd walked by the picture and bio of Dr. Al Canna on the wall, she stared at the man with brunette hair, a trimmed mustache, and designer eyeglasses. His smile was sideways, although not intimidating. But his penetrating light-brown eyes seemed menacing to Pearl.

To her, it had seemed like the man in the photo was staring back at her, no matter what angle she had looked at the picture from when she passed by it. She remembered it vividly. It was creepy, and she was never going to forget about it.

But when Kai came to mind, Pearl couldn't fight the intrigue she felt. He seemed to be out of place in the Center's Hippo Project wing, and she truly hoped that she hadn't caused any grave trouble for him by sneaking away under his watch.

She sat the water bottle down and picked up her apple to take another bite. She continued to consider the talk she overheard between Canna and the young medical tech who was her observer.

"It's her hippocampus, it is absorbing data of all kinds at accelerated rates. Consequently, she is having severe episodes of cerebral hemorrhaging. Short-lived, but severe.

"And, she has excellent resiliency," Kai spoke with certainty. As Dr. Canna's interest peaked, his body language shifted. He became more composed. He interrupted Kai when he inquired,

"Excuse me, what's the report?" he asked Kai.

"The first step was successful, and the intended areas of memory were deleted. Her hippocampus, however, simply will not reformat," Kai advised his on-site authority.

"Furthermore, now her brainwaves are incontestably displaying hyperactivity. We were unable to program her new

identity, Dr. Canna. She would make a great candidate for the Rhode Island branch, under Maquiller," he concluded, with sudden trepidation.

Pearl stared up at the ceiling in the office building. Briefly distracted from her thoughts, she noticed her surroundings.

She was in a deserted office building, yet there was some mysterious familiarity about the place. She appreciated the daylight that was shining throughout the room, considering her unsightly adventure in the woods.

She took the last bite of her apple and then returned the core to a freezer bag where she kept another apple and an orange. She still had a few granola bars, too.

She had known it would be wise to keep those things when she collected them Wednesday afternoon. But the circumstances had generally deterred her hunger.

Pearl was trying to manifest someone who could help. She was fairly certain that she was not supposed to have heard that conversation between Kai and Dr. Canna. But she knew that what was being said in that hallway made her even more rapt.

Noticing that her appetite had also returned, she decided to open a granola bar. She chewed her first bite as she recollected moving a little closer to the door so that she could hear Kai and Dr. Canna better.

"What does she believe her name is?" Dr. Canna asked Kai. His tone made it sound like a routine question.

"Pearl Lerell," Kai responded. He'd been newly employed by the center, just about reaching the end of his ninety-day probationary period. What he had yet to learn on the job was Dr. Canna's modus operandi concerning a malfunctioning subject, like Pearl.

"But, isn't that her programmed name?" Dr. Canna asked, still doubting that she was going to be a rare case. "So, she is programmed," he concluded in error. "She's just experiencing temporary side effects."

"Yes, it is," Kai said. "But it's only because that's what I told her, and she believed me," he added. Pearl's jaw dropped as she strained to hear them better. "Her programming may be delayed. But, as you know, it also may never happen." The look of confidence on Dr. Canna's face slowly faded, and Kai realized that he had just made a huge mistake by speaking too much.

Canna's protocol for a failed procedure only led to the indefinite detainment of the subject. This simply depended on the sub's overall usefulness. The success of his research depended on his ability to retain *useful* subjects like her.

Canna would only keep a malfunctioned subject in the Center to study them like a lab rat until the fragile experiment finally rendered them impotent. At that branch location, it was unfortunate to "malfunction," or better put, be "un-programmable." It was an even bigger threat to be considered a *hyperactive nonprogrammable* sub, according to Dr. Canna.

Pearl threw the granola bar wrapper down as she stared through the air, spacing out. She wondered what her fate would have been if she had stayed at the Center, willing to cooperate. Her heavy ruminating continued.

Kai's voice cracked up as he searched Canna's countenance, "What do I need to do with her?" he asked his superior, as he regretted disclosing Pearl's results. Dr. Canna had decreased the conversation volume as Subject Sixteen's review grew more and more unattractive. Then, Dr. Canna swiftly straightened his face and changed his tone to sound very optimistic when he replied,

"We should keep her for a while, in room 321. It's the wing for special study subjects like her. You'll need to have TJ escort her to the room, and I'll let him know to get the room ready," he concluded. From the distinct chatter between Kai and Dr. Canna, Pearl could only make out the words "keep her... in room 321," but she definitely didn't need to hear anything else.

She couldn't have handled being put in another room for another minute, and finding out that Kai lied to her about her name didn't help.

She slid out of the cracked door in the post-programming section of the research center. On the way out, she grabbed the file folder in the box attached to the wall just outside the door of her room. She moved quietly, hoping to not be detected.

As she fled, she looked back behind her and she saw a part of Dr. Canna's white jacket sleeve as he talked with Kai in the adjoined hallway near her room. She slid down another hall just as soon as she could. She knew she had to get the hell out of there, no matter what.

Kai had dreaded the task of subduing a sub, and he saw right through Dr. Canna's fake bright tone. All of the other subjects he'd observed went through the program successfully.

True, their memory was stripped from them and they had been given a new identity or a new life. But their new lives were good lives. At least, that's the recurring thought that made it all bearable to Kai during his employment in the Maquiller Center.

Unfortunately, Pearl was one of those odd cases Kai had heard about in training. About 1 in every 200 subjects had some sort of issue after the process, and all subjects in that half percent did suffer immensely. But a sub like Pearl was even rarer, even within that half of a percent.

Kai had hoped that he would never have to witness the dark side of the Hippo Project. His hopes were crushed that Wednesday in Opal Firs. It was clear that Kai didn't know a lot about himself, the Hippo Project, or Project H.E.A.D.

Pearl definitely sensed the reluctance in his presence when she was there. Although she couldn't pin down an exact reason, she knew that there was a good story behind his behavior. She tried to imagine what had happened once they learned that she was gone.

Kai walked back into the post-programming room and gasped when he saw that Pearl was missing. At that second, he'd figured he would be fired immediately. But it also caused him to smile a little, as he figured Pearl deserved a head start. A part of him sensed she would actually be better off out there.

Suddenly, Kai's faint smile faded completely when he latently remembered that his work at the Center was far from done, and his own mission needed to commence immediately. He also understood that he couldn't cover up for his missing subject for very long. He shut the door behind him to gather his thoughts.

He leaned his back against the door, taking the weight off of his weak legs. He began to stroke his trimmed light-brown beard with his left hand and closed his eyes, envisioning his scenario.

It did not look good at all. For the first time since he'd started his venture there, Kai felt the plain white walls closing in on him.

*******End of Chapter*******

Chapter 4

The Bathroom Stall

(Wednesday, June 20th - 12:12 p.m.)

Kai splashed his face with cold water at the men's bathroom sink. He needed to find Fowley Court, his fellow adopted brother and colleague who had been working as a data analyst at the Maquiller Research Center in Opal Firs for about six months. But Kai needed to pull himself together first.

He took a deep breath and splashed his face once again. The water from the chrome auto-stop faucet continued to run for another few seconds while he grabbed a paper towel to dry his face.

Alone in the restroom, he looked himself over one last time before he headed to Fowley. He searched himself for the confidence to complete a mission almost a month earlier than planned. *What a nightmare,* he thought as he chucked the balled-up paper towel into the waste bin.

He could've caught up with Pearl, but he hesitated. Something about her was all too familiar, and he was glad that she left. That is, until he'd realized that the mishap could cost him his job that very day. He figured she slipped out right behind him when he went to store her things and had already found the outside of the Center, if the alarms weren't already ringing.

"This is crazy. I messed up. What were you thinking?" he exclaimed to himself in the mirror as he slapped his palms into the sides of his forehead. When Pearl had slipped out during her post-procedural window, she activated a countdown to Kai's own chaotic expiration that was sure to unfold by the day's end.

While he was glad to see her go, he had inadvertently put something much bigger in jeopardy, Maquiller's orders as well as the Cr8's plan. He reached into his pocket and pulled out a white leather change purse and a cell phone.

He unhooked the two faux pearls that snapped around each other to open the small purse. He pulled out Pearl's former identification card, a Washington State driver's license.

Her real name was Mari Hera. She was 5'6" in height, and 130 lbs. She had black hair and brown eyes. She was also an organ donor. Kai realized that the Center, especially him, knew more about her than she did.

Mari Hera needed Kai Paw just as much as Kai needed her. He lowered the license back into the change purse and put Mari's phone back into his pocket.

He could hear footsteps approaching in the hall. He walked toward the door to exit and was almost smacked with it, as another man swiftly shoved it open.

"Excuse me," Al Canna said as he beheld Kai with no discernment. He briefly searched for any obvious injury to either of them. Kai's eyes widened a little bit, as Canna was the exact person he was trying to avoid.

"I was just about to check on Sweet Sixteen and those post-exam files. Are her vital signs updated from this morning?" Al Canna inquired with his dry humor being accompanied by a business-as-usual tone as he slid by Kai to enter the men's restroom.

"Dr. Canna, Subject Sixteen will not be awake for a few hours. She became pretty sullen and hostile. I had to put her to sleep for a little while," Kai lied. He was hoping his face didn't display any signs of treachery, or sweat.

He tried to return the humor, "She'll be bright-eyed and ready for visitors by late afternoon, and the file will be updated when she does," he assured Canna. He then grabbed the door handle, flung it open, and swiftly exited before pivoting around to face the door. "Thank you," Kai nervously added an unfitting end to an uncomfortable conversation, and just as the restroom door was shutting. It was indeed awkward.

Canna badly needed a stall, so he was completely unbothered by Kai's awkward behavior and short-windedness. Kai had just delivered the fakest trying-to-be-nonchalant sentence he had ever spoken in his entire life, and Canna didn't even notice.

Once he entered the hallway, he acknowledged that the nerve-racking encounter with Canna was just mere practice at another thing he would also need to execute that day, a very brilliant performance. Albeit he wasn't sure if he could be convincing.

His steps became springy as he whistled down the hall as he would any other day. He serenaded the hallways with a tune he had learned when he was a young kid.

As time went by and he grew up, the tune had gotten stuck in his head sporadically. It was something that resurfaced in his life that did not come from the supernatural, and it continually popped up in his head at times.

In recent days, it had become calming to him as well as nostalgic. He walked along a corridor that connected one wing of the Center to the other, humming with the natural reverb from the big, bright, white walls. As usual, he paused mid-tune to try to remember where he had learned it in the first place.

The wing Fowley worked in was the run-of-the-mill side of the Maquiller Research Center. Many marketing research clients used the facility and campus to conduct their own research.

The world-renown Maquiller Center continually conducted several ongoing health studies relating to various subjects such as cancer treatment, depression and other mental disorders, sleeping disorders, allergies, and experimental vaccinations. It was common to find these types of topics on their list of active studies in any given six-month period.

The other wing is where Kai worked. It was split into three sections and was dedicated to all follow-up treatments. One part was for subjects in the Hippo Project and in the post-programming window thereof.

Another section was for experimental vaccination subjects, and the other third part was a general area for all other kinds of follow-up matter in the Center. But even there in the Hippo Project wing, there were rooms that even Kai had yet to see. There was a hallway with a dozen rooms that had been designated for the subjects that needed *further review,* as often as Canna required.

Kai swiped his badge to enter the wing, and again to enter the office that housed all of the data analysts. That office also held the overall management of study findings, and Human Resources. The offices in that wing had a typical workplace feel to it, and even the daylight shined brighter in that wing.

He walked toward Fowley who was working at his desk, in the back left corner. As he approached, he began to talk to him over other people at their desks and any running office machinery, "Hey, are you going to lunch or what?" he asked Fowley.

"Yeah, give me just a minute. I'm sending the morning reports to the boss man." Fowley replied as he studied the upload progress on the screen.

Kai was surprised to see him running his reports. "Are you kidding me? I thought you normally finished the morning reports no later than noon, right? After all, they are called the morning reports, Kai spoke as he snickered at him.

"Here I was thinking I'm the only one running late," Kai kiddingly rushed his brother with his hand language. "C'mon, I have to talk to you about something," he added.

Fowley smirked and rolled his eyes, "You always have to talk to me about something. What's new?" he asked. "You finally get a yes from Ria?"

Sammie Pyre, who sat next to Fowley in the D.A. department, chuckled at the joke which had been a common theme. Fowley laughed as he pointed past Kai at a shelf with miscellaneous office supplies on it, asking, "Will you please hand me the staple remover on that shelf?"

"What are you laughing at?" Kai asked Sammie, elevating his chin and eyebrows. "How's Thomas doing?" Sammie's facial expression switched to pity for Kai as he grabbed the desk tool from the shelf for Fowley. Kai walked over to hand it to him.

"Thanks," Fowley told him as he reached for it. But both Kai and Fowley were stunned when a blue laser briefly zapped them between their fingertips as Fowley grabbed the staple remover. The static the two created made an audible and bright zapping noise, something like that of a compact stun gun.

Shaken, they nervously looked around to see if anyone else saw it happen. When they concluded that no one else noticed, they calmed down. Kai whipped his neck around to face Fowley with irritation, trying to whisper,

"You just zapped me. What the hell, man?" Kai stated harshly. Unsuccessfully, he tried to hide his deep breathing and composure loss from the scare.

"Shh," Fowley replied holding two fingers to his mouth. "Calm down," he whispered in his own tranquility. Kai had never gotten used to the static that Fowley naturally created sometimes. But it had been happening ever since 2008.

"Well, control it," Kai demanded, knowing that most of the people they worked with were unaware of their superhuman capabilities. Even though the quick charge was just a mild instance of Fowley's superhuman ability, Kai knew he was capable of much more and didn't want to expose it. Sammie just sat in her chair, rolling her eyes at both of them.

"Are you two finished?" she asked with an expression of acute boredom. "And, to you," she said, twirling her index finger toward Kai. "I was laughing at the same thing I've been laughing at for the last three months. Kai, you can't keep chasing these weirdo online chicks. You ever notice how they're all models' who are in between jobs?" she jokingly asked Fowley.

Fowley couldn't hold back his laugh, or his perspective, and he confessed, "It's cool if you're cool with it, man. But, Sammie's right. Ria is a strange one."

"Strange," Sammie exclaimed with realization. "That's the word I was looking for." She looked at Kai with a serious face and expounded, "I'm sorry I called the girl weird. I meant strange. Forgive me."

Sammie and Fowley looked at each other, then laughed so hard that he almost interrupted the file transfer that was just then reaching 95 percent on the progress bar.

"See? Stop, Sammie," Fowley shouted as he grabbed his abdomen and tried to lighten up his deep giggle, "I almost interrupted my file transfer." The three adopted siblings started their regular loads of *dirty laundry*.

"Don't try to change the subject, Sammie," Kai spoke, and he smiled in such a way that Sammie knew he was backing off of a sensitive subject. Instead, he just looked at her with a weird high eyebrow and a closed mouth. Fowley had his eyes fixed on his computer screen,

"Come on," he impatiently commanded his computer as he tapped his index finger on his work desk.

Sammie made her demeanor serious, "Again?" she then smirked at Fowley. "Kai, on second thought, Fowley and his luck with technology. It is crazy comical," she stated, confused. She glanced over at Fowley and said, "Your employment here is ironic, although fun to watch," she kidded.

Fowley picked up his own personal laptop that was on the floor below his desk and slid it halfway inside of the vinyl case he used to carry it. He had always brought it with him everywhere, it seemed. Fowley was much more likely to forget his wallet at home than his laptop.

"For whatever reason, every file transfer is slower today," he said in a mildly defensive tone.

"I know right? And that's why I ran mine earlier than usual, Fowley. The system stalls all the time," Sammie teased. Her long, light brown bangs covered half of her face. She used both hands to brush it to either side before forming a big bright smile and rosy cheeks, to accompany the smart-ass comment.

"No," Fowley said with certainty. "This is nothing at all like a normal stall, this is like molasses outside in winter," he explained.

"You should come with us for lunch," Kai invited Sammie to join them. She didn't always go with them as she had a husband with whom she liked to catch up with on her breaks, if they weren't fighting. Kai made his expression still and serious toward her for a very quick second.

Sammie caught the message in his expression, and it was enough for her to know that she needed to go with her two bearded brothers that day. "Wherever we're going, it will not be the cafeteria downstairs," Kai added with normality.

"I know right, it's awful," Fowley added. They all cackled, then Sammie put her finger over her closed mouth,

"Shh," Sammie attempted to hush the two. The trio had always drawn attention to themselves and their daily trash-talking routine. In reality, they all brought out both the worst and best in each other and had been since middle school. She brought order in her words, "Don't talk badly about it, we might actually have to eat the food in there one day."

"Yum, here's hoping," Fowley's sarcasm lingered in the cheesy grin he flashed Sammie as he stood up to put on his jacket. He put his computer in sleep mode, and zipped his laptop in its case as he grabbed his things,

"Transfer is done, and so am I. Let's go," Fowley said to Sammie, who had already grabbed her jacket and purse. She plotted herself next to Kai on the edge of her desk. The two had waited in anticipation for Fowley's transfer to complete, but they had yet to fully stand up with him.

They were waiting for him to announce something else he had forgotten to do. He often needed to redo tasks at the last minute as a result of rushing. Yet, he always procrastinated until he had to rush. They could hardly stand the irony, and Fowley could never admit it.

"Fowley, are you ready?" Sammie joked.

"C'mon, get it together," he whispered a phrase that a younger, absent-minded Sammie had gotten used to hearing in her high-school years. With a slight grin, he breezed past them both frontward to the double doors and out to the street.

As soon as they turned the corner and were not in the company of coworkers and supervisors, Kai's entire demeanor changed. He looked around cautiously for anyone outside of them who might hear him. He then stopped and turned his head toward Fowley and

Sammie so swiftly that they became stunned, and they paused their steps.

"Listen, we have to do it now," he announced. Sammie gasped, and she looked as if she'd seen a ghost. In the least, the announcement was very haunting to hear. Fowley stared at Kai as he swallowed the knot in his throat, still waiting for a punchline.

"What do you mean we have to do it now?" Fowley replied. Sammie stood next to him still stunned, and her jaw still faintly dropped.

"I mean that one of my subjects got away from me, and I'll probably be fired by the end of the day," he looked at them apologetically, and with saddened eyes. "And, here's the thing. She's hyperactive," he exclaimed quietly. Sammie finally joined the conversation,

"When you say 'hyperactive' do you mean," Sammie was interrupted by Fowley who couldn't help his eagerness,

"Is she just like us?" he asked.

Kai scratched his beard, as he searched for the appropriate wording. "Not sure if she's exactly like us. But, yeah. She is hyperactive, just like us," he replied.

"Then again, you guys have to remember, I never meet subjects until they are in the post-procedure stage. So, there's no telling on how she will evolve, or if she was already hyperactive beforehand," Kai informed the other two. His head shook, and he pondered on it.

"That's right," Fowley exclaimed. "I've heard of a person who became superhuman after the programming."

"Yeah. I remember that too," Sammie added, looking at Kai for confirmation. Kai had been nodding at them.

"That's what I'm thinking," he said to them. But then Fowley's eyes opened wider when his morbid memory came back to him, and he asked them,

"Didn't that guy die?" Sammie looked at Kai as the memory came back to her, too.

"Spontaneous combustion," she and Kai recalled, speaking at the same time.

In his contemplative mind frame, Kai tried to find the right words, saying to them, "Well, a fragment of her limbic system, the hippocampus in her specific case, is exceptional in its capacity. She's hyper-intelligent, at the least. That guy who died tested pretty low in that regard. Guess I really just need to find her, he admitted.

"Canna would've imprisoned her for his research, or he would have killed her in the shaky process," Kai spoke as his breathing became shorter, and anxiety pushed his thinking forward. "So, we must finish it all today," he concluded.

Sammie shuddered and she couldn't help but to express herself as tears swelled up her eyelids, "I'm not ready. I wasn't ready," she cried as the tears flowed down her cheeks. Fowley immediately attempted to calm her and remind her that they must stay temperate. He leaned in close to her ear,

"Your tears are only *showing* what we all are thinking. Please, lose the tears sister," he said. And Kai concurred with a rhythmic nod as Fowley spoke to her.

She had begun to wipe away her tears with her hands. When Kai saw that there were too many tears for her method, he pulled out a restaurant napkin from a small stack that he had always kept in his coat pocket for emergency spills -and the like.

Sammie wiped her tears away before she recapped her burden. "But I'm married. A month from now he'll be leaving for two weeks, and I really didn't want him in town for this," she said in her fallen countenance.

She continued on, "We haven't had the chance to check the exits in your wing. What if this doesn't go right? What's about to happen, Kai?" she keenly inquired while fighting new tears.

"I've already done the exit walkthrough. I didn't really have the choice," Kai assured them. "It's exactly as I thought before, so the layouts we have are already correct," he added.

"Well, it's a good thing that I just now, and I mean just a half-hour ago, finished forwarding the encrypted files to headquarters," Fowley was able to almost smile about something. But Sammie's paranoia was still lingering.

"Are you crazy?" Sammie yelled. She looked around, a little embarrassed of her tone as she briefly peaked in her volume.

She pulled in closer to Fowley's chest. She was 5'4" and Fowley was 6'4" in height, and she stood on her tippy toes near his ear to speak quietly. She asked him, "You mean to tell me that you've just used a Center computer to send the records to HQ?" She could barely use her indoor voice as she incorrectly rephrased his words.

"Of course not. And don't repeat that ever again," Fowley shouted, shaking his head in disapproval and trying his hardest to stay unruffled. "No, Sammie. That's the transfer my laptop was processing, he informed her.

"I was hoping to use my friggin' lunch break to get my laptop put away safely. But now we have a major change of plans, don't we?" he exclaimed purely out of annoyance as his eyes dimmed some. He closed them as he ran his hand over his mustache and beard, clearly mending his own nerves.

"You still need to transfer Canna's files from his PC," Sammie calmly reminded him.

"So, how about we go get something to eat and discuss how we can do that. We also have to protect Kai's job, at least for a few more hours," he said, nodding his head at them both before he continued.

"I also need to get my laptop to a safe location at some point, very soon. And, most importantly, we need to get you to your husband," he smiled awkwardly at Sammie. "Where in the hell is he anyway?" he inserted the sarcastic inquiry.

Sammie shook her head in bitter disgust at Fowley for a second. Then, she finally cracked up faintly at the fact that her marriage was possibly a bigger mess than their situation. As in, she didn't even know where her husband was just then anyway.

Sadly, that was the gist of their relationship. Arguments and absence, along with bitterness and turmoil. Their good days were great. But they were also few and far between.

"Let's eat at the bistro. It might be the last time we do," she said with a kind of bittersweet tone. "We knew it was coming, and now this is it," Sammie accepted the fact as she started walking ahead by herself toward the café they had frequented. Kai and Fowley caught up to her, and Fowley put a brotherly arm over her shoulder,

"Yes, I guess this is it. This is nuts, Kai. I hope you're ready for this," Fowley stated, and he was becoming amped. Kai and Sammie replied in perfect unison.

"I'm not," they chanted once, negating Fowley's aspiration at the moment. Fowley, who was slightly saddened by their response, realized what they meant and acknowledged it.

"Yeah, I guess not, huh?" He twisted his neck to check his tension. "Well, I'm expecting to know what to do when it's time to do it, he countered as he strolled alongside them.

"And it's a café, not a bistro," he added, to correct his slightly younger sister.

Sammie pondered on Fowley's words for a few seconds, then she had a sudden burst of intrigue when she inquired of his honest opinion.

"You really think we could pull this o-," she started to speak, but she couldn't finish her sentence. Her breath was taken by something she was seeing. Sammie abruptly stopped, and Kai with her. He looked at Sammie and inquired,

"What?" She didn't respond, so he followed her eyes to what was striking her. They stood there on the sidewalk, staring up at the clouds in the sky. A large patch of cumulus clouds had formed a sign of some kind, and it was explicitly clear.

It was a large patch of clouds that seemingly glided as the wind carried them. Traveling rightward in the sky, the first part of the patch was shaped like an elephant.

Fowley pointed to it, "An elephant?" he identified it.

"Yeah. Clearly, it is," Kai replied. "It's perfect," he added, speaking of its shape. As Kai spoke, the elephant cloud patch started to break apart. As it dissipated, another section of the cloud cluster had found its perfect shape.

"That's amazing," Fowley said as they gasped all at once. A new shape was made clear from the cluster.

"And a fox," Sammie pointed out the shape, but that wasn't necessary. They all saw the fox. They all watched the cloud break up.

"That's crazy," Fowley exclaimed as they started to walk forward again, not wanting to hold up the sudden group of pedestrians creating sidewalk traffic. But as they started to walk, Kai abruptly halted again staring skyward as he uttered,

"No way. Is this real? This is really happening right now." He was gawking with his eyes on the sky. They all looked back up and saw the entire patch formed together as one huge turtle. "A turtle," Fowley confirmed in awe, and none of them could look away.

The turtle maintained its shape for a full fifteen seconds, although the clouds glided hastily. When it finally dissipated, the three looked to each other. A little disoriented, they were not sure of what to say.

"That was so bizarre," Sammie whispered, shaking her head for the lack of sense in what they saw. "Maybe our angels are looking out for us," she willed.

"Sweetie, we'll be lucky if our angels don't resign today," Fowley kidded with a straight face. "But, if they want to make a cameo, I'd be very cool with it," he accepted and smiled, scanning the sky at all angles.

He lowered his head back down to them, "Are we ever gonna eat?" he asked. They resumed the walk quietly until they arrived at the café, but they strolled at a slower speed than they had ever walked that block before. They knew that they were going to need a longer lunch, a bigger plan, and a lot of luck.

****

Pearl sat very still on the floor in a storage closet with her head in her folded arms and her elbows over her knees. She was certain that the Center had alerted all on-site security of her disappearance somewhere in the past thirty minutes. She had yet to find an opportunity to get out. As she'd roamed the hallways hoping to find an exit, she found that the door at the end of the corridor was the only one with no human security blocking it.

It also wasn't doing Pearl any justice by showing herself to every security camera in the building. She searched most diligently for an exit, or at least a room to hide in for a minute.

She hoped she'd continue to be lucky enough for the guards to overlook her on camera. She had barely dodged a couple of them, and a few in-house officers, in person.

She was now closer to the section of the building that didn't have the same dire needs for security because it housed low-risk to no-risk study groups. Still, there were a few guards who were posted somewhere in the lobby as long as those doors were unlocked.

She had been growing uncomfortable. She was careful not to move, knowing it would trigger the sensor that turned the automatic lights on. Her body was becoming stiff.

The storage room housed lots of shelves holding basic medical supplies. She had found some scrubs in the supplies and put them on over her sweats. She also had put some first-aid supplies into a plastic storage bag to have it on hand, if needed.

What she didn't have was a way out of the main entrance doors, as of yet. Every door she'd found would have sounded an alarm if she had tried to open it.

Normally, a sub wouldn't have made it as far as she did, but the complacent security guards who were monitoring the hall cameras were distracted by their own vices in the surveillance room. They had already missed a few different opportunities to spot her creeping in the halls. They simply failed to be alert.

She needed to breeze past the medical receptionists, attracting little-to-no attention. She would also require an employee badge to enter the main wing lobby in the first place.

She had narrowly avoided one employee who had come in to grab boxes of tissues and rubber gloves from one of the shelves. At that time, the automatic lights had come on and Pearl was suppressing her fears for the entire moment until the staff member left.

Pearl had been in the back corner of the storage room in an upright-fetal position, afraid to move. After experiencing the close call with the employee, and a severe migraine attack, she wasn't ready for the brightness. In that moment in the storage room, Pearl was also lucky to learn that the pitch-black dark combatted her episodes.

She knew she couldn't stay there. When she finally understood the risk she was taking by still being in the building she became more panicky, but much braver. She calmed herself and visualized the building she was in. Pre-routing her steps out of the place, she was confident that she could somehow sneak away.

She'd figured she could blend in with the employees during lunch-hour traffic as they entered and exited. She then visualized the contents of the storage room as she remembered what items were in there, and exactly where each item was located. She'd devised an inventory list in her head.

She had decided to take some employee's black backpack that was not so sanitarily hanging on a hook about three feet away from the scrubs closet on her left. For protection, she would also take a scalpel blade from the locked cabinet with the glass window that was about six feet in front of her.

In addition, Pearl had imagined that the eye-rinse solution on the shelf above her head could prove useful. She'd also planned to grab the bag of first-aid supplies that she had already packed up and placed on a shelf that was about five feet to her left. She was also taking the flashlight next to it.

She needed the backpack for storage, and to look normal enough to blend in on the way out. She was finally ready to make the attempt to leave. Pearl took a deep breath, then slowly counted to three. She stood up, and the lights turned on.

As Pearl reached the corridor to the main wing, she crossed paths with an employee. The preoccupied young woman in scrubs and white sneakers had yet to look up from her phone when Pearl brought her hands up to her own eyes, as if to wipe away tears.

The woman looked up, feeling caught off guard when she said, "Hi," She was waiting for a response to tell whether Pearl was crying, or just wearing irritating eye make-up.

"Hi," Pearl replied, choked up in the voice.

"What's wrong, are you okay?" the medical assistant moved in closer to her.

Pearl nodded her head, and she lowered her hands to reveal the many tears that had run down her face. Pearl's anxiety was truly peaked, and it only made for a more believable performance. However, the tears she cried were not her own.

She was just glad that it wasn't security or Kai in the halls, and she exploited the situation for her own sake. Pearl saw the young woman and broke down crying,

"I'm so sorry. I don't mean to," she started to say, but the woman interrupted,

"Don't be," she said with an authentically concerned tone. "Do you need help with something?" she inquired. Pearl deepened her breathing, but she got it out.

"I'm sorry, I've just learned that I'm having a baby. I'm glad about it," she said as she faintly smiled through her tears. "But, the father doesn't want to have anything to do with it," she blurted out. Then she dropped her face into her hands, sobbing crocodile tears.

Shrewdly, she had poured the eye-rinse solution into her eyes before she walked out of the storage closet. She just hoped that the act could work on the first employee she bumped into.

"Come on. Let's go get you some tissues. Are you on lunch break?" the medical assistant queried.

"Yes, I was going out to get some air," Pearl explained as she appeared to be very embarrassed, and trying to pull herself together. "Thank you for asking if I was okay," she added with appreciation.

They started to walk in the corridor together. Pearl tried to stay quiet for fear of saying something stupid. She grabbed a tissue from the little front pocket on the leather backpack and began to dab her eyes.

"What's your name?" the woman asked as they walked.

"Kim," Pearl responded. She couldn't think about anything, except how close she was getting to the door. So, she behaved as smoothly as she could. She answered with "Kim" because she had seen the name twice already that day, and it felt familiar.

"Well hi, Kim. I'm Joy, find me if you need anything at all," she told Pearl, as she reached her arm out to scan her badge. They were approaching the double doors to the main wing. Pearl didn't want to leave any awkward spacing in the moment, so she grabbed the door and held it open for Joy, with a smile.

She hoped that her face effectively expressed her ability to control her composure, so not to worry Joy any further. As she stood next to the open door, she motioned for Joy to go first. Then, with a dry face, Pearl said to her once again,

"Thank you. Really," she almost whispered as she nodded once more, and smiled with a little mortification. Joy just smiled back and replied,

"That's okay, it's what we do sometimes, right? Do you still need me to get those tissues?" she asked once they had walked through the doors.

"No, I found some in my backpack. Thank you," Pearl replied as she waved the facial tissue for her to see.

With a calm and confidential demeanor, Joy advised. She spoke gently when she said, "Don't you worry, it gets better."

Joy casually turned to walk away, and Pearl noticed something flying very closely behind her. A loud and lively butterfly was buzzing around the bun she wore on the back of her head.

It was an extremely radiant, pinkish-purple butterfly that was about two inches wide, and it followed her down the hall. Joy was unbothered by its buzzing hum as she disappeared through the door of a connected hall. Pearl noticed that the young woman couldn't hear the insect at all.

Pearl thought she might have an issue or two with her perception. What she had just seen was simply bizarre.

Joy walked through the doors, then off to the left. Pearl walked through the doors then right out of the front entrance.

She walked hastily through the lobby. She avoided any eye contact, afraid to take any chances with exposing her identity. She pushed through the revolving door. The second she touched the pavement she noticed a new air that was much crisper.

She immediately started to walk to get as far away as she possibly could from that strange place, and daunting experience. She couldn't even remember how the day began, and it was slowly becoming less and less in the forefront of her thoughts.

She scoped a small parking area that was for Center employees. She noticed a flashy, deep-red car. The chrome trim made it really stand out. The vanity license plate read, "DOCIZN." Pearl smirked, but she wondered if the car belonged to the same man with whom Kai was speaking in the hallway.

Pearl accepted the fact that if the answer wasn't somewhere in the file that she possessed in her new backpack, she may never know. But she was okay with that. Her only mission was to get away from the Maquiller Research Center, and never return.

*******End of Chapter*******

Chapter 5
Bitter History

Each Maquiller Research Center branch was a limb of a much bigger entity that specialized in various medical advances all in the name of research, innovation, and personal gain. Over the years, unsettling practices had become prevalent amidst the professionals involved with the Hippo Project. Pure greed is what influenced the entire operation.

The Maquiller Center had quickly become, and still was, like a big glass house divided against itself. The two head professionals detested each other, but no one could cast the first stone.

Hazardously, as a hyperactive subject who rejected programming, Pearl couldn't be appealing to either side of it. Whether Maquiller or Canna, Pearl's new nature made it a very short walk to tragedy for her.

Whenever there was hyperactivity found in a subject, superhuman characteristics were usually not far behind. While Maquiller may administer the serum to keep those special strengths at bay, he wouldn't be inclined to keep a subject trapped like Canna tended to.

Maquiller had the ability to retry programming if the procedure had previously failed. He was likely to re-approach new programming from another angle after several serum treatments. Canna was much more hands-on in his personal approach.

Contrastingly, Dr. Al Canna was more interested in what it was about a failed subject that made them nonprogrammable, and he wanted to know what made them tick. So, he found out by testing them.

In turn, Al Canna used that tick to help steer a secondary method of reform to curb hyperactivity, pain-inflicting conditioning. Canna's main problem was that only one of the two professionals had the answers to his groundbreaking research questions, and it was not him.

For him, the cognitive understanding of a sub's physical resilience was the only contribution he could make to the Opal Firs location when he had first taken his seat there. The Rhode Island branch was the main location for the programming process. But Dr. Al Canna had begun to use a newfound memory-programming method of his own in 2001.

Maquiller only cared if a subject held any memory of going through the programming experience, but Canna's subjects had to meet two vital requirements to be released. Firstly, they had to be unable to exhibit anything beyond average human strength. Secondly, they must either have no memory of the research process whatsoever or be fully programmed altogether.

As Canna did not have access to Maquiller's effective serum, his research was very *trial-and-error* in its style. He'd developed a serum of his own, but the effect it had on the superhuman was much more debilitating than Leroi's concoction.

Maquiller's handy serum and built-in programming triggers could halt a subject in their tracks, Al Canna had no such muscle in his method. So, his goal was to prevent their free movement in the first place.

Maquiller targeted humans who he had reasons to believe would exhibit exceptional skills, or gifts, after the procedure. Over time, the attempt to make super humans had become perplexing for Maquiller.

Not every blameless subject who completed the procedure had become hyperactive, and not every hyperactive subject exhibited possession of any kind of super skill. It threw Maquiller off, however, it had never stopped his goal to build himself a powerful army to stand behind him.

When it came to rarer subjects, some didn't even know what great skills they possessed. The others, who didn't exhibit their strength, were afraid of making it known to anyone. Nonetheless, Maquiller's concluded stats were wacky.

Of the two, Maquiller was more advanced in the research, and he'd intended to keep it that way. To be simply put, the two professionals were rivals. It was only a matter of time before one of them attempted a big move to bigger power. That time was imminent.

Several other studies had resurfaced for the same purposes, but with a different name each time since the original inspiration in 1977. Things had turned regrettably darker than the original innovator's true, and slightly humbler, intentions.

Robert Kin was an aspiring 41-year-old American neuroscientist who had come from a family of medical practitioners, scientists, and soldiers. In 1976, a year after the Vietnam War had ended, Kin became determined to find a breakthrough procedure. One that would allow him to reprogram the memories of a subject who had been traumatized by the violence and gory images specifically related to war battles.

He had also figured that he could achieve the same results in a few other instances in which a person had experienced a horrific trauma otherwise. As it had turned out, Kin was correct, and his method ultimately aided some assault victims who needed help managing memories of their own.

While they could never forget the attacks, they could redirect their focus around the flashbacks that frequently held them captive. Many of the first successfully programmed individuals out of these victims went on to become volunteers and employees for the Social Services community.

His uncle, who was near and dear to him, suffered incalculably from Post-Traumatic Stress Disorder and exhibited some of the most severe symptoms Kin had ever witnessed in all of his time in research. The condition saddened Kin, but it had also moved and motivated him deeply.

The procedure he had in mind would be relatively harmless to a person already suffering from very acute P.T.S.D. Or at least the risks were low for the Robert Kin theory.

He never aimed to create any alteration outside of his focus on the amygdala, hippocampi, and a small part of the temporal lobe regions of the subject's brain during his procedure. This would have allowed the person to still live harmoniously with the people they loved, and to resume the activities they already enjoyed doing.

Kin had successfully completed the procedure on his uncle, who had been anxious to try it. Leroi Maquiller then successfully proposed a partnership with Kin, guaranteeing a forward leap to help veterans all over the United States. Shortly after, the Maquiller Research Center had achieved all kinds of great successes, publicity, and endorsements.

Founder Leroi Maquiller and Co-Founder Robert Kin renovated a property in Rhode Island and created their own dedicated research building and lab. Kin had the product and Maquiller had the funds to maintain the means to produce massive results.

That year, even local politicians jumped on the bandwagon, each promising to fundraise on behalf of the Maquiller Center Fund for the duration of their terms. The technology had become a possible catalyst for major neurological breakthroughs.

But Robert Kin was dead by 1978. He died after leaving the Rhode Island Center, the first of all the branches, with Leroi Maquiller and Company. That night, they were to attend a meeting among the heads of staff.

Kin "suffered a heart attack," the police and medical examiner had concluded. But Kin's wife Rachael had received a weird call from Robert just moments before his estimated time of death.

He called her just to say that he loved her, which only happened when they had an argument. The thing that concerned Kin's wife was that everything was great between them. Rachael knew better, but found it hard to trust anyone to tell.

Rachael, who was also the mother of Kin's two children, settled with the Maquiller Research Center after a long and painful battle, which included a few counter offers regarding monies owed to Kin. The amount of money that Kin's family received was relatively fractional to the profits made from his research "breakthrough," as professionals worldwide agreed it was.

But all Rachael wanted to do was to get enough to flee to some place new, where she could feel safe with her children. So, she did what she knew she needed to do to protect them.

Over time, the intelligence inside of the Human Resources Department of the Corporate Center in Rhode Island had concluded that Maquiller himself had become drastically different.

He'd changed dramatically, for the worse. Yet, they had neither the power nor the guts to do anything about it. He had become a bitter dictator roaming free in a world of secrecy where the people surrounding him had even bloodier hands than he did.

Because he was able to carry out his most violent deeds through the hands of others via the programming, Maquiller was able to sleep unbothered at night. Meanwhile, the victims of his scheme suffered immensely from the guilt of those deeds.

Sleep was elusive to many of those people as the deeds they had committed would be with them all the way to their graves. Sometimes, very early graves they were. Maquiller was a man-made monster who wanted all of the power and wealth to be gained, without the guilt that came along with the practice.

Between 1978 and 1998, a few attempts to bring down Leroi Maquiller were made. But they had always wound up unsuccessful at exposing him, as the witnesses were silenced in various ways. Thus, the inquiries themselves had become lost like grains in a sandstorm and dissolved like every other *far-fetched conspiracy theory* ever concocted.

Then one day, Leroi found a breakthrough in his scientific research. He had gained the perilous ability to program an entire life story into another human being, programming content that was much closer to one hundred percent of the subject's memory capacity. The history of it all became an unnerving tale to tell, and so few have told it.

Once again, the reputation of the Maquiller Center rocked back and forth in the gossip and other unproven conspiracy theories about the dark influence that the facilities may have had in the four cities that housed one of its locations. Nonetheless, in 1998 the Washington State-based branch had launched the predecessor to the Hippo Project.

Project H.E.A.D. (Health Education for Alzheimer's and Dementia), was their first study launched with the goal to strip the subject's memories altogether, and then reprogram the original memories back to them along with new perspectives, new talents, new goals, and ultimately, new lives.

For the most part, those subjects would tell all that their quality of life had been restored. The very first trial started with recruiters screening for elderly citizens suffering from Dementia or advanced Alzheimer's disease.

In most cases, the subject's family desperately wanted a cure because it had been harder on families that required extra care for a member in their household who was struggling with one of the two diseases. Those families were a little skeptical, but still hopeful enough to be optimistic when they enrolled their loved ones for the brand-new experimental trial.

In the first phase of the trial, twenty subjects had undergone the new procedure, and eighteen of them exhibited a "mostly normal" memory to all those around them. There was a minor exception regarding small details in tastes or perspectives that the subject had acquired during programming. The other two remained the same.

Remarkably, while no connection was directly made, it had been noted that those same two subjects were also the first two of the twenty in the study group to die, and it had been presumed to be from natural causes. But overall, the other families were highly impressed at the hands of science.

It was believed that the study had also exposed a strong correlation between healthy brain functionality and a healthy physical existence. There was a lot of promise in the research that Maquiller completed in that trial. But within his own dark reasoning, Maquiller wanted to pursue a younger set of subjects rather than continue the great work done in the first phase of Project H.E.A.D.

There were one hundred subjects in the second phase, and they were mostly young adults. These were people who generally had no issues with memory loss, but did have some criminal history, struggled with drug addiction, or was a ward of the state with no next of kin. The marketing was customized to be alluring to a young citizen who might gladly take a $2500 stipend for a shot at remembering a sad life differently, or a whole new life altogether.

Many of the one hundred subjects would have never considered themselves good candidates for the study, understanding that not one of them was a traumatized individual. Even though they had maintained healthy memory states, the staff still convinced them that the procedure was likely to affect their quality of life in a very positive way that appealed to each participant personally.

Those subjects filled out questionnaires inquiring about their ideals including, preferred career or skills, preferred location, and so on. Outside of those subjects, three did not participate voluntarily. They were given no say in the matter.

With the exception of those three subjects, each participant was given an intricate physical before the procedure to note any shifts in athletic abilities during the post-procedure window. Outside speculation had begun to question whether there was any need to reprogram perfectly healthy adults. Maquiller had begun to receive backlash from almost all walks of life, and it frustrated him deeply.

In that round, the initial deletion of memories had only been successful in eleven of the one hundred individuals with whom the study staff screened and completed the process. Goose Gary was one of those eleven subjects. In fact, he was one of the three forced subjects. As for the 89 subjects who had retained their memory, the reprogramming step had bombed as well, transferring less than .01% of the intended new identity or data.

It was likely to happen. Their own authentic memories remained stored in their rightful places, making little or no room for anything new or contradictory. With no considerable alterations made to them, all 89 were released. Of the eleven with successful memory deletion, one subject rejected the coding step.

His result was much like Pearl's, but without any hyperactivity anywhere in the cerebral cortex. In fact, his brain activity lowered drastically as he had no association to any memory to steer his intelligence.

He was partly a vegetable, but he retained his physical ability. He had been kept in observation for an extended time. His family reported him missing, while the Center kept him in a room away from everyone and everything, not offering much to guide or fix him. He was only useful to them for as long as it took for them to find out why he might have malfunctioned.

After seeing that the young college student was not a threat to their operations, they released him to his worried family. The unlucky young man couldn't even recognize his mother, father, or his siblings.

His recovery method was to go home and try to relearn who all those wonderful people were to him. The Center explained that he had been found on the street with no knowledge of who he was and was brought to the Center for his safety, and possible treatment. They offered his family an offensively small monetary stipend which they passed off as a donation of goodwill, and it was atomic even.

That young man was Leith Nomea, a medical student who had bought a dream that promised him exceptional knowledge and skill in his desired profession. By the time news outlets had reported on it, it was believed that Leith had become overwhelmed with school, and had suffered some kind of a breakdown.

Every source attributed in the report spoke of a young man who was feeling pressured academically. But not one source detailed his participation in *breakthrough research*.

Project H.E.A.D. was an unmonitored study trial with an inconsistent set of subjects. It originated with a group of hopeful elderly subjects and their families, but ended with homesick preschoolers and kindergarteners; the grandies.

All thirteen grandies were programmed that same year, not long after Maquiller had become enraged over his trial's Phase-II results. He was fuming.

During phase two of Project H.E.A.D., Maquiller had found it to be difficult to program a subject with a large pre-existing memory set. He couldn't achieve it with his technological capabilities.

He then organized a hunt for the youngest subjects he could find, hypothesizing that a toddler without well-developed memory would make for easier programming, and better quality thereof.

But by then, Maquiller knew exactly what he was looking for. He had purposely aimed to recruit a certain kind of child for his research, and he had been able to gather five other small kids, as his *control group*.

He had targeted extraordinary children, who he believed possessed distinctive traits. He believed that to have them in his possession was to have power, as well as revenge against a group of special human beings who had all refused to partake in anything pertaining to research. These people were within the bloodlines of the eight grandies who were made superhuman.

Maquiller paid relatively small amounts of money for insignificant criminals to gather up his new subjects.

New, young subjects whom the nation's citizens would add to a heartbreaking list of *missing children*. It wasn't that difficult for Maquiller to find his subjects, let alone his candidates for the odd job of abducting them.

There was a total of four adult men who were responsible for kidnapping and gathering the children. Each *snatcher* had been followed and under surveillance every step of the way. Once Maquiller finally had his thirteen subjects retained, he no longer needed their services. Every snatcher, except one who had suddenly abandoned the assignment, was murdered shortly after -all in the same week.

The grandies had been raised as Leroi's own children. In a sense, they were kept close to him to save him in some spiritually awkward way. In 1987, both Leroi's wife and child died in a freak accident, leaving Leroi completely broken then -if he wasn't already broken.

Eleven years later, he finally made the attempt to fill the voids his wife and child left when he'd decided to foster the grandies. It's not what he originally had in mind, but once he had seen what they are he knew he wanted them all to himself.

Eight of the grandies had been made superhuman, or "hyperactive," in the invasive programming process. However, each and every grandie held the belief that they were adopted by Leroi Maquiller.

Whenever he held any of them in a research session it was because he wanted to observe their unique abilities, and maintain their loyalty. The grandies had never been given a reason to believe that they had gone through the program process themselves.

The other five were also successfully programmed but did not exhibit any unusual abilities during their post-examination. These five were still able to successfully complete preprogrammed tasks assigned to them.

Maquiller assumed guardianship of all of them, but it was obvious to the five that he favored the *special* grandies. Naturally, those five grandies had gradually become bitter toward the Cr8 because of Maquiller's subtle favoritism. Relentlessly, they had dedicated a lot of time and energy to win Maquiller's approval, if they ever really could.

The third phase wherein the grandies were made was fully backed by Dr. Al Canna, M.D. He was a pharmaceutical-rich, world-renown psychiatrist who afforded a portion of the remaining funding needed to maintain Maquiller's research. There was enough money between the two of them to keep the operation confidential and stable.

Canna hadn't known about Maquiller's method for gathering some of his subjects, and Leroi left him in the dark on those matters, initially. The proof eventually surfaced, and Canna took full advantage of his new upper hand over Maquiller.

In return, Canna stayed silent and took his position as Hippo Project Head of Staff at the MRC Washington-State branch. In recent months, he made plans to separate his own research from the Maquiller Center altogether to ultimately become both a climber and a competitor.

Back in December of 1998, Al Canna suddenly bucked up and bullied Maquiller into a bargain and partnership. That day, Maquiller learned that Al Canna had more than enough proof to expose his scandal with the missing children.

The first external, non-programmed person to obtain proof that Maquiller was indeed corrupt was Al Canna. Without delay, Al Canna presented his advantage to Leroi, but he'd presented himself as an ally looking for a career boost, and not a rivaling informant. Maquiller was desperate and willing to work something out with him.

However, Maquiller and Canna disagreed about a lot of things -especially how to utilize subjects who experienced abnormalities. Their approaches to research and results for the programmed subject contrasted sharply.

Yet, neither of them wanted to deal with a botched subject, ever. The nonprogrammable subject was the equivalent of a failed experimental attempt.

That would mean that the subject couldn't do Maquiller's bidding for him and that was a deal-breaker. The indication of life and death for that subject depended on whether the subject could remember the programming process, or not. With that, ignorance was bliss.

If Maquiller had ever sensed that a sub knew they were tampered with, he would have them killed. A small, but sad, share of unsuspecting subjects died in that arena of Maquiller's paranoia.

Canna wanted nothing much to do with anyone who couldn't conform in his world, programmed or not. His personal belief system and delusional social circle left him no room for a lack of stealthy results. He wanted to change the world, but only to *his* liking.

While he programmed his subs with the outside world in mind, Maquiller kept his successfully programmed subjects close and busy. A more precarious Maquiller was motivated to keep his programmed children, as his own. But his own twisted version of a successful family business underlined his end goal.

In the midst of it all, he generally wanted the grandies to be happy and healthy. As long as they proved to serve him, they were free to roam about.

They were allowed to be kids, but they were indeed on a tight, and very short, leash. There had always been someone lurking around them back then, but for their well-being -and Leroi's discretion.

Uncooperatively, Canna found major negligence in allowing any subject who is exhibiting superhuman characteristics to run about in the world among common people. He answered to a different set of masters, and the fear of mass rebellion ailed them.

To the grandies, Canna was like the school system that always blamed the student and never the ridiculous curriculum. While they weren't exactly on Canna's blacklist, they had always worried about the few they knew who have been. And way deep down inside, Canna was envious of each one of the Cr8 members.

While Canna was indeed interested in growing his own riches, he was more inclined to create a world in which all the inhabitants moved as a single unit with a single mindset, via mass-programming strides. This wasn't going to happen if he ever went up against an individual who could actually defend himself.

It drove him mad when Maquiller began to send the grandies to the Opal Firs location to work because he'd felt that he would be too close under Leroi's radar. Even though they were successfully programmed, he'd still maintained a hesitant attitude when it came to the grandies. Perhaps he was just jealous of them, but he didn't like them.

On the other hand, Maquiller was a deeply troubled captor who really wanted to create his own personal "army of servants," made up of the children whom he had reserved as if they were his own. Years had passed, and the grandies still didn't know they weren't Maquiller's "adopted" family as he'd always claimed. But in recent times the grandies had grown skeptical about his story, although they've lacked hard proof.

When examining each of the two professionals closely, some might find it difficult to conclude which one was the lesser evil of the two. Over time, a malfunctioning subject's treatment while in the program simply depended on which of the two professionals headed their specific study trial and branch location.

Kai and Fowley both have had premonitions about Leroi Maquiller's history with the Center. They both have dreamt strange dreams. Since their arrivals in Washington, their dreams had become more frequent, and a little more telling.

But never was the story of the kidnappings shared with them, and there were only a few knowing Center individuals who were still alive by the time the grandies grew up. Those few Maquiller Research Center affiliates were never going to tell, by any means.

Although those few may have wanted to protect the Cr8, they could never calculate the extent of the grandies' loyalty toward Maquiller. None of them wanted to risk facing the consequences of exposing a grandie's circumstance to the grandie. Besides, they all had taken an oath, and they would forever keep that promise.

Kai, Sammie, Fowley, and TJ made up the four-man team that had been collecting data from the Maquiller Research Center in Washington and sending it to the main headquarters and home branch in Rhode Island. They all were preparing for further instructions from Maquiller as their mission was coming to an end. But now, Kai would need to probe for instructions prematurely -in light of the circumstances.

Their relationship with Maquiller is why they've slowly but surely followed each other across the country. They've always had the feeling that the big picture would become clear, and they just wanted to be together when it happened.

They had all grown up under Maquiller's influence, and still were. But with Kai being the last of them to transfer to Washington, the team finally had all of its remaining members and could execute a better plan.

They knew that they could pull off the last task, even if they were a little early. But this time they had a plan of their own, and they hoped it would set them completely free. Their special group had rules to operate by, but they were still learning them.

It was clear that they didn't like to use their powers, but with time it became inevitable. They had also learned to respect their powers over the years, as they practiced self-control often.

They had already discovered their own excess individual strengths at some point years ago, and they all knew that it was too much. "No gore," was their motto. But occasionally, the surmounted fear caused a grandie to become oblivious to such consciousness when backed against the wall.

The programming caused them to complete tasks that they had sometimes found to be surprisingly harsh, and hard to live with. A programmed being could implement an entire crime wave and then find themselves sitting at their desk at work two hours later, delayed in digesting what they had done.

Any programmed subject out there in the world could have such a day. The rules that the Cr8 followed, they sometimes didn't make. Contrastingly, the rules that they did make they sometimes couldn't follow. It simply depended on the circumstances that surrounded them.

The average subject had been programmed with horrible tendencies that were sure to surface at some point in their coding timeline, and Maquiller did not lighten the load for his grandies. He used them for tasks that would damage a rival financially or politically, as well as physically.

The grandies had all vowed to each other to keep the secrecy regarding their powers or hyper intellect. They gladly *walked on eggshells* in this world, and they humbly embraced the paradoxes therein.

Over and over, their lives were out of their hands. The members of the "CR8," as they had decided to call themselves in high school, began to recognize each other as outliers very early on in their childhood somewhere around ages six to eight. It was at that time that all eight of them knew that they wouldn't have any other friends in the world like themselves, ever.

In 1998, Maquiller's Program Content Writer, Louis Heart, had become disgruntled during the last phase of the H.E.A.D. project. Louis scheduled vacation, hoping he wouldn't be assigned beyond the first successful phase. He had realized his convictions about bringing younger subjects with healthy memory sets intact into the project, let alone the grandies.

Maquiller had grown colder toward the staff surrounding him and occasionally lost all signs of common decency when dealing with them. One day, Maquiller had decided to cancel Louis's vacation at the last minute to reassign him. He scheduled him for the third phase of the H.E.A.D. project, which introduced the small children as subjects.

In his vengeful fit, Louis added extra programming codes that ultimately would make two particular grandies turn on Maquiller with the sole mission to kill him. It wasn't detected among his colleagues in the Center who worked near him that Louis was boiling beneath the surface, and Louis had no idea that what he had done was going to cost those two grandies their lives at some point down the line.

Later in 2009, when the grandies were teens, Cr8 members Dee and Tonny both had awakened with the sudden urge to kill Maquiller. Their behavior was erratic and the program code they were living out was not at all compatible with the character their specific programming had instilled. It flopped.

There was much inner conflict that was made apparent to those around them. They had also displayed awkward disconnects or internal glitches, sort to speak. It was undeniable that they had lacked simple confidentiality.

They attempted to enter Maquiller's work office straightforward, with no discretion regarding their mission to harm him. The security team was able to subdue them and lock them up using a special serum that pauses all brain activity.

Subsequently, they had lost bodily control. It had turned them into vegetables, temporarily. Maquiller later ordered them to be detained in lock-down status under his elite security team and to be made hypoactive altogether, while he investigated the ordeal.

However, while the two teens were in the care of the security team, they both died from an overdose of hypoactive serum. The guards who were supposed to have been caring for them became negligent and abusive. One day, the guards upped the amount of serum that they administered to the two grandies. The fatal dose shut down every vital organ in their bodies.

Exaggerating the grandies' rebellious behavior, the guards convinced Maquiller and his reporting staff that they had accidentally overdosed the teens. Maquiller was left to believe that the grandies were not improving, and he covered up for his security team.

The rest of the Cr8 could never understand why Maquiller let the security team get away with murder. True, they had thought that Tonny and Dee were going to be kicked out of the Maquiller house, maybe. But never had they imagined a death sentence, and they were sorely displeased with their adoptive father.

Despite what had been told to them, they all felt that Dee and Tonny were wrongfully killed. In fact, they felt the presence of those two grandies leave them, right when it was happening.

Truth is, Maquiller no longer had any trust for Dee or Tonny. While it was upsetting to lose two of his grandies, a weight was lifted off of his shoulders when he'd learned that they were no longer. The rest of the grandies could sense his emotion, and it shifted the way they saw their guardian from then on.

Nonetheless, Maquiller continued to investigate the glitch that ailed them. After decoding the programming transcripts for Dee and Tonny, Maquiller had learned that his former content writer for Project H.E.A.D. in 1998 was the wrongdoer.

Months later, Louis was walking to his car in his apartment-building parking garage when he was suddenly jumped by two men. Louis was stabbed repeatedly, just like several other victims of a locally active serial killer near that same time.

In late April of 2008, bodies had been turning up all month long in various places near Providence, Rhode Island. The individuals who Maquiller hired to hit Louis thought it would make for a smoother storyline to copycat a serial killer, rather than to fake an accident.

The remaining "grandies" from the Cr8 group did learn of Louis's death from the news. They immediately had doubts that a serial killer was responsible for it, knowing how corrupt the Center was. In those times, the Cr8 felt actual disgust toward Maquiller, the Center, and everyone employed there.

Two more members of the Cr8, Rose and Kielo, died in a freak accident a few months later. They were canoeing and got overturned in rough water. From what had been reported to the Cr8, they both had drowned.

Unaware of their own programming, none of the Cr8 members knew that Dee and Tonny were experiencing severe internal glitches. From their view, the two had come to hate Maquiller and the authority figures around them chose to leave it right there -uncorrected.

Both Kielo and Rose had taken Louis's death very hard. And even though he was very much involved with the Center like anyone else they knew, they knew that Louis had grown weary of the operation, and bitter toward Maquiller. After Louis died, they had become wicked in their own ways and refused to abide by the principles of the Cr8, let alone Maquiller's rules.

While they both were extremely powerful, they mishandled that power by operating under anger. Shortly after Louis's death, they had committed a few deeds that required recompensing. The rest of the Cr8 was forced to accept the fact that they may never know for sure if Maquiller was responsible, or if the drownings were simply universal atonement.

On that day, their lives were turned upside down, yet again. In reality, their lives were truly turned upside down the day when each of them were stolen from their real parents and programmed to disremember them altogether.

In that same week when Kielo and Rose died, Kai had watched a documentary on missing children. He hadn't even been looking for anything in particular, he was just intrigued by the stories. But Kai had an epiphany when the host and narrator of the film mentioned a birthmark on a four-year-old boy being the only thing his parents could be sure of, considering his current-time age progression.

He used a hand mirror with his back to his wall mirror and realized that he still had an awkward patch of skin on the back of his neck, right underneath his hairline. He had always been curious about it. It wasn't a birthmark, but it did look weird like one that had possibly been removed from that very spot.

From that day forward, Kai had an undying gut feeling that neither he nor any other grandie was who Maquiller said they were. However, without authentic memories, Kai continuously second-guessed the possibilities that sprung into his mind at such times.

The Cr8 also knew that one day they would ultimately cut ties with Canna on behalf of Maquiller, and from Maquiller on behalf of their own dearest friends who were merely pawns until the end. They knew without a doubt that the karmas of Al Canna and Leroi Maquiller were both inevitable and imminent.

*******End of Chapter*******

ODD GEMS Soaked by Suri R. Moon

Chapter 6

Canna's Cryptogram

Kai, Fowley, and Sammie quickened their steps as they approached the entrance to the building. After taking a longer lunch that day, Kai quietly ran through the outline that they had agreed on at the café, saying,

"So, I will go to Canna and let him know what's happened. Fowley will complete his last transfers to HQ." He looked at Fowley with nervousness as he continued, "Please complete the transfer by all means, and please do not transfer anything concerning Subject Sixteen," he begged.

Kai wanted to be careful not to take Mari out of the frying pan of Al Canna just to toss her through Maquiller's ring of fire. Fowley nodded back,

"I got it. I'm on it," he replied. Sammie nudged Kai with her elbow as she spoke,

"Please, Kai. Whatever you do, make sure that Fowley and I know if and when you've changed over," she said waving her phone. "Send a text? Say, 'Hi. I'm in,' when you are?" she proposed the code language.

"Will do, that goes for all of us," Fowley added. He looked over to Kai with slight worry, "I talked to TJ. He said he's 'been ready,' and I know it's the truth," he reminded them.

Sammie and Kai looked at each other with mild trepidation while they nodded in agreement with him, knowing that TJ had been waiting impatiently for the downfall of Canna's operation.

Keeping his eyes on a very anxious Kai, Fowley continued, "But you, Kai. You have to understand that you might not get into that part of your wing. No matter what, keep your cool and keep us posted," he outlined. He glanced at Sammie to make sure she was listening, then continued to speak,

"And, please do not put TJ in danger," he added.

"Okay. I'll try," Kai snapped back wildly throwing his hands up.

"He's the only access we have to those rooms, and them. And, he told me to tell you that he wrote Canna a message on the wall in room 321. He said maybe you could use it?" Fowley said as he nervously eyed the main entrance door while trying to keep his deepened voice quiet.

Kai was nodding his head pensively, trying to see how a message might help his act. "What does the message say?" he asked Fowley.

"Hell if I know, that's all he said," Fowley replied to Kai, who was still nodding. Then Fowley abruptly stated,

"Wait. Well, it's a puzzle, or riddle, or something. He said that, too," he added just as he remembered.

"A puzzle?" Kai and Sammie asked in unison.

"Yes, a puzzle. Let's do this?" Fowley asked impatiently. Trying to focus, he shook off the trivial matter as he swallowed the knot in his throat. He looked over at Kai and loudly snapped his fingers near his ear to get his cooperation.

Kai finally paused his thoughts and exhaled before he complained, "He's always doing something extra," he exclaimed as they all rolled their eyes at the truth he spoke. Kai began to move forward, while Fowley and Sammie stepped closely behind him.

The three entered the building with fast and heavy footsteps. Sammie and Fowley walked off toward their office while Kai swiped his badge to get into the corridor. Fowley unexpectedly yelled over to Kai, who was pulling the door open.

"Tell Ria hello for me," Fowley shouted with a smirk, and Kai realized that they all were being beside themselves and way too serious. Sammie realized it too, and she laughed loudly at Kai to express some kind of normalcy. Kai moved forward with a forced grin to acknowledge the comment, but the pressure he was under made his grin a bit tight.

Kai walked past the reception area of the Hippo Project wing, checking for any alerts regarding Subject Sixteen. Everything seemed quiet, and the receptionist was separating paperwork for filing at her station. He walked past her and down the hall to Canna's office.

He closed his eyes and took a deep breath with his lips just a few inches away from the closed door. He opened it and walked in, sharply switching his demeanor to convey defeat. He raised his voice to give a great sense of urgency.

"Dr. Canna, Subject Sixteen is missing. She's gone," he exclaimed as he waited for Canna's reaction.

"What?" Canna replied, thinking he'd heard Kai incorrectly. Kai nodded his head to reaffirm as he looked Canna in the eyes. "At what time did you notice that she was missing?" Canna probed.

"Just now," Kai replied swiftly. "Like you advised, I had TJ come and take her to room 321, right before I left for lunch. I'm not sure how, but she got past him," he reported.

"But TJ was injured. He says she attacked him when he went in to take her lunch, and he was forced to disable the wing-door lock. But, there's no sign of her, sir," he explained.

"Did she take anything with her?" Canna asked him. Kai was visibly breathing heavily as he communicated,

"She has her file. Well, she has the general file, not the comprehensive file," Kai said, trying to keep his facial delivery as concerned as possible. Deep down, he was extremely satisfied with Mari Hera having a shot at escaping Canna, but he continued to speak with dread.

"Also, TJ told me that she did write something on the wall in room 321 that he doesn't understand. It's like an intentional puzzle or riddle, and I have no idea…" Dr. Canna interrupted Kai's bold lie with sharp authority.

"So, the writing's on the wall, huh?" Canna stretched his neck to release tension as he eyed Kai in such a way that gave his words more depth. Canna wasn't talking about the subject; he was referring to Kai's probationary employment and the soon-to-be lack thereof.

"Yes, it is," Kai answered, pretending to be oblivious to the extra layer of Canna's sarcasm. "Hopefully, you will know what she means by it," Kai spoke hopefully as he fidgeted with the key to room 321.

He soon acknowledged what he was doing, and he stopped. He looked down at the key in his hands, and he didn't even remember grabbing it off of Canna's desk.

When he looked up, Canna was staring at him with intrigue. The doctor's eyes went back and forth between the key in Kai's jittery hand, and the grandie's confused facial expression. He handed the key over to Canna, who practically snatched it from him.

Once Canna had the key, Kai took a step back. Canna grabbed his phone receiver at his desk and made a call to the head of his security team and ordered them to his office. Kai figured that Canna was going to have him escorted off the property. He was growing irritated with the fact that Canna hadn't even shifted his body language at the news of his missing subject.

A very short while later, seven uniformed men entered the office. Two were off-duty police officers who were contracted with Al Canna, at times. The other men were all in-house security guards, including a few who had grown way too comfortable with abusing what tiny little powers the Center had given them. Nonetheless, they were loyal to the Center, and Canna.

Canna pulled out the intake file that was created when Mari Hera was brought in and gave the file to his Head of Security, and his confidant, Miles Knott. Miles, who headed the security agency that employed most of the Center's guards, opened the file and removed a picture of Mari.

In the photo, the subject clearly didn't want to pose. There was nothing about the expression of pain and fear on her face that conveyed a message saying she might have been a willing participant.

He passed around the photo of her with mascara running from her eyes that screamed for help. The next guard shared the picture with the next and so on, until they all had a great idea of what Mari Hera A.K.A. Pearl Lerell looked like. They also studied the basic info needed for such protocols.

Michael Cup, the newly employed guard at the center was last to get the photo. At first glance, he flinched when he saw the woman in the picture. He immediately recognized Mari Hera, and he quickly regained his composure to cover up his natural reaction from the others.

When no one was looking, he slid the photo into his pocket. He thought it could later be useful as proof of some kind. He closed the file folder and casually laid it on Canna's desk as Canna stood up to give his orders.

"We know how this works. But, this time, be careful. She might be disoriented, delusional, and violent. Run the cameras back and find out what time she exited, and in which direction," he directed them with his eyelids closed as if he were barely able to exercise his patience.

Two guards immediately left the room to pursue the task. Once they were gone, Canna ordered, "Get rid of them when this is over," he addressed Miles. He nodded his head toward the two guards who had left the room before continuing on.

"The reward is $100,000, to the one who brings her back dead. But, it's $500,000 to the one who brings her back alive." The group of henchmen looked at each other, knowing exactly how badly they all wanted that bounty.

"Visit her daughter at the home address. In fact, bring her back here. Let's be sure that the sub's memory truly is stripped, and she doesn't go home," Canna commanded as the two off-duty officers left the room in search of a 14-year-old girl named Kim Hera.

Kai and Sammie had already prepared for Kim Hera to be at risk. At lunch, the two constructed a hopefully believable text from Mari's phone commanding Kim to go straight to a friend's house when she was done with her after-school activities.

They saw that Mari had an alarm to remind her that she had a dinner-and-a-movie date with her daughter at six o'clock. Imposing as her mother, they assured Kim that she was "caught up at work until much later," and offered a deep apology for canceling their plans.

Kai stood in the room with Canna and the remaining men, hoping that Kim Hera would follow their indirect instructions. Her life depended on it. And still, the text message they had sent to Kim Hera didn't seem to keep him from feeling queasy and uneasy about Canna's orders.

Canna finished the meeting off by assigning the others, his head guard included, to the street team. This is the group of guards who would hunt for Pearl Lerell and bring her back, whether she was alive or dead. Canna spoke to the remaining three,

"Get several more men with you and go," he ordered. Then he looked over at Kai and said, "And you can go with him," Canna pointed to a new guard whose name he couldn't remember. The guard looked at Canna and Kai, before introducing himself,

"I'm Michael and yes, I'm new here," Michael met eyes with everyone, especially Kai and Canna. Kai said nothing back to him, but kept his eyes on Canna.

"I'm sorry. What do you mean?" Kai asked him, wide-eyed and confused.

"You. Get your car and the two of you can pursue *your* subject, Mr. Paw," Canna yelled, and he seemed glad to assign him to such a task. "Welcome to the game," he added.

Canna smirked as he examined the key to room 321, then he stood up to leave his office. Kai just stood there, unsure of how to proceed.

"But are you sure that I'm a, um," Kai tried to articulate his concern, but Canna interrupted him once again to say,

"You go get her. Trust me, son. I don't have any issue with ridding a grandie or two," he orated in a sharp, threatening tone as he stared beyond Kai and the new guard Michael, as if through the wall and into the next room. Miles maintained a pitiless face as he held his arm out toward the door so that everyone would leave the room before him and Canna.

Kai and Michael went out the door. Michael's pace led Kai to speed up. Kai was fearful, and the plan was already falling apart. But just when he'd thought that he had no control over the situation, he looked back over his shoulder and saw Dr. Canna walking in the opposite direction down the hall toward the high-security area.

The elevator in that part of the center, so Kai had learned from TJ, would take him to the rooms that housed the hidden subjects whom the Cr8 were plotting to free. Every potentially superhuman or hyper-intelligent, nonprogrammable subject Canna had ever encountered dwelled there. Excluding the ones who are now dead.

Kai sent TJ a quick text, *"I'm sorry I sent that crazy lady with you. Hope your head is okay. And Dr. Canna is coming to check the message she left,"* he typed, giving TJ the story to corroborate. He knew that his brother would catch on to him quickly, and go along with it. That day, TJ would have done whatever it took to free the imprisoned subs.

Al Canna needed those subjects to further his studies, and to protect his ideals. Especially now that he was looking to compete with Maquiller himself, he was not going to release them any time soon. Sadly, those subjects could have possibly been extraordinary people, if given the chance.

But Al Canna created a serum that induced a hypoactive state in those subs, keeping the subject from experiencing their own new special abilities. None of them had ever displayed any special skill set, but their hyperactivity levels were alarming, and Canna wanted any of their super skills curtailed. That alone was enough for Canna to have them detained.

TJ Vewitt, however, had been waiting a long time to get the Cr8 mission underway. He was responsible for dosing the subjects with their daily medication as well as immediate security concerns, controlling who entered and who exited that floor.

He didn't want to, and it took a while before he understood what the serum even was. From the very first day that TJ had learned what the serum was, he awaited the time to come when he would be able to stop dosing them so that they could find their strengths and distinctiveness. "Hopefully, that someday is *today*," he'd daydreamed often.

While he was a superhuman man himself, he oversaw subs of all ages in his position, all while never knowing that he too had once been in their shoes. When he'd realized those subjects were given the serum to keep them from using their powers, but he wasn't, he wrongfully distinguished himself from them.

He wasn't that dissimilar. He, like any grandie, was simply "programmable," and the detained subjects were not, even though their former memories had already been erased. However, what they had in common was much weightier than their differences. They were all blameless for their threatening strengths.

None of them knew that their memories had been erased by Al Canna's team. TJ had never told them that they'd completed the procedure because that could have breached his agreement with the Center, prematurely. While TJ kept one secret hidden from the special subjects, the Center was keeping the same secret from him and the other twelve blameless grandies.

If he had told them, TJ would have ruined the Cr8's mission to free them for good. He would have put the Cr8 in grave danger, without a doubt. But June 20th, 2018 was predestined to be a different day.

Still, during his time there, he couldn't help but get close to those special subjects out of his own curiosity. Just like the rest of the grandies in the Cr8, TJ suppressed his own hyperactive tendencies daily.

But he did it by choice. It broke his heart to realize the involuntary suppression of the imprisoned subjects who were hidden in the Center.

Sure, there had been a couple of malfunctioned subs who were sent home to be with their family, but not without a bogus lie about what happened to the sub and how the Center *"stepped in to help,"* they would say. But in any case, a subject going home to their family was just too rare.

Perversely, Canna and his research team going out from time to time to find subjects who had no one who would come looking for them was a normal weekend. Although it was very rare for a subject to be both superhuman and nonprogrammable, Canna generally stayed prepared to keep such subjects in his view for the massive insight he would gain from them.

Canna wanted loners, or people who would have no one to inquire after them. He also wouldn't hesitate to kidnap, subdue, and condition anyone who came too close to exposing his awful tactics. There was at least a handful of people in the town of Opal Firs who used to know a thing or two about Al Canna, but they no longer do.

It took Canna ten years to collect five subjects of the nonprogrammable-superhuman kind. He preferred to program adults, as he looked to develop a special workforce. Whenever he had successfully matched an individual to the career that he programmed them for, it was big money to his name.

He had the possibility of bountiful profits. Canna had the potential to build a large, and subjective, workforce in just about any industry. He'd once projected that he could cut workplace turnover rates by seventy percent.

Although Canna had found his own technique to successfully program an adult, it was not without flaws and complications. A small percent of Canna's subs died from internal glitches, or were drastically changed to the point of acute personality shifts. But the thing that mattered most to Canna and Maquiller was that no participant actually remembered the procedure.

Their operation was filled with deceit and despair for the love of power, money, and outright rivalry. In 2018, twenty years after its first draft, the Maquiller Research plan was no different from how it was in 1998. It was a job made for a recruiter with ensnaring skills, and a professional with truly vile ethics.

****

The normally lethargic look on TJ's face had quickly brightened up when Fowley told him that the Cr8 was moving forward a month early. He had wanted to stop dosing the subjects at least a week before the plan was in play. He was hoping that they might exercise their superhuman talents by the time Canna was exposed to them with unlocked doors.

Remorseful for the thought, TJ decided that would have been a tad bit too cruel. He was after Canna himself, but that day was not about only him. He did not want to lose sight of his sole mission to free the imprisoned subs, and not further their hardships.

The Cr8 had already laid down the blueprint. Rightfully impatient, the five subjects who were being held there at the time had become ruthlessly single-minded about finally getting out. With or without their super strengths, they were all ready to get the revenge they had been seeking.

Instead of distributing medications that afternoon, TJ had cleverly used the brief sessions allotted for doses to prepare each of them one at a time. Canna would soon be in the lockdown area and TJ was about to unlock the doors to every room amidst the disgruntled subjects.

While he himself was prepared to be hands-on, if necessary, he had an obligation to give the subs a good head start to escape. Indeed, a couple of them had a whole lot to say to Dr. Canna. But somehow in the midst of the operation, TJ felt disgusted when it came to Maquiller. In TJ's mind, Canna was terrible, but Maquiller was the one who empowered him to be that way.

Still, the orders given to him by HQ were the orders he would follow. If he followed it well, he would free the five captives as well as make a run for somewhere far away himself. Somewhere between his unknown internal programming timeline, the need to release the captive subs, and the Cr8's collective wish to rid themselves of Maquiller, he knew he had to follow through that day with his emotions pushed aside.

Of all the grandies in the Cr8, TJ Vewitt is the one who detested Al Canna and his harsh ways the most. TJ had been anticipating Canna's daily rounds ever since he hung up the phone with Fowley, but he still jumped a little when he finally heard Dr. Canna's footsteps approaching.

He searched his desk area and setup to make sure he was ready. He was, but he was also nervous.

Dr. Canna came to the hallway entrance door and he pressed the button that buzzed TJ's station. Then, TJ held the button that allowed a Center medical professional like Dr. Canna to press their hand against the screen to identify their prints and open the door to the one hall that was missing from every Maquiller Research Center campus map. Canna entered unusually silent, when normally he would be whistling a tune.

On a normal day, Canna was verbally abusive to any subject who asked any meaningful questions. That day, Canna was the only one seeking answers -and from the same subs he had abused. He knew he wouldn't get answers from them.

His only selfish interest in the nonprogrammable, superhuman sub was to figure out how to either program them or re-create their hyperactive talents within another subject who was programmable –an idea he stole from Leroi's playbook. Overall, he just wasn't brilliant enough to handle the superhuman being straightforwardly, but he was still dedicated enough to capitalize on it.

TJ flipped the switches on the control board that unlocked each individual sub's room on that floor, from end to end. Room 321 was a mess, and the door was left wide open. Canna stood at the doorway as he looked down the hall at TJ, who was sitting at his station holding an ice pack to his head.

He looked at Canna and shook his head to signify that he had made a grave mistake somewhere in the operation. He scrunched his face, pretending to have been injured by the crazed missing subject. Canna didn't say much, he just declared to TJ,

"I'll deal with you later on." Canna shook his head at TJ with disgust before stepping into the room to see the message on the wall. A puzzling, random letter-character sequence was written in red in the center of the wall.

Al Canna was stumped. He studied the characters of the writing as he grabbed a black pen and a few pieces of blank white printer paper usually found in the rooms. The letters seemed to make a note, or message, of some sort.

He laid the paper across his clipboard to copy the characters from the wall onto his pad with his black pen. He began to draw the sequence of characters, realizing that the writing on the wall was a cryptogram puzzle.

Whoever sent the message wanted to make sure that Canna got it. A few letters were already decoded, intentionally leaving him hints. After a quick moment with the letter-swapped puzzle, Canna began to figure out a part of the cryptogram.

According to the hints, "B" represented "L". Canna had become intrigued enough by the puzzle to try and figure out what it meant, and he successfully decoded one word; "will."

He put his slightly incoherent focus into it, rambling as he became more determined to solve it. As he worked the logic and made progress, his subjects fled from the rooms in that concealed part of the Center, right behind his turned back.

All of the subs in "special units" were beyond sick of Canna and the Hippo Project. They had seen, or heard, each other go through horrifically poor treatment by the heartless egomaniac. Canna insisted on their torment because of how much money the skill of conditioning would be worth to him later.

Canna had overstretched his sub, Jade Noble, in every aspect as well as to the maximum. Sometimes he took his research well beyond her limits. The term P.T.S.D. was accurate to say when describing the side effects of it, and the effects were sadly numerous for Jade.

During their disheartening *research sessions,* Canna regularly told her that he would one day cause her "to forget all about it." He had a habit of making loose promises to Jade and the rest of the struggling subs alike, knowing that hope was just like oxygen for each of them. But until that long-awaited day comes, he needed them all to help him "make the world better."

The five subjects in the hidden wing didn't know that their memories had been stripped, but none of them contested the fact that they had none. None of them disputed the fact that they were desperate for help, and longing for answers.

They all believed that the Center had found them in their extreme states of confusion, and had been attempting to help them recover. They all patiently waited, some for longer than others, for that ever-so-elusive cure that was guaranteed to them.

The serum they had been ingesting the whole time there in the Center made the lies that were told to them from inside much more believable than the truths that awaited them on the outside. Truth is, they were in for a long, hard lesson in the outside world.

Ironically, if it weren't for Al Canna's cruel nature, they would have been happy to seek assistance from such a prestigious source. Canna was like a corrupt soldier who needed to fall on his own sword. In this case, Canna's wickedness helped him trip.

He had been amazed by Jade's unbelievably high tolerance for pain. Her resilience was just as high as her tolerance, and Canna thought it was "unprecedented," as he had always worded it. But her compassion for Al Canna was naught. No one, not even TJ, knew Jade's true level of hate for Canna.

It was really a kind of toxic disgust she felt toward him. Day after day, for three years, she had hoped to hear him say that "the time has come," for her to be released, to begin rehabilitation.

The time may have passed, but it never did come. However, it was clear that Wednesday, 6/20/2018, was by far an entirely different day with a totally different story for which no one really knew the ending, or the means –for that matter.

ODD GEMS Soaked by Suri R. Moon

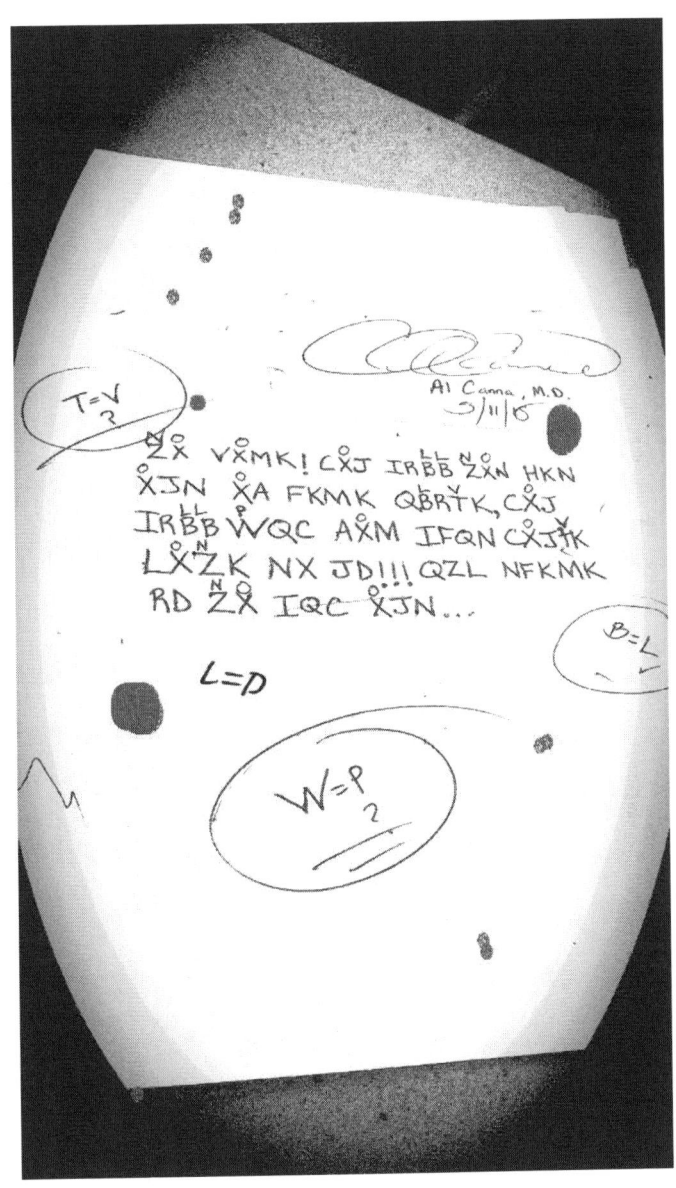

The answer finally clicked, and Canna dropped his clipboard on the floor after he realized what the message stated. He then looked up dreadfully at the wall, wondering who would write such a thing. *"No more. You will not get out of here alive. You will pay for what you've done to us. And there is no way out."*

Canna turned pale with sickness, and he felt a gut-shaking cloud of doom overcasting him as he slowly walked backward toward the door. He took his last step back as he turned around to escape the setup he was realizing a little too late.

But as he swiftly pivoted, he walked right into Jade Noble's blade. Jade standing there behind him would be no surprise to anyone in the hidden wing. But the placement of her knife blade was a shocker, and it was jammed right into Canna's stomach.

Jade pulled the blade, which she had obtained a week prior, out of Canna's hunched torso. They made eye contact, and the correlation between her look of satisfaction and Canna's look of confusion said at least two things.

One, Jade was truly deeply disturbed. And two, Al Canna didn't comprehend what he really had coming to him for everything he had done to her, and the rest of his subjects. Even at that moment, when the victim had all the chance she could want to say what she needed to say to her aggressor, Jade just smiled silently. Her faint grin said enough.

Finally, Jade was not held back from running; the thing she had wished she could do for three years. Although she was cleared to run for freedom, she chose to stay a little while longer for revenge. She had become someone new in her realization of the situation, and it had everything to do with Dr. Al Canna, M.D. -and his own demons.

He just stood there weakly on his feet as his upper body swayed back and forth. His eyes began to roll toward the back of his head. She jabbed the blade into him once more and the second time resulted in a holler of pain, fear, and a morbidly grim insight.

She retained her knife as Canna leaned forward then fell to the floor in room 321. Without a word, Jade watched him as his breathing slowed down.

She turned to leave and almost bumped into another subject. Their eyes met, and they immediately noticed the mutual ferocity. She quickly moved out of Ray Goddem's way. It was clear that she wasn't the only one who had been driven mad by Dr. Canna.

Jade glanced at the blade on the knife in Ray's hand. It was a big, sharp blade and the top one inch or so was ridged. Ray looked at her with sincerity when he told her,

"Get yourself outta here. Leave," he spoke with authority, and there was an eerie calm in him. Jade thought it was awkward because he was such a gentle, more timid man before. He moved past her to enter room 321, and he slammed the door behind him.

Jade tried to book down the hall, realizing that she didn't actually want to hear Canna scream again. She had always imagined what it would sound like if he did, but it wasn't the type of therapy any of them needed.

He was already gurgling in his scream before she could even get to her door, and it was clear that he was being stabbed multiple times. TJ remained hands-off with both Ray and Jade, and he had hesitantly speculated what parts he could see from his station. Delayed, he grew into his own acceptance of the event, as well as his obligations.

TJ was surprised that Maquiller didn't order the Cr8 to kill Canna. Yet, he was definitely relieved that the responsibility to kill him wasn't put on them. But he finally caught wind of Maquiller's intelligence, as he watched everything play out.

If Maquiller wants to get rid of someone, he ended them. But then, at his station, TJ saw that Maquiller's plan was to have Al Canna killed by one of his own subjects, all along.

As Jade ran into her room to get whatever she was going to take with her, TJ sat at his monitoring station as calmly as the situation allowed him to. But he wasn't so calm inside. TJ was remembering the orders Maquiller gave to him, and he knew the craziest part was yet to come.

He briefly looked up at the security camera which he had covered with a T-shirt the minute he saw Jade creeping quietly in Canna's direction without her packed knapsack. He checked to make sure that it was still covered.

In no wise would TJ, or any grandie, ever boldly challenge Maquiller or Canna. Staying undetected and striking fast was a reasonable approach to either of the two professionals. That, and then running away, was the boldest initiative they had ever thought to take.

Jade came back out of room 329 where she'd been kept, trying to keep her composure. She talked to TJ for a quick moment as she passed by him. She didn't want him to get into trouble for their deeds.

She knew he didn't like Canna, but she never really knew exactly how much TJ despised him, or why. TJ held up his hand at her to deter her anxieties. She turned to her friend,

"TJ," she started to shake as she spoke his name. She was scared to go out into the world alone, but that day she had to. Both TJ and Jade had hoped that the resources he was able to get to her would be enough for a time. "Thank you," she told him with extremely mixed emotions.

"Shh. Get away from here, and definitely stay away from Maquiller. Never ever go there," TJ instructed her, as it was truly his own wish for Jade. He wished them all to leave the Center and go live whatever life they had remaining that might be salvaged, especially Jade Noble.

Just like Kai was with Mari, TJ was glad to see Jade go. And the barely surviving, seventeen-year-old girl ran out of the wing while TJ opened the door long enough for her to exit.

He silently wished her well, and a part of him was scared for her and all of whom had been kept there. It was all a huge and crazy task, which everyone involved had agreed was well worth the risks. TJ picked up the phone and called Leroi Maquiller, who answered after a couple of rings.

"What's going on?" he asked TJ, his tone expressing confidence in his grandie.

"Well, he is definitely done," TJ talked as he looked at the closed door of room 321, wondering when Ray was going to come out. TJ grew curious and inquired, "You knew exactly how it would play out, didn't you?" TJ asked Maquiller with hopes of understanding his twisted mind, for once.

For several seconds there was silence, no word spoken from either end of the line. Then, as if TJ's question were never asked to him, Maquiller picked the conversation back up, saying,

"Very well," Leroi replied with an off-putting vibe and no regard to the question. "Is it over?" he inquired. His deep voice and nonchalant tone became clearer. Although TJ felt a small wave of disappointment in Maquiller's sidestepping, he smiled to himself knowing all was far from such.

"It's done. But, no. It's not over," he stated. "I hope they all will find their way to you. They can't wait to meet you," he added with a little charm, and a smirk of roguish satisfaction knowing that the five newly-freed subs would be traveling anywhere but Rhode Island. Maquiller was both pleased and short-winded when he said,

"Very good, let me know when it's over. We'll talk to you soon, son," he said to TJ, then disconnected. TJ walked to the door of room 321, arguing for Ray to make his decision to stay, or to leave like the rest of the subjects.

TJ knew they all would have a death wish the minute Miles Knott found out about the breach, so he pushed at Ray. "You don't have to go with them, Ray. But, you do have to go, man," he yelled through the door.

But Ray didn't respond. So, TJ called out again, "Ray? Please do not be here when we return," he hollered out, pleading through the closed door of room 321 one last time before he needed to get himself prepared for the Cr8's next steps. Still, there was no answer from Ray on the other side of the door.

"Please know that I understand you, but I don't suggest you just quit right here, Ray." TJ then hopped on the computer at his station to grant Ray, Fowley, and Sammie access to the exit.

Once he completed those permissions for Ray's handprint, the system crashed. TJ wondered if he accidentally triggered the system in some way, and he became even more rushed in the moment.

Unable to grant access to his Cr8 siblings, TJ would have to get them into the hidden wing himself. He wanted to be careful to not have any interference from Canna's guards until after they were done transferring Canna's body, so he locked down the wing once again. He grabbed his own backpack and fled the wing to go meet with Fowley and Sammie.

But Ray didn't leave behind him, at least not right away. He refused to leave, and he was more than happy to be the one who stayed behind to help wrap things up. To Ray, a man who had been in the hidden part of the Center for more than seven years, there was no interest in running.

All he ever wanted to know is why he couldn't remember his life beyond the previous several years. Without any knowledge of himself, past or present, he was just a man who had spent the last seven years of his life in misperceptions induced by Canna's mischievous science.

He was only interested in getting rid of a monster he had thought of as nothing more, or less, than sour evil. He noticed the cryptogram that Canna had solved, and was surprised at the message it unveiled. He looked to the wall with the writing wondering,

"Who did that?" he asked himself just over his breath. Ray read the threatening note a few times over and he didn't sense that it was written by a subject.

He had begun to wonder if the bloodbath he made while exterminating Canna had hindered someone else's plans. If so, there was nothing he could do about it at that point, and hopefully that somebody will accept the ending that Ray and Jade orchestrated for Al Canna.

He looked at Canna's cryptogram once again with wonder, and then his corpse. The body was lying on the floor, covered in blood. Ray sat in a dark place for a little while, and he knew that he wasn't getting the satisfaction he'd thought revenge would give him.

Canna's desperate eyes were still open, exhibiting an element of shock. Weirdly, his brown eyes were still piercing like they were in his bio picture that was on display in the Center's secondary-wing corridor.

Ray Goddem sat quietly and calmly on the edge of the bed in room 321. He wasn't doing much more than staring at Canna and the gory mess he had made. He was mentally preparing himself for a lifetime of problems, prison, or whatever other woes may come.

He just reclined on the bed and closed his eyes for a moment. Feeling defeated rather than victorious, Ray began to contemplate his next steps. He decided that he would flee the Center, but stay just close enough to help deal with whatever bag of crazies that was next to come.

*******End of Chapter*******

Chapter 7

Dirt and Water

Pearl rested in the dim afternoon sunlight with her back against the brick wall on the side of an Opal Firs gas station, not far from the Maquiller Research Center. She had checked the inside of the black leather backpack, taking inventory. She found a twenty-dollar bill, a tuna fish sandwich, granola bars, and a bottle of water -along with everything she had hoarded from the supply room.

She had already eaten the sandwich and drank half of the water. She just stood there alone, contemplating what to do next in a paved walkway between the gas station exterior and a wall of big rocks. The pathway was only wide enough for a pedestrian or two.

A tall man with light-brown hair, and a very edgy demeanor, was pumping gas at the pump closest to the walkway. It allowed Pearl to see parts of the man and his pacing movement. She held the bottled water as she searched her surroundings.

A demanding gust of wind blew through the walkway, causing Pearl to fold her arms tightly to avoid the untimely chill. The air was cool in Opal Firs, considering that it was the last day of spring. The sun shined off and on as the clouds slid past it, creating moments in the afternoon when it appeared to be a lot warmer than it really was.

Jacketless and uncomfortable, Pearl knew she couldn't bear to stay on the side of the store much longer. It was dim and wet in Opal Firs that day, and the sun's pale gold, short-lived cameos in the sky were intermittent.

She saw a few empty beer bottles and figured it might be usual that someone had been hanging out on the side of the convenience store. As she looked around the walkway, out of nowhere came blaring sirens that halted just in front of the gas station.

She presumed that the Center authorities would be looking for her, and she didn't know what to expect. She began to panic. But when an officer began to speak into his bull horn, she knew that she was not who they wanted.

His voice came through loud, clear, and intimidating. That officer, who was still near his car on the street, commanded the man who was pumping gas,

"Put your hands in the air where we can see them," the officer yelled. The man then ran off unexpectedly, dodging a few bullets as the police fired at him. He entered the walkway before Pearl could get the backpack in her arms to run. Pearl and the suspect locked eyes, standing just five feet from each other.

In the midst of panic, the two couldn't find any trust as they both were clearly running from something. He nervously reached into the inside of his jacket to pull his gun from his waist holster. In a much swifter action, Pearl picked up one of the empty beer bottles and attempted to catapult the glass at him.

In less than half of a second, she wound the bottle back and pitched it forward. But as she did so, both the bottle and the remaining substance inside turned into sand. It morphed into a deep-purple-colored, grainy substance landing all over Pearl's shoulder, arm, and right hand.

Some even reached the front of the man's shirt, but he didn't detect it. The alleged criminal only saw the beer bottle that Pearl picked up to chuck at him. To the best of his perception, the bottle had vanished into thin air. He became so stunned that he couldn't even pull his trigger.

In that off instance, Pearl noticed an officer aiming his gun at the man. She became frightened and ducked down, just in time. The officer fired, and a bullet went through the man's back side and out the front of his left shoulder area.

Pearl screamed so loud that the firing officer became aware of her standing in the walkway as well, so for her safety, he didn't fire a second shot. Pearl took off running, and she knew how lucky she was to do so.

The man in the walkway was dazed. He released his weapon and the gun fell to the ground. He stared down at his wound which was healing at an unbelievably rapid rate.

Stunned and confused, he looked to where Pearl had been standing before she disappeared. He realized that he was able to lift both of his hands in the air. He was supposed to have fallen, but instead, he was still standing with both hands raised when two officers crept to the walkway entrance.

They closed in near him while he was still in shock, and tackled him onto the pavement. As the police read the man his Miranda Rights, he just surrendered in astonishment. He was speechless anyway.

As the officers handcuffed him, he lifted his head off of the ground and looked ahead, trying to find a clue regarding his bizarre ordeal. There wasn't anything there in the walkway, except the two remaining beer bottles and random trash.

In his thoughts, it was both the best and the worst day of his life. This man is one who no longer believed in miracles by the time he actually witnessed one. He was truly shaken up.

Pearl could have stood there for much longer trying to figure out what had just happened. But she fled through the other end of the back-parking-lot area of the store.

She ran out to the street where there were more pedestrians, a couple of which who were wearing scrubs like her. She thought she might temporarily blend in better.

She slowed down when she got to a busy corner and studied her new surroundings. It was a very noisy place to be as there were small shops and bistros along the block as well as vehicles on the road passing through the intersection. Only then did she reflect on the situation at the gas station.

"What was that? Did I really just see brown glass turn into purple sand?" she asked herself, unable to accept the unnatural. She knew that she had too much on her plate, considering the Center, her memory loss, the migraines and seizures, and the guards. "And, now this," she said in a huff, referring to the shimmering, vibrant purple sand.

A woman and her seven-year-old son were standing across the street at the corner, waiting for the crosswalk light to change. The boy wore tan cargo pants, an orange sweatshirt, and a thin, dark-blue jacket over it. He held some sort of spherical ball or toy which consumed his attention. The boy fiddled around with it, manipulating its form to make it open and close again.

Pearl noticed the boy, then she looked around to examine the escape options she might have, if necessary. Although there weren't any ambulances in sight, she could still hear sirens. Her searching brown eyes kept moving around, waiting for something to suddenly change once again and all at once.

She looked down at her right palm to find that some of the sand remained, and was still sparkling. The amethyst-tinted glimmer was so intense it reflected off of Pearl's face.

And the shimmery dirt grains didn't budge when she tried to dust her hand off. She tried once again, and she still couldn't shake the sparkly grains.

Suddenly, the rain began to pour. Pearl noticed a few people on the street stopping to open their umbrellas, or to cover their heads with hoods.

She stepped into a doorway of a small video game shop to stay dry while she thought about where to go next. The crosswalk signal changed, so the woman and the boy began to walk across the street.

They were hand and hand when the toy that had charmed the boy fell from his hand and rolled away into the middle of the street. The little boy broke from his mother's hand to chase it, holding no regard for oncoming traffic. Just seconds later, every pedestrian on the block yielded to the blood-curdling scream.

When Pearl looked over, a white sedan was stopped, and the woman was screaming as she hovered over the boy. A few people who were stopped near the doorway where Pearl stood began to pull out their cell phones to make sure someone called 911.

Other witnesses whispered amongst each other, and everyone became shaken up to some degree. One elderly man looked over at Pearl, who had forgotten that she was wearing scrubs, and pointed to her saying,

"Hey, aren't you a nurse? Do something," he volunteered her, and it caused several others to stare as well. They all waited intensely for her response.

Pearl didn't know how to tell them that she wasn't a trained medical professional, and she was powerless at trying to not hear the boy's mother screaming. She looked over at them, and the wailing woman was beating on the bumper of the car that hit her child, as the front left tire was still pressed against the boy.

Pearl sighed and hoped to receive strength for the cause. She knew she was determined to help until the paramedics, or any *real* medical professional, arrived. When she took the first step from underneath the dry area of the video game store doorway to run to the street, everything ceased moving.

There was absolutely no detectable movement by anyone or anything, anywhere. Pearl was oblivious to the motionless scene, and her mind was thoroughly preoccupied.

Pearl ran over to the child and his mother, gripped the car by its bumper and threw it aside about six feet away from him. The strength-stricken cast flung the white full-size sedan upward onto its two rear tires. The car then pivoted and slammed into a mini-SUV that was traveling in the next lane over.

Amazingly, nothing and no one was even remotely disturbed by the awful crashing racket she created in doing so, not even Pearl herself. She had crossed over into a hyperactive state, and her eyes became like two sheeny amethysts. The only important thing was the task at hand. Or, so she thought.

She then immediately set her undivided attention on the unconscious boy. But she then became momentarily distracted by a haunting visual that just didn't seem right in her peripheral view. Devastated, she began to tremble, as she looked around her.

Slow to notice what was happening, Pearl spun herself around in astonishment, as she finally realized that she was the only one moving. The fat raindrops were frozen in mid-air and every person or thing, in mid-action.

The young man who had called for help was paused in the middle of a sentence while on his phone with the 911 dispatcher. Pearl kneeled on the ground next to the boy, and across from his motionless mother.

A river of tears was rolling down the woman's face, and a couple of tears that had squirted from her eyes were also paused in the air a few inches away from her eyelids. Everything was still. Oddly, Pearl briefly wondered to herself if time had also stopped as she marveled over the inexplicable breath-pausing spectacle.

She grabbed the back of the boy's neck, about five inches below a huge and nasty gash that was bleeding all over the pavement. She looked up and saw that his mother's face was frozen with an expression of utmost devastation. There was absolutely no facial expression more disheartening than that one.

Pearl was becoming freaked out on a whole new scale, and she just couldn't believe what her eyes were showing her. Pearl had to look away from everything else, especially the heartbreaking face on the woman, to focus on the child. Still clueless about what to do, she just held his head up by the back of his neck and spoke to him softly,

"Please, c'mon sweetie. Please be okay. Please be okay. Please be okay," she pleaded repeatedly with the unconscious child as she stiffened her arm, preparing to hold him for as long as she needed to. She began to cry at the possibility that the kid was dead. As her tears formed, she considered just running away then while everyone was still unmoving.

But she then began to hear the boy's voice. She looked down at him and he was still unconscious, but she could somehow hear his little voice anyway saying,

"Mommy. Mommy?" he called out repeatedly. The *sleeping* child was calling for his mother, and Pearl heard him as clear as spring water. After pleading with him to come back for another several seconds or so, she finally felt movement.

She looked down at the boy, and he opened his eyes. Surprisingly, the wound on the back of his head had closed up and his clothes were scrubbed clean right before her eyes.

Stupefied, she watched as his blood disappeared from her hands and clothes, and everywhere else it had splattered. The little boy was terrified when he saw all of the unmoving people, and he was beginning to go to pieces. Pearl instinctively sensed that the kid was neither programmed, nor like herself.

He was just an innocent being who was witnessing an effect of the first realm while still living in the second, which was an extremely rare occurrence beyond infancy. Pearl hadn't a clue, and she couldn't imagine how hard it would be for the kid to explain the scene to his mother later.

She just accepted that for some reason unknown to her, the kid was supposed to see what he saw. She stood the boy up on his feet and told him,

"Don't be scared, okay? Look around you, what you're seeing is a miracle of some kind," she informed him. The boy couldn't stop trembling. So, Pearl tried to encourage him,

"I can see it too, and I don't even know what it is. But, don't be scared because all of this was here for you to see," she spoke in a soothing tone as she held his skinny shoulders in her hands.

The kid was speechless as he gaped around him while Pearl thought it would be best if she encouraged him to think of the event as "magical" and "inexplicable" because it was. She didn't know what else to say, but she stated,

"You don't even have to explain it to anyone. Just don't ever forget it, all right?" She smiled at him with much admiration. He was an amazing sight to her sore eyes, and she whispered, "Exactly who is this kid?" as she goggled at him.

Pearl rose up from her knees that were both sensitive from being pressed to the pavement. She stood upright, letting out a sigh of mild aching. She commanded the boy to stay with his mother no matter what.

"Okay," the kid said as he displayed an unworldly smile on his face with neither a worry in his mind nor a clue of how close his close call really was. "What's your name?" the boy asked her. She looked at him and almost answered him, but he had reminded her of all the things she couldn't remember, and she became bothered.

Her eyes reverted back to dark brown, then she noticed that something else in her peripheral sight was not quite right. In contrast to all of the still matter surrounding them, Pearl sensed movement. A man who had been quietly standing nearby gasped when he realized that the boy was still alive, and well.

He too witnessed the accident, and the impossible. The small act of him raising his hand to cover his mouth in his astonishment was enough for Pearl to detect his presence.

Pearl locked eyes with him, and it triggered fear in both of them. Troubled by the man, Pearl looked back at the boy who was waiting for an answer.

She didn't know what to tell him, and she froze. Pearl then let go of his shoulders and ran away. She ran around the corner to flee from the scene, wherein she had been a strange guest star of some sort. She looked down at her hands one last time as she moved, and even the purple sand was gone from her skin. She marveled over it for a second, then she kept moving.

As she fled that scene, the man in his early forties with short black hair started to follow her with mild hesitation, considering his own safety. He abandoned the acoustic guitar he had been playing while sitting in a closed-storefront doorway that *partly rainy* afternoon. He was compelled to follow her.

At first, he had remained still like everyone else, to avoid exposing his presence after he saw what she had done to the white car. But once the boy was safe, he couldn't control his emotion and therefore gave himself away.

After certifying the boy's incredible recovery, the man wanted an explanation. He wanted to understand what his eyes had processed. After all he had witnessed of her, he was determined to see where she was heading next.

He gazed ahead of him as he sped up in his steps behind her. "Who is this?" he whispered to himself as he marched forward on Pearl's trail.

He had seen the expressive signs in the clouds earlier that day just like any other who could see them. In his life, he had seen a lot of things of both uncanny and strange sorts, in fact. But he had never seen anything like the event he had just watched unfold.

He needed to know why the world seemed to pause everything for her. As he maneuvered in between the people and vehicles that were still dormant throughout the block, he got wet as he broke up every airborne raindrop he walked into.

Pearl got around the corner and a few blocks away when she stopped running, to catch her breath. She had to dry her face with the sleeve from her sweatshirt. She also was colliding with the still raindrops with every stride she took.

On the inside, she had more mixed emotions than the inside of a high-school locker room. Before she could even begin to wrap her ruptured mind around everything that had happened between the Center and the car accident scene, she heard someone yelling at her.

"Hey, Pearl." Kai and the new guard Michael Cup were nearby on the street. Kai was driving around the corner to close in on her as he called out.

Pearl shrieked, and she resumed running in a different direction to ditch him. It was then that Kai suddenly unveiled his own surroundings, and his heart was beating against the inside of his chest when he realized that no one, including Michael, was moving.

The stationary people and cars on the road led Kai to a street that he couldn't drive down. Finally, Kai's car stopped and became still, like Michael and everything else. So, Kai jumped out of the sedan to try to catch her on foot.

He left the car in park near the curb with Michael in the passenger seat. Michael was mute and stock-still, like a department-store mannequin.

He was holding one arm up, and pointing ahead, and he was entirely oblivious to the whole unworldly phenomenon that consumed him.

"Wait. Pearl, I'm not going to hurt you," Kai called out as he tried to run after her, hoping she could hear him. Pearl cut in between buildings and she was getting farther from them. As she ran, she looked up and noticed a Boeing 747 jet stopped midair in the sky above and she felt a wave of extreme fear that the plane might lose its suspension and plunge to the ground.

Nonetheless, she kept running. Frequently, she wiped the excess water caused by the breaking raindrops from her eyes as she sprinted through them. She was already soaked and had become even more drenched by then. Her heart was beating too hard when she finally stopped and slid through the door of a coffee shop and bookstore.

As soon as she walked through the entrance of Emerald Coffee and Books, the uncanny phenomenon was reversed. She screeched piercingly out of fear. She was surprised when everyone abruptly resumed movement as if nothing had ever stopped.

A couple passed her at the doorway to exit, staring at her with confusion and concern. The entire front half of Pearl was soaked as if someone had splashed a huge bucket of water at her chin. Despite the clear presence of rain, Pearl was drenched beyond logic and people were staring.

The few people in close proximity to her who had just resumed their mobility stopped all over again, dumbfounded at the sight of her. She felt like running again. But she was at least glad to have lost Kai who was definitely looking for her out there, and she figured she could wait it out for a little while in the bookstore.

After unsuccessfully trying to catch up with her, Kai stopped. He was out of breath, and he needed to get back to his car. He figured he was surely blocking traffic, with everything moving once again.

He just wanted to talk to her, but he reasoned that just maybe the seemingly failed chase gave her more time. *That's okay, too,* he thought.

So, he started to head back. But when he tried to turn himself around, he bumped into the heavily tattooed guitarist who was also pursuing Pearl himself.

"Excuse me," Kai bellowed from the impact as he nodded upward at the man. He saw something in the man's eyes that startled him. The dark-haired man saw something about Kai's aura that made him yield also, even though he was initially more short-tempered in the instant.

Surrounded by all of the suddenly moving matter, the two just looked at each other with familiarity. The guitarist replied with inquiry,

"You're looking for that woman, aren't you?" he asked.

"What woman?" Kai shook his head, trying to be nonchalant and unaware.

"That lady who just ran over here. You were yelling something at her," the man insisted.

"Do you know who she is?" Kai asked, unsure if the scrubby-looking fellow could be trusted. But by his apprehensive demeanor, Kai felt that the man might know something useful. The man was pinching the bridge of his own nose, trying to word his response before he spoke,

"No, but I should. I definitely should," he said staring pensively over Kai's shoulder, lost in his thought. Kai recognized that the man he was talking with may have witnessed the bizarre events in the sky that day, so he asked,

"Who are you? Why are you looking for her?" Kai demanded to know. The man looked around him and Kai at the people who had been inanimate, but were moving once again. He realized that Kai had also witnessed the freeze, and was someone to be honest with.

"I'm Leith Nomea," he replied, and he reached his hand out to shake with him. "Maybe we should talk?" he invited Kai, who shook his hand precariously.

Kai glanced toward Pearl's direction one last time and checked to see if she was there. Seeing no trace of her, he pointed with his head to signal Leith to walk with him. The two of them headed back to Kai's car.

Just as they began to quicken their steps, Kai tried countering the discomfort from the large raindrops that were now pouring down heavily again as he wiped them away from his face with his hoodie sleeve. Leith, who was wearing a brown baseball cap, pulled it down over his eyebrows as he held his chin near his chest to avoid getting his head wet.

Several blocks away at the accident scene that both Pearl and Leith had left behind, the movement of all things was restored. The boy's mother embraced him in the pouring rain as she cried grateful tears because he was alive and okay.

The other bystanders stood together for a while longer, disoriented. But they still considered the kid and his mother with their inexplicable gladness.

The mother and her boy walked away from the noisy intersection while the driver of the white sedan that would have killed him stood in the middle of the street, arguing with the driver of the mini-SUV. They couldn't agree on who was at fault for their awkward fender bender, and they never would.

****

She wanted to buy herself time in the warmth of the bookstore, so Pearl did just that by buying herself a Café Americano. She paid $2.00 for the coffee, then walked around to check the place out. The coffee stand was near the bottom of a wide staircase that went to another floor.

She stared up at the top of the steps where there was a framed map on the wall. She couldn't see the content of the picture clearly from so far away. She took a cautious sip of her hot coffee, wondering if she was allowed to go up.

"That's the bookstore up there," the storekeeper and assistant manager Pamelah told Pearl, as she observed her. Pamelah laughed lightly explaining, "Everyone comes in here for the first time and they always stand right where you are, wondering if they can go up there.

"Just staring up there. Like it's blocked off with yellow tape or something," Pamelah said, with a light giggle. "And yes, you may take your coffee up there with you," she added as she walked back to the register to assist another customer.

"Thanks," Pearl said to the mind-reading barista with an affirmative nod as she lifted her coffee cup in the air toward her. She sipped the coffee once more then walked up the steps. When she reached the top, she learned that the big map she was eyeing in the center of the wall was a map of Washington. It was a huge, framed copy that covered the entire state.

Pearl was just studying it, but she started to feel weird after a few seconds. Her brain immediately began to absorb all of the details. In the extreme rush of data, she started to suffer a seizure episode, and she could no longer see clearly.

Some kind of cerebral contraction overcame her stance and she lost control. She fell backward down the steps, spilling her hot coffee all over herself.

Her limbs went flying about, and she was terrified. She had no physical control over her body as her nervous system seemed as if it had shut itself down. The seizure was enough by itself, but falling down the steps made it much scarier. Wondering where she was going to land for the entire trip down made it devastating.

"Are you with me?" she heard a man asking her. Pearl opened her eyes, and the store owner Nomad Artman was holding her head in his arm. Pearl sat up dazed and unsure about what to tell him. "Do you know your name?" Nomad asked, checking her for any obvious head injury.

She hesitated, but only because she knew that the name she had was not hers to begin with. To lighten the embarrassment in front of the gawking patrons she answered,

"Pearl is my name, and I'm fine. Thank you," She stood up to her feet and found out in that instance that her left knee, right elbow, and lower back were all in a lot of pain. Plus, she was covered in coffee which had initially burned her right through her clothes.

In agony, she leaned over to retrieve her black leather backpack. Nomad tried to help her pick it up, but she snatched it up first. He said to her,

"If you are able to make it to the second floor, I think I can find something you can wear." He lifted one arm to point upward to the bookstore while using his other to help keep her on her feet, as she wobbled a little.

Pearl went with him; she really needed to get the attention away from her before the Center caught up to her. She also wanted to get far away from the main entrance windows right there on the first floor.

As she walked past the Washington State map a second time, she noticed that she wasn't fazed by it at all. In fact, she had an informative set of thoughts; *"It's about two hundred seventy-nine miles from Seattle to Spokane, about two hundred twenty-three miles from Richland to Everett, and roughly one hundred ninety-nine miles from Marysville to Vancouver,"* she stated under her breath, barely moving her lips.

Once they stepped onto the second floor, Pearl became unnerved when she saw rows and rows of bookshelves, movies, and magazines. She attempted to ignore the titles as she walked by them. Even though she tried not to look, books were everywhere in sight, and the lighting in the bookstore was bright.

She repeatedly caught an accidental glimpse of some random book title. Oddly, each glimpse seemed to carry with it a bigger message that she couldn't resist heeding.

It Was Meant to Be was among the messages. *A Guardian's Work* was another title, and Pearl had concluded in her gut instinct that the messages were referring to Nomad Artman.

Within her intuition, she began to feel as though she may be able to trust someone, and she felt hopeful. But she wasn't sure if she was ready to divulge her entire situation to him.

Nomad led her to the place that his small bookstore staff called the "office-break room," as it was the only room with an employee sitting area -if one could call it that. He offered her a chair to sit on while he looked for something different for her to wear. He returned shortly after with nothing, saying,

"There's a first. Nothing for clothing in the lost and found," he announced regrettably as he contemplated on how to help. He then realized what he could do, and he turned to Pearl with a resolution,

"In the bookstore, there are a few clothing items, mostly T-shirts. But I will get you something from there. And you can just have it. I'm Nomad Artman, by the way." He stretched his hand out, and she reached out to shake it.

She couldn't hold her arm up long, as it triggered pain in her elbow. In pain, she awkwardly pulled her arm back, and Nomad immediately apologized,

"I'm sorry. I wasn't thinking to make you do that. You might need a couple of aspirin," he offered, opening the aspirin bottle on his desk.

"Thank you, I will hopefully get the chance to repay you," she replied. It seemed as though her bad luck at the stairs had fortunately led her to something she really needed, a change of clothes.

Nomad walked off into the store. Pearl looked around the office trying not to pay much attention to anything. She didn't want to have another episode, so she covered her eyes with her hands.

Luckily, the darkness she created did help revert the bubbling symptoms of another attack. He returned to the office room a couple of minutes later with a black-and-white, cotton pinstriped jumpsuit and a dark-green hooded sweatshirt. The zipped sweatshirt read, "I Love Washington."

The pinstriped jumpsuit was shorts for the bottom half of it. It was workable on its own, but awfully tacky when paired with the fifty-two-degree weather or the green hoodie. On that day, however, anything different was better.

"Sorry about the one-piece, pinstriped thing. Generally, I only have T-shirts and hooded sweatshirts. Cups, keychains, maps, postcards, calendars, coffee mugs, et cetera," he listed. "And this was the only thing with a bottom," he said as he handed them to her.

He was trying to be accommodating as he suggested, "There's a restroom behind you, feel free to change up. If you want some water or something," he said as he pointed toward the cold drinking-water tank near the door. She stood up and spoke,

"Thank you, very much. And hey, I'm sorry if I scared you back there on the staircase. I think it was a seizure or something," Pearl apologized for the drama, shaking her head.

"Yes, it was. A seizure, or something," Nomad answered back instantly, and with confidence. "No worries. I'm glad you didn't die in my store," he kidded as he laughed a small laugh. Pearl wanted to laugh, and her old self usually would have. But contrarily, her response was slow and grave.

It was all Nomad needed to witness before he dialed his humor down a notch, or three. Pearl walked into the employee restroom and shut the door as Nomad watched.

Given her morbid mood, Nomad wondered about her. He was concerned about her well-being. But when he heard the restroom door lock from the other side, he recognized that Pearl was too.

When Pearl returned from the restroom where she had disposed of her scrubs and the sweats she had on underneath, Nomad was sitting at his desk holding a book by a popular horror-novel author. He looked up to acknowledge Pearl and he asked her, "Have you ever read this one" and he passionately shoved the book into her hand.

Pearl looked down at the title and she fanned through the book with her thumb. In doing so she inadvertently uncovered the whole storyline, including the ending.

She caught an off-putting sensation from the surge. She suddenly looked up at Nomad, stunned by her own foul.

She didn't mean to make a sour face, but she did. Her telling facial expression prompted Nomad to ask,

"What was that?" he was shocked by the element of surprise on her face. Pearl didn't want to say anything. She didn't know how to tell him that she had just read, and digested, the entire story. So, she just stated the obvious.

"This is a very, very thick book," she exclaimed, fanning the pages once more.

"I know right, most of his novels are," Nomad agreed, nodding along with Pearl in the obviously strange context of their conversation.

"I'll bet this book would make a good movie," she realized aloud. Nomad looked at her like she was an alien as he replied,

"Um, yeah. It *is* a movie as well. It's based on this book," he told her as he laughed, astonished that she really didn't know about the book or its popular subsequent film. For a few seconds, Nomad continually nodded his head toward her, as if trying to prompt her to admit that she was just kidding.

She became uncomfortable when she saw his expression, so he casually added, "I'm really hoping that the main character doesn't die at the end. I, for one, will be highly disappointed if he does." The conversation was downright odd, at the least.

The TV mounted above Nomad's desk was on, but muted. There was a breaking news story that caught his attention. Nomad picked up the remote and restored the volume to hear the basic issue of the story,

"The suspect allegedly robbed a bank, then stopped at the gas station just across the street to fill his tank. Reports noted that he left his house on the risky venture, and then later realized that he forgot to fill up his gas tank beforehand. The Internet has been flooded with comments referring to the man as the 'dumbest criminal ever'," a brunette woman reported into the camera, trying to hide the smirk behind her serious visage.

She handed the report over to a man anchor who was still airing live at the gas station. He stood just yards in front of the walkway where Pearl had recently eaten her lunch, and watched the police shoot the bank robber on whom the news anchors were reporting. The man reporter delivered every sentence with spiked enthusiasm,

"*Earlier today, a local man, who is now being charged for the Emerald Credit Union robbery just across the street from here earlier this afternoon, was shot by an Opal Firs police officer during his arrest. The man, in his thirties, was shot through his left shoulder when he tried to remove his gun from his holster,*" the bald man reported. His face changed drastically from intrigued to astonished before he continued.

"*But, here's the thing. The suspect's gunshot wound was fully healed just seconds later. Local authorities have had more than just the robbery to interrogate the suspect about this afternoon. We will definitely have more on this story later,*" he added before ending his segment and passing the report back to the broadcast newsroom.

Nomad Artman was doubled over in laughter as Pearl looked at the screen with her jaw dropped. Nomad muted the TV sound again and put his head in his hand, still laughing, "Oh, no shit? Did you just hear that?" he asked her, although he was still watching the muted news report.

"What a dummy. Why would somebody rob a bank, and then stop directly across the street for gas?" he questioned, and he had a sincere aura about him. It wasn't hard to tell that he genuinely wanted an answer.

"And, what's up with the gunshot wound healing? I find that hard to believe, unless there was a," he paused in his thought, shaking his head.

He turned around and looked at Pearl whose jaw was still wide open. Her eyes exposed her worries, and Nomad began to pick up on it as she disclosed her truth to him,

"I was just there, not long ago," she exclaimed in disbelief that the man's gunshot wound was healed. "I saw the bullet go right through him." She was soaked in confusion and enchantment about the report.

She was astounded that the man had survived the standoff at all, to be frank. Nomad let out a heavy breath with a vague smile as he replied with wonder,

"You saw that happen?" he asked her with his undivided attention, watching her as she began to pace back and forth.

Pearl suddenly grew antsy again as she paced in Nomad's office, and she wished to get herself much farther from the Center than she was. But she didn't know where to go. She plopped back down into the black office chair on wheels and sighed as she started to come clean to Nomad.

She caught his attention while he was inserting a bookmark in his novel to mark his page. In reality, he knew that something was mentally ailing Pearl, and he just fiddled with the book so that he didn't make her feel too pressured to speak about it. Regardless, Pearl conveyed her situation to him.

"Look. Okay, here's the thing. My name isn't Pearl," she confessed to him, hoping that he would still hear her out.

"It's not?" he asked, vaguely dumbfounded.

"No, it's not," she replied, staring over his shoulder into nothing. She felt like the truth was easier to say if she could avoid having to read the look on his face when she said it.

"So, what *is* your name?" he inquired. The simple question made her jump as she acknowledged her bigger problems.

"That leads me to the second thing," she paused to breathe before she proceeded. "I can't remember my name. In fact, I can't remember anything about myself," she admitted, deeply saddened. "I was in a research center or clinic-like facility until just a little while ago, today. It was so," she abruptly started to cry mid-sentence.

Nomad grabbed a tissue from its cardboard box on his desk and was about to hand it to her when he saw that one, single facial tissue wouldn't help her multitude of tears. He then grabbed the whole box and handed it to her.

"Here, have them," he offered, realizing that she was definitely going through something heavy. Pearl had her face in her hands when she looked up at him with her distressed eyes and said,

"I think they stole my memories. I mean, one of them told me that my name was Pearl, but I believe he lied to me," she cried as she shook her head. "I don't know what I'm doing, who I am, or where I'm going. I remember nothing before this morning" she declared.

"I keep having migraines or seizures, or both," she said, motioning toward the stairs that she had fallen down moments before. "And, now I have people from within the clinic coming after me, and I think they're going to kill me," she finished her thoughts with a deep breath outward, knowing that what she'd said to the complete stranger was a mouthful.

"Wait, who stole your memories? And, who's trying to kill you?" Nomad asked.

"The doctors. Hippo, it is called The Hippo Project," she tried to explain it as she reached into the leather backpack and pulled out her file. She shoved it into Nomad's hands, pleading with him, "I don't know what to do, or where to find help. Help me, please?"

Nomad read through the file as Pearl quietly sniffled, attempting to let him focus on what he was looking at. Nomad read through it, and something caught his eye. He was fiddling with a strand of his wild, dark hair as he read. He then moved a wavy strand to stay behind his ear and out of his face when he flipped to the second page.

Under the *"active status"* information field he saw the result, *"nonprogrammable"* and something immediately clicked. He slowly looked up at her with conviction in his mismatched eyes, one brown and one blue. Nomad amiably communicated to her,

"I think you were definitely meant to come here," the certainty in his eyes gave Pearl the impression that he was not to be debated.

"I was? Why do you say that?" she asked as she leaned in toward him.

"I remember something called Project H.E.A.D. from a long time ago. It was a study at the Maquiller Center in Rhode Island, and I read somewhere that," he began to say, but hesitated. "But, I was --" he hesitated again.

Then, a second later he shook his head as if he had to shake a thought out of it.

"That doesn't matter now. Listen, that thing that happened out there with you falling? Seriously, what the hell was that?" he lowered his chin with his eyes fixated on her, trying to induce a truthful answer.

Pearl shook her own head at the absurdity when she tried to verbalize it, "I saw the map of Washington and I think I remembered it. Like, all of it. But it's like it caused me to have a seizure episode from all the, I don't know. Too many details, I guess?" she tried to articulate.

She really struggled to convey it, but she continued. "It's like it was too much for me to take in all at once," she explained. He sat straight up in his brown leather chair and inquired,

"You remembered it? You mean like every town?" he probed with wide eyes, waiting for her response.

"Yes. And, I had the miles between cities completely memorized when we walked by it again. Also, when we walked through your bookstore? I felt nauseous as hell," she admitted to him as if she were glad to get it off her chest.

Then, she grabbed the horror novel he was reading and shook it near him when she confessed, "And, you should probably start on a different novel because this one doesn't end the way you're hoping. Sorry," she offered. Nomad grabbed the book back from her hand. He was amazed, but he had to test his belief. So, he asked her,

"You mean to tell me that you read this book right when you thumbed through the pages? Ten minutes ago?" he asked her with an unbelieving demeanor. Pearl nodded her head and he continued on. "So then, what year was it printed?" he asked with a smirk.

"1984," she replied as she let out a sigh of relief, glad that he asked her something her eyes had actually seen when she flipped through the novel. Nomad stood to his feet and spoke,

"What in the world is going on? Who are you?" he asked rhetorically while Pearl kept on nodding along. He tossed the book on his desk, grabbed his black jacket, and flung it on while he told her, "I know someone you really need to meet. Let's get you away from here."

They went down the steps and into the coffee shop. Pearl moved slowly as she noticed that her fall was more damaging than she had originally calculated amid her adrenaline spikes. Nomad moved fast and well ahead of her, and he momentarily disappeared into the storage area behind the cash register.

They were both obviously cautious about their surroundings. Pamelah studied their serious demeanors, and she asked Nomad, "You're taking off?"

"Yes, will you please hold the store down until I get back?" he begged, calling out from the other room. Pearl was standing off near some collectible gifts, admiring the hanging crystals. In reality, she was hiding away from the huge storefront windows to the best of her ability.

She tried to be inconspicuous. While waiting on Nomad, she spotted an abnormally brilliant amethyst wand that piqued her interest. It reminded her of the purple sand that was stuck to her hand just before the car hit the boy.

It was about ten inches in length and hanging on a metal hook by itself. She was just about to reach up and take it off the hook to examine it when Pamelah startled her,

"Careful not to touch anything," Pamelah begged her. I've already broken two this week. Nomad would kill me," she said exhaustedly to Pearl. Pearl took her hand back with a rapid jerk, embarrassed.

She was trying to deter any attention away from herself, and she wasn't doing so well at it. Nomad came out of the back room and handed Pamelah the keys, advising her,

"Please lock up if you need to. I will be back," he told her. She nodded in agreement as she went into the back room with a big brown cardboard box. Nomad waved Pearl toward him at the door as he looked out the windows for any sign of trouble.

At some point while Pearl was in the bookstore with Nomad, the rain had ceased. She followed him out as he exclaimed once more to his assistant manager, "Thank you, Pamelah. I'll be back."

Pearl zipped up the green hoodie all the way to her chin and pulled the hood over her head. She was awaiting the cold gusts of wind that were visibly blowing stray papers and trash around outside. The gust attacked immediately, but oddly; it wasn't cold.

Nomad stood on the sidewalk looking back at Pearl, who believed that her senses were failing, saying,

"We have to go. What is it?" he asked her as she stood by the store doorway quiet, but obviously bothered. She replied to him,

"I thought I would be freezing in these shorts," she said. "Am I losing my senses?"

"I doubt that," Nomad said with a knowing kind of grin. "Let's hurry up and get you to the car before you change your mind," he coached. Pearl unfolded her arms that were poised for her personal freeze defense and stepped out onto the sidewalk.

They marched off to the car. They stepped away from the storefront rapidly, and they left the door swinging wide open.

Seconds later, a sudden and strong gust of wind slammed the entrance door back shut. The vibration from the shaking door frame caused the same amethyst wand that had captivated Pearl to fall from its hook and hit the floor.

Pamelah raced out of the back room to see what all the noise was about. Before she even walked around the counter to see if any of the crystals had fallen, she looked for the one that Pearl was studying before she left. Pamelah saw that it was no longer hanging on its hook, and she curled her lips inward in anger.

She had already started to dread having to pick up another piece of damaged merchandise. She walked heavily around the marble counter, expecting to find her third merchandise misfortune in a week. Instead, she was shocked to find the amethyst crystal wand on the floor, unbroken.

Whatever it meant, it was a good sign to her. She carefully picked it up and took it to the storage room in the back. There, Pamelah chose to put the wand away in a safer place, and for a different time.

*******End of Chapter*******

ODD GEMS Soaked by Suri R. Moon

Chapter 8

I Smell Smoke

Kai and Leith were getting close to the car when Kai's phone rang, and he anxiously answered, "Hello," he said as line static bothered his ear a bit. He pulled the phone an inch or two away from his ear until the static dissipated. A voice on the other line came through calmly,

"What's that noise, where are you?" Sammie asked, practically whispering to him.

"I hear it, but I don't know, are you still there?" Kai responded, hoping their connection wouldn't fail. Kai glanced at Leith out of the corner of his eye to see if he could hear her talking through the phone receiver as she continued,

"I'm in. But, I messed up, Kai," she admitted to him from the start.

"Him too?" Kai inquired to see if Fowley was also operating hyperactively. Kai understood that a grandie wouldn't shift into a hyperactive state unless they were on defense. So, he was already expecting to hear some bad news. Sammie brought him up to speed,

"Not yet, but he will be soon. One of the guards attacked me, Kai. They were interrogating me. I'm so sorry. I couldn't help it," she concluded with a self-aware tone in her choked-up speech. "And, Canna. He's," she began to expound, but hesitated before taking a deep breath. "Out. He's out," she finally blurted.

She looked at the office door, considering that someone might be listening on the other side. Agitated, she shrunk her voice down to a plain whisper, "He's way out. Kai, they're coming for us over here," she confirmed to him as she looked over at Fowley. He was sitting in Al Canna's office chair, printing out files and cloning documents from the computer folders.

Sammie was on the phone, Fowley was in the chair, and four security guards were lying on the floor, dead. They were all badly burned from top to bottom, and a steamy stench was still emitting mildly from each corpse. Firearms were on the floor near two of the bodies, where they had dropped when Sammie screamed fire at the guardsmen.

They were all cooked to a crisp when they attempted to separate her from Fowley during their abrasive interrogation. One of the Research Center's high-clearance officers had found Dr. Canna's dead body in room 321, after responding to reports of the obstructed security camera in the hidden wing. The guards used an alternative way to enter the wing, meant for emergencies like such.

Being mindful to keep the issue a secret, the guards decided to find TJ and the rest of the grandies, whom they never fully trusted. Kai's eyes widened in anger and fear for his family, and while he was in that highly emotional state, a colorfully coated beam from within him rolled over his eyes.

His hyperactive transition caught him off guard. It was happening much sooner than he'd ever anticipated. At that moment, he knew how much he loved the Cr8 because his emotions had to be running very wild for him to shift into such a mode.

His blue irises lit up in a bright golden yellow tone, for a brief instance. He looked away for a couple of seconds so that Leith couldn't witness the transition. Recovering from the momentarily awkward withdraw, he finally responded to Sammie, saying,

"I'm on my way. If not inside, I will meet you at our spot outside. Keep your phone close," he said.

"Okay," Sammie replied. She was about to hang up when Kai suddenly blurted out,

"Wait, Sammie. Just so you know, I'm in," he declared.

"Good. Please just hurry back," she replied. She then turned to Fowley holding her hand over her cell phone mouthpiece, whispering with agitation, "Hurry up. We have to go," she said to him with tight lips.

"What do you think I'm doing?" he snapped back at her. Annoyed, he inquired to her, "What would you like to do with them?" and he pointed to each of the four dead bodies.

"Nothing. What do you want to do? Hide them too?" she asked him. "We already have one of those on our to-do list today. And, being that we're not yet done with that one, I'd say that one is more than enough to focus on right now," she said as she regained her own temperance.

"After all, we're getting out of here anyway, right?" she added, looking as if she were trying extremely hard not to pull out her own hair.

"Yeah. We're getting out of this," he replied calmly, nodding his head to affirm the truth. "No more of this shit," he added as he exhaled a breath and flashed a vague expression.

"Yep. The shit has already hit the fan, and is now what you see lying on this office floor," Sammie spoke, trying not to be loud. She then heard a voice from afar, saying,

"Hello," Kai hollered for the third time into the phone. Sammie had temporarily forgotten that she was still on the line with Kai.

Though she'd barely heard him the third time, he was loud enough to get her attention as soon as she stopped talking. She lifted the phone to her face and said,

"Sorry about that. Just hurry up and get here." She rolled her eyes at herself for having been so anxious in the moment.

"I'm on my way there," he said, and he disconnected. Kai was both nervous and hyperactive, an awful combination for any superhuman being. Kai hadn't tried to *fully* exercise his abilities since he was 15 years old, and he had his own reason to be wary of his abilities.

The event that caused his morbidly negative outlook toward his powers happened right after the very first calibration for the grandies. It was an unexpected accident, and it didn't end well. After that, Kai never spoke of the incident again, and he never planned to.

When it came to the rules, they had no choice but to create principles to live by and try to live by them. But when it came to the grandies, Kai knew he wouldn't have much mercy on anyone who tried to harm them. The rules sometimes seemed obsolete, and against all common sense, at those times of direct danger.

Being both humanistic and superhuman was a rare commodity in the world around them. Both of the concepts were scarce in Maquiller's world. They had to develop their moral guidance outside of Maquiller and the Center. But they also had to look out for each other.

Kai put his phone away and turned to look at Leith, who was already staring at him with concern. He was wondering what was wrong. He wasn't fooled by Kai's unnatural, casual behavior. But Kai gave him no explanation.

He just picked up his pace and kept on walking. When they reached the sedan, Michael was motioning for him to hurry as he yelled,

"Did you find her?" he asked, with a nervously hasty demeanor about him.

"Does it look like I caught up with her?" Kai responded sharply in his momentary exhaustion from the unsuccessful chase. Cup disregarded Kai's attitude and moved on to the next issue at hand, exclaiming,

"Well, we have to go, right now. We have a big problem at the Center," he conveyed. He was still clenching the phone as if he had just ended the call with the branch. "Don't ask, because I don't know what happened, yet."

Kai marveled at him, noticing his lack of knowledge about the statue-like state he'd been in just several moments earlier. It was almost funny watching Michael, who by then was so animated in his angst. The contrast was like night and day.

As Kai and Leith jumped in the car, Michael kept talking,

"But, I can tell you that there's something wrong with Dr. Canna, and some of the guards too," Michael expounded.

Kai silently replied with a mere expression of surprise on his face. Michael turned around to eye Leith, then he asked him,

"Who the hell are you?" Leith didn't answer, he just looked at Kai for some sort of approval to share his name. Without a word, Kai started the car and sped off to get back to the Center.

****

Back at the Center, Fowley and Sammie had finally completed the file transfers to HQ, and they were heading to take custody of Al Canna's corpse. By then, some of the other guards in the Center had already found the four bodies in Dr. Canna's office. They began the search for Maquiller's grandies without any doubt that they were responsible for the tragedy.

When the two grandies had left Canna's office, they left the dead guards on the floor. Jerek Riddle and his group of men later found the four dead security team members, and he immediately enforced the emergency protocol.

They sent all of the Hippo-wing staff and out-patient, study participants home, telling them that it was a biohazard precaution to be taken for their safety. After that part of the wing was reported fully evacuated, Riddle ordered the guards who were with him,

"Leave the bodies there. Let's go find those grandies, right now," he demanded. He and his men took off to find the only ones who could have possibly pulled off something so outrageously grotesque. They went looking for them, and they left the door to Canna's office wide open.

Of the four dead guards, one did not stay dead for long. He stood himself up, and slowly found his way into the halls of the facility. That one horribly charred guard was roaming the facility, and he was anything but dead.

Minutes later, the undead guard was in one of the Hippo Project wing hallways, unsteadily striding forward. Ami Wentawaye, the wing's housekeeper who didn't get the evacuation memo, was rolling the mop bucket out of a room she'd just cleaned.

She was stepping backward carefully, not wanting to spill any excess water on the floor. The charred guard was approaching the open door just as Ami was backing out of the doorway. After being hunched over the bucket, she raised herself upright and stretched her back.

When she looked over, she saw it. A gravely burnt Center security guard with slimy eyes that had sunk into his face. With every step he took, ashes from his clothing particles flew off of his body. The ashes flew chaotically throughout the hallway, causing the bits to settle randomly.

Ami screamed like she was six years old, waking up from a nightmare. She was frozen, and she couldn't move her feet. Her breathing couldn't keep up with her heart rate. She was stuck.

But then she realized that the undead man wasn't after her. "Huh," she sighed when she saw that he was aiming to walk past her.

"What the shit?" she bawled. Even though she was utterly confused, given the normal zombie stereotypes in all the horror movies she'd seen, she took decisive action. She quit the job.

But she wasn't going to let a zombie go free to scare the wits out of everyone else. She'd just concluded that her employer was in the business of, "doing business that nobody has any business doing," she muttered, mad at science. No, not mad -she was livid.

She grabbed the mop handle as he crossed the doorway, and she used it to roughly shove the zombie through the door and into the room. The charred guard hit the floor, and the icky matter from the burnt clothing, flesh, and bones dirtied the floor she had just sanitized. She was sort of pissed off.

She ran back into the hall and shut the door, to keep the zombie in. Then, she took a small memo pad and pen from her uniform pocket and wrote her letter of resignation. She stuck the note on the wall near the door, and she left.

She was going home to get her son, and they would go stay with her cousin in Georgia. She planned to give the Center a courtesy call to let them know that there was a zombie in room 505, once she was far away from it. At the very least, she figured,

"Security should be catching this shit, anyway," she said to herself on her way out.

****

Fowley and Sammie finally found the unmapped elevator in the hidden part of the Hippo wing, after making a few wrong turns trying to locate the right hall. Fowley pressed the button, hoping that TJ had unlocked the security that monitored the elevator and required a hand scan to open the door.

The ascending cabin moved slowly to get to their floor. After a lengthy amount of time, Sammie and Fowley stared at each other, thinking the same thing: There might be more floors to the Center, and more secrets being kept.

The elevator cabin finally arrived at their floor. The door opened slowly, and TJ was there to meet them.

"I couldn't hack the security feature and grant you access, so I guess I'm going with you two. Get in," he told them in a hasty tone of voice.

Right as they were about to step into the elevator, five more armed men cornered them. These are among the guards who had stayed behind at the Center while the others searched for Pearl. TJ took a step back toward the corner of the elevator car, hoping the guards wouldn't see him.

Fowley didn't want to give away TJ's presence inside, so he shook his head just enough for TJ to see that he should let them handle the armed guards and keep his unrevealed position. Sammie kept her eyes on the guards as she positioned herself behind Fowley. TJ let the elevator door shut, and Fowley turned to face the guards as if he had simply missed the opportunity to get in.

The guards had already become wiser to put on full fireproof gear. They had decided to wear the high-quality emergency gear, after finding out about the ill fate of their in-house colleagues. They crept forward as the elevator door shut.

Of the five guards, Jerek Riddle was by far the most experienced Center employee and he already knew that the grandies were a different kind of human. While Jerek was ignorant regarding the details about each superhuman grandie, he had been around long enough to learn a little bit about the extent of their potential.

In fact, being the only living person outside of the Cr8 and Maquiller to witness Sammie's fire-screaming habit is what landed him his over-paid position in Opal Firs. That, and his willingness to be programmed.

"How did you get the elevator open?" Jerek asked him. Fowley just stared at him with a dull expression and no intention to answer him right away.

He closed his eyes for a brief moment, allowing the opaque silver coating to cross over his irises, as he primed himself for a fight.

As he felt his irises process the beam and return to their original color, Fowley was also afraid. It was the fear of knowing what he could do to them. Considering what was happening within the walls of the Maquiller Research Center that day, the fear was insurmountable.

****

Meanwhile, also in the section of the wing with the hidden elevator, there was an office that conducted a large portion of the Center's clerical work. The office was just on the other side of the wall and down the hall from the hidden elevator and staircase, but the employees who worked there were not aware of the secreted hall.

Amber, who was both the head supervisor in that office and a Maquiller Research Center board member, was sending out an email from her desk. Out of nowhere, her olfactory glands were hijacked by a smoky scent. She stood up, lifting her nose in the air to follow the smell.

She opened her office door with trepidation and a pounding heart, believing that she might find the place in flames. But when she entered the hallway from her office door, there was no visible fire.

She walked straight over to the second-floor railing, gripping the metal as she searched for smoke. From that view, Amber was overlooking the highly visible, open-area-style office on the first floor, which housed the 44 employees who worked under her.

Nothing was out of the norm, from what she could see. But even as her eyes were not confirming danger, the smell of smoke continued to intensify in her nostrils.

Just as she was going to reenter her office to call someone and have them check out the grounds, she noticed a fire above her. The rapidly enlarging flame seemed to be eating through the ceiling as if it were working its way across the roof.

As Amber watched it, the fire suddenly started to catch and spread wildly, and much faster, across the ceiling. She screamed in terror at how fast it was traveling, but then abruptly stopped her wailing.

It was gone. It had just extinguished itself. Promptly, her assistant and one other employee whose desks were close by rushed over to her to see what was wrong.

"You smell that?" Amber asked them, surprised that no one had said anything yet.

"Smell what?" her assistant inquired, shaking her head in her lack of understanding.

"I smell smoke," she yelled, thinking something was wrong with their noses if they couldn't perceive such a thick scent. She then withdrew her certainty, afraid that she might seem unstable. Many of those 44 employees coveted her job, and she did not want to add any fuel to that fire either.

She pulled herself back from the two of them, still plagued by the invisible smoke. By then, she was fighting off the urge to cough, and she began to suffer acute internal confusion. She looked back up, and the flame was once again burning through the ceiling above them.

Then, Amber remembered that she had the gift of premonitions, and it had been especially heightened for about a month. But what Amber forgot was that she did complete the Center's programming procedure.

It was required for any employee who was promoted to an official position of authority in the Center to complete the procedure. Amber was the only employee in that clerical office who had done so, about a month prior to June 20, 2018.

What she was experiencing was an effect of the first realm, which usually wasn't so intense for a false gem. However, her grievous encounter there in the office was something that occasionally happened when a naturally intuitive human went through the programming process, which intensified their gift.

Still oversensitive to the smoke, Amber prioritized to protect both her sanity and her employees. She temporarily closed that department of the building, as her gut was suggesting. She sent out one email, sending all 44 workers home for the rest of the week, with pay.

Amber was a woman who wasn't as afraid of looking stupid on Monday morning, as she was afraid of being responsible for somebody's fiery death, including her own. If there was ever a time to pull her boss card, June 20th was the day.

After ten minutes or so, that office was completely empty and quiet -as was the Hippo wing. The rest of the Maquiller Center continued on with their day, business as usual.

****

At the elevator, Jerek was holding a device that resembled a large universal TV remote, and it was used to control the elevator, in the case of an emergency. He had already stopped the elevator car with TJ inside. He waved the device at Fowley and Sammie with a devilish grin on his face, as he pressed the button and said,

"Okay. Now, whoever is in that elevator is a dead man. Whoever helped you two traitors get into this hallway will be dealt with just like the two of you," he declared with cold confidence.

"You already know this," he yelled loudly out of frustration with his freakishly whiny voice. Jerek was a husky man, and the sound of his voice just didn't match his physical appearance at all.

There, in the elevator hallway, Fowley had to focus on the gift he had, rather than his surroundings. There was a gray tint over everything like he was seeing through the filter of a photo editor.

He concentrated exceedingly hard on centering himself. When he finally did find that core, he felt a shift in the energies around him and he blocked out every sound.

Inside the elevator, TJ had become uneasy when the cabin stopped and began to ascend back up to the deadlock situation near the elevator call station. Anxiety set in, he was assuming that something happened to Sammie and Fowley.

"Oh shit," he said, as he considered that the guards might be controlling the elevator. "What the hell am I gonna do?" he anxiously asked himself as he wiped his hand over his face trying to be ready for what was to come.

TJ also wasn't yet very keen on his skillset, and fear overcame him when he thought about the enclosed area he was being returned to. He was unsure if he would be able to defend himself, and he braced himself for a real challenge.

Respectively, the same could be said of Fowley, or any Cr8 member –for that matter. When it came to their skillsets in relation to their gifts, they all were still very much at a novice level, or quite rusty.

The cab halted again, and it began to move downward. TJ then realized the hope that either Fowley or Sammie was controlling the elevator. But when the elevator stopped for the third time, ascended for a few seconds, then suddenly stopped again, it confused him right back to square one.

What TJ couldn't see is that it was Fowley against the machine. It was a frustrating match between Fowley's telekinesis and Jerek's hand-held elevator controller.

TJ had quickly become agitated by the constant reversal of direction while stuck inside. He finally became annoyed by the sound of the elevator's squeaky wire ropes.

He became mildly ailed with motion sickness as the cab stalled and reversed direction, several times. Ultimately, he became triggered, and a frosty, aqua-colored beam glossed over TJ's irises as he ascended and descended.

Finally, the elevator began to move up without interruption, and TJ was getting ready for the worst. He was completely terrified. He'd just hoped that Sammie and Fowley were okay, and that he wouldn't have to lay a hand on anyone.

At that time, Fowley was avoiding any verbal exchange with the guards in front of him. In his mind, he was too busy trying to manifest control over the guards' weapons, whichever weapons they were prepared to use.

He had been practicing the telekinetic manipulation of mechanical devices. When he found that powerful stillness which only a hyperactive gem could conjure, he opened his eyes wide, looked straight ahead to the guardsmen, and calmly declared,

"How we opened the elevator door is none of your damned business," he finally replied with rich oration, and with laughable tardiness. Dismissively, the security staff continued to give Fowley orders, but he couldn't hear a thing except for a low hum in his ears.

Seconds later, water began to form on the floor around Sammie and Fowley, spreading outwardly toward the group of men. No one saw the water forming, there was no carnal detection of its presence to anyone there.

It created a shallow puddle around the grandies, leaving a dry patch only right where they stood. The undetectable water spread itself out. It stayed shallow in some areas, and it deepened in others.

"Why don't the both of you just stop? Stop right here. And let's figure out what you're looking for," the same guard attempted to negotiate. The guardsmen, Sammie and TJ all alike were clueless about the sudden shift in Fowley's hyperactivity, as it was too subtle to sense.

When the elevator stopped the door began to open. As the door slid open, TJ became poised to attack as he watched. Once the opening of the door was wide enough, Sammie jumped into his arms, startling him.

She immediately turned around and screamed for Fowley to get in with her. Staying out of the guards' sight, TJ quietly tried to calm her down.

But Fowley was operating in his own manner, and his focus was unbreakable. He couldn't hear Sammie's pleading or the guards' commands as he held out his right hand toward the group of men. Big-eyed and stunned, TJ and Sammie watched Fowley, as the elevator door unexpectedly closed shut on them.

"Did he just shut us in here?" TJ asked, examining Fowley's intention. "No, no, no. If we're leaving, we're leaving together," he vowed.

"Fowley," she yelled through the door, then slapped her palm against it. "Maybe it was just the door, timing out?" Sammie spoke her thought as she studied the call buttons on the wall panel.

"Nope, it was Fowley," he said, repeatedly pressing the "door open" button.

"Okay," Sammie replied. "So, let's just reverse the door, right?" she brainstormed.

"Of course. Let's do that," TJ said, as they both tried to focus on the elevator car. After thirty seconds or so with no movement or change, TJ rolled his stiff neck around to loosen up, and he declared,

"So, this might take a while. This isn't really my thing, you know. Let's try again?" he asked her.

"All right. Let's try again," Sammie replied with obvious worry. The two took a moment in the elevator to stretch like they had seen Fowley doing before practicing telekinesis when they were younger, trying to loosen up and find the focus they needed.

Sammie looked at TJ admitting, "I really don't know how he does his, you know, telekinesis or whatever. I was too afraid to get good at it," she spoke shamelessly.

Sammie was such a *scaredy cat* growing up. As great as her powers were, she was still just as scared that day at the elevator as she was timid in her childhood. Despite all of the times when it had been made clear to her that the Cr8 could definitely protect themselves from threats, she still preferred to hide.

When she was fourteen years old, Sammie was a first-hand witness the night Fowley had made an oncoming car brake itself. The driver was severely intoxicated and clearly about to run them over.

In his telekinetic defense, Fowley suddenly halted the car, hurling the drunken driver's back-seat passenger through the windshield. The driver, a Virginian man in his thirties broke

out running. It was more like staggering, but he left his injured passenger behind, nonetheless.

Twenty-six-year-old Sipp Apple landed into Fowley's arms, where he died. At least, the first time.

The dead became undead within fifteen minutes of his first passing. When he stood back up on his feet he was, in fact, a zombie. This type of zombie is a "slainch," as the grandie later coined the term. Scared, they phoned the police.

A slainch is a zombie that only seeks to devour his own maker's flesh and to kill the power of their light. No one else but the hyperactive being who created the slainch would ever be the target, and that fact was still unknown to the Cr8. Fowley was the primary, and only, target in its path as the zombie lunged forward with sloppy strides toward him.

Fowley, Sammie, Rose, and Kielo had been standing at the accident scene grouped closely together. Confusingly, it was not so apparent that the undead man was coming for Fowley, and only him.

When the police had finally arrived to investigate the scene, they saw that their expected corpse wasn't as motionless as they had imagined. What they had walked up on was a group of "hysterical teens, and a delirious zombie," as they later described in their reports. After firing numerous rounds into the slainch, the frightened police officers ran away just like everyone else.

In the end, it took desperate measures to stop the slainch. Extremely panicked, Sammie screamed fire on the slainch, and she burned the undead back to dead -for good. The slainch had been reduced to a pile of ash.

When they all ran away, Fowley had been sure to keep a handful of the slainch's ashes. He later poured some of the ashes into a local river. He had deemed the ceremonial closure important enough. He left the rest of the ashes on Sipp Apple's front porch in an urn he'd made himself, to give the man's family what belonged to them.

That night changed the talk of the town for quite a while. At least weekly, some prankster would claim that he or she saw a zombie. It was the most bizarre thing that had ever happened in that small town in Rhode Island, and the stories that stemmed from it wouldn't be going away any generation soon.

It was a very sad time for Fowley. The incident was traumatic, but the magic was real. Every now and then, Fowley secretly checked on the deceased man's surviving family. It seemed to help with the guilt, but what happened that night was never forgotten by any of the grandies who were there.

Nonetheless, a decade later, Sammie was still as nervous as they come. The things she'd seen, and done, were still not enough proof to make her relax.

None of her own personal knowledge was remotely enough for her to speak, or feel, with much optimism involving powers. Right then, in the elevator with TJ, Sammie's rant only confirmed that she was the same worried person she'd always seemed to be back in the day.

"So, I hope we can do this. But, I've never really tried before," she started to babble on. "And I definitely don't want to hurt anybody else," she confided in him, shaking her head, and biting her bottom lip.

"TJ, I'm prepared for a search party, but not a death wish. I mean, if we complete this, he'll kill us all. Won't he?" she questioned him regarding Maquiller.

TJ didn't even try to get a word in. He just stared at her while she just ranted on and on, wasting time -in his mind. For the moment, he wished he could block out the uncertainty, the negativity, and the disbelief that spewed from his adopted sister's mouth as he thought, *Will she ever shut up?* She finally brought her rant to a close,

"So, when I say that 'I hope we can do this' I'm saying I hope we can do the whole thing. I hope that we'll truly be free from all of this. And I hope that those five subs whom you gave freedom to will stay free as well because I know there will be trouble. I just know it, she cried.

"I'm sorry, I'm just scared about it all," she exclaimed, then she sighed to finally catch a breath. TJ wondered after her, and he abruptly pulled himself from his thoughts as he spoke,

"Interesting," he responded emotionlessly. "Well, I think you might wanna get good at it now?" he suggested impatiently. "Or, maybe you'd just like to hide in here all day," he added with a sarcastic tone.

"Yeah, sure. Let's try it again. And shut up," she replied, jabbing at him.

"You shut up. Please." He dished it back at her, and there was something about it that started to give them the calm they were looking for just then. The two became quiet again, ready to make another attempt. It was then that TJ noticed the wetness of the floor inside of the elevator.

"Why is the floor wet?" TJ suddenly inquired.

"What?" Sammie replied as she finally noticed it, too. "I don't know. Weird."

"Well, did you step in water, or something?" he probed. Slightly annoyed, as the wet floor was not the most important thing on her mind at that second, Sammie answered him saying,

"No, I don't think so. Sure it wasn't you?" she asked.

"Nah, it didn't look like this when I was in here alone," he stated with certainty. "Whatever. Let's listen out and try to hear what's going on," he suggested. He tried pressing the button on the panel to open the door again. Still, nothing happened.

None of the guards had expected such a weak effect when they saw the voltage in Fowley's hands. He'd zapped them with the bright silvery surges for several seconds. He'd stopped, lowered his hand, and allowed the current to retract when he had thought it was enough.

But the guards weren't fazed after just a very short moment of low-voltage shock, and discomfort. A stun gun could've done more than his zap did. Fowley didn't want to kill them, but his electrical charge wasn't as damaging as he'd hoped it would be.

The haughty guardsmen looked at each other in disbelief, then laughed at the minuscule damage dosed to them. "C'mon lil grandie boy," another guard taunted Fowley as he had heard Canna speak of him as a soft touch. "Let's talk about this," he insisted with authority.

"Not gonna happen today. Please don't test me, I am begging you," Fowley replied in an advisory manner as he locked eyes with Jerek, and shook his head with disregard. Jerek, reached inside of his fireproof suit and pulled out a smoke grenade canister rigged with a serum that was injurious to any superhuman gem's powerful abilities, and possibly their basic health as well.

Jerek became infuriated, fuming when he saw Fowley's carefree visage. It made him all the more ready to neutralize a grandie whose uniqueness he had coveted for most of his pathetic career.

But when he activated the smoke can, he became inflexibly stiffened in his stance. His jaw was dropped, and locked with his mouth wide open. The smoke traveled straight away from the can into Jerek's nose and mouth, where he inhaled all of it. Fowley's sharp concentration caused the veins near his own temples to enlarge underneath his sweaty forehead as he emptied the can into Jerek's nose and mouth.

His flesh burned on the inside, and blood trickled out of his eyes, nose, and ears as the canister itself was sucked flat. The other guards, and Fowley, screamed nauseously at the unsettling and gruesome backfire.

The remaining guards quaked in fear when they saw that Fowley was completely unarmed, and unharmed. They examined the can that killed their partner, and it made no reasonable sense.

Although his intention was very clear, they marveled at the evidence that Jerek had inhaled an entire smoke grenade can that was filled with a potent concoction designed to disable a human of exceptional strength. He'd gulped the whole canister straight inward, then flopped onto the floor dead in less than ten seconds.

Speechless, and harshly disoriented, they returned their attention to Fowley. But only with more rage than before, as they all were furious over their loss.

Fowley regained his more temperate demeanor, careful to stay focused. But the guards translated the sudden lack of emotion as a challenge to be taken.

They didn't give resistance a thought, and they did go after him to clutch him by hand. The guards had become afraid to fire their own weapons.

They all carried the hypoactive serum in some way, shape, or form. They were always prepared to use common tactical weapons to make discreet serum attacks with. The Center made a priority of secretly training its security team to be ready for such applications via common weaponry, as well as everyday household items.

Canna's protocols confirmed that he simply never trusted the grandies or any other superhuman beings.

The guardsmen were hoping to get close enough to Fowley to disable him. But in their frustration, and emotional recklessness, they went after him tactlessly.

They all charged forward together, hoping to pile up on him and tackle him down. And so, without perceiving their surroundings, they all fell into the suddenly perceivable water that had earlier surrounded the two oblivious grandies.

When the guards stepped into the water between them and Fowley, they dropped six feet deep into the floor, or better put, the pool that had mysteriously constructed itself mid-hallway. Fowley's heartbeat skipped when he suddenly comprehended the pool that was all of a sudden present between him and them.

Before then, no one had detected the water on the floor. But as soon as the guards made the conscious decision and blatant attempt to attack the grandie, the water made its presence known.

Fowley hollered out when the water from their uncontrollable dives splashed up against him. He was just as punch-drunk as the four ill-fated men who had just landed right onto death's lap.

The guards all were electrocuted, and they were dreadfully charred by the dormant voltage that was inadvertently stored inside of them with Fowley's bright silver electrical spark. When paired with water contact, the seemingly low voltage that Fowley had planted in them with his hand turned out to be well more than any death row inmate had ever received.

The electrical surge by far exceeded what had been deemed necessary even among the lawmakers who endorsed capital punishment. Then, Fowley marveled, as he watched the water recede away like a draining bathtub. As the water was just about emptied out of that space at mid hall, Fowley was able to see the floor there again.

He looked over the floor that was still wet in some areas, and the dead bodies. Jerek Riddle had stayed dry, as his corpse was farther away from the area where the pool had formed. Fowley's thinking was intense, yet unclear, as he tried to grasp what had just happened.

Fowley looked at the charred guards' smoking but wet corpses. In that moment, he noticed something else that was equally strange. Oddly, he couldn't smell the smoke that rose from their lifeless bodies. He knew something eerie was going on at the same time.

It was *presence by purpose*, a concept that the grandies learned over time which implies the inability to see the source of a solution until well after the solution source has already solved the problem.

And sometimes, it was a solution source that orchestrated the completion of a necessary task that one couldn't complete for himself. It was not the first time Fowley had experienced it live, and it wouldn't be the last. But it was always a dumbfounding event each and every time it happened to him.

"How can this be? Does this smoke not have a scent?" he asked himself beneath his breath, amazed. But he then reasoned to himself, concluding that he must have lost his sense of smell for the moment.

He had drowned out sound as well, and he was just then getting that sense back. Nonetheless, things were exactly as Fowley had always feared they would one day be. Except, things had escalated much faster than he'd imagined.

Fowley couldn't have felt worse. Even if it was in self-defense, and out of clear or absolute danger, a part of Fowley died whenever someone else did. In the very least, a little bit more of his persona seemed to darken.

He undoubtedly battled some degree of depression that no one around him had the power to heal, paradoxically. But the first rule the Cr8 had grown to both accept and respect, however chaotic, was this; *"Confirm that you're right, then go right ahead."* They all agreed on it.

However, Fowley always had a heavy heart about it. It was why he could never kill with his own hands, or weaponry. Fowley had the type of childhood traumas that made him second guess every little thing he did.

Although his paranoia was justified, it was also a handicap that contributed to his outlook. It habitually crippled his progress in real time.

But then again, there was something to be said about a man who could win any fight without initiating fatal contact with his opponent. He'd always thought that maybe if he weren't so clumsy with his power, he would be a pretty cool guy.

His rules were unusually advantageous to his opponent. He'd preferred to be a defense-only fighter, and any kill weapon must be provided to him, and not brought by him. This uncommon attitude of his is what made the others in the Cr8 marvel at his skill.

That is how he lived and learned. Even though he sensed it, he could never verbalize his knowing that he had always been granted a certain set of uncanny advantages whenever he was defending, and not attacking. That Wednesday was no exception.

Still stuck in the elevator, TJ and Sammie looked at each other, worrying about what was happening to Fowley. They had given up trying to move the elevator car. Sammie opened her eyes and moved her hands away from her ears, which she'd covered when she heard all of the screaming and commotion.

Sensing that the standoff had ended, TJ tried the "door open" button to reopen it. It worked, and the two of them sighed at each other in their ironic exhaustion from trying all along.

When it was completely open again, they were staring at Fowley. They were amazed that Fowley was still standing, and he was unhurt. He too was shocked at the aftermath, as he gaped at the deep-fried guards.

Eager to see what he was fixated on, TJ and Sammie got off of the elevator to find that all of the guards were dead. TJ was stunned, and he responded to what he was seeing,

"Eggs over Mercury," TJ said in a monotone voice.

"What?" Fowley replied, unsure about what he meant by it.

"You fried them. Hard," TJ expanded for him as they examined the scene. Sammie thought to herself that the four stiff guards in Canna's office may have gotten off easy. She was puzzled as she spoke,

"This is ridiculous," she said to herself under her breath, looking over Jerek's remains. Seeing the spotty wet areas on the floor, she pointed to it as she brought it to TJ's attention. "The floor's wet in here, too? But how? There wasn't any water on the floor like this before," she exclaimed as she tried to recall it.

"When did this water get in here?" she insisted on knowing. She scanned the whole horrid scene, as did TJ.

Jerek's floppy body was on the floor in an awkward, and humanly impossible, position. Blood was still running from his eyes, nose and mouth. His eyes had sunken far into his skull. And the other guards who had been cooked a little closer to the elevator door finally began to cause a stench in the hallway air.

"Oh. There it is," Fowley said as he covered his nose and mouth with his sweater. "That reeks," he shouted. Both TJ and Sammie surely agreed with him, as they had already covered their nostrils upon entering the hall.

"Sure does. We gotta go. Come on," TJ spoke as he got himself as far away from the stink as he could. He stood in the elevator ready to move on right away.

TJ was overall dazed by the outcome. He didn't have many words and his silence said a lot about how he felt. Sammie stood in the elevator doorway, pulling on Fowley's arm as she cried,

"C'mon let's get moving. Please, let's go." They got back in and as the door was shutting, Fowley exhaustedly exclaimed to them, "I can't believe the shit I just saw." He let out a breath that he seemed to have been holding for way too long.

"Now, exactly what was that? How'd you do it?" Sammie shouted in wonder as her heart raced. Fowley was too excitable in disbelief and hadn't registered her questions. He continued to recount.

"Good question. What was that?" he asked himself, though he looked at TJ and Sammie. He elaborated, "The direction of the smoke in the grenade was my doing. But, damn," he said. He pondered on the details, still in his adrenaline rush.

"What do you mean?" Sammie asked him, waiting for details. Still ignoring her questions, Fowley resumed his recount,

"The voltage beam, to hem them up so that we could run. That was me, too. But I didn't know they were gonna fry like that," he said.

"Incredible. I wonder how long a surge could stay dormant in the body before water becomes ineffective," he started rambling to himself about the horrid exploit while he scratched his black beard, not realizing his displaced sanity in the moment.

"And the water?" TJ added to the list. But then Fowley shifted his demeanor considerably, knowing that he wasn't responsible for the sudden pool of water. Fowley responded,

"But that wasn't me at all." He paused, and he sighed in fear. "Actually, I thought that maybe you had done that. You know how you do," he spoke to TJ. TJ shook his head to negate the notion.

"I wasn't trying to --I didn't mean to do *that*," Fowley tried to explain to them. "Did you see it?" he asked them. "Shit was sickening," he yelled with agitation and bulging eyes. TJ acknowledged Fowley's changed mood as he probed,

"Hold on a minute. You're saying that you didn't manifest the water that we just saw on the floor?" TJ asked as he shook his head, genuinely unsettled.

"You have no idea. 'Water on the floor' is a drastic understatement," Fowley advised him. TJ then looked over at Sammie, wondering if maybe she had created it with her energy, knowing he himself didn't do it. Before he had the chance to ask her, she answered,

"Don't look at me. I was too freaked out to think anything." Both TJ and Fowley nodded with pure belief. The mood became uneasy for them all. "Let's just get this thing done," Sammie said, ready to move on.

However, she hadn't seen Fowley do anything like that in quite some time. Fowley turned to Sammie, looking into her eyes, so that she would see that small trace of what they called a "hyperactive gleam," in his eyes. He said to her,

"To answer your question, I have no idea how it happened. If I had my way, everyone would still be alive when we leave. Call Kai, get him back here," he told Sammie and TJ, closing his eyes while trying to get past his growing disappointment. Sammie was digging in her backpack, but TJ was quicker to pull out his cell,

"I got it. I'm calling him now," he said as he dialed out. Kai answered right away. TJ was supposed to be out of the building, but was speaking with urgency,

"Hey, yeah we're here. And we're all in mode. Are you?" TJ asked Kai, expecting an affirmative reply.

"Oh shit. Okay. Um, yeah, I am," Kai replied to confirm that he'd crossed over into his own distinctive mode. He was caught off guard when TJ called him, instead of one of the others. An impatient Fowley called out to Kai over Sammie and TJ,

"Okay, hurry up and get yourself back here. We're barbequing the place, and we have to get everybody gathered here before it gets worse," he hollered into TJ's phone.

"At this point, if we get out of this it's going to be as a unit," TJ said into the phone, also addressing Fowley and Sammie. He knew very well that their battle was going to follow them everywhere they went once they left the Center. TJ hung up the call with Kai and tucked his phone back into his pocket.

The bad news was that their cover was definitely blown, and the drama was already bigger than any of them could imagine. There were already ten dead in the Center, yet their job was only half done.

On the bright side, however, the good news was that TJ, Kai, Sammie, and Fowley were still alive. They were closing out a chapter that they had been eager to end.

They still needed to get Dr. Canna's body out of the building, along with the files in Sammie's tote bag. The bag that she was carrying and protecting would expose Canna, his terrible practices, and the real intentions behind the Research Center.

Leroi wanted Al Canna gone at all costs. Maquiller was expecting to frame him for the wicked deeds they both were equally guilty of facilitating. But what Fowley and TJ had in their backpacks was just a little more paperwork to shed a lot more light on the bigger picture pertaining to a more seasoned manipulator, Leroi Maquiller.

TJ, Fowley, and Sammie were carrying pages and pages of reports, diary entries, and examination results that would undoubtedly break many hearts once it was released to the world. They were going to create a colossal, and catastrophic, implosion within a big group of self-made bureaucrats. For the first time in their lives, they were absolutely okay with the chaos they felt they needed to bring about to start over without Maquiller.

They were content with the family they had made so long as they had each other. Still, it didn't take away any of the fear or anxiety that they all were feeling to some level.

Maquiller had instilled in them to take the good with the bad, and they usually did. But there was nothing good in their lives as they were, with Maquiller. They just carried with them many memories that they had wished they could forget. They were also regretting all of the dark deeds that they would've never committed without his slick programming.

There are many awful memories that would belong exclusively to Leroi Maquiller if he had ever done his own dirty work. Instead, all of the trauma, the nightmares, the guilt, and the deeds themselves, burdened the Cr8.

Not just them, but every programmed being Maquiller had ever *practiced* on. In some way or form, they were all like puppets on strings.

No one knew what would ultimately come to pass in the long run, and no one could control the horrible possibilities. However, it was ironic that the same horrible possibilities made them the tightly knit family they had become, and even more so that day in Opal Firs.

"So, that's that part," Sammie concluded. TJ was stunned more than anything else.

"Wow," he uttered, shaking his head. Fowley, who was a bit calmer right then, said,

"I know. I know. I know," he nodded his head and repeated the phrase enough times for Sammie and TJ to worry. Then he suddenly broke his nod as he looked at Sammie, telling her,

"You know, I never knew that you actually *screamed* the fire out of your eyes, too. That was very interesting," he said to her with an intrigued expression. The weird topic change was accompanied by a casual attitude that just showed up unexpectedly.

He used his hand to try to illustrate the flame blazing in front of him. Sammie was slightly confused at the change, but she and TJ responded together.

"You didn't know that?" they replied, surprised.

"No, I didn't. Wasn't sure how that worked, cause I missed it last time," he admitted, shaking his head.

Sammie smirked slightly at TJ. He sensed the new shift in Fowley's demeanor again. He held his lips together tightly so Sammie would know that he was aware of Fowley's unpredictability, but not speaking on it.

"Wow. This is already crazy," she replied to Fowley.

"Tell me about it," Fowley exclaimed somewhat snappily. Sammie then changed her tone, as she studied their surroundings.

"What is going on?" she said, looking around the motionless elevator. Fowley also began to gather that something wasn't right. He finally asked,

"Why aren't we moving?" Then, TJ suddenly huffed, immediately grasping that no one had pressed the button to move the elevator. He reached out and pushed the button, and the elevator began to descend. For a short tick, all three of them avoided making eye contact.

They were embarrassed that they had slipped up and lost vigilance at a time like such. If not ever before, they felt like true amateurs -just then. The three of them just stared ahead in disbelief as the motor rails turned the elevator cab downward to the Center's hidden floor, to collect the body.

*******End of Chapter*******

ODD GEMS Soaked by Suri R. Moon

Chapter 9

Thorns

Pearl sat in the passenger seat as Nomad tapped his thumb on the steering wheel, waiting at a red light. He glanced at the digital clock, it read 3:03 p.m. They had been riding in awkward silence, and they both were locked into their own thoughts.

Pearl was still very much in pain from her fall, and by then she was trying to fight another migraine attack. She grabbed a pair of sunglasses that Nomad had sitting in the small compartment near the dash.

The radio station played hits from the '80s, and the playlist was yet another trigger to Pearl. The lyrics of all of the songs immediately became stuck in her head as they played, and she had remembered every word by the end of each song. So, Nomad turned the volume down.

Nomad knew the less talking he made her do, the better. So, he was letting her be -for the time being. The stoplight turned green, and he accelerated as Pearl finally asked him,

"So, who is this person I must meet?" she inquired out of curiosity. His sunglasses made her look goofy; they weren't a good fit for her face. But they helped block the daylight which intensified her headache.

"His name is Goose Gary. He lives about twenty minutes from my store. He seems to be the only person I know who has any knowledge about the Center," he replied, looking back at her. "He used to work there, maintenance or something," he added with a vague shoulder shrug.

Nomad was a man who could keep a secret, and he rarely had a choice in the matter. He was someone who retained important information, if he had received any. Even though the first realm was always the source, Nomad didn't know where he had received such knowledge from, or why –for that matter.

It was not unusual for Nomad to be given vital information concerning the gems, although he did not yet know that he himself was one. He stopped the car again, stuck at another red light.

Nomad Artman had just as little information about his story as the grandies did about theirs. The grandies believed that they had been working at the Center for their adoptive father. They were not inclined to believe they were ever programmed, as they had always been told that "they were born special."

They would have understood the prefacing history behind their malfunctioned programming had the grandies known more about the gems, and their modern-time correlation with Maquiller's scientific research.

Nomad believed he had always been a single man. Both of his parents were deceased before the procedure, and Maquiller's content writers had chosen to maintain that part of his story.

He was wired to complete Maquiller's tasks, just like any other successfully programmed subject. But he learned how to fight off the urges when it mattered the most. He too was given premonitions and other insight to forewarn him of the oncoming evil.

Effortlessly, all he had to do was exist, and the gems would eventually draw in together, somewhere close around him. The subtle way that the other odd gems would eventually surround him would be in a subconsciously magnetic capacity.

He was the *magnetic liaison*. When the right time arrived, the magnetic liaison was the geographical anchor to attract those gems who were drawn into a calibration.

While every calibration designated a gem as the liaison, the liaison had never been the same gem twice, ever. No matter what distance a gem needed to travel, all gems eventually find their liaison by the time of the calibration.

Nomad didn't know a whole lot, but what little information he did receive was sometimes a matter of life and death for himself, or someone close to him in his path. But he hardly ever knew who, or when, until it was time. It never ceased to amaze him.

For Nomad, it had all started in 1998 when he was abducted from a jail cell. His real name became unknown to all, as his identity had been completely scrubbed from every vital system.

He had been arrested, and charged, for "driving while intoxicated," according to police. One minute he was sleeping off his sorrows behind bars, and the next minute he was convinced that his name was Nomad Artman.

His new identity had a squeaky-clean criminal record, and Nomad Artman had a brand-new business to start up in a new location. Wrongfully, he believed the new coffee and book shop was his own idea, and desire.

Ironically, he wasn't even a heavy drinker, he was just having a bad day and didn't want to be at home with his hostile wife who still resided in Rhode Island. He was forced to complete the research procedure while his wife of just one year was at home, packing all that she could take with her.

They were divorcing, and he had been the last to find out about it. He never would have put himself up as a test subject for weird science, but it didn't matter to the two arresting officers in his DWI case back East. Unfortunately for Nomad, they were greatly connected to the Center. He was money in their pockets that night.

"Nomad?" Pearl spoke to him, wondering what he was thinking about. His facial expression had turned to disgruntled. He was lost in his thoughts, but he finally noticed that he'd been staring ahead, spacing out.

He'd always felt like he was lacking the truth, and he was certain that he lacked a majority of the facts. He was caught up in his own scars for a minute. He glanced over at Pearl, briefly wondering if she knew how unique she was.

The light turned green, and Nomad shifted his body language. He shook his head as he began accelerating, appearing to be clearing some haunting thought away as he said to her,

"Anyway, Goose might be able to tell you what to do, and how to pull it off. I hope," he added. Pearl nodded her head with optimism, and she didn't even judge his spacy stare. She was just as dazed as him.

She studied him as he drove. She noticed how big his thighs were when she glanced at how snug his denim jeans fitted him. She scanned his front seat for any random information, but his cab was completely neat, and nothing considerable stood out.

So, she continued to study him, trying not to stare. He was wearing a silver ring on his right hand that had an eye-catching center stone, an emerald. She wondered if it was something significant as she resumed evaluating him.

She silently giggled to herself when she saw the small tattoo that was set low behind his right ear. It was a dagger, and it pointed upward to his hairline near the backside of his ear.

A vine of some sort was wrapped around the dagger handle. At the first glance, it looked like an earring dangling from his lobe. But as it was, the ring was the only piece of jewelry that Nomad wore.

She caught herself staring. She then looked out the window, trying to cover up rudeness that he wasn't even paying any mind to. As they made a left turn, she looked up to the sky out of the passenger window, and something ridiculously mind-boggling caught her full attention.

There were small waves of water forming in the sky. She blinked her eyes repeatedly because she was doubting them.

The waves began to softly crash into each other. The sky around the sun, which had finally seemed to stay present, was becoming a deep sea-green color. Earlier, it had been a typical Pacific-Northwestern blueish gray.

Wherever the waves crashed, they produced purple clouds that swiftly dissipated, as they were more like bursts of purple steam. Pearl closed her eyes hoping to calm the anxiety that was overwhelming her, but she couldn't look away. Speechless, she stared up, feeling helpless, as the tiny bodies of water began to create much larger waves that moved vehemently in the sky.

Pearl had her nose on the glass window, trying to see how big the phenomenon was. While it seemed colossal, Pearl calculated that it was most likely airborne over the entire town of Opal Firs, at least.

She trembled at the sea-green sky, and the surreal animated suspension of the lively waters that one could only fear would break and flood everything below. It was by far the most awesome, and yet the most terrifying, thing to watch.

There were no words for what she was observing, except maybe *apocalyptic*. Nomad had become worried about her, and he called out her name for the second time,

"Pearl," he exclaimed louder than before, and he snapped her out of it. "What's up? What's wrong?" he asked.

Pearl was afraid that he might not see what she saw, but she knew that she should at least try to explain it. She pointed at the windshield glass, upward at the sun.

Luckily, she didn't have to explain because Nomad's face was already stuck with his jaw dropped as he peered out the top of his car windshield. Pearl was surprised that he also could perceive the waters above. She pondered on whether the sight was for the whole world, or just the two of them.

"What is that?" she asked him, looking back to it again. The sun's light became tinted, and the sunlight created a different color where it shined on the whole town of Opal Firs. The tint was somewhere between a shimmering light, pale pink blended with radiant gold.

It would be best described as rose gold. The rose-gold sun wasn't shining any brighter, or dimmer, than usual. In contrast, the air was a little chilly for that time of year to Pearl when she rolled her window down to poke her head out. Weather aside, it was absolutely amazing to see and the sight of it caused Nomad to quiver.

"Maybe we should take a picture?" she asked him, full-blown fascinated. Nomad pointed to the glove compartment, saying,

"My phone has a camera. The phone's in there, but don't be surprised if you can't get the shot," he advised her, letting out a light laugh. Pearl wondered what he meant, but she opened the glove compartment to take the phone out anyway. She grabbed his cell phone, but then noticed a box of colored pencils that seemed out of place.

The all-black interior of the car cab suddenly faded toward the background, upstaged by the glowing box. *Colored pencils?* She thought about the strange box of pencils, wondering if Nomad was an artist of sorts. The colors popped so intensely, and Pearl tried to understand why the box was so spellbinding.

Nomad saw the excessive glow coming from the glove compartment out of the corner of his eye, and he jerked his head toward it. As Pearl was still gazing at the pencils, Nomad reached over and slammed his glove compartment shut. She flinched at his sudden reaction and snappy movement.

She stared at the closed glove compartment, still envisioning the surreal luminosity that came from a basic box of coloring pencils, and she was baffled. Nomad was holding his jaw tight when she searched his face for an explanation.

Then, she looked out of the opened window, and goosebumps grew all over her skin. She fiddled with the phone in silence for a while. She finally activated the camera, then she aimed the phone at the waters above.

She got the shot, and the shutter sounded. But there was absolutely nothing abnormal about the picture. Nothing that they were witnessing live transferred to the saved media image on the phone.

"So, that's what you were laughing at. Great." Pearl acknowledged her mishap as he looked ahead. He then glanced at her for a second before laughing again at the unsuccessful photo op. Not losing his seriousness, he engaged.

"What'd I tell you?" he asked her, as he kept his attention on the road in front of him.

He was one-hundred-percent certain that they needed to get to the Center. Though he did not know why, or how, a strong hunch had convinced him that Goose would show up there at some point soon.

When he saw the unyielding display above him, he knew something was happening, and he knew it was something that Goose would also perceive. He looked to Pearl with reluctance as he said,

"You're probably gonna hate me for saying this, but I think we really need to get back to the Center," Nomad declared, concluding his thoughts. Pearl whipped her head around to face Nomad who had begun to accelerate on the small highway. Checking his mirrors, he got over into the right lane. They were then on a stretch of road that appeared to have a narrow shoulder and a shallow ditch.

Pearl was horrified. She had no good reason to return to the Center, at all. As far as she knew, she would only bring herself more trouble by going back with him. She asked,

"Can't you just call him? And let him meet us somewhere that is not the Center?" She suggested her alternative with a tone of worry, and she shook her head to negate his plan.

"No, I erased his number. I don't even know why. But I don't know his phone number," he replied, slightly agitated.

She had to make a quick decision, and all of her worries began to build up inside of her. So, she looked over at Nomad saying, "I'm sorry I can't go with you," speaking with genuine regret.

"Wait, what? Trust me, you really need to. And you'll be glad you did, I promise you that," he advised her, wondering what she was about to do. She looked ahead and saw that the shoulder was going to run out not far ahead of them. She felt that if she didn't jump soon, she wasn't going to.

"Stop the car," she requested, attempting a peaceful approach. But Nomad didn't press the brake or slow down, at all. He tried to calm her, checking to see if she was having another attack. He tried to convince her,

"Pearl, I won't let anything happen to you. And Goose would only be a help to you," he pledged. But Pearl couldn't get past the fact that she had her mind made up about returning. She wouldn't be going with him.

Pearl swiftly unhooked her seatbelt and clenched her leather backpack. She opened Nomad's car door at forty-five miles per hour and threw herself from his vehicle.

Wildly, she rolled well past the shoulder, and into the ditch that did not turn out to be as shallow as she'd calculated. It was a twenty-foot drop into the thick blackberry bushes that grew unrestrained alongside the small highway.

She was already pricked from top to bottom by the many thorns. It was fluky for her to have had such a cushioned landing on top of the backpack.

"Ouch," she exclaimed to no one in particular, hoping that verbalizing her pain would lessen it. She was wrong. She just made herself still, afraid to get herself stung by any new thorns for the moment.

She had just *ditched* the one person who had actually been helpful, let alone herself. She felt utterly stupid, stuck there in the branches as she whispered in pain, "That might've been a mistake."

Nomad pulled over and closed his passenger door. He was about to try to see where she landed, and if she was hurt. He saw that the blackberry bushes had grown upward uncontrollably, and densely. He couldn't see Pearl, but he imagined all the thorns and the pain she would be in.

Twenty feet above her, light traffic passed by. Nomad was examining the deep drop from the side of the road where there should have been a fence, or some other barrier, to prevent a fall like Pearl's.

Then, he noticed something from the shoulder of the road. As he was about to call out for her, he was distracted by two men in a car. They were bobbing in and out of their windows, clearly looking for something or someone.

Knowing they also could be looking for Pearl, he casually retreated to his car. He turned his eyes to catch a glimpse of them, and from their sense of direction, he knew that they most likely didn't see Pearl jump out.

One of them was in uniform, and one was in plain clothes. They had begun to slow down a bit, as Miles Knott and Nomad locked eyes. But Miles ultimately turned his attention away with no interest in him. After they had passed, Nomad waited another fifteen seconds or so.

He then looked back down into the bushes, searching and shouting for Pearl in the darkened area. He yelled out numerous times, but there was no answer. He hoped it was because she had found her way out of there, and he gave up after a while, concluding,

"Well, she's gonna have to figure it out, I guess," he spoke to himself.

He really wanted to follow somewhere behind her and make sure she was safe. But he looked back up at the sky and saw that the waters had already become more brutal.

The steamy purple clouds were forming more frequently than before as adjoining waves became larger. Nomad jetted back to his car and jumped in. Before he drove away, he looked over at the closed glove compartment -thinking about the pencils inside.

"Why me?" he asked himself. He took a deep breath with his eyes closed, and he began to shake in fear. Then, he stopped.

He stopped obsessing about what he had no control over, and he shook it out of his head. He put the car in drive, and mashed the gas pedal. He sped off down the street with his only intention being to get to the Center.

Pearl waited for Nomad to leave before she could try to move. She was afraid that he would find her if she made too much noise.

"Shit. I need help," she said to herself, as she learned that she was exceedingly pained in her right ankle. Even though she could have retracted her mistake by answering Nomad when he called out to her, she had already mentally reaffirmed her decision to not return to the research facility.

As much as she was already hurting, she gradually became hysterical at the fact that she was going to have to afflict pain on herself even further to get out of the branches. She began to laugh, panic-stricken, as she acknowledged the painful predicament.

She barely moved four inches upright before new thorns began to scrape at her. She leaned back in defeat and cried into her own ears. She definitely was going to have to try again. As she reclined there for several more seconds, she wondered who she could lodge a complaint to.

A sudden rustling noise in the near distance shook her up and swiftly shifted her perspective. Then, her pains began to play the background to a new threat. Deep in the darkened area of the wild blackberry bushes, Pearl feared the unknown thing that was somewhere close by.

With her heart pounding, Pearl looked to the sky. It was barely visible through the branches above her. She then located a patch in the bushes where the crazy oceanic display was much more visible, and she knew which direction she would have to move toward.

Like a chicken in a rotisserie oven, she slowly turned herself over, onto her stomach. Once she was resting with her chest on her backpack, she began to stand up. Groaning, she could feel multiple thorns poking through the green hoodie and her skin.

Deepening her breaths and concentrating, she pulled her hood over her head and got her leather pack onto her back. She raised the fabric with her hands and used her unzipped hooded sweatshirt as a shield for her face. Looking ahead to the spot where she might find ample wiggle room, Pearl took the first step in what was the most painful fifteen yards she'd ever walked in her whole life -that she knew of.

When she finally made it out of the other side of the blackberry bushes and onto a small grass field, she was covered in thorns. Bleeding through cuts and pained with a sprained ankle, Pearl was a horrific mess.

Breathing heavily and smiling faintly, she was happy to have endured that short-but-horrible walk. But her breathing was interrupted by that heavy rustling noise, once again. She quickly turned around to face the threat, and she was standing face to face with a huge raccoon.

Before she could even react, the raccoon seemingly gasped at the sight of her. The 25-pound, wild mammal scampered away in terror, leaving Pearl feeling both stupid and creepy. She weighed the pros and cons, then moved on knowing that things could have gone differently.

****

Kai, Leith, and Michael were marching toward the back side of the Center when Leith suddenly flinched at the sky. Kai and Leith followed just yards behind Michael, who was disturbed and in a hurry to get back to the security room. The inharmonious waters above were mute, even though one could easily imagine how the rough waves would have sounded, if audible.

"What is going on? Do you see this?" Leith asked Kai. Just then seeing the big oceanic exhibition for the first time, Leith gazed in awe at the sky.

"Shh," Kai instantly became animated as he shushed him, shaking his head. Kai feared that Michael could hear them. Kai had already noticed it, and he was trying extremely hard to ignore what he'd seen. He was mentally barring the sea-green aquatic display at every overwhelming glimpse of it, for the sake of his own social-behavioral interactions.

Leith knew better, and Kai's reaction simply reminded him. Not everyone could see what he was so mesmerized by, but it caught Leith way off guard, and he slipped. Mysterious things had happened to Leith before on a minuscule level, but he had never seen anything so undeniably otherworldly before that day.

None of them had ever seen such breathtaking effects in the sky above like the one over Opal Firs that day, and everyone who could see it trembled with good cause. Kai stopped, and he looked around as to finally let himself acknowledge the rose-gold glow that the unusual sunlight was beaming onto everything around him.

He'd stayed quiet about it because he sensed that Michael was not distinguishing the parallel realms. That day, Kai was not in the mood for explaining. They approached the same entrance that the office employees exited through when they had left out of the building less than an hour prior.

Kai turned to Leith and commanded him saying, "You have to wait out here, across the street. We will come back."

Leith gathered that he had no authorization to enter the building. He just sighed, massaging the back of his neck as he wondered what was happening. Several seconds later, he just let it go and said,

"All right, but I really need to know what's going on. You have to at least tell me if everything I'm witnessing is tied in together. Please," he begged Kai in a whisper. Kai nodded, with good intentions to compare notes with Leith later.

They both ignored whatever expression Michael had on his face, as he seemed to be interested in their conversation. Kai knew that Leith just needed clarification, if not some sort of confirmation. Leith nodded back and then jogged briskly across the street as Kai and Michael scanned themselves into the building.

As Kai and Michael walked, Kai was looking for the right moment to lose Cup so that he could contact the Cr8. Before they reached one of the main halls, Kai started to form his sudden excuse when he looked over to see Michael flashing a badge back at him.

Michael promptly tucked his badge away from any possible security camera angles. Kai stopped walking, and he contemplated whether or not he would have a problem with Michael.

"You're a cop?" Kai asked him in a whisper, shocked. Michael Cup was an undercover detective who was just as interested in Al Canna as any of the Cr8 members.

Detective Cup was intrigued, and at times, completely obsessed with the chain of missing children along the East Coast in 1998. He'd frequented the help of Mari Hera, who was the clever journalist in Seattle who had interviewed him a few times over the past ten years of his career. She led him to Washington State, and to the Cr8.

It was clear, that week was probably both the best and worst possible week for anyone to start a new job at the Center. Ironically, it was also likely to have been the last opportunity for Cup to meet Kai, TJ, Sammie, or Fowley before they would be gone. Besides, he would have never learned that Mari Hera was in trouble.

The Rhode Islander had been anxious to talk with one of them, and he gloated to Kai,

"I know who you are, and what you're doing. But, I also understand why," he assured him. "So, first off, you should know that we're on the same side of things, he asserted.

"But, you'll have to trust me," he advised right away, as he knew there was no time to waste in their matter. "In fact, I know who Mari Hera is," he added. Kai looked at him with intrigue as he inquired,

"You know Mari?" he asked him. Cup pulled the file photo of Mari out of his pocket. He showed it to Kai once again, saying,

"That woman is the reporter who has been helping me investigate your case. She has been looking for you just as hard as I have and truth is, she knows more about you than I do -I believe.

"Mari, or Pearl, or whatever she's answering to -she is worth your trust. Why she was a subject here? Beats me, he confessed.

"But I would like to make sure that we get to her before they do," he spoke with a cautious tone as he took the photo back from Kai. After he put the photo back into his pocket, he continued,

"But I must get back to the security office, and report to them that Pearl got away from us," he stated decisively. Cup paused to emphasize the importance of his statement, then he continued speaking,

"Also, that we had gotten separated until we bumped into each other outside, just a few minutes ago," he directed Kai. Cup spoke with hand quotations to highlight the story which they both would need to corroborate, if they wanted to distract the security team.

"I'll back you up on that. Wow," Kai responded with uncertainty, still dumbfounded to learn that Michael Cup was a detective. Michael halted his steps as he was walking away. He hesitated, pulling a small stack of folded papers from his inner jacket pocket.

He unfolded the stack, and the paper on the top was Kai's original birth certificate. He examined it once again before he turned around, and walked the stack over to Kai, saying,

"Sorry to be so quick with this part. These are your original birth certificates, for you and the others." Cup was focusing past Kai, avoiding any emotional eye contact, as he spoke. The people on the birth certificate are your real parents."

Cup gripped over Kai's hands tightly as Kai clenched the stack, and it underscored the importance of the papers in his hand. Kai was stunned, and he couldn't figure out why Cup would be lying to him.

Jumbled, Kai just shook his head. Trying to find words, he asked,

"Is this real? And Mari Hera? She was investigating us, too?" Kai just stared at Cup with skepticism, and speechlessness, as Cup continued unfolding,

"So, that is your real name. Just in case you've been feeling lost, or just wondering about things, you should know that it's not uncommon to feel like things are off, he advised.

"Very cute name," he concluded with a grin that bordered chuckling. Kai accepted that Cup was a little entertained by his birth name, but he was too obscure to care right then.

"What the hell?" Kai blurted out, after examining his birth certificate. "Who are you, really?" he snapped in disbelief. Cup, who had been expecting some skepticism, replied,

"A good friend who has been searching relentlessly for you and those other missing children for years. Kid, you were abducted twenty years ago," he divulged. Kai bit his bottom lip, surveying Michael Cup and the things he was claiming.

"Honestly, I'd always hoped that by the time I found any of you, you would have already established your own personal suspicion regarding your identity," Cup added, searching for verification in Kai's eyes.

Kai was stupefied as he briefly looked around, then asked the detective,

"You're serious?" He was a notch calmer than his initial reaction, and he spoke several decibels lower.

"As a heart attack," Cup replied, giving Kai one firm nod of the head.

"How do you expect someone to believe that shit? How could you be so sure?" he asked with a fifty-fifty mix of skepticism and optimism.

Detective Cup laughed lightly at Kai's raw response. He then replied,

"How could I not be sure? I will explain more to you later. I've only found the four of you so far, but this is a milestone for my agency, he genuinely stated.

"The rest will naturally unravel, I hope. But you call it whatever you'd like," he advised as he turned around to leave the conversation right there. But he then hesitated, and he turned back once more to say,

"And I will try to handle the security cams the best I can. It will make some trouble, but hopefully enough trouble to keep everyone distracted. So, you all stay clear of this area."

"Wow. Um, thanks?" Kai said to Cup, still experiencing bewilderment as he watched the detective walk away. "I can't believe it," he said to himself just under his breath, thinking Cup couldn't hear him.

Cup was still walking away when he turned around to make swift, but sincere, eye contact with Kai. He said to him in a calm manner,

"Believe it or not," and he continued to move forward in his own charming confidence.

Detective Cup walked away briskly, leaving Kai flabbergasted. Cup knew it wasn't a good time to tell Kai that he had been kidnapped twenty years ago, or that his name is not really Kai. However, he wasn't going to miss the chance to make the matter known.

By the time Detective Cup disappeared into another hallway, Kai had recognized the information bestowed on him as truth. Though he was still dumbfounded, Kai was rapturous to have confirmation of his sporadic hunches about Maquiller. He called the others immediately.

"Hey, are you here?" Sammie asked impatiently, answering before he'd even heard a ring.

"Yeah, I'm back, and you'll never guess what just happened," he replied, expecting her to probe for more details.

Sammie, who hadn't heard a word Kai said except, "Yeah, I'm back," lit up, relieved. She yelled into the phone,

"Good. Get the car and meet us outside at that side door you showed us earlier," she guided him as TJ, Fowley, and Ray Goddem stuffed Canna's dead body into a vinyl zipper bag sized for an adult human. The dead weight and bloody mess made for a hard time trying to wrap him up, and not leave a trail when they move him outside to the car.

"Hold it together. I have to get the vehicle first, remember?" Kai reminded Sammie.

"Dammit. Hurry up, we can't keep him here like this forever. Please be quick," she pleaded. Kai hadn't quite decided how he was going to get Canna's car from the parking spot and into his possession, but he suddenly had an idea, saying,

"Okay, I got it. Talk to you in a little bit," he said. He hung up on Sammie and chased Detective Cup down.

Kai came to the hall where the security control room was located. He lightened his steps to a soft creep to stay undetected by a couple of guards who were running away from the security room.

The guards were surely rushing to get somewhere. As they hurried away, Kai slid in closer. He waited until they were far enough away before he approached the door.

He moved toward the room and saw that the huge window was mirrored from the outside. He couldn't possibly know if Cup was in there alone, or if other guards occupied the room as well. He didn't want to bring unnecessary attention to Cup, but he needed to get his attention.

Kai got to the door and put his ear against it to see if he could hear someone inside. He heard the sound of someone rummaging around for a minute, then it stopped. It was likely that if someone was in there, they were alone.

He waited a minute longer to make sure there was no sudden dialogue. From the inside of the room, Detective Cup laughed in pity, as he watched Kai at the security control room door.

Kai was trying to be quiet, as well as invisible, and Cup was humored to see him eavesdropping on security. Cup leaned forward in his chair, examining what he was seeing.

Kai was becoming faint in his opacity, slowly on his way to becoming invisible. And when he saw it, Cup sighed in frustration with the security room monitors, unaware of Kai's superhuman bearing.

To Cup, the playback feature in the security system distorted the content on the screen. He just assumed it was one of those days that he had been forewarned of by another guard. He got up to go see what Kai wanted.

The camera that monitored the control room door was discreetly placed in the hallway. It was meant to be undetected, and Kai didn't consider that whoever was in the control room could see him eavesdropping at the door.

Kai struggled with his power set, as all of the Cr8 did. But if Kai Paw had improved any of his skills, invisibility was the one. He'd almost mastered it, and he had come a long way in exercising the skill.

Not always successful at obtaining pure invisibility, he did sometimes exhibit the ability to simply blend in plain sight. Though it was accidental, the ability to *blend* had proven to be a helpful power.

It was beneficial to their alliance that Cup didn't know of Kai's powers, so Cup's misunderstanding of Kai's appearance in the hall was luckily for the better.

He was listening at the door with one palm resting against it. He was jarred when Cup quickly swung it open. He looked Kai up and down, questioning why he was there.

Kai reversed the progress he'd made in becoming invisible as the door flew open. Michael hadn't noticed it at all, yet Kai was nervous to realize that Cup knew he was at the door.

Kai could never be too careful, as he'd learned that any individual could perceive a shift like that -if done right in front of them. He'd realized that he knew nothing about Cup, so he preferred to keep Cup out of the loop concerning those uncanny things.

Michael snatched Kai into the room, to keep him out of sight. He was annoyed as he exclaimed,

"What'd you follow me for? You trying to get me busted?" he asked him.

"No, of course not," Kai responded firmly. "Why would I do that when you're clearly here to help?" he added, hoping the detective would stay calm. "I need your help with the cameras," he explained to Cup.

"What do you mean? I was going to disable them all," Cup said. Kai was relieved to confirm Cup's plan, and he agreed with him saying,

"Yes, great. Please do, and as soon as you can? Especially the camera in the main entrance parking lot," he asked hoping to persuade him to act immediately. "So, have you found out what happened here today?" he inquired out of his own paranoia, and curiosity.

Cup wasn't willing to keep up the false charade, and confessed to Kai, "You already know what's happening here today, possibly better than anyone," he said. Kai froze up completely, realizing how much Detective Cup might have known.

"All right. I suppose I do," Kai said, shaking off the embarrassment as Cup shared yet another piece of information.

"Now, I don't know what TJ has done to the cameras in that secret hallway, but Miles Knott and Al Canna are the only people with access to that area besides him. If there was ever an emergency, Jerek Riddle as well. I'll trust he knows what he's doing," he said.

"You know TJ, too?" Kai asked in surprise, as TJ was hardly ever with him and the others.

"I've heard a lot of it at that little café you all like to go to," he replied. "Truth is, I know quite a bit about what you're doing right now."

"The café? You were at the café? When?" Kai asked, completely unaware of Cup's presence there.

"Today," Cup exclaimed. "And the rest of your conversations at the café have been extremely boring," he admitted with heart. Cup slightly pulled back his manners when he added, "No offense," and he spoke as he held his palm up toward Kai.

"So, exactly what do you believe we are trying to accomplish here today, Detective Cup?" Kai asked him straightforwardly.

"I know you all want to free those subjects down there. You want to free all five of them, and I hope you do. But I'm here to help free you, and your 'siblings' alike," he replied. "All four of you."

Kai looked over his shoulder to observe all of the security monitors, and he hung his head when he spotted the one that was filming the control room door, and possibly his transparency shift.

"That monitor has been messed up, I hear. And it was distorting while you were standing out there. Figures." Cup complained on, but Kai eased up considerably. He suddenly felt like he was back on his plan. He said to Cup,

"Thank you. I'd better go. See you later?" he asked for confirmation.

"Sure. Be careful with whatever you're about to do, son," the 55-year-old detective advised him. Kai dashed down the hall, as Cup shut the door. Once the door was shut, Cup turned around to view the malfunctioning monitor. There was nothing, and no one, in the hallway.

Cup noted to himself about Kai, "That kid sure runs fast." Cup let the thought go.

TJ called Kai, and they were connected after one ring. Kai answered saying,

"What's up?" he asked as he walked toward where they all were to meet.

"You have to move the car right now. We're running out of time," TJ warned.

"I know, did you get his keys?" he asked TJ.

"Yes, but there's no time, you have to move that car over here without them," he explained, with concern in his voice.

As it went, Pearl's escape preoccupied the Center's security team, much to the grandies' luck. But there was still an expiration to their window of opportunity. They needed to move much quicker than they were. The time Pearl had bought them was undoubtingly running thin.

Kai hadn't moved an object with his mind in a long time, and only once when he had finally done so. Fowley was much better suited to move a vehicle, telekinetically. But Fowley was tied up with moving Dr. Canna, so Kai had to pull it off instead.

"All right. Let me get over to the car," he accepted the challenge as he chewed his jaw in his stress.

"All right. Relax, man. You remember what Fowley taught you, right?" TJ asked for confirmation. Kai nodded his head for a few seconds before verbally affirming saying,

"Yeah, I think so," Kai replied as he swiftly pivoted, walking hastily toward the front entrance of the building, where the VIP parking lot was. With a dodge here and there, alongside his spotty invisibility, Kai was able to stay off of the other guards' radar as he exited the main lobby.

On many days, Dr. Canna would have parked in his reserved spot in the parking garage below the main lobby. But whenever he was running late, he would use the VIP parking lot near the main doors for faster building access.

Kai approached the lot and immediately spotted Canna's car. The glitzy sports sedan stood out like a sore thumb among the other cars.

Kai began to focus on moving the car out of the parking spot. But he couldn't quite get centered. The noise of the nearby passing traffic hindered him, and he couldn't quite gain the momentum he needed to use such a combination of powers.

So, he tried once again to become fully invisible, and to anchor it. His second attempt was successful. After comfortably sustaining invisibility, he was at least able to truly concentrate on moving Canna's car.

He sat down on a big rock on the side of the lot and began to pull himself into a meditative mind frame. It was one thing for him to maintain his invisibility, but it was difficult to prolong his telekinesis on top of that.

With his eyes closed, Kai concentrated hard on drowning out the sounds of all the traffic and people along the block.

Finally, the gift he once exercised came back to him. He remembered what Fowley told him the first time he had ever moved an object with his mind. Fowley, who was the first to achieve the skill, taught a sixteen-year-old Kai about harnessing the energy to make it happen.

After Kai had become extremely frustrated and discouraged, Fowley got that Kai's addiction to video games could prove helpful. So, one autumn evening, he told Kai that when it was hard to focus, to just pretend it was all like a video game.

"Just hold up your controller, and control," Fowley had coached him. With much effort, Kai was able to lift a pumpkin off of the ground and smash it against the side

of the house. Not just that, but that autumn had changed a lot of things for the grandies.

Kai sat on the rock, lifting his imaginary controller. He put the car, which was already parked into the spot backward, into drive. He slowly began to move it forward. Just as he was becoming celebratory, he noticed someone in the vehicle moving around frantically.

The scrubber inside of Canna's car had been ordered by Miles Knott to scrub the vehicle clean of any DNA samples that did not belong to the head physician. He had already gathered two different DNA samples that were not Al Canna's. He was still vacuuming the back seat when Kai scared the living daylights out of him.

The scrubber was just about to rid the incriminating evidence that he had gathered. His goal was to misdirect any investigation on Canna, if need be. He had done a marvelous job, and the car was extra clean.

He tried to open the door, but they had automatically locked when Kai changed the gear. Kai decided to let him suffer the scare. He pulled the sedan out onto the street, and he picked up the speed.

The guard's face stuck to the glass of the back-seat window. He screamed out of panic, as Kai took him for a spin. Jerkily steering the car in a sharp turn onto a side street, he caused the guard to fly to the other side of the back seat.

The guard's nose smashed into the window on the opposite side. Kai hoped that the security officer would be wise. He'd hoped that the guard would get out, and run away without drawing attention.

His hopes were accommodated, and the guard fell out of the rear passenger door onto the pavement, very dramatically. He was disoriented as he looked back into the car to figure out what was happening. The guard freaked out when he recognized that he was all alone, and he fled instantaneously.

The scrubber ran away in fear while nobody was looking, wishing to stay unseen. He whimpered to himself as he ran past Kai, whom he could not detect. And Kai could only hope that the man would wipe the blood from around his nose before reentering the facility.

Once the frightened scrubber guard was out of his sight, Kai ran toward the car. Trying to get to Canna's vehicle before other cars became stuck behind it, he ran as fast as he could. He jumped into the car and resumed control.

As he pulled up to the alley entrance, Sammie and Fowley appeared relieved. She had been worrying that Kai would struggle with the task, and she was glad to see that he made it to them. Kai jumped out of the sports car as Sammie opened the rear passenger door for the others. He immediately forewarned Fowley and TJ,

"You two have to remain completely covered from head to toe until you're done," he told them as they carried Al Canna to the open car door in the leak-proof body bag. He cautioned them to not leave any fingerprints, or any other giveaways, on the scene. Sammie then looked them up and down for any potential issues, as Kai put on gloves to help them position the research center's dead head doctor onto the seat.

Once they positioned the body in the car, they opened their backpacks and began to toss various informative papers and files around the rear of the car cab. Fowley zipped his backpack up, still hoarding a stack of papers. He directed TJ,

"That's good enough for now. Once we are close to being done with the setup, we'll throw the rest around the front seat." TJ contemplatively nodded in agreement, and he too zipped up his bag, reserving the rest of his documents, journal pages, files, and other various telling papers.

"Please do not leave anything in there that doesn't belong," Kai concluded as Fowley unexpectedly gasped.

He'd thought he heard Canna move just as he was about to close the rear door.

He couldn't associate the eerie scratching noise with anything else near him, so he imagined the worst. He quickly gathered himself and fanned off everyone's concerned reaction, saying,

"My bad. I'm just tripping. Let's just get this done, please." Fowley's paranoia was a part of who he was, and that moment wasn't very out of the ordinary to the others. They knew that Fowley was always startling himself, so they refocused their attention.

Sammie turned to Ray Goddem with the sack that was premade for him. She pressed it into his arms, telling him,

"Stay out of sight," and then she looked to the sky, pointing. Ray looked up at the clashing waves that had formed and intensified over that past hour or so. Even though the sight was scary, he had felt relief once outside.

Something about the threatening sky brought with it a great level of hope for an ending to all of the chaos. It was chaos that Ray had helplessly witnessed from inside the walls of the Center.

Ray was the least shocked of them all about the phenomenal sighting. Whatever was happening wasn't over, and Ray Goddem sought a definitive ending which he felt was vital.

To him, the ending needed to happen before he could ever find a peaceful new beginning. A part of him was prepared to give up and die, and the other part of him wanted to start over more than anything. He was silently hoping that the water up high was there to bring about either.

He grabbed his sack from Sammie and walked away telling them all, "Just in case there isn't a next time, thank you. Thank you, to all of you. And I- I'm terribly sorry," he stammered, as he shook his head.

He took one more deep breath, as if to prepare for a challenging undertaking. Without another word, Ray then ducked around the corner and out of their sight.

Kai waited for Ray to leave before he expounded about their birth certificates. Something about Ray's unknown history made Kai feel a need to be secretive about his important news, so he waited until Ray was out of sight to share the thing he had a hard time holding in for that moment.

"Here you go," Kai said to Fowley as he handed him his alleged birth certificate. Fowley was already sorting papers, and he had to free one of his hands before he grabbed it.

Fowley reached over his own shoulder to take the paper, squatting over his bag of files at the moment. Without a word, Kai handed Sammie and TJ their own birth certificates, too. Before anyone could say anything, Kai put his finger over his mouth and told all three of them,

"We have a lot of work to do. Do not mention this until the work is done. I will tell you this, I believe that those documents are what you think they are," he divulged with an emotionless face, glancing at each of them.

Sammie immediately formed her lips to say something, but Kai halted her, saying,

"No. We are not talking about it now, understand? Focus," he demanded in a loud voice, irritated. But Sammie made her argument,

"Then why the hell did you give this to me now?" she asked with good reasoning, as she stared down at her name. "Is this me? Just tell me, is it?" she inquired to him.

"Yes. But I only gave those to you all so that you will have them if I just so happen to, I don't know, die today?

That's all," he exclaimed sarcastically, and they all remained quiet. Fowley folded his certificate, and put it in his pocket as he stated,

"We have a lot of work cut out for us today. Let's take care of it," he proposed as he looked at Kai, appreciating his intentions. TJ, who had been silent ever since he had grabbed the paper from Kai, said to them,

"The paper in my pocket is all the more reason to get this done, right now," he spoke with a piercing decisiveness in his tone. He looked over to Fowley and said, "Let's get it together," as he swung the driver-side door open. He got in, not waiting for anyone to respond before starting the engine.

Fowley, checked the back seat of the car, making sure that they had everything that they were supposed to be taking with them. He stopped sorting his mental checklist long enough to tell Kai,

"If this doesn't end this guy, I don't know what will," he said as he eyed all of the documents that were already spread over his body bag. Fowley then finished his checklist, until he was confident that there wasn't anything missing. He then hopped in, and they drove away.

The plan to use Canna's car was the best choice for maximum exposure of the crooked doctor. The Cr8 had suspected that there could be a great deal of evidence inside that may prove to be helpful, and they already had it *in the bag*.

Sammie left her backpack with TJ, Fowley, and the corpse. She then set out to find Mari Hera's daughter Kim, hoping to keep her protected.

TJ and Fowley drove away with the body bag to set up the elaborate scene. Kai crept off on foot. Still fully invisible, Kai laughed at the late realization that the others didn't know he was imperceptible to anyone else.

The Cr8 could always see him. The worst-case scenario would have been for one of the Cr8 members to appear to be having a heated discussion with themselves, until a natural human pointed it out. That was one of Kai's signature pranks regarding his adopted siblings.

He crept all the way around the building in his invisible state, just in case something hindered Detective Cup in the control room. Kai was briskly walking away when he remembered the sky.

He'd been so caught up in the car hacking and the plan, he'd turned his eye from other important things. He hadn't even noticed how much closer the waves had come to them since the last time he'd looked. It was slowly, but surely, coming down to land.

Still mute, and abrasive, the waters had intensified a little more. Just like at any other glimpse of it, Kai got goosebumps.

He needed a moment to think. He walked slowly, and he was in his thoughts about everything that day had brought with it. He came across a small and simple rock, and he started to kick it ahead of himself as he walked.

He became consumed by his conversation with Detective Cup. Tears were burning his eyes, but he was sure to fight them. He didn't have time to think about his real parents, or Cup. But he just wanted to take a few deep breaths at the newfound knowledge of their possible existence.

He was afraid of getting into a mess at the Center, and never having the opportunity to learn his truth. He had every reason to make sure that he walked away from the Maquiller Research Center alive, but he was simply discouraged whenever he caught a glimpse of the sky.

A kid, who was walking nearby with her father, caught a glimpse of the small rock rolling on the pavement on its own, and she yelped. The little girl ran over to pick it up, and she showed it to her dad, fascinated by it. Kai finally stopped kicking the stone.

Kai knew he had to face the sky. He couldn't keep his head down, ignoring it all day. He knew that they simply needed to finish what they had started.

It was then that he felt even more helpless on what to do about the sky view. He felt even more pressed for time.

Abruptly, in the middle of considering the oceanic vision, he remembered Leith. Leith was still hanging out across the street from the building alone.

As he hastily started to navigate his way back around to that side of the building, he turned back and looked at one of the outside security cameras. It was pointing toward the sky, and he considered if Detective Cup was really able to interfere with the cameras. Kai definitely hoped so, and he also hoped that Fowley, Sammie, and TJ were going to be okay.

Fowley and TJ were thinking the same thing of Kai and Sammie at that same moment. They worked like that sometimes. Recounting their steps, they had acknowledged that nothing was really going the exact way they had planned it, and it created a certain level of concern amongst them.

In the midst of all the drama, TJ almost forgot to call Dough. Charles Dough was the man who had produced many identification cards and vital records for the subjects to whom new identities were assigned through the Hippo Project.

He had a sophisticated system that he used to hack the Department of Vehicle Registration, as well as a few other vital agencies. He had made a stack of alternate identifications for all of the grandies.

He also had his own personal reasons to detest Leroi Maquiller for the many monsters he had made throughout the times. Charles Dough was one himself, although he too was sadly unaware of his very own programmed existence.

Fatefully a loyal friend of the grandies, Charles had vowed his assistance to them wholeheartedly when the day came for them to make drastic changes to the corrupt operations. The time had arrived. His conversation with TJ was quick, and positive in its context.

"I have had your stuff prepared for a month now. Pick them up whenever you're ready," Charles confirmed, excited for the Cr8 to make a move.

"Okay, I'm not sure how soon we'll come, but we'll be there soon. Thanks, man," TJ replied, ending the call.

"That guy definitely has some superpowers," TJ joked after he hung up the phone, putting both hands back on the steering wheel. Fowley agreed,

"Yeah, man. Hell, I wouldn't wanna piss him off," he added. Their light laughs were limited, as they couldn't laugh past the task at hand. As they rode along, a strange noise whispered from the back seat, out of nowhere.

It sounded like Canna's corpse had moved, creating a quick rubbing sound of nails on the vinyl fabric. Fowley and TJ looked at each other, spooked. After spending several silently terrifying seconds waiting to hear the haunting noise again, TJ finally spoke,

"Okay. If he moves, you gotta keep him down," he said as he adjusted the rearview mirror so that he could see the body while he was driving. He accelerated back to the speed limit after realizing how distracted he must've looked, driving at 10 mph in the 40-mph zone.

"I'm sure of it," Fowley promised as he cautiously stared the body bag over, waiting for some unlikely surprise. TJ and Fowley were off to park Canna's corpse, and they had become even more hurried, and for more than one horrid reason.

*******End of Chapter*******

Chapter 10

Hurry Up and Wait

On the inside of the security room, Cup was leaning back in his chair, already looking at nothing but static on all screens. The guards who were supposed to be working the room had fallen for Cup's fake emergency that caused them to run out into the halls. They were armed for a subject who was "running around the wing with no pants on, and scaring the employees," as Cup had worded it.

He had watched through the bulletproof window of the security room as they scurried away down the hall. Being that one was playing on his cell phone while the other had fallen asleep reeking of weed, Cup didn't feel bad one bit. Once they had exited the security room to go search for that "bottomless madman," he simply locked them out.

Unknowingly, Michael helped give the Cr8 the elusiveness they needed when moving the dead body, and Canna's vehicle. Once the other guards were out of the control room, Cup was able to fully disable the cameras throughout the premises.

The guards of the Center had no incentive whatsoever to report any of it to the local authorities. Every guard knew that the protocol would not allow it in such situations, especially the incidents regarding a subject from the Hippo Project. Such things were handled discreetly from within.

He knew that TJ had taken care of the cameras in the hidden wing. The two deadbeat guards in the camera room told Cup that they had been trying to reach Miles Knott for at least an hour about the non-working cameras. The only thing visible on those screens for those cameras was whatever cloth TJ used to cover the lenses with.

Michael made a call on his phone, and a woman answered on the other end. He straightforwardly asked her,

"Did you pick up the bag?" The woman on the other end affirmed the completion,

"Yes. About two hours ago," she replied, waiting for his reaction.

"Did you get it to where it needed to go? Did you add the note regarding Mari Hera?" he asked her, biting his lip in some sense of suspense.

"Yes, approximately 45 minutes ago. And yes, I included your message, sir," she answered back. She then relayed a message from his real agency, The Missing Children's Organization, and she said to him,

"The agency is really proud of you, Michael. Really proud," she informed him, respectfully.

"Thank you. I will see you when I get back to Rhode Island," he spoke through a faint smile. The biggest part of his mission was over, and the rest would unfold in due time.

But a part of him wanted to stick around to make sure that the long-time-missing children truly grasped the nature of their situation. It was that same part of him that wanted justice for their families just as much as he wanted Maquiller's big collapse.

The grandies would have made their own job a lot harder if they had allowed themselves to be on camera doing anything that they hadn't staged for the camera themselves. In his uncanny fate, Michael Cup was another person in the right place, and time, to be a key collaborator with them. Very unaware of what was happening, or what it all meant, Cup still didn't doubt for a second that he was right about what *he* was doing there in Opal Firs that week.

****

Outside, Kai approached Leith, who was lost in his own considerations when Kai walked up. He felt bad for forgetting that Leith was waiting on them. In truth, he had spaced out with too many things on his mind at that point, especially Fowley and TJ.

He couldn't ease up for one second until he knew they were done with their task. Kai leaned up against the building next to Leith, who was smoking a cigarette as he stared at the sky.

"Crazy, isn't it?" Kai asked him. Leith jumped and he frantically searched around, trying to find the man who had just spoken to him.

"What in the hell? Who said that?" he demanded with his back turned to Kai's presence. Once again, Kai remembered that he was invisible. He immediately brought himself back to be seen when he responded,

"I'm sorry bout that. It's just me." Leith spun to face him. He staggered backward out of both amazement, and fear. He fell onto his backside when he tripped himself up in his stumble. He had no words when he saw Kai leaning up against the building.

Leith's heart was pounding, and his mind was racing as he questioned what he had gotten himself into that day.

"How'd you do that? Honestly, what was that?" Leith shouted in his suspense.

Kai remained calm, and the intrigue he felt caused a slight grin on his face. He was surprised at Leith's inexperience. He directed him,

"Look up," he told him, pointing to the waves. "That is something you can see, but not hear. Why be so scared about hearing something you can't see?" he asked out of his own logic.

"Not exactly the same thing to me," he defensively replied, still taken off guard.

"So, what's your deal? How are you able to see signs? Especially that one." Kai's curiosity was raised around the loner he befriended that day.

"I've been seeing signs for as long as I can remember," Leith said. He shrugged at the thought before he continued, saying,

"One day, something happened. And I forgot everything and everyone I ever knew. I've been seeing odd things ever since," he explained. "But I have never witnessed something so blatant before. Today has been way beyond the norm," he appeared to be pensive as he spoke to Kai, reflecting.

"What? Were you a subject at the Center? And what do you mean? What happened to you?" Kai gently pressed the topic.

"From what I know, I had suddenly begun to experience severe memory loss. A woman had found me that way, unable to remember my own name. She got worried, I guess, Leith recalled.

"She took me to the Center near Providence to seek help for me," he continued speaking with feeble confidence. "They say I was in an accident," he added. Leith detected Kai's countering demeanor, and he asked him,

"You think differently?" He searched Kai's face with his desperate eyes, hoping for another opinion on the matter.

"I don't know what I'm thinking. Maybe you're superhuman," Kai theorized aimlessly. "Who even knows anymore?" he asked in his sad countenance, hanging his head to the ground with his baffling newfound perspectives.

"No," Leith replied quickly, and sharply. "Special? Maybe a little. But superhuman? I am not that," he stated with the certainty of someone who had diligently tried to exercise superhuman skills, and failed.

It was the first time Kai had ever met a non-superhuman being who could see the same signs the Cr8 did. But since Leith could see such an intricate display clearly made for a unique sample of individuals, Kai would ruminate about it over and over until he found out Leith's real story.

Kai suspected that Leith was indeed a subject at the Center. Leith's name sounded familiar to Kai when he had first introduced himself, but he wasn't sure where he was remembering the name from. Nonetheless, Leith's description sounded very similar to Pearl's current state, and Kai took note of it.

Either way, Kai figured that if Leith was indeed programmed, then they all should be very afraid. He also considered Pearl, and how little she knew about her own situation. He realized how close she was to closing their story, before Canna got to her. Kai's mood darkened with the ugly truth.

Kai knew that if the grandies are missing children from 1998, then the Cr8 had been living a lie for twenty years, unknowingly. But the only way they would be unaware is if they were programmed to be. He was becoming heated.

He pulled back the harsh theory of being an *installed* individual in the very same experimental project that employed him, and his adopted siblings. He pulled back for the sake of his sanity and he moved the conversation to focus on something else, the skyward scenery.

While he was with Leith across the street from the Center, they spoke freely about the development above them. Leith still had his eyes tending to the sky, and he behaved a little too feverishly to blend in.

Kai gave up on trying to keep him unbothered about that, or any other thing Leith had seen that day. He knew that the nervous man wanted to know more, but first Kai wanted to feel out how much Leith already understood.

"Did you see the clouds yesterday?" Kai asked him out of curiosity.

"I did. You guys saw that?" he replied.

"I saw them. The shapes were so perfect," Kai recalled, and Leith agreed. They both looked up at the waters above them, and Kai asked another question, "What do you think this is?" he asked him, not taking his own eyes off of the sky.

"I don't know," Leith admitted. It was the only thing he could say with confidence.

"I'm in awe, but not really surprised?" Leith spoke as if he'd thought he would be more emotional to see something so vast. He didn't doubt that universal judgment was coming to someone very soon, although he didn't know who, or why.

While he himself had no solid information, he also perceived that the sky signs were clearly trying to get a message to him as well. That gut feeling was undeniable, and Kai was feeling the same way.

"Whatever is going on, it is not going to happen until everyone who's supposed to be here gets here. She's one of us too, I sense," Kai stated toward the sky though he was speaking to Leith.

Leith took his eyes off of the waves to search Kai's face to see if he was referring to Pearl. Then he replied,

"I don't doubt it at all, man. I know she's definitely superhuman." He almost laughed, nodding his head. "I saw her throw a car off of a child just this afternoon. Just flung it away from the kid like it weighed a feather's worth! I can't do that," he explained, using an excited tone to color Pearl's effortlessness. Kai was surprised,

"Is that what you were trying to talk to her about?" he asked. Leith nodded. Then Leith asked him,

"Why were you chasing after her?" Kai shook his head, unable to give him a detailed answer. Instead, he just used his index finger to direct Leith's attention back to the sky-bound water.

"What we are looking at, I believe, is the making of the perfect recipe for universal recompensing. But it seems to just keep developing as if it won't complete until everyone who needs to be here arrives," he theorized to Leith.

Leith was the only person to whom Kai spoke those words that day. He knew what Kai meant, but was compelled to ask,

"How do you know?" Kai gave him a goofy grin, and said,

"I don't know where it comes from, but I believe I'm right," he answered firmly.

Kai continued to speak with his eyes still fixated on the overwhelming waves that were undetected by any common man. "This has a lot to do with it, and I do know that whatever is brewing up there cannot manifest down here, without Pearl."

"That's her name?" Leith asked him.

"Yes, and no," Kai replied bluntly, making Leith settle for the unsatisfying indirect answer. He rolled his eyes and sighed, having neither the energy nor the mental capacity to tell the long story.

He kept talking, "I just don't believe that this will complete until we are all here, and that's just my hunch," he added.

With his back still against the building, Leith rolled his shoulders to stretch his muscles. Kai was still theorizing, and he proclaimed,

"And even you. There are no accidents concerning these things from what I've heard," Kai summed up the scenario the best he could. "This is new to all of us. But I'm pretty sure it all comes down to just showing up, and paying attention," he explained.

"And don't ask me how I drew that conclusion either," he added, shaking his head as he laughed. Kai knew how cocky he must've sounded, but it didn't make him feel any less correct.

"So, there's still something missing? Well, what do we do?" Leith sighed at the irony with so much intrigue toward the matter.

He stood up straight from the brick building he had been leaning his back on. Kai joined him in the moment's morbidity as he spoke with as much discontent as Leith did,

"Yeah, something is definitely happening, and it's been a thorn in my side, you know?" he spoke exhaustedly.

"Yep, I definitely do," Leith agreed, stretching his uncomfortable neck. Kai looked up one more time and spoke aloud to declare his inevitable acceptance of the uncontrollable,

"I guess we just have to wait for it."

****

It was 7:11 p.m. on Wednesday when Kim Hera came home. She was worried about her mother, whom she hadn't seen or talked to since very early that morning. After sitting at her friend's house for as long as she could, she dashed to get home.

She quickly slid her key into the door and unlocked it. She opened the door and poked her head into the foyer, shouting, "Hello? Mama?" She had just seen her mother's black coupe in the driveway and was sure that she was in the house.

"Mama?" she called out, expecting Mari to come running out from one room or another to tell her all about the crazy day she had. But there was no one there, and Kim began to worry again.

She continued into the living room and walked over to the corner where her mother's home workstation was set up. She looked over the desk to see if there was anything that stood out. She was studying the many multi-colored sticky memos that were stuck on the desk and computer monitor.

The memos included the names of doctors, public officials, neuroscientists, university professors and staff members of the Maquiller Research Center, research-study subjects, the Missing Children's Hotline, and a Detective -Michael O. Cup. Kim knew she would have to give her mother a chance to call or text her back before she could report her missing. But she would call every number on that desk if she had to.

Kim had run out of options concerning who to call, besides the many sources on the sticky notes. Neither her Aunt Kelly nor her cousin Nessa had heard from Mari at all that day.

Mari and her sister only touched base about once a month, so their lack of insight wasn't completely surprising to Kim. So, she tried to reach her mother, again.

After an extended series of rings, the call eventually forwarded to Mari's voice mailbox. Kim had given up leaving her messages hours before that, plus the "mailbox was full and could not accept messages," according to the greeting.

Kim then began to feel a presence in the house with her. Not sure if she had actually heard something in one of the bedrooms, she wanted to be ready to protect herself.

She opened the drawer that was built into the entertainment center, and she armed herself with the stun gun that her mother had bought her for her thirteenth birthday. Then, Kim started to creep quietly down the hallway.

She first opened her mother's bedroom door. She pushed on it, yet she stepped back, alarmed at the possibility of someone jumping out at her. The door swung open, and she barely poked her head in to look around. When she saw no one in there, she then turned around to open the door to her own room.

Kim walked into her room, seeing that was empty. She walked over to her open closet door and eyed the clothes she had hanging up. She examined the outfit that she had already put together for the next day.

She took down a purple, newly creased blouse -if only for a quality control check on her ironing job. She hung the long-sleeved blouse back up over her closet door where she had also hung her starched white slacks.

Being already near her window, she reached out and made a peek hole with the blinds just to see if anyone was out there. It appeared quiet outside with no one to be seen, just her mother's car.

She turned around to go back out to the hallway, and she was frightened out of her wits. Sammie, who was suddenly approaching her from the bathroom at the end of the hall, had caught Kim way off guard.

Sammie held both of her hands up toward Kim, trying not to come off as a threat. She spoke as softly as possible to the girl she'd recognized from the photos in Mari Hera's phone, saying to her,

"Relax. My name is Samantha Pyre, and I work at the Maquiller Research Center. I am not going to hurt you," Sammie tried to tell her. But the fourteen-year-old daughter of a shrewd journalist who had gained a few enemies over time was too quick with the draw. She stunned the grandie with more than a million volts, and Sammie didn't even see it coming.

She zapped Sammie with the stun gun for about five seconds, then pulled it back. But Sammie immediately recovered, and startled Kim even more than the first time. Kim's facial expression was blank for a few seconds before she lost it.

She belted out the most distinctive high-pitch scream, and the sound quickly became more harmful to Sammie's ears than the stun gun voltage was to her torso. Sammie, who couldn't bear the chaotic noise, softly put her hand on Kim's throat and it muted her scream.

Kim gave up. She stopped screaming, but she backed away from Sammie in terror. They both were equally shocked that Sammie was able to mute the sound. Even Sammie herself had never done that before then.

She had an epiphany about her. Kim's scream was just as scary as her own, in her opinion. She was almost completely distracted by it, and she barely retained her focus in the weird instance of silence. Still, she reiterated.

"I am not here to hurt you. So, please stop. This is about your mother," she unveiled as fast as she could cram the words in before Kim freaked out again.

"My mother?" Kim tried to ask her with suspicion. But her voice was still silenced. Sammie touched her throat once again, and Kim's voice came back. Kim yelled,

"Where is she? And who are you?" she immediately continued, still quivering. Kim needed convincing, and Sammie needed to try harder.

"She is in trouble, but she will be okay," Sammie tried to explain it as gently as possible. "But I'm here because *you* might be in danger. I cannot tell you all the details because I don't know all of the details," she continued.

"Where is she?" Kim screamed. Sammie huffed, and replied sharply,

"I don't know yet, but if I don't get you out of here the people who are after her will be coming after you. I understand that you are indeed scared and confused, but you are definitely going to need us. We need you, too." Sammie tried to help her understand as best as she could.

"I don't believe this. I don't believe you," she shouted as she clenched her unhelpful stun gun. "I'm calling my mom," she shouted as she grabbed her cell from her back pocket and dialed her mother's number.

When the phone began to ring in her receiver, it also started to vibrate in Sammie's pocket.

"I have her phone, Kim. I swear to you, you're just wasting time. All I can tell you is that your mother has gone through an ordeal today. And, I wish you would have just stayed over at your friend's house as directed, Sammie admitted.

"Truth is, I just wanted to get you and your mother reunited. That is the big task at hand, Kim," Sammie pleaded. Almost in tears of compassion, Sammie waited quietly for her response. She couldn't pretend that Kim wasn't wedged between a rock and a hard place.

Mari Hera was very close to bringing out a big story, and she talked to Kim about it very often. On many days, too often, in her opinion. But Kim's level of interest in her mom's work increased that day, vastly.

This was the first time that her mother had ever missed their dinner-and-a-movie date. Kim didn't have much but her intuition to go on, and she chose to listen to Sammie because she knew that Sammie could have easily harmed her -but didn't.

"Let's get you out of here. And I promise we will find her," Sammie pledged to Kim as Kim grabbed her jacket, preparing for a cool night outside. They hopped into Mari's car, which Sammie planned on ditching as soon as they got close enough to meet up with everyone else again.

After Sammie started the engine, she looked over at Kim, and she made a face that exposed the fact that she still had to share yet another part of the issue. She batted her lashes and bit her bottom lip while she looked for an easy way to tell Kim,

"One more thing, your mother might not recognize you when she sees you," she said, realizing that there was no good way to tell her.

"What? Wait, what are you saying?" Kim probed.

"The information on your mother's desk is a good start. But, in a nutshell, your mother's memory was erased, and now she might believe that she's someone else," she divulged. Sammie shook her head, knowing how crazy she was sounding. But she continued anyway, saying,

"And I suggest you never utter the name Mari Hera, aloud in the street. At least, not right now," she warned her. Kim paused for a tick, carefully studying Sammie. Kim knew that she needed to get a better understanding of the issue, so she asked her,

"Did those people at that research center do something to my mother?" Kim probed a second time. Sammie hesitated, then she replied,

"Yes. But there's more. The procedure wasn't successful as intended, and now your mom may very well be something different," she revealed. Kim was still unclear,

"What do you mean by, 'something different,' is she human?" she sighed with a slight giggle when she heard herself utter the question.

Sammie put the car in reverse and started to back out as she responded, "Oh yeah. She's human, all right," and her manner changed to match the heavier portion of her reply.

"In fact, she's probably superhuman. Heroic even, possibly." Sammie checked the mirrors for any followers, then drove forward. She continued, "And it's probably you who will be able to help her remember, if anyone can." She glared in her rear-view mirror studying the gray sedan that was parked on the street.

Two houses down, Miles Knott and another officer sat in their car. They had seen Sammie driving away from the Center in Mari Hera's coupe, and they followed her all the way to Mari Hera's house. The two off-duty officers who were sent to find Kim went out casing the most popular hangouts frequented by local teens when they didn't find her at home.

Miles and his partner, Rob, were just about to enter the home when Sammie came near the big, street-facing front window. Her swift and unexpected movement had caused Rob to trip over a gardening tool in the yard.

He'd fallen onto his backside, and he struggled to remain inconspicuous. It was the jarring noise that had brought her attention to the front yard.

She didn't see them, but Miles refused to take the risks involved with challenging a superhuman grandie head on. Or the risk of being exposed while sneaking up on one, all the same. After the unsuccessful attempt to enter the house, the two frustrated pursuers waited in the car for another opportunity.

They saw Kim when her ride dropped her off, but Miles couldn't confront her then. She was with her friends, and he didn't want to make them witnesses to the matter at hand. The two men concluded that if they could just get close enough to Sammie to administer the hypoactive serum, they could collect Mari's daughter.

So, they just planned on encompassing the girls, then closing in on them. Miles knew that the sooner they did so, the better. But it was detrimental to him and his partner that Sammie couldn't see them coming.

If she did, then getting close wouldn't be an option. Staying alive would be just as improbable, and getting Kim into their custody, impossible. Miles had to be sneaky, and smart.

He started the car, and proceeded to follow Sammie. He soon began to communicate with the other guards in town, formulating the perfect opportunity. He wasn't going to leave any room for error with the dramatic plan he was crafting.

Sammie shook her head and stopped talking for a weird minute, while Kim's thoughts overcame her as she digested the news. Then, glancing again at the gray car that stayed behind them, Sammie resumed speaking calmly,

"I'm sorry to have to tell you such madness, but it's true," she said. She lifted her hand toward the ignition. "Please don't let me forget to give you this key when we're done," she requested, pointing to Mari's single spare key that was in use. She'd found Mari's spare car key in a magnetic key box that was stuck to the bottom of the coupe.

"And you see that?" Sammie asked her, pointing at the key again. "That's why I don't do the whole hide-a-spare thing. You should never put your key on your car, unless you want someone to steal it," she tried to school Kim. Conversely, Kim responded,

"Why not keep an emergency spare on the car? It's not like everyone's out there stealing cars. That's just you," she countered. "Besides, what if you ever locked yourself out?"

The kid's right, Sammie thought to herself. Part of her admired the girl's outlook, yet part of her already wanted to mute the sassy teen, again. Either way, she was going to need Kim's cooperation in order to help. She said to her,

"If I locked myself out of my car, I'd use one of those third-party guys who shows up wherever you're at and breaks into your car for you. I'm clearly not alone on this carjacking thing," Sammie replied, with a wink. She then nonchalantly pulled her focus back to the gray sedan that was undoubtedly following behind them.

****

TJ and Fowley were at the deserted beach strip, burying Canna in his work. They were busy with their setup scheme.

They confirmed that the property was deserted like Goose Gary said it would be. TJ Vewitt scoped the entire property to ensure that no one was anywhere remotely close to the parking lot.

There was an old shack that was all boarded up about fifty yards from where they parked Canna's car. It was once a diner, many years ago. Other than the empty boarded-up diner and the small strip of beach near the woods, the two grandies were alone.

As they removed the body from the leak-proof bag they had used to seal the mess in, blood spilled out of the rear door and onto the ground beneath the car. With an edgy demeanor, TJ griped at Fowley, whose end of the bag was leaking.

"Leak in the car, not on the ground," TJ shouted in frustration. Fowley looked down, and he straight 8away stopped the dripping. He was annoyed, paranoid, and obviously inexperienced with moving dead bodies. He exclaimed,

"This is stupid. This was a stupid idea. What the hell was I thinking?" he asked. For the second time that day, TJ had quickly grown sick of hearing the depressing negativity that one can only conjure when panicking. He replied,

"It's way too late now, killer. Don't lose your head over it. This is just the first half of the game," TJ advised. TJ was only interested in getting out of there, and he couldn't leave room for any more slips, or anxiety.

He was mumbling to himself about how far he was going to run after the Cr8 mission was complete, until he caught a glance at the displaced waves that were developing in the sky. TJ was astounded. His tone had completely changed when he said,

"Bro," he spoke with faint volume. He cleared his throat as he watched the waves crash, and fear was shaking his very core. He called for Fowley's attention again. "Fowley," he shouted, much louder than before.

"What," Fowley snapped as he backed himself out of Canna's rear door. "I thought you said you wanted to hurry up and," Fowley stopped his fit, as he was silenced by the waves. They were both inarticulate for a minute.

After the shock had passed, they looked at each other, and said, "Let's get the hell outta here." They threw the remaining documents all about the inside of the cab, then locked up the car. They walked away slowly, studying the suspended sea-like waves in the oceanic-green sky.

There were no words to describe what they were feeling. Naturally, they had both become rushed once again, to go stay near the others.

They lowered their heads to avoid the blatant water works above them, and they slowed their steps to a complete stop. They began to wonder why they didn't have a car to get back.

"We forgot to plan a way back," TJ said, devastated. Fowley was already spewing obscenities over their inconveniencing blunder. He then calmed down, and realized,

"If we get busted, it'll serve us right. How could I forget?" he stated, trying to not be so angry. "Hey, hop onto my back, we'll just fly?" he offered, being childish. TJ shook his head, saying,

"That, I'd like to see," he kidded as they picked up the pace of their inevitable walk back to the Center. While they walked, TJ was trying to cure an itch in his right ear.

Fowley stopped to check with him asking, "What's wrong?" TJ was scoping their surroundings again. He looked back in the distance at the car to see if he could detect anything off. There was nothing.

"I'm cool, but my ear is itching," he replied. "That usually means that something's off somewhere around me," he explained. Fowley heeded his grandie brother, and decided,

"C'mon let's book," he suggested as he searched his awkwardly quiet surroundings.

"And don't look up right now," TJ advised, still rubbing his ear against his shoulder to cure the menacing itch. Fowley nodded.

Even though neither of them saw anything out of place, they both felt that something about the beachfront parking lot was not quite right. Just to be safe, they advanced to sprinting anyway.

****

Kai, Leith, TJ, and Fowley stood outside of the Center, near the intersection that cornered the building. They were standing in a hidden alley nook, in front of the rear door of a small Thai restaurant. All of their heads turned, as Nomad Artman walked up.

They had never seen him before, to their knowledge. But there was somehow an at-home familiarity among them when they saw Nomad approaching.

They just stared, waiting to see who the unknown man was coming for. Just like them, Nomad was experiencing a sense of knowing of the four men. It was just like it had been when Kai first bumped into Leith, there was a yielding vibe about them all.

"Goose told me, this is where I needed to be. Am I right?" Nomad spoke with a hopeful grin. "He said he's gonna meet us here later?" Nomad spoke to them, hoping that someone would know what he was talking about. Kai stepped forward, and replied,

"You're Nomad, right? He told us you were coming," he said as he extended his hand to shake with him. Nomad shook everyone's hand. When he shook hands with Leith, their faces expressed acquaintance toward each other. They tried to figure out if they'd seen each other before.

When he shook hands with Fowley, he got zapped. Nomad jolted away from the grandie when he felt the unexpected surge. Fowley was embarrassed and startled.

"Sorry," Fowley hollered, frustrated. He looked over at Kai, who was holding his jaw tight, and he exclaimed to him, "Don't even say it." Kai musingly closed his eyes and dissipated his thought.

"It's okay, I'm all right. Right?" Nomad replied. Kai and Fowley laughed lightly, and assured him, "You're good. It's just a static thing," Fowley said, while Kai nodded in agreement.

Nomad was pensive. He was bearing so many weird questions he had wished to ask them in person. His precariousness started to influence his overall mood, but he tried to be diplomatic and find out who's who.

"Do you happen to know what's going on?" he asked them. He lifted his eyes up and allowed himself to be amazed at the reversed gravity that kept the erratic sea-fueled phenomenon pinned. He did it to make the others comfortable with discussing it, and to find out if they could perceive it.

When the others saw that he was in the same position as they were, they did loosen up some. At least, they knew they wanted to learn more about him. He looked at Kai with a grin that one could only form when meeting someone whose presence succeeded their reputation.

"So, you're the one who wrote Goose all those letters when you were younger?" he asked Kai with wholehearted interest.

"Yep. I'm Kai Paw," he replied with a warmish tone. "I've heard of you, too. You've known Goose for several years now, huh?" he inquired.

Nomad nodded in response. They had both heard things about each other, but weren't sure if they were supposed to. So, their head nods and sighs extended back and forth for an awkward amount of time while they searched for something general to talk about.

It felt as though the world was the smallest it had ever been to any of them. But it felt right to Nomad to meet them, and it also made sense to him that his venture to the Center was seemingly predestined.

"You run that bookstore, don't you?" Leith said, finally recognizing Nomad.

"Yeah. And you're the guitarist. You play across the street from me sometimes, right?" The two had never exchanged a word before, but they had seen each other dozens of times.

"What's your name? You said Leith, correct?" he added for confirmation.

"Leith Nomea," he answered, nodding at Nomad. He then continued with his questions,

"So, what's your connection to the Research Center? What's your deal?" he asked him. Leith was astonished at the sudden dialogue between him and Nomad, and he couldn't hold back his questions.

For as long as he had been around, he hadn't had that much conversation with anyone in a while, let alone extraordinary humans. "Are you programmed?" he asked Nomad outright, hoping to catch his initial, or honest, reaction.

"I don't know. I hope not. But, I would like to know what's going on," Nomad responded. "Crazy day, is it not?" he added, conversationally. Leith replied with a nod back at him. Fowley and Kai began to compare their notes with Nomad's chronicle regarding the suspended water.

As they began to carry on, Leith was becoming contemplative. He was trying to figure out why he had such things in common with the others. He felt as though he should be there, but he kept wondering why.

Something is happening to us. Something is happening to me, he thought. Leith was indeed a false gem, and he just didn't know.

He did know that there was something to be learned *that* day, considering his crazy day. Leith was humbled, and he felt auspicious to be surrounded by people who understood even a fraction of his disaster. They had become quiet, so TJ broke the ice again when he asked,

"What are we gonna do now?" he spoke as he looked around the block outside of the Center. "We need to get away from here," he exclaimed.

"We cannot go far from here. We are expecting the others. Sammie, Pearl, or even Goose Gary might show up," Kai reminded them.

Fowley looked at TJ, then the two of them looked at Kai with curiosity. Kai became annoyed by their awkward stares.

"What?" he finally shouted, raising his arms.

"Make us invisible," Fowley demanded.

"Exactly," TJ confirmed the request. He looked at Fowley and nodded affirmatively.

"We have never done that before. We've never even tried it," Kai objected. But Nomad sided with TJ and Fowley, and he told Kai,

"That doesn't matter. Not right now. Instead of thinking about it, shouldn't we just try?" Nomad asked. "Just about everything that has happened so far today, has been unprecedented in some major way. Am I wrong?" he asked them all. They shook their heads, considering the truth he said.

"Okay, let's try it. Quick," Kai responded, motioning for them to follow him. They stepped away from the street, and farther into the small alley behind the brick building. When there were no other people in sight, the men all interlocked their arms, standing in a circle.

While they stood there, interlocked on the side of the building, Kai made himself invisible. Once he achieved it, he furthered his focus to bring the others, and the others meditated on becoming imperceptible with him.

After the moment had passed, they all seemed to be invisible, although they could still see each other. There was no way for them to know how long they would stay unseen, but it was by far the smartest defense they could muster while they waited for everyone. They walked back out to the sidewalk.

Fowley soon noticed that Leith was still visible. A woman had walked by them, and she noticed Leith. She smiled, and she offered a casual hello as she walked past him.

She sees me, Leith thought to himself. Leith waited until she had completely passed before he turned to their general direction, saying,

"I can't see any of you," he exclaimed, and they were all stunned. Fowley spoke,

"That woman saw him," he expounded to Kai, TJ, and Nomad. They had missed the very quick exchange between the friendly lady and Leith, but Fowley brought it to their attention. "He's not invisible, why?" he asked the other three.

Leith was confused, and he stayed quiet as he was expecting to hear their theories about why Kai's invisibility didn't stem out to him. They all shrugged their shoulders, completely unaware of how those things were supposed to work.

"It's okay, stay close to us. And don't give us away. I say we should wait in our other office down the street, he proposed.

"That's where Sammie would go, and we would be safe there if we begin to reappear," Kai advised Leith, who agreed to stay close -and quiet. He replied to Kai,

"Why am I not surprised about this? It's okay. Just stop talking to me, and I'll stop talking to you. Then, I won't have to look like a lunatic on the way there, he suggested.

"The guards around here shouldn't know who I am, anyway. I have never been at this location before," he explained. Kai warned him,

"Well, still be careful. Several of the employees here were once employed at the HQ branch outside of Providence, he informed him.

"If they can't see us, we're safe," Kai reminded them. All was well, so long as they could make the guards at large pass them by on the street. For the time being, staying unseen was the best way to do just that.

*******End of Chapter*******

ODD GEMS Soaked by Suri R. Moon

Chapter 11

Stuck

Many of the buildings in the town of Opal Firs had been made with large stones that helped comprise their foundations. The prevalent evergreen trees in that town created a great contrast with those buildings in some of the pricier parts of town.

Sammie was driving on a semi-busy highway when she checked to see if the men in the gray sedan were still following behind them. Still calm, nonchalant even, she looked over at Kim in the passenger seat and asked,

"Kim, you know those people who I said were probably coming after you?" she positioned her question for the bad news to follow. Kim looked over her shoulder and saw the men in the car behind them. Still looking, she spoke,

"Yeah, why?" she said, anticipating a troubling update. But Sammie prevented her from staring at them, saying,

"Don't. Do not look with your head. Just your mirror," she instructed Kim. "They're in the car behind us. Do not scream again, please," Sammie pleaded, cramming her request into one really fast sentence.

Behind them, Miles was on his phone with one of his officers who were in a white SUV heading east as Sammie and Kim headed north. "We're heading north on Old Seaway Road, approaching Topaz Street right now. The girl is in the black coupe. Close it in, and cut them off. We'll snatch the girl and slow down Maquiller's kid," he commanded.

Sammie and Kim were approaching Topaz Street as Sammie noticed that Miles had hung up his phone. The light in the short distance turned yellow. Flaking, Sammie was paying too much attention to the guards behind her, and too little attention to the light at the intersection ahead of them.

Kim was nervous in the passenger seat and she had slid down about 6 inches, bracing herself for the worst. Sammie approached the intersection, but she was studying her mirrors. Kim finally looked up to see the traffic light at the intersection ahead of them, and the yellow light turned red in that very second.

Red light, she acknowledged the red light in her stuck brain. Sammie was going way too fast. Kim figured they were going to crash into something, or that something was going to crash into them.

Her heart froze up, and she struggled to speak. When she regained control, she belted out,

"Red light." Then, there it was again. That high-pitch scream that Sammie couldn't bear. In her chaos-driven decision to dodge an oncoming car, Kim removed her seat belt.

She frantically jumped over onto Sammie's lap, to avoid being crushed on impact. As they drove through the red light at Topaz, a random driver heading east sped through his green light and t-boned Mari Hera's car.

The blue four-door sedan slammed into Kim's side of the black midsize coupe. It bulldozed their vehicle until Sammie's door was rammed into the back of a van that was parked near the next intersection over. The coupe was crushed on both sides, and they were pinned in between the blue sedan and the van.

Looking at the smoking engine, and the limited amount of space she and Kim had, Sammie slowly began to move. She immediately positioned herself to see if Kim was hurt.

Her heart was pounding, and she was waiting to hear Kim's annoying vivaciousness. But she didn't hear a thing.

She had to shake off the glass from the shattered windows so that she could sit up to see Kim better. When she looked over at her, Kim was lying still in her shock. She made herself a little more upright, and examined herself for injuries.

Miles pulled over immediately when he saw the crash. The guards who were heading eastward in the white SUV met them at the scene. They were traveling just two cars behind the blue sedan.

Kim was amazed, speechless. She couldn't believe that she wasn't hurt. They were still mashed together, she spoke very calmly to Sammie,

"You told me not to scream, right?" Her eyes looked as if she was holding back the urge to ring an ear, or two. The driver of the dark-blue sedan that t-boned them jumped out and ran away from the accident scene.

He looked scared, like he was running for his life. He didn't say a word to anyone, he just ran. Unclear about why the man was abandoning the crash scene, Miles and his men paid it very little mind as they approached Mari's coupe on foot.

Sammie then looked over to see the guards gathering around them. She didn't feel as bothered as she normally would've been. She said to Kim, slightly irritated, "Kim, I can't believe you removed your seat belt."

"What'd you want me to do? It worked out, didn't it? Look at my door," the fourteen-year-old girl sassed as she stared with adrenaline at the blue car that was smashed into the passenger side. Sammie was looking out of the windows, thinking about how she was going to get Kim to safety.

In broad daylight, the guards were willing to take Kim and Sammie, even if a few people were to see them. It was at Sammie's disadvantage, as she wasn't going to expose her superhuman characteristics to the public. She was stuck.

When Kim saw that the guards were approaching, she panicked. She belted out that brutalizing high-pitch scream as she used her jacket to clear away glass. She then tried to escape through the windshield opening.

Miles and the others pulled their weapons on Kim upon her exiting the car. Two of them grabbed her, and they shoved her into the back seat of the gray sedan that Miles drove.

As Sammie crawled out of the windshield frame, she began to speak to Miles, "You don't want her, she will be no help to you," she tried to explain, sliding off the bent hood of the car with both hands up.

"You're right, she'd be useless to me. But, to Al Canna? She's leverage. You know that we just need Pearl," he replied. Kim wondered who Pearl was as she tried to hear them from inside of the gray sedan.

Sammie still had her arms raised when she looked over at Kim in the back seat. The two guards were still standing close to the sedan to monitor the girl. She made eye contact with Sammie, then she noticed that the engine was still running.

Sammie nodded upward vaguely hoping that Kim would have the chance to take off somehow, and she gave her a head start. She then began to distract Miles by telling him,

"Al Canna is null," she clued them in on the facts of the day.

"What did you say?" he asked her coming in a little closer to her, and suddenly acknowledging the small group of onlookers. All of the men with him, stepped a little closer to Sammie, stunned by what they had just heard.

Sammie took a bold step closer toward him to tell him, "Al Canna has no need for anything or anyone, anymore," she replied with a very eerie voice and slow pronunciations. Then, leaning in one more time, she whispered to him, "Canna's dead. And, if you touch me, so are you."

It was then that Miles was reminded that Sammie was a grandie under Leroi Maquiller, although she appeared to be one of Canna's employees for business purposes agreed on between Canna and Maquiller. Given the amount of autonomy Canna had granted Miles, it was way too easy for Miles to forget his place in a grandie's life.

The other three guards stepped in closer near the two, ready to attack Sammie on Miles's command. One of them said to Sammie,

"Take it easy. It's not even you we're after, Sammie," he tried to reason. "Why are you protecting this woman you don't even know?" he asked for clarity.

"I do not have to explain myself to you. Not to any of you," Sammie said, and she drew the line clearly. The three guards became more resentful toward Sammie, who was making a scene.

When in doubt, Maquiller's rules mattered more, and Miles was fully aware of it. Sirens were becoming louder, as the local police and an ambulance, had been called. "I'm taking her with me to the Center, as instructed. We'll see you there I guess," Miles explained to Sammie with a resentful smirk.

Trying to leave the scene before the police arrived, Miles told the guards to fall back. They lowered their guns, ready to retract. But when they turned around to leave, they wheezed to see that Kim had driven off in Miles's car.

Sammie watched the backs of their heads. She was holding in her laughter, as they became outright irritated. Miles and the three men out there with him stared at each other, dumbfounded that no one had heard the low-purring engine accelerate away.

"She took off, what the hell? We were just carjacked by a fourteen-year-old girl," one guard stated the obvious as they all shook their heads, staggered.

They then turned back around to face Sammie. But she was gone, too. She had vanished just as quietly as Kim did. Left on the scene with heavy explaining to be done, Miles and his three henchmen retreated to the white SUV and deserted the intersection of Old Seaway Road and Topaz Street.

Startled, the four men got into the SUV, speeding off with squealing tires to get back to the facility. Miles Knott was determined to confirm Sammie's words concerning Dr. Canna, and to find out what happened to his long-time friend.

****

After sneaking away from the accident scene, Kim ditched the gray sedan. She walked toward the Center until she reached a small, corner coffee bar at an intersection. She went in, and she ordered tea to help buy herself somewhere to sit for a little while.

She'd already navigated herself to get closer to the Maquiller Research Center, using a phone app. She was hoping that she would hear from Sammie, and soon. She pulled out her phone so that she could map walking directions to the Center, knowing that she and Sammie were heading somewhere close by.

There were no words for the confusion that she had been feeling that day. Sammie had informed her that her mother was in danger, and also that her memory had been erased. Kim knew it was because of everything her mother had been researching.

The woman behind the counter was a little too attentive to Kim, making her feel out of place. *What is she looking at me like that for?* Kim thought to herself. With raised eyebrows, the waitress asked her,

"What are you doing around here this evening?" she asked. Being low key, Kim made up a story about waiting for a ride. But the nosy waitress didn't seem convinced. She tested Kim, asking,

"Would you like me to call someone?" she rolled her eyes as she spoke. Kim lifted up her cell phone, and replied,

"No, thanks. Got my own," she spoke with a smirk.

Thirty minutes into the visit, and Kim was paying no mind to the meddlesome waitress. She peered out of the window and sipped from her cup again.

She looked up at the sky, and she admired the shade of blue. She looked at the clock on the wall, and she saw that it was about ten minutes until the late sunset. She continued gazing as the people who were still out walked up and down the street.

She had been hoping for sunshine after the heavy rain that morning. The sun did come out, and its faint golden glow had almost completely disappeared at 8:22 that night. Kim was disappointed that she couldn't enjoy it with her mother.

She looked up at the cars that were stopped at the traffic light. She moved the upper half of her body around, bobbing her head to see a particular car that was idle at a red light.

"Jackpot. It's them," she whispered to herself, as she set the cup down on the table. It was Miles Knott and his men. Kim figured that they were heading to the Center, so she jumped up from her table, accidentally spilling her tea all over it.

Apologetically, she looked up at the waitress behind the counter. The waitress was still looking at her, with an expression of disdain. When she saw the tea spill, she shook her head at Kim with disregard.

Being the teen that she was, Kim pulled a one-dollar bill from her pocket and tossed it into the puddle of bubble tea that was formed from her spilled cup. Without a word, or another look, Kim walked out.

She had to run to keep up with them. The light had just turned green and they were picking up their speed. Kim found herself getting lucky that the guards were catching every red light, repeatedly giving her the chance to catch up. After following as close as she could for about twenty minutes, she found herself at the Maquiller Research Center.

She retreated away from the guards, but she began to search for Sammie. She'd hoped that she could find her somewhere outside of the place. All of a sudden, Kim remembered that Sammie had her mother's cell.

Mad at herself for not being able to think past her anxiety earlier, she shook her head as she yelled out at herself, "Shit, Kim." She dialed her mother's number right away. She started to walk around the big building that occupied one entire block, hoping to bump into Sammie.

It went straight to voicemail, then she began to worry about Sammie, too. Meanwhile, Sammie was outside of the Center hoping to find Kim. Mari Hera's cell phone was dead, and she hadn't given Kim her number.

The plan to keep Kim safe was seemingly falling apart. She tried to turn the phone on, hoping that she might have enough battery for one phone call. The phone turned on, and it displayed "1%" remaining battery life.

She quickly dialed out to Kim. She paced impatiently waiting for Kim to answer.

"Hello, Sammie?" Kim answered. Sammie cut her off, instructing her,

"Be outside of entrance number "3." It's the east entrance. I will come and get you, and please don't draw any attention," Sammie crammed her instructions into the call before the battery died again.

Considering proximity, Kim began to search the double doors of the closest entrance. She found the entrance number, "1" above the doorway. She moved away and followed the building around, eventually passing doorway "2" as well.

As she was approaching the third entrance, Sammie was hiding in a nook on the side of the building outside. She stepped out from the nook and walked with Kim, upping the pace.

Kim said nothing and just kept walking. Sammie was looking up, obviously fearful of something that Kim couldn't detect. Kim wasn't sure what to say, but she felt concerned for Sammie.

Kim wondered if she was okay, as she searched for a threat that might have made Sammie so hasty. "Quick, just keep walking. We're almost there," she said sternly to Kim, still glancing upward frequently.

A block later, they came to a short stairway that went down to a place underneath a pho restaurant. When they entered, the rest of them were there. TJ, Kai, Fowley, Leith, and Nomad all looked up when Kim entered with Sammie.

Kim just looked at the group of strangers with suspicion. It appeared as though they were having some kind of meeting. The probability that it was about her mother seemed high, and Kim was single-minded to hear all of what they knew.

"Who are all of you?" Kim asked straightforwardly. Kai let out a deep breath,

"Hello, Kim. That is a very long story. Maybe we should start with your mother?" he replied, presuming the girl was Kim. He shifted the topic, as Pearl's safety was still in jeopardy and he didn't want to waste time.

"Yeah. Where is she?" Kim snapped back.

"We honestly don't know. But what I do know is that your mother won't make it far before she ends up back here, at the Research Center," he promised her. Kai knew that the developing manifestation impended her mother's presence.

"What was your mother doing this morning? Do you know where she was going when she left the house?" Leith interjected, just as she started to respond to Kai.

"Who are you?" she asked him with a sharp tone, to acknowledge his rudeness. Leith apologized,

"I'm so sorry," he said as he shook his head in embarrassment. "Leith Nomea," he answered with a faint hand wave. Kim's eyes opened wider.

She recognized his name from one of the sticky notes on Mari's work desk at home. Leith also jumped a little at her intense reaction to his name.

"I don't know what she knows about you, but she's known of you. My mother might have been researching you?" she said to Leith. He almost rolled his eyes, as he was taken off guard for a second when he heard the words, "researching you" for the millionth time in his life.

He wasn't very surprised. Over the years, many journalists mistakenly thought they had a helpful idea for an article, but they always ended up even less knowledgeable than when they had first started their research. For what it was worth, he nodded and replied,

"Yeah well, I'm not surprised. I've had quite the ordeal," he said to them all. "And, very much like your mother, I had forgotten everything important to me," he shared that much.

It was enough to silence a room full of people who still had their memories. Or at least some form of their memories. Leith knew that his story was a mystery for anyone who had followed it. Kai resumed his attention on Kim, elaborating.

"Your mother is somewhere out there," Kai told Kim. "I just hope you understand why we wanted you to be here for her when she gets back," he added, hoping she would understand her value in their process.

"We will not let anything happen to you. Just please stay with us, and do not separate yourself. Only then can I personally promise to protect you," Sammie pledged.

Nomad was standing near the window obsessing with the sky, and Kim couldn't just wonder anymore, "Why is everybody staring at the sky?" she demanded to know. "There's clearly nothing up there," she exclaimed as she began to grow uncomfortable by their abnormal behavior.

"Honey, if you can't see it, we can't tell you," Fowley told her. "It's really that simple. And secondly, it's nothing that you have to worry about," he said to give her some perspective.

Kim took an empty seat, talking to him with curiosity, "At school, I once heard some kid try to convince a group of us that his uncle from the East Coast has superpowers. I heard him say that his uncle was always watching the sky," she explained to them.

She briefly looked at Nomad, intrigued. She had never seen him before, but she somehow felt like he might be the one with answers to her questions.

"Is it real?" she asked, turning back to Fowley. He responded,

"Like Sammie said, we won't let anything happen to you," and his smile gave Kim a kind of confirmation. She then became extremely quiet, as if trying to digest what she'd just been told. Fowley reiterated, "And meanwhile, we just patiently wait."

Nomad gulped nervously as he commanded the others, "You might want to come see this." They all went to the window and crammed in to see. The sun had developed very intricate facial features.

Just like the moon at times, the sun's own pleasantly surprised facial expression was highly visible in its altered, rose-gold state. What was normally foolish to stare at became enticing, and temporarily harmless, to behold. Kim was scared for both herself, and them.

All four of the grandies in the group instantly thought about how they had frequently looked at the face of the moon when they were younger. They had even called it "the moon man" when referencing the earthly lunar light.

They were astonished to be able to look directly into the rose-gold sun, without the sunspots. It was the first time they saw its face, and it was clearly smiling wide. With that, and the petrifying waters that threw violent waves in every which direction around the smiling sun, they all registered the confirmation that the unworldly event was imminent.

"What are we going to do to find Pearl," Nomad asked the group.

"Wait. Who is Pearl?" Kim finally had the chance to ask. They all just looked at each other, then they looked at Sammie, who should have explained it already. So, Sammie owned it and spoke up,

"Pearl is your mother," she illuminated to Kim. "Or, that's what she believes her name is because that's what she was told. "Just brace yourself. Your mother is not the same person she was when you last saw her, okay?" she instructed Kim.

Kim didn't nod in agreement, or shake her head in discontent. She became ponderous, still trying to find an understanding of what she was supposed to expect.

"We will have to keep the news on in case we can get some help locating her that way," Nomad said. Kai added,

"We will also have to keep taking turns watching these local blocks for when she returns."

"Someone needs to get Detective Cup out of the Center before she is back," TJ reminded Kai. "And someone needs to stay here with Kim." Kim suddenly pinpointed the detective's name, "Cup."

His name was also on one of the many sticky memos on her mom's desk. She was surely becoming exhausted just from thinking and worrying. It wasn't just Kim Hera, every last one of them knew that night was going to be a long one.

"TJ looked up out of his deep thoughts, and asked them, "What about Goose and Ray?"

Kai was quick to answer. He didn't want to share more than he needed to about Goose and Ray.

"They will be here in time, even if they are just in the background unseen. They will most likely be present somewhere on the premises," he clarified to everyone.

"We just need to watch the water, and we should know when the time has come," Kai gathered. "And, I will go get Michael Cup, at some point." TJ nodded at him, saying,

"And I will go with him," he volunteered, knowing he had a better handle on the Center's floor plan. Kai nodded back. The tentative plan to stick together, and stay unseen, was the wisest they could come up with, in their state of affairs that night.

****

~ (June 21, 2018 9:09 a.m.) ~

Pearl was still in the vacant office building. She was deeply saddened by what she had learned from reading Ruby's journal, as well as Devan's letter of resignation. She read their words over and over, just to make sure she had a true understanding.

Ruby S. was indeed a center employee, but she was also the teen-aged runaway who helped lure a four-year-old girl named Lilli into the hands of the Project H.E.A.D. snatchers in 1998.

True, Ruby was not a snatcher, but she definitely was a key accomplice when it came to Lilli. She had been a greatly challenged foster child herself when Leroi Maquiller took her in, and changed her life.

But over time, when she had been around long enough to see the long-term consequences for her actions, she had learned that her position under Maquiller was no different than the poor little girl she had tricked. She talked Lilli into following her to go peek at a "secret garden," as Ruby had described it to her. Lilli was steered into an alternate life that a child so young could never ask for.

Ruby herself had willingly undergone the invasive programming process, at Maquiller's influential request.

Eventually, she had turned into someone completely different. She had found herself dealing out Maquiller's remedies to his rivals, in various ways. Sometimes, a "rival" was just an individual who flat out knew enough to damage him.

She could never forget the images of those victims whom she had slain under the program's coding. Sadly, the crimes, the gore, and the guilt existed only in Ruby's mind, and not Maquiller's.

That was the danger of it. Maquiller regularly used the people around him to take on his burdens, and the darkness that accompanied them, in his stead.

In 2017, when Ruby's programming began to haunt her on a much more severe level, all she could think about that day were the disturbing images she had made when she slew her victims.

Those haunting images had finally broken her. She had started keeping a journal as an attempt to cope with the horrible flashbacks she was having daily for years. In March, she had reached the decision to leave the Center one way, or another.

For one of the journal entries in late March, she had signed her name as Ruby S. at the bottom, after she wrote,

"I don't know what to say anymore. It's been nine months, and keeping this journal is not helping. In fact, it's like I'm just making a book of horrific reminders for myself. No one will ever understand how sorry I really am for my part in this nightmare. I despise Leroi Maquiller. And he obviously despises me- and always has.

The main thing that I really need to do, and want to do, is to go to Sammie and explain things to her. But, I sometimes wonder if it will help her, or just worsen matters.

She has to know that I had no idea of the recruiter's intentions. I was told that if I helped them, I myself would finally have a place to call home for always, and they promised that Lilli would return home safely to her family before too long.

I probably would have never had the gall to confess what I've done, but when I'd heard her crying in the restroom stall at work last week, I knew I had to. She was wearing those cute brown Mary-Jane-style pumps she wore often, and she had tried to cover up her crying when I walked in.

I wouldn't have noticed who it was in the stall crying their eyes out, but I noticed her shoes. I'd also recognized her voice, even though she was weeping instead of talking. The cry that I heard when I had first walked in was just like the type of wailing I did after I'd killed my first victim, under the programming.

It was, and still is, the most conflicting set of emotions. It is also a very dark state to be in all alone. My heart was broken for her, and every other child that was fostered by Leroi Maquiller.

I know that sometime soon, I will tell her what she needs to know. I just have to be prepared for it to turn everything upside down. Hell, a part of me hopes it does..."

-Ruby S."

Reading Ruby's journal entries triggered Pearl's own flashback. She suddenly saw a vision of the black metal headgear that the medical staff had removed from her head after she had awakened from the procedure the morning before.

They peeled off four circular quarter-inch plates; two that clung onto the temples of her forehead, and two similar pieces that dug into her hairline on the back of her neck. Also, a half-inch plate that was flipped down to press against the top of the forehead was flipped upward during the gear removal.

She remembered scaring the medical staff when she'd awakened much sooner than expected. Some of the gear and devices hadn't been put away yet, though the subject was never supposed to see those items.

The two staff members who were with her at the time quickly put the equipment away, and they had agreed to not tell anyone that she'd seen it. They were just as worried about their lives as they were about their jobs.

Her memory became very vivid, and she trembled. She remembered the eeriness she'd felt when they removed the gear.

She then remembered her first migraine, and the intense seizure that came shortly after. She began to wonder if Ruby S. went through the same initial side effects.

She recollected the two staffers who had removed the equipment finally leaving the room, and only seconds before Kai had come in. He was there to begin her post-procedural examinations. He'd entered the room slightly smiling, offering her breakfast.

His presence was calming to Pearl. As if it had mattered, she was glad to have had a moment in which she was comfortable enough to digest her new, and unexpected, surroundings.

The pages throughout Ruby's diary were about to be key in exposing the Hippo Project, Project H.E.A.D., Al Canna, and Maquiller. Just the documents that Pearl held in her trembling hands by themselves could socially implode the Center. Pearl held Ruby's diary close to her heart, and she cried hard tears.

She sensed that it had taken much bravery for Ruby to even get those thoughts onto paper. She had chosen a few specific pages that shared pertinent information to help lead authorities to evidence supporting the accusations written throughout the journal. She chose several more entries that shed light on Ruby's bitter relationship with Maquiller.

She was careful to only circle the pages that would lead to hard evidence such as files, photos, videos, payment receipts, etc. The only thing that Ruby's enlightening writings didn't lead authorities to, was her own dead body.

Luckily, Pearl had a general sense of where to find four of them. She started to pack up as she jumped to her feet. Before she put away Devan's letter, she read through it once more, to make sure she wasn't missing anything.

****

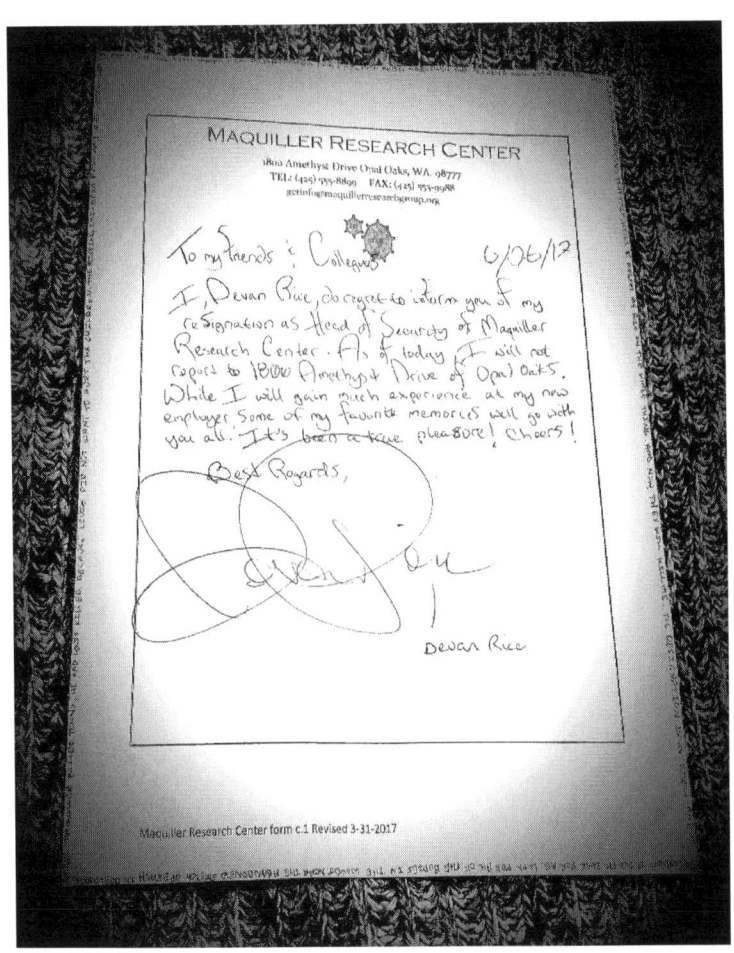

The letter was basic, and there wasn't any obvious information to help expose the matter, the first time she had read it. But upon her final inspection of the letter, Pearl saw the tiny writing that went all the way around the edges of the paper.

Around the edges of the stationery, a cry for help was written in diminutive penmanship. She was astounded that she hadn't seen it before then, but there it was.

"*Maquiller had Louis killed because he didn't want to hurt the children...the missing children... now they will kill me...Search in the woods near the abandoned stretch of beach in Opal Firs...I regret my role in the whole thing.*"

The message was choppy, and the handwriting was so small that Pearl was going to need a magnifier if she wanted to read the rest. But she knew that the letter was viable evidence, nonetheless.

She held the page closely to her face, still studying the message. The letter would be a big help when taken into consideration along with the former Center employee's decapitated body. It was up to Pearl to make sure that the letter she had was evidence paired with the corpse she'd seen.

Pearl packed everything away and lifted the leather backpack to mount it onto her back. She was getting ready to take the documents to someone who would be able to help her.

Just as she was starting to leave, six guards came rushing into the office building where she had been hiding out. She looked them over, and her heart started beating heavily when the thought of them possessing Ruby's journal and Devan's letter occurred to her.

In the group of guards, there were five males and one female. They were all well poised for an attack, and Pearl was scared.

The thought of them taking her back to the facility consumed her. What little she had was too much to lose.

"Don't move. We do not want to hurt you, but it is not good for you to be out here alone, Pearl," one guard tried to negotiate.

She panicked, and she instantly felt sick from it. Although the guard closest to her told her to stay put, she ran. Just like she had been all day.

She ran into the next room, and they followed right behind her. The door to that room had no lock. So, she ran through that room and into another. It appeared to be a perfect room for storing a company's computer server, or other goods and supplies.

As it had been left, there were painting supplies, basic tools, and big white buckets of eggshell-colored premium paint. Alongside those items were basic tools, and it looked as if efforts had been abandoned mid project.

Pearl realized that the room had no windows, nor a second exit. She stood just inside the doorway. But when the guards were just a few feet behind her, she slammed the door shut and locked it.

Within seconds, she found the light switch and flipped it on. The guards on the other side of the door repeatedly beat on it. She could hear the mischievous laughter from a couple of them.

She definitely had an episode bubbling up, and she was unable to reverse it. One of the guards finally shot through the door lock, while she was on the other side of the room. She was shuddering with acute anxiety and a menacing migraine.

For a few seconds, her irises became a radiant purple, before they returned to dark brown again.

Her back was against the wall, and the slow steps of the guards became highly frustrating to her, as it only built up an awful tension between her and them. The guard who seemed to be the one in charge said,

"You really shouldn't have made us chase you all around Opal Firs," He was deeply disappointed, exhausted, and very rude. "And for what? Just to end up right here," he bellowed at her as he clenched the cramp in his side and shook his head.

But then Pearl saw something lighting up behind them. It was a fuchsia-lighting butterfly like the ones she had seen in the woods, and buzzing around Joy's head at the Center. One guard, James Lidd, stayed in the background behind the other guards, frightened.

"Did you not see her eyes?" he exclaimed, after witnessing her hyperactive gleam. The other guards stared at him and each other, trying to figure out what James meant.

In their own minds, the other five guards were plotting on how to give Pearl a dose of hypoactive serum. They did not want to kill her, they wanted to collect the bigger bounty.

Pearl Lerell was worth five times the bounty amount if brought back alive. They completely disregarded their timid partner's hesitation. "What are you talking about James?" the guard in charge asked, as he moved closer to Pearl. "I didn't see anything," he added.

The other four guards stood between them shaking their heads because they too had missed the queue. James, taking heed of what he saw, took slow steps toward the door as the others moved in to retrieve Subject Sixteen.

While she had no expectation that the butterfly would do anything directly significant, she smiled a big smile. She wasn't sure how, but she knew it all was going to work out. Just then, it was all that she needed.

The guards doubted whatever she was so smiley about because they saw nothing when they turned around to look. They assumed that she was either "disoriented," as her file in the Center had stated, or she was just trying to stall them. Pearl prepared herself for a fight, and she was willing to defend herself.

Unexpectedly, just as the leading guard came charging toward her, the lights went out. Pearl stepped off to the side, dodging the guard who then stumbled to the floor in the pitch black.

At first, Pearl didn't mentally register that the butterfly was helping, so she was afraid of the abrupt darkness. But in two ways, the insect did assist her.

She noticed that her once worsening migraine had almost fully subsided by itself already. She had also remembered every little detail, and every object, within the room.

She had a huge advantage in the dark. The violent brawl that the guards initiated was unbearable to the ears, and it seemed as if they were utilizing every square foot of that room.

Pearl was devastated, but not about the fight. She was taken aback by the sound of it. There were moments when she knew it wasn't going to be pretty when the lights turned back on.

Even in the pitch-black dark, the sound of a limb being ripped away from a human was horrifying. Even more so knowing that the limb was detached by her own bare hands.

Only fifteen seconds had passed before the tussle was quieted and the lights came back on. Pearl looked for it, but her butterfly buddy was nowhere to be seen. Covered in blood and afraid of what she had done to them, she straight away started to walk out of the room.

But when she got to the door, she didn't have any peace in not knowing what she was capable of. She really needed to know what she had done. Pearl slowly turned around with dread, and she instantly gagged at the gruesomeness. She was briefly in shock, and it took a lot out of her to fight the nausea.

Looking back, she didn't even think it had sounded as horrific as it looked to her in the aftermath. She had smashed the front guard's head into the floor with a big white bucket full of eggshell paint, and his neck was almost completely severed.

The amount of blood was overwhelming, and it had splattered all over the room. The red blood and eggshell paint were swirled together in some places, creating bizarre designs in the spill. They were all too grotesque to look at.

She closed her eyes and looked away, regretting her sick and foolish need to see the scene for herself. She refrained from examining any more of the five guards. It was time to run.

A noise startled her, then she noticed that James was still alive. He was standing away from her in a corner, and the shriek he couldn't hold in alarmed her. He was shaken up badly, but it didn't stop him and Pearl from making eye contact.

The other guards' blood had splattered onto James, and his clothing. But for some reason, even the devastatingly gory scene couldn't take his attention off of Pearl. He knew she was scared about what she'd done, and it was plain to see that she was shaking in fear, too.

When she saw him, she cried. She didn't want to harm anyone, but she did. She hadn't even wished to fight them, and James knew it.

That *knowing* was a thing that someone either possessed completely or not at all. They had just taken in the same knowledge; despite which team they were playing for. Both James and Pearl learned just then that those who possess the knowing have it to use for their own better judgment or safety, as James did.

Pearl had no motive to attack James, and he really didn't have a reason to blame her. She was glad that he somehow knew to stay away. She knew that she couldn't have resisted defending herself.

She wondered over his knowing, in fact. "Please, forgive me," she cried to him. She took a step toward him, and his back hit the wall behind him, hard.

When he jumped back from her, the butterfly that turned the light out quickly flew from behind him. It had been hiding behind James, and it clearly didn't want to get crushed. Pearl marveled to see it again.

James was so nervous, and he didn't know what she was going to do. Pearl was distraught and overwhelmed, but she had no intention of harming him. She saw that he was still afraid, and she didn't want to worry him any more than she was worrying herself.

The new truth was that she was going to regret looking at the slain guards, forever. Comprehending that James was no longer interested in trying to capture her, she just wanted to leave. She stared at him and the glowing butterfly, not concerned with the possible outcome.

Pearl hung her head low as she backed away from him, then she left the room. She used her hands to block her peripheral view for fear of being reminded of the monster she was, and she left out of there with tunnel vision.

She was careful to not pay attention to the other guards, who were undoubtedly in no better condition than the first three. Just when Pearl Lerell thought matters couldn't possibly get any worse, there she was as mentally unstable as she could possibly feel.

The super strength she'd exhibited when she opened the skull of one guard with a metal paint roller, she could not yet understand –or control. She still couldn't believe that the simple-looking paint roller had been drilled at least a few inches deep into his head when the lights came back on.

She caught a vague glimpse at a single, bloody leg near the back corner of the room, but she didn't want to think about that either. She was so scared of herself. Her strength was brutal and merciless.

I'm a freak, she thought through her short breaths. She would never forget what she had just done, or the extent to which it was measured. The term *self-defense* meant absolutely nothing to her, at that moment.

She just wanted to run away from the whole nightmare at once, but Pearl was afraid that she herself was becoming the monster in the nightmare. When she stepped foot outside, she looked up at the clashing waters and shuddered. The rain had stopped, she was hoping it hadn't.

The outrageous sea-green exhibition of waves had lowered noticeably, and it made her think about all of the things that had occurred in such a short time frame. She was no longer the same person she was thirty minutes before, or the person she was forty-eight hours before that, whoever that was.

Pearl made three stops. She went into a thrift store where she could change clothes, after throwing away the bloodstained hoodie. She spent $10.80 on an ugly brown sweater and a pair of black leggings that were both on clearance.

The clothes were hideous, but it was way less conspicuous than being covered in paint mixed with blood. Luckily, she then found a store with a print station that offered fifteen free pages, and she made copies of Ruby's most useful journal pages, and Devan's letter.

She also paid a quick visit to KGEM, the local news outlet that seemed to be on the biggest billboards in Opal Firs, Washington. As she approached, she saw a young man with blonde hair entering the building. She got his attention when she asked him,

"Hi, are you familiar with the Hippo Project, by chance?" she asked him in an attempt to feel him out, and to break the ice.

"No, not remarkably familiar. Why do you ask that?" he inquired, curiously.

"Are you familiar with the neuroscientist, Leroi Maquiller? Or, a psychiatrist named Al Canna?" she tried again.

"Oh, you're talking about the guy who was catching heat because he'd allegedly programmed his subjects to commit crimes?" he recalled a common story, amazed at how ridiculous it sounded when he said it. "Yeah, I've heard of him. Around here, you can only go so long without hearing a bogus Maquiller story," he explained to her.

"Anyway, it was all a hoax. Those people are trying to do good for trauma victims at those Research Centers. Are you researching it, or something?" the stocky young man attempted to probe once more.

Pearl had to try hard to stay unruffled at the young man's ignorance. She knew he wasn't the one she needed to give the evidence to, but she did mentally record his conversation.

As she struggled to answer him, another man was about to walk into the building. He was a well-dressed gentleman, and he was being tailed by yet another glistening butterfly.

She sighed in relief as she spoke under her breath, "That's the one." She looked at the inquisitive young man with a slight grin. "Excuse me, thank you for your time," she said to him, before stepping away to catch the older gentleman at the door.

When she got to the door, she learned that she could not enter with him. Without an ID badge, she needed to quickly make her intentions known. She tapped the back of his shoulder and greeted the gentleman.

"Excuse me, mister?" she met him with a softer voice. His fearless smile was genuine, and he appeared to be in his early fifties. She didn't pay much attention to the details of his appearance; he was her guy.

Wasting no time, she handed him the copies in a manila folder. "I'm supposed to give you this," she declared to him, and she immediately began to walk away. But as she got a short way down that block, the stylishly dressed middle-aged man called out to her,

"Is this what I think it is?" he shouted his inquiry with a certain confidence about it. He opened the folder and whispered as he handled the contents, "Oh my goodness, where did she find this? He searched the sidewalk for her and when he spotted her, he shouted,

"Wait. Where are you going?" But Pearl continued to walk in a hurry. He looked down at the pages that confirmed one of his many suspicions about the Center, regarding Devan Rice.

"Call me later?" he yelled behind her as she got herself away from the KGEM building. She began to wonder why the stranger was behaving as if he knew her.

He was both ecstatic and pensive when he shouted, "Thank you, Mari," he called out one last time. He shook his head at the bizarre encounter with the undercover journalist who had interviewed him regarding his missing brother.

That letter, and the hand-drawn map she'd made for him, was everything to that man. The information he had just been given would lead him to his brother Devan's body. Intuitively, Vergo Rice already knew that his brother was dead, and he had been concealing the painful revelation for quite some time.

But the rest of the family had been needing closure. They needed it so that they could have an appropriate farewell for their deceased loved one. He exhaled, knowing that it was finally time to say goodbye to his little brother, and hopefully bring justice to his situation.

He wasn't sure why she walked away so quickly, but he was content with what she had highlighted on both the resignation letter and the handmade map that could steer a search party to Devan. He was glad, but he was saddened. Regardless, Vergo knew just what to do and exactly where to start.

Pearl turned around to make sure that he was really talking to her and not one of the other pedestrians passing by them. He was already gone, so she kept walking.

She kept her head down as she hiked, trying to ignore the compelling formation in the sky. In fact, the intensity had tripled since the day before, and it was also closer than it was initially. To Pearl, it felt like a weird dream that she couldn't awaken from.

She became so confused that she began to sprint to get anywhere but the KGEM building. She thought to herself when she slowed down to a walk a short time later, *is my name really Mari?* She wondered over it, trying to register what had happened back there with the man whom she couldn't identify.

She was still trying to keep a mental record of the marine sky, the purple sand, and the corpses in the woods. There was also the slain one in the car, the man at the gas station, the *sleeping* boy who was struck by the white car, the motionless phenomenon at the accident scene, and the butterfly swarm.

By then, the five gruesomely massacred guards in the vacant office building were just as high on the list, and all in just a day. Pearl was well over overwhelmed.

Then, there was James Lidd, the witness. She knew he wasn't going to report that incident outright. The world at large was not ready to hear the tale involving those guards, without mass panic.

When she thought of the five of them, she still couldn't fathom how she could have been so vicious. She wondered what James Lidd did after she had left the bloodbath.

Pearl acknowledged that her ability to quickly soak in information, both audibly and visually, allowed her to utilize every potential weapon in the pitch-black dark. But her physical ability was destructive, and she knew it. Her strength was what scared her the most.

She was completely dumbfounded when it came to her outrageous capabilities. She was jarring herself and increasing her own heart rate just from the visual flashes she'd been trying to shake ever since the fight. She had seen enough blood to last her a few lifetimes just that morning alone, and she was becoming unraveled.

What was done could not be undone, and what was seen was also irreversible. As far as she'd gathered, the waters above were no less than an oncoming atonement of some far-out kind and there was no doubt that her seat was in the front row and center.

By then, she was still feeling rude, and reckless, for jumping out of Nomad's car. She knew she had to go back to the bookstore to find him, and hopefully his reportedly insightful friend, Goose. After everything she had been through over that past day, she was glad to find that she still had just over seven dollars left.

She hacked a cab ride after she had been fortunate to find an idle taxi driver whose intended passenger flaked out on their ride request. Pearl approached the driver, who was smoking a cigarette as she leaned up against the taxi.

"Are you busy?" Pearl asked with hesitation.

"I thought I was, my customer's a no show. Where are you trying to go?" the brunette woman asked. Pearl felt the need to explain her situation some, as she knew that she didn't have enough money. She said,

"I really need to get somewhere. It's not that close, and I don't have that much money," she said, expecting a hard no.

"You look like hell," the cabbie stated the obvious. "Are you safe?" she asked. Pearl almost hesitated to answer the question. But because she knew that she could defend them both if need be, she answered with conviction,

"Absolutely. I just have an emergency that cannot wait. I'd really appreciate it," she said with a certain needy tone that made the lady cabbie sigh with sympathy. After she was done huffing, she commanded Pearl,

"Get in," she said, shaking her head. Pearl hopped in saying, "You have no idea. Thank you so much. I'm going to Emerald Coffee and Books." The middle-aged, lady cabbie gave her a nod and they pulled off.

Pearl rode in the back seat silently, still spacey and pensive about what was to become of her. She was keeping her eye on the meter in the cab, knowing that she only had about seven dollars in her pocket.

Twenty-five minutes later, they were pulling up to the front of Nomad's establishment. Upon arrival, Pearl was bewildered when the cabbie announced her total,

"That'll be $7.20," she announced. Unexpectedly, the suddenly knowing driver became another part of Pearl's mystery. The total that the cabbie charged was exactly how much Pearl had left. Though she was baffled about the driver, or why she undercharged her, she figured it had to happen.

Pearl wasn't especially glad about not having a tip to leave her. There really was no room for her to feel bad, but she said to the driver anyway,

"Hey, this was a really important trip. I'm so sorry I didn't have enough, I really am," Pearl apologized to her. But the driver turned around in her seat to face Pearl, saying,

"There's nothing to feel bad about," she informed Pearl. "I hope your day gets better, honey," the cabbie said to her with a grin.

Sure enough, a lighting fuchsia butterfly was vying behind the cabbie. Flying near the driver side of the windshield, the butterfly glowed brightly to clearly make its presence known. Pearl smiled back, then exited the cab.

She paused outside of the bookstore, wondering how she was going to construct her apology to Nomad. She knew she had to do it, so she took a brief pause to get over it. After she did, she went in.

She stepped through the entrance, and immediately looked over to see Pamelah staring at her with a strongly disquieted expression on her face. She waved over to Pearl, who then stepped up to the register, as there was no one else in line. Pamelah leaned across the counter glancing around for eavesdroppers, and she asked,

"Where is Nomad? I had to call in extra help today." She looked very agitated that he wasn't there. "He hasn't been answering his phone either. What the hell man?"

"He hasn't been back here?" Pearl probed, surprised.

"Nope. He hasn't. Where'd you guys go? Is he okay?" Pamelah started to pile up the same questions that Pearl was already asking herself. Pearl just replied,

"I don't know, we got separated yesterday. He didn't call, or anything?" She asked her question as she shook her head, realizing that she may actually need to go back to the Center.

"Actually. He did call me, yesterday," Pamelah remembered. "He needed me to look up some guy he knows," she added. Pearl probed,

"Did it happen to be Goose Gary, by chance?" she asked, anxiously.

"Yes, Goose," Pamelah confirmed, expecting that it would help Pearl find him. Pearl spoke with surety,

"Well, I don't know where he is now. But, I will find out," she promised Pamelah as she threw the bookstore door open, in a hurry to leave.

As she walked down the block of the bookstore, she realized that she was heading to the exact same place she had been so desperately avoiding. Remembering the level of discomfort she'd felt while she was there was beginning to make her feel sick to her stomach, and flustered.

She walked down a less traveled street, and she came to a wrecking yard. She stood at the huge gate that enclosed many broken-down vehicles. She looked at all of the cars and trucks.

Some were totaled, with massive body damage. Others seemed to just be old, or possibly abandoned. One car stood out, the black two-door coupe. The damage to the small car was staggering, and it seemed to Pearl that whoever had been driving at the time of that accident probably didn't survive.

She shuddered at the car. She just felt sadness for the person who wrecked it. She took the beat-up black leather backpack off her shoulder.

She turned it around and unzipped one of the small compartments to take out the mysterious rose keyring. She studied the keys in her hand, trying to brainstorm on what they might go to.

She looked at the wrecked coupe once again. She scanned all of the vehicles in the *car cemetery,* as she defined it in her mind. Feeling inexplicably sad, she put the keyring away, and she swung the black leather bag back over her shoulder. Then, she resumed her walk to the Maquiller Research Center.

*******End of Chapter*******

Chapter 12

We Meet Again

(June 21, 2018 11:45 a.m.)

Pearl remained on the other side of the street as she searched around the Maquiller Center building with her eyes. She wondered how many of the people passing by it actually had any knowledge of the Hippo Project. Or even some sort of knowledge of the dark works within its walls.

It looked like any other medical facility or clinic, and the foot traffic around the outside of it made it appear to be reputable. But there was no unlearning what she knew of the place. She began to look around for someone, or something, helpful.

****

Inside of the building, Detective Cup was making haste in search of something. Mari Hera's eluding security was the reason that Cup was able to manipulate so many of the security team's functions, and he knew it. After leaving the security room the day before, Cup had locked the door in hopes of keeping the two sloth security guards from getting back in.

He knew it would only last until their help arrived, but it gave Cup the head start he needed, to explore more of the building. Word was, there was another floor that wouldn't be on any of the Center's radars. Only an exceedingly small elite team of outsiders had ever visited the floor, with Dr. Canna.

Cup wanted to see if he could find the place. If his source was correct, then he needed to obtain Canna's fingerprints to enter. He was on his way to visit Canna's office for a decent print sample.

He had never left the building because he knew that he would be confronted when he tried to re-enter the facility later. So, he had trapped himself inside the Center well past his shift's end and spent the night undetected. Come Thursday morning, he continued dodging the rest of the security team and resumed his search of yet another possible Center secret.

He casually opened the door to Canna's office, and almost peeped inside. The stench of burnt flesh was lingering inside of the office, and it made him yank his head back. Holding his index finger under his nose, he shut the door fast.

He scanned the area to see if anyone had seen him. When he saw that no one was around, he became concerned. There was absolutely no one around, and that was bizarre by itself.

There was no medical receptionist at the front station near the entrance of the wing. "Where did everyone go?" he asked himself. He decided to abort the mission of getting Dr. Canna's fingerprint.

He walked past Canna's office and followed the hallway. He was hoping to follow a helpful path. He noticed the excess amount of filth that covered the floor. After noting the Hippo wing's need for housekeeping, he came across the note that Ami Wentawaye had left sticking to the wall outside of room 505 the day before.

He was perplexed at such a short and abrupt quit letter. He reached his hand out and turned the door handle. He pushed the door open, and the first thing he saw was a mop bucket and a very dirty floor.

He stood at the doorway, staring down at the nasty matter that stuck to the floor. A sudden noise from the end of the hall near the reception area jolted Cup. He quickly entered the room and held the handle down while he quietly shut the door behind him.

He was breathing deeply with his forehead against the inside of the door. He wondered what the noise at the end of the hall was. He was plotting his next steps.

As he was in deep study, he heard a noise. A crispy, but distinctive, noise was coming from within the room. He pushed himself off of the closed door, slowly turning around to see what he was about to find.

The crispy-burnt zombie took two steps forward, staggering toward Cup, or the open doorway. Cup was already gone.

"A zombie?" he asked himself, regarding what he had just encountered. As he swiftly moved away from the undead man, he figured that the Center was indeed engineering unthinkable things. Right or wrong about who made the zombie, both Ami and Michael had good reason to get out.

As he ran down a hallway in the unexplored parts of the wing, he knew that his time in the Center was extremely limited. Cup was searching for the closest exit, as was the zombie that he had carelessly freed.

****

Still staring at the building in her contemplative mood, Pearl began to feel faint at the bleak idea of ending up back in the custody of Al Canna. The building looked so much dingier in the daylight, after reading the ridiculously depressing-but-insightful words of Ruby and Devan. Out of nowhere, someone called out to her.

"Pearl. Over here," Kai shouted from the half-open door in the small vacant office that the grandies had been leasing, using it to monitor the Center. He stuck his head out and waved her down, motioning for her to come to him. "Please. C'mon," he pleaded with her, inconspicuously.

As she approached him, she knew that she no longer had anything to lose by hearing Kai out. Before she reached the door, Nomad practically wedged his head and shoulders into the doorway in front of Kai so that Pearl could see that he was already there. When she saw him, Pearl knew that she was right where she'd needed to be.

She was relieved to see him. She increased her pace to a jog to meet them at the door, and she went in with them. Kim instantly ran toward her with her arms out, crying,

"Mama." Kim's eyes teared up as she tried to reach out to her. But Sammie held her back, reminding her of her mother's current state.

"She doesn't know who you are Kim," Sammie said, pulling her into her arms to keep her still. "She doesn't know any of us," she added.

Pearl looked at her new surroundings. She looked around the room slowly, gazing at each of them. She looked at Nomad, who had come in and stood near a window, and she figured he was watching the progress of the sea-like sky as well.

"I thought you would have way more scars on your face," he lightly joked. He was astonished by her flawless appearance, considering she'd jumped out of his fast-moving car the day before. She then was jolted by the memory of crawling out of the blackberry branches, and she had forgotten about the many cuts that were no longer all over her face and body.

"It's a very long story," she spoke in a sassy tone, unsuccessfully trying to break in a smile. "I'm so sorry," she said to him, with a sigh. She was embarrassed to say it, but she definitely meant it.

"It's all right. If you're all right," his face held no judgment as he responded. "You are a little crazy though," he communicated, unfiltered.

Pearl snickered, seemingly unbothered. But she knew that she was very far from "all right." She had no urge to confide in them about her gruesome episode because she knew that she would make herself sick trying to elaborate about it all. Kai walked over and stood right in front of Pearl.

"And, I'm sorry. I'm sorry you have to go through this," he spoke with compassion as he looked back and forth between Pearl and Kim. He dug into his pocket and pulled out her driver's license. He handed it to her as he told her,

"That's you. At least, that's who you were before all of this," he told her as she examined the ID that allegedly belonged to her. He ran his hand over his beard before he continued speaking, "This is Fowley, Sammie, and TJ, my siblings," he announced.

He pointed to each grandie as he introduced them, and they all casually gestured toward her as they said hello. Pearl looked at the group of "siblings," and became intrigued to know their story, as they all looked so different from one another. Kai interrupted her in mid thought, somberly saying,

"Your daughter is also in danger. But we know that you would be challenged to address that yourself right now. So, she's been sticking close to Sammie," he disclosed. Pearl didn't appear to have any kind of acquaintance with Kim.

But Kim just stood there hoping that it would click, and her mother would recognize her. She was shaking her head, trying to understand why her mother hadn't done so already. She became deeply saddened and scared.

"You lied to me about my name?" Pearl asked Kai with an accusatory tone. Kai was taken aback, not knowing that she'd heard him talking to Al Canna.

"I know," he admitted, shaking his head. "I stole your driver's license and phone when I was told to take your belongings to the storage piles," he explicated.

"I wanted to know who you were, before. I'd heard of some subjects being given new identities as part of their participation, and," Kai started to explain, but Pearl interrupted him, exclaiming,

"Whoever I was before this was very unpopular apparently. I've been running around like a crazy case for twenty-four hours, and not one person recognized," she paused her claim before she finished the sentence.

The man at KGEM called me Mari, she remembered. Kim rolled her eyes, contrasting her mother's statement about being "unpopular" because the teen knew all too well that her mother had a few potential enemies.

"It's not safe to use the name Mari Hera anymore. But, if it helps to know, I like the name Pearl," Kai said with genuineness. "And, I wouldn't say that you were completely unpopular, he advised her.

"Either Maquiller or Canna had it out for you, perhaps?" he considered with one brow raised. "Me and my siblings already know who you are, so you must be someone," he calculated. Anyway, we'll help you and your daughter get new identities, soon enough."

Kai lowered his head in thought before he looked at Pearl, and spoke, "I'm sure I should be telling you about Leroi Maquiller," he started to say. Pearl immediately responded,

"You mean the asshole who founded this crazy shit?" Pearl asked, raising her voice a bit. Sammie's face expressed compassion for Pearl while she studied the unfortunate woman.

Kai nodded, "I guess he is that too, but he's also our adoptive father. Well, he was up until now, as far as I'm concerned," he spoke confidently, nodding his head in certainty. He then continued, "Your programming may not have been successful, but you can be sure that you have become something else," he said, once again nodding his head.

"And, you should know that the water in the sky isn't his doing. That is way over his head. No pun intended," Kai insisted.

"What are you saying? Who are you anyway?" she became agitated as she inquired. She didn't even let him answer her first two questions before asking, "Then what *is* going on? What's happening to me?" she exclaimed to the room full of people.

She turned to see the girl who called her "mama," and she felt saddened. "And, I have a daughter?" she demanded reiteration.

"Before I help you figure yourself out, you will have to know a little more about Leroi Maquiller," Kai explained to her.

"You mean the asshole?" Pearl asked with discontentment.

"He is a lot more than just an 'asshole,' so be ready to learn all about that. Truth is, he's a beast." he replied. Nomad turned his eyes to Kai, and he watched him for a few seconds before he blocked the topic, asking him,

"What do you want to scare her for?" he exclaimed. "Find another topic to start with. Look at her," he yelled as he held his hand out toward Pearl, who was already trembling with nervousness. "You have plenty of places to start, Nomad suggested the wisdom with sternness.

"How about you start with what the hell is happening? And, the rules. What are the rules? How can you not know them by now?" he demanded clarity from Kai and the rest of the Cr8 siblings. But right after he'd spoken, he adjusted his demeanor as if he'd surprised himself by even mentioning the word, "rules."

"We don't know the rules," Kai snapped. "They have never been given to us. We have had to make do with what has felt right, and wrong, this whole friggin' time." he expounded. "But, I can tell you about some of the random things we've learned over time," he added, looking at Pearl.

"Okay. Shoot," she responded sharply, with folded arms that harnessed her skepticism.

Kai stuttered, "Well. I, I. It's not an easy thing to ex-," Nomad interjected to share one piece of information that he himself was sure of, and to buy Kai some time to think about his answer to Pearl.

"Goose Gary and I became friends after he'd mistakenly called my bookstore. We used to answer the phone with a greeting, saying, 'Thank you for calling Emerald Coffee and Books. How may I help you?' And, we'd say it the same way every time," he told them.

He walked over to a metal folding chair in the empty office building, and he sat down. Looking at everyone, he continued his story,

"I was holding a very special comic book in my hand. A comic book that has been out of print for decades," he explained while he took off his jacket.

"It was, and still is, very valuable to me. I had been wanting a copy for a long time, and I had finally gotten one. So, I was simply excited about having it," he said as his mind changed, and he stood up to walk back over by the window.

"I was distracted by my fascination with the comic book, and I messed up delivering the business greeting. What I said was, 'Thank you for calling Odd Gems,' instead," he recalled to them.

He smiled while talking, "And, the man at the other end of the line said, 'You don't mean *Odd Gems*, the comic book? Do ya?' he asked me," Nomad spoke as if he wanted to remember the whole phone call verbatim.

"After talking with him for a few minutes about it, I'd realized that he had every Odd Gem comic book that

I didn't possess. It was highly improbable, impossible really," he proclaimed to them all. "Anyway, that's how I met Goose Gary," Nomad concluded.

As if it were an alarm set to remind the grandie, Nomad's story made Kai jump up abruptly to ask, "Where the hell is Goose?" Everyone looked at each other in surprise, acknowledging that he was still not present.

"He should have been here by now for sure," Fowley acknowledged.

"Call him," Fowley pressed Kai to dial Goose's number. Kai tried to call, but it went directly to his voice mailbox greeting. Kai disconnected the call, frustrated at his third unsuccessful attempt to reach Goose. Stressed out over it, Kai announced to the rest of them,

"That's the third time I've called him, and he's not answering," he talked with temperance. "All I can say is, he knows exactly where we are. I guess he'll get here, when he gets here," Kai expressed, with a little doubt in his voice.

"Question," Pearl suddenly stated to everyone, waving her arm. "So, nobody knows what's happening between us and the body of water that has been freaking suspended over our heads since yesterday? Anybody?" she demanded information.

"Shhh," they all shushed her.

"We don't talk about it. But, to answer your question, no. Nobody knows. Hope that helps," Sammie said, trying to end the conversation before Kim joined it. Kim was thinking too deeply about what was going to happen to her already small family, so she didn't catch Pearl's outrageous claim.

Kai decided that Pearl should know a little more about Mari Hera, and he said to her, "A man named Detective Cup was working with you. You both were investigating a string of kidnappings that had occurred all in a thirty-day period in 1998, he stated.

"He found us. Cup found us," he said excitedly, and he unfolded his birth certificate to show her. "You've found us. I know you can't remember, and I'm sorry. But, I'll try to help you remember, if possible," he vowed to her.

Pearl didn't see any help in doubting his intentions. She paused with a brooding facial expression for a few seconds. "Where is this Goose?" she inquired. Kai then remembered his phone call to Goose early that morning.

Right away, Kai queried to Pearl, "Were you the woman in the abandoned parking lot this morning?" He searched her face for an honest response.

"Why?" she asked, defensively. Sammie locked eyes with Kim, and she relished the irony that she wasn't the only one there who would break into a car. Her grin was only slight, but Kim still caught the expression and rolled her eyes. Unaware of their exchange, Kai replied to Pearl,

"Because, if you're the one who saw the body in the car, I wanna know," Kai's mood shifted as he knew she was safe with them, but he wanted to know how much she was going to be honest about. "If you're the woman who is able to create Purple Opal sand, I wanna know. Quite frankly, I wanna know what it's for," he admitted straightforwardly.

Leith concurred, "If you're the woman who did both that, and threw the car off of that kid, *we* wanna know," he added. The others just looked at each other, clueless. Kai continued,

"And, if you're the woman from that parking lot, then you've already met Goose Gary, and *you* might wanna know," he concluded. Nomad grew concerned all the sudden, asking Pearl,

"Wait, was it you trying to break into that car? Goose told me about that." Pearl became uneasy, startled by the question.

"Yes, but I was just trying to get something important out of it," she replied, still defensive in her tone.

Nomad recounted his phone call with Goose, he then knew that Goose had kept the part about the Purple Opal sand to himself. Being that there were a couple of good reasons why Goose would withhold such great information, he still questioned Pearl's intentions.

"What was so important that you would break into a car?" he probed. Pearl dipped her chin, and she explained.

"A document with my name on it was inside of a car," she told everyone. Kai looked over at Fowley, and he straight off put his face down into the palm of his hand.

He had remembered to remove all of Pearl's digital information from the database, but he'd forgotten to pull her paper documents from the stack before throwing the papers around in the car. She spoke on, with frustration,

"There was a dead body in the back seat of that car," she blurted. "Yeah, a dead man in the back seat of a car, and a document of some kind with my name on it was lying just a foot away from him," she explained herself. "I was trying to get that paper, whatever it was."

Neither Fowley nor Kai said anything more about the paper. It was too late, and they knew it wouldn't help to argue. Pearl continued,

"I didn't want the car or anything else in it. I just wanted the document," she cried out, stating the predicament she'd encountered. Nomad's jaw was dropped, and he finally inquired,

"A dead body?" he asked for clarity, while everyone else moved in closer to hear her better. "Yes. A corpse in the back seat of a car full of documents that I couldn't even see clearly from the window. I panicked, she hollered out.

"I hope I didn't leave any fingerprints on anything," she exclaimed, deeply troubled. The grandies looked at each other, knowing how worried Pearl was. She kept recounting the incident,

"Anyway, I couldn't get in -after all. I tried throwing a big freakin' rock through the window. The rock broke, and it turned into this," she cried out as she pulled a small amount of the purple sand from the leather backpack.

They all gathered to get a look at it, as it still gleamed with its glowing purple shimmer. Nomad backed up in shock. He looked around him at everyone there and cried out, *"Odd Gems,"*

Pearl asked him, "You mean your comic book?" Nomad looked at all of them as if he'd just cracked a sacred code.

"Yes. The comic book," he stated calmly, still pensive. He was a painter in his former life, and he still loved to draw post-procedure in 2018. Nomad recognized Purple Opal sand from the comics he owned, and he realized that he may very well have the rules they had been needing to know.

Kai was very interested in the comics that Nomad had. Goose had shown him a few of the Odd Gem comic books he owned. But Kai remembered Goose saying that he doesn't have the one that explains the power behind the sands.

"You have the comic about the sand?" he asked Nomad.

Nomad nodded his head, correcting him, "You mean the sands. There are more colors to a spectrum, son," he advised Kai.

Sammie was only half listening. She was clutching the birth certificate that Kai had given her when she got their attention. She spoke with some uncertainty, "Wait a minute. Today's my birthday?" she asked Kai. He didn't know what she meant.

Sammie waved the document in the air toward them as she continued to speak,

"This birth certificate says I was born on June 21st," she exclaimed.

"Well, Happy Birthday to you." Nomad responded in a formal tone, and the others also acknowledged the awkward occasion. Then, Nomad probed, "But, why are you carrying your birth certificate around with you?" he asked, looking at the grandies with confusion as to why Sammie carried such sensitive documentation on her.

She was still looking at Kai and Fowley as if she had just swallowed a horse pill, with no beverage. Then, she looked at Nomad and said, "I just received this today. Truth is, we're still trying to understand," she admitted.

"Me too. Seriously, I don't know any Detective Cup," Pearl said, severely disappointed that she couldn't remember. In silence, she took several steps away from everyone, fighting a meltdown. "Happy birthday to you," she said to Sammie as she walked away from them, shaking her head.

"I think that maybe all of us were programmed, at some point. I mean, we know that I was, for sure," Pearl reasoned. Kai tried to comfort her, saying,

"Well, you should know that Detective Cup definitely knows you, and it sounds like you've helped him immensely on our case. So, thank you. Truth is, I suspect that everyone here could use some better insight," he admitted.

"Oh, yes. Please," Pearl affirmed. I am certain that I'm the failed experimental sub, so maybe you're all successfully programmed subjects -whatever that means," she said, annoyed by the complexity of the topic. Leith spoke up for himself.

"I also had no clue about who I was, at one point. I still don't. I've relied on my family to help me salvage my life, but it didn't work, he confessed.

"I'm really not who I used to be, but I don't know who I used to be, anyway. It's very strange," he offered his story to Pearl. Leith added the bottom line,

"I believe wholeheartedly that I was a subject in the Center, and not 'found' this way as they had told everyone. Kim took a step or two closer to everybody, and she said to him,

"You're right. My mother knows about that," she said, pointing at Pearl before she continued. "She has a lot of info about you and your run-in with Maquiller. Your name sounded familiar before when you said it, but now I remember you," she declared. Leith nodded, and asked,

"You have information about my story? I would really, really like to see it sometime," he stated with sincerity. Kim nodded,

"I think she would be happy to do that, so yeah. If we get out of here alive, you may read whatever we have. I'd be glad to help you," she said, committing to the offer.

The four grandies looked at each other, each of them remembering the dark days they've tucked away over the years. As they connected that darkness to the Center, their moods became dark, and they were heavy at heart.

"When given the opportunity to compare notes, all of the gems in the empty office found their appropriate conclusions. Either they had been under the programming without their knowledge, or they had been severely damaged in the programming process.

Either way, they all had gone through the invasive procedure, and they were all rendered mentally hindered, or gaslighted, in some major way. At least, until that day. Sammie's epiphany made her shout out to the others,

"Oh my god," Sammie blurted. "We're not monsters. We're programmed."

The verbal confirmation was heavy to bear. Nomad, Leith, and Pearl became enlightened to the very thing that likely ruled their own individual quirks.

Everyone was angry, and everyone realized how much they had in common. Pearl looked at her arms, and goosebumps had grown all over them. She spoke in a faint voice when she said,

"I knew it," she whispered as she recapped that past day. She raised her voice a little higher and told them, "They tried to program me, and something happened. Something went wrong, now I can't remember anything about me." Kai nodded as he responded to her,

"That's what I wanted to talk to you about when I'd found you. I was always planning to get you somewhere safe," he admitted to her. "I know you're superhuman, like us, he noted.

"But, I swear my mind never had one wave of thought that I too was programmed. That is something that has built up to this point for me," he concluded, no less frustrated than anyone else.

"Me neither," Fowley added. Sammie and TJ shook their heads to suggest their ignorance on the matter.

"Maybe, that's what she was doing at the Center, it would be on the cameras, right?" Sammie asked. Kai stopped her thought when he said,

"Detective Cup has retrieved any useful video footage, I'm sure. He's here for the same reason that she is," Kai said, referring to Pearl. "I feel good about it," he said as his perspective broadened.

"I was told that we were born special and that we would be in danger if we shared that information with anyone," TJ testified.

"So, we've never talked about it to strangers," Sammie added. "All this time we've thought that we were freaks whose parents didn't want us," she spoke in a choked voice, fuming and disordered.

Kai held his left hand over his mouth, considering the chaotic episodes he'd been through. They were now understanding that their programming was the cause. They began to spiral downward in their demeanor. They were connecting the outrageous behaviors they each had sporadically exhibited, to Maquiller.

Kai looked back to Pearl and said, "The detective we're speaking of, Detective Cup? He called you Mari Hera, for the record," he confessed to her. Kim excitedly jumped in without delay, exclaiming,

"Yes, mom. Your name is Mari Hera," she confirmed, hoping that her whiny voice would be familiar to her mother. She was met with a blank reaction.

She was about to tear up, overwhelmed by all the madness. She just couldn't grasp the concept of being unrecognizable to her own mother. She didn't say anything more in that instant.

Fowley had never been so livid. None of them had been that angry in a long time, if ever. He stood up from the cheap wooden chair he'd been sitting on, picked it up, and smashed it onto the floor. Sammie and TJ, who were standing by him, lifted their arms to protect their faces as the chair pieces flew about.

"Son, I have seen you all twice now. Once, before I turned 34 years old. You all were about, I don't know, fifteen, maybe fourteen years old then, maybe," Nomad divulged. The grandies stared at him in confusion, as they vaguely remembered Nomad as well.

"And, here we are again with just twelve days until my 44th birthday," Nomad said to Fowley, who was about to curse a mouthful at Nomad. But Nomad broke first, telling them,

"Sorry to withhold that from you all. I just have to be careful before I speak. Whatever you kids went through ten, or even twenty, years ago is beyond my knowledge.

I wasn't a part of it, and you should know that. But we are tied to each other for reasons obviously bigger than ourselves," Nomad enlightened Fowley, and the others.

"However, I was asked to evaluate you all back then. I knew Maquiller had adopted thirteen unlucky orphans, so that's what he'd claimed. But he only wanted me to talk to eight of you," he recalled for them.

"Where did you see us last?" Fowley asked him.

Nomad gave it a quick thought, then replied, "Like I was saying. In Rhode Island, I worked for the Maquiller Research Center, as an outside associate," Nomad's sentence was interrupted.

Out of nowhere, a crow ran itself into the window of the office, and it startled everyone. The reflective glass confused the fowl, and it flew itself into the window - thinking that it was attacking another rivaling bird.

"It's just a bird," Fowley said. "Although, that territorial behavior shouldn't still be happening on the first day of summer," he added, to acknowledge the irregular event. Sammie thought to herself, *not again*. Yet, it disturbed her because the thought made no sense to her, though it naturally came to mind. It was *déjà vu*.

Caught off guard, they all considered the awkward black bird for a short instant. Then, they all casually disregarded the incident. Nomad kept talking,

"So anyway, it wasn't long before I was set, ready to move to Washington to open my new business. I was even staying in a hotel at the time because I'd already moved out of my old residence. But I took those counseling sessions with you kids, as a favor to Maquiller.

"I checked you out, asked you some questions, recorded your answers, and gave it to him," he walked them through the event. "From what I could see, you kids were fine. So, that's what I reported," he told them.

Leith followed up with an epiphany, sidetracking Nomad as he said to him, "I was drawn to your store. I chose your store to set up in front of the first time I had ever decided to play my guitar in public. I made enough money that day to buy a new guitar amp," he recalled with satisfaction.

"I still set up across the street sometimes," Leith said to Nomad. "But, you were always familiar to me," he said. He turned to everyone else, "Sorry, my point is that everyone else also seems to have migrated from Rhode Island after him, from what I've heard."

"Even I had left my family in Rhode Island years ago, to come to Seattle. I had accepted a new job, thinking that it would be good to get out on my own for a bit, he continued.

"I moved to Seattle then, and I'm still here in Washington today. You some sort of crazy people magnet?" he asked Nomad, in conclusion.

"I can't be sure, but it has been considered," he replied to him, tapping the tip of his index finger against his own temple. Then he grinned, and said, "Nah, you're not crazy, Leith," he told him with sincerity, shaking his head.

"Is Goose from Rhode Island too?" Sammie asked Kai and Nomad. The two looked at each other, and neither of them could remember where Goose was originally from.

"I don't remember him ever saying where he was from," Nomad realized, and said so to the others. Kai was in a similar state of mind, saying,

"I wrote him several times from Rhode Island, but I don't know if he himself had ever lived there. I don't think I ever asked," Kai stated to him. Nonetheless, Leith was still mentally putting together the puzzle pieces that he had received that day.

"So unreal. They never found me that way, after all. They made me this way," he spoke to Kai, then he hung his head in sadness.

"I believe you're right. This all means that I too was most likely a subject. If so, I have no memory of when, or how. Fuck." Nomad was uneasy. Then, he addressed the Cr8,

"What we need to know is what has brought all of us here right now," he stated. "In fact, what happened to the rest of you?" he asked, out of curiosity. The grandies looked at each other with much trepidation, and it was clear that they weren't going to answer either question with ease.

Nomad noticed their elusive responses, then he let it go and continued his thought, "Maybe, we're gathered together to give Maquiller a dose of his own medicine," he said with his chin downward. Pearl looked at Nomad as he was staring at the floor, pondering. She asked him,

"Yesterday, you started to tell me something about the Center when we were talking. What was it?" she inquired with great curiosity.

"Doesn't matter, my position in the whole thing apparently isn't what I thought it was. What we know now is that we've all been targeted for some reason," he outlined the theme.

"We've all had our lives hacked. Do you all struggle with unexplainable behaviors yourselves?" Nomad swiftly looked up to study their faces, trying to catch their natural responses. The looks on their faces confirmed his suspicions.

The grandies may have been working on their plan to expose the Center's bad practices, but there in the secret meeting place is where rage began to bubble. What the grandies were doing before was for the well-being of those who couldn't help themselves. But the operation unexpectedly became way more personal than they could have imagined.

"Hell, all five of Canna's subs should be here, especially Jade Noble. Now that we know we're all in the same position, it would have been good to stick together," TJ said to everyone, shaking his head in disappointment.

Sammie saw TJ's sadness, and she was compelled to say, "Well, at least Canna's five now know that they've been tampered with. A part of me just wishes that we had told Ray to stay with us," she expressed her regrets.

"Actually, I never really left," Ray replied, startling everyone when he suddenly began to speak from the doorway of the adjoining room in the vacant office where they were. He stepped through the doorway as if he had come into the office through a different entrance.

"I've been around. I just couldn't leave. I wasn't gonna let anything happen to you all because of what I did," he spoke with a peaceful tone, lowering his head.

"Wait, what exactly did you do?" Pearl asked him, concerned. He looked at everyone else to confirm their undivided attention, then he declared,

"I killed Dr. Al Canna. He was an awful man. A monster, really. I'm sorry, but that's what I did," Ray answered.

He didn't want her to know all of the details, but he clearly was going to make sure that no one else could pay for his crime. Ray Goddem knew what he wanted to do, and he was just sticking around closely to ensure his timeliness.

He wanted to turn himself in, but he knew that it wasn't beneficial to the Cr8. So, he figured that when the time was right, he would do the right thing. He made known what he thought of his own role in the situation at hand.

"I'm not like you all. I don't have any special, quirky thing with me that I know about. I'm hearing all kinds of things about you all, Ray revealed.

"No, I'm just a pissed off study subject who wanted revenge, and got it," he declared. Contrarily, Fowley shook his head, saying,

"A pissed off study subject who has managed to complete a task that any of us could have been required to do. You have no idea.

"You are very much one of us, Ray. Look, we all just found out today that we've been programmed," Fowley tried to tell him. But Ray was convinced, and he had his own plans.

"You just don't see it now. But when that water breaks, you probably won't see me again," Ray spoke with certainty. "I've killed a man." They all stayed quiet to consider the peace he had with his own words.

Kai offered a theory on why they all had to be there. "Originally, there were eight of us grandies. What if the rest of us who are here right now is the new Cr8? What if Goose isn't coming?" he asked them, looking at Fowley and Sammie. TJ agreed with him that it was possible,

"Yeah, maybe these people are replacing Dee, Tonny, Rose, and Kielo?" he shared his thoughts with everyone. They all looked flabbergasted, even though no one could disprove the possibility. Kim was utterly muddled.

"Yeah," Kai agreed. He started to add something seemingly important to their theory, but he was abruptly interrupted by a tremor that shook the ground beneath them. All of a sudden, there was a commotion going on outside of the office building.

Shortly after the tremor, there was a terrifying boom that rattled their ears. The people outside of the office screamed all at once, and it made Kim shriek.

They all rushed out of the office door, and to the street. When they went out, they saw people all over the road, running from the Center.

Some were running to safety from the presumed earthquake. Some seemed to run for a different reason. The mix of emotions among the people was mind boggling, and the group watched in terror.

They all looked up. There was a colossal lightning bolt suspended in the sky, and it was paused midair before reaching the ground. At the opening where the waters separated, the gigantic violet lightning bolt appeared to stem directly from the rose-gold sunlight.

TJ didn't wait for anyone; he straight away went back into the building to check for employees who needed help evacuating. He made it halfway deep into the hallways of the Hippo wing. But as he approached the double doors to a heavily staffed department, he heard it.

A grievous roll of thunder accompanied the monolithic lightning strike. The two marvelous effects occurred simultaneously. The huge electrifying bolt zapped straight through the rooftop of the Maquiller Research Center, sparking fires even three floors below the roof level.

TJ was in a hallway on the first floor when he heard the lightning strike. The sound of the broken ceilings and floors rumbled as the entire building shook. TJ aborted his pursuit, and he unsteadily headed back toward the exit.

The building caught fire right away, and the blaze became big and threatening within just thirty seconds of the lightning strike. The instant pandemonium was too much for the two police officers who were first to arrive at the building. Those policemen had pulled their car over, and they hopped out to help a woman who was hysterical, as she struggled to tell them that the building was "exploding."

Even as she cried out to them, another employee came running out of the double doors toward them, screaming about an injured man who was heading out of the building. In his description, something wasn't quite right about the burn victim.

"He looks dead," the man exclaimed as he rested his hand on his head, right on top of his brain. The police thought that the man was experiencing acute side effects of trauma. Meanwhile, the zombie was exiting the building at the street entrance where Sammie, his maker, and the others were gathered.

Sammie was looking up to see the huge fire that had straight off started to blaze at the top of the Center. It wasn't as easy to see from the corner, but the flame was growing so rapidly that it was just a short matter of time before it would take the whole place down.

Sammie checked all directions, trying to scope out the severity of the scene. A moment had passed before she noticed it.

A slainch had emerged from the corpses in the Center, and it was coming straight at them. Sammie couldn't believe her eyes.

Pearl and Kim saw the slainch at the same time, and they both screamed at the top of their lungs. Their screams were similar in sound. Although she couldn't mention it at the moment, Sammie noticed.

Kai turned to see what was wrong with them, and he saw that one of the guards was coming out into the street. *Dead. No, undead,* he thought to himself. He finally calculated what he was witnessing. "Slainch!" he screamed out to warn the Cr8.

The slainch wobbled toward them loosely. There was clearly no noticeable human instinct, and his sucked-in eyes suggested that he was brain dead. He was staggering away from the Center with his arms out, seemingly ready to attack any random warm-blooded human within his reach.

"But they were dead," Sammie testified to the group. "They were dead," she repeated, surprised to see such a being for the second time.

The slainch was still charred from head to toe. He was still coming after his maker, moving sloppily toward her. His strides were extremely rickety, and his aim seemed unpredictable.

The newcomers had never experienced such a thing, and the grandies' experience was so long ago, they had almost forgotten what it was like. They were all highly disturbed.

They ran around the undead guard, screaming as they crossed the street toward the Center. As they booked, Kai divulged one of the first rules he would share with them.

"A non-programmed human who is killed by a hyperactive being becomes a slainch. It was in Goose's comics," he spoke loudly to explain the sighting to them all.

"What the hell is a slainch?' Nomad shouted over the madness. "And, exactly why should we be afraid of him?" he added, pointing out the slainch's abnormal behavior.

The undead man limped right past a few people on the street when Kai stopped to observe him. One by one, the people stopped screaming as they realized that they were not the target. The slainch dragged itself forward, but it seemed as though it was only moving in Sammie's direction.

Several seconds had passed, and he still hadn't answered Nomad's question. Coming out of confusion, he then realized that the slainch wasn't after random flesh. "He's only after Sammie," he said to himself under his breath.

"Kai, what the fuck is a slainch?" Nomad inquired again, but louder.

"A zombie," Kai exclaimed, trying to teach them, and run toward his endangered sister at the same time. "Sammie, look out," Kai yelled at her. She responded,

"What?" she yelled back at him, trying to study the disturbed look on his face. She struggled to hear him.

"The slainch. He's trying to get to *you*," Kai warned her. Immediately, Sammie separated herself from everyone to deter the guard zombie. Leith watched in horror as he clenched the front of his black tee shirt.

"I'll have to tell you about that later," Kai said to all of them as they ran toward the entrance.

They weren't able to go into the center as officials were already blocking the entrances, but Kai was already trying to get Detective Cup on the phone. He was pacing on the sidewalk as it rang.

He was wondering if Cup had already left the building. Then, a loud roll of thunder got the attention of all of those under the majestic waters.

When they all looked up, the wrestling waters had become too vicious to be ignored. Kai put his phone away, gazing into the waves.

Pearl, Kai, Nomad, Fowley, Leith, and Ray were all severely thunderstruck. The sparring waves were clashing so hard against each other that it was becoming inevitable that the suspension would soon break.

The inaudible, suspended waves had been awfully breathtaking for almost an entire day. But then came an unexpected dead silence. They all were made deaf, and unable to hear anything in the surrounding chaos.

It was even more disruptive to see all the mayhem around them, without the sound. It removed a layer from their sense of safety, as they couldn't hear any possible dangers approaching. It was stunning to their senses, but it didn't last long.

Sammie still kept a safe distance from her slainch, but she was highly disturbed when her hearing went out completely. Decisively, she'd figured that if she can turn sound on and off, she could control the sound. At least, in her panic, she hoped so.

She stopped dodging the zombie just long enough to extend her hand to the sky. Without a word, she wished for her hearing to return to her. She made a huge mistake.

The silence was broken. The suspended, violent sea waves were finally roaring, and it demanded their ears. They could hardly hear each other scream, and they were screaming loud.

A few people watched as Sammie moved quickly to keep the slainch going in circles, but she had just made it much more challenging. She could barely hear anything besides the crashing waves, and her attempt to turn the sound back off was void.

TJ came running across the street, with his hands over his ears. As he ran, he followed everyone's eyes upward to the sky, and he was startled at the progression of the waves. He swung his head up so fast, and leaned back so far, that his feet slipped from underneath him.

He just stayed there, willingly resting with his back against the asphalt. Surrendering, he let his brain absorb the closeness of the sea-green waves as he looked at them straight on. He was frozen in a daze, finally hearing the sound he'd been awaiting, with fearfulness.

Fowley and Kai helped him up and rushed off with him. The burnt slainch was still pursuing Sammie. She continued to give it the *run around* until they could figure out what to do.

By then, normal humans on the street who were spectating the fire had run off in all directions at the sight of the slainch. A young man ran away warning everyone in his path,

"Zombies. Zombies are coming," he yelled to anyone who would listen. The young man was clearly determined to go prepare for an apocalypse. TJ gave Fowley a bottle of water, and Fowley already knew what to do.

He poured some of the water into TJ's hands, TJ began to shape it into a spherical ball. Once it was the size of a baseball, he launched his water bomb at the undead guard that was dragging itself toward Sammie. He pegged the slainch with the aqua ball, and the undead guard became frozen like ice.

They weren't sure how long the freeze would last, but TJ knew that the frozen slainch wasn't going to defrost anytime soon. He looked like an ice sculpture, and he would have made a great exhibit for anyone holding a camera.

The freeze was to keep it tamed, but just for a short time. Nonetheless, the ice-coated slainch would be seen by the common eyes of the earth. That day, the frozen slainch was sure to spark a new story-time legend that would last for generations.

Fowley smiled at TJ and gave his approval of the trick. Fowley was the only one who knew how long TJ had been trying to manipulate water. To Fowley, it looked as if he had finally gotten the hang of it.

He had been practicing ever since the deaths of Kielo and Rose, when he had developed an acute case of aquaphobia. Over time, his practice with water naturally eased the threat. Luckily for him, the phobia was cured well before June 21, 2018.

Other substances and materials were easier for TJ to shape. But TJ's biggest challenge over the years was simple H_2O. It was the first successful aquatic manipulation that Fowley had ever seen TJ do. But the excitement for it was short-lived.

They were about to celebrate, but they looked up at the waves. Those waters were something that TJ could spend a few lifetimes trying to tame, to no avail. The unearthly waters weren't controllable from any earthly standpoint.

No one on land would ever possess the ability to counteract that kind of phenomenon. One might know how to direct rainfall or induce a huge wave, but the waves they were witnessing there at the Center were different from any of that.

Kim stood underneath the ferocious waves that were roaring low in the sky, completely unaware. She was worried about the whole group. She was still trying to understand what was happening, and what everyone was looking at in the first place.

She saw the firemen trying to put out the fire that was blazing through the top of the building. She saw the flames, but she could neither see nor hear the waters that consumed her mother and the others. In a quick breath, Kim boldly grabbed her mother's hand and held it when she saw Pearl's face painted up with fright.

In the ears of Pearl, and the rest of the group, the volume of all the chaos outside of the Center was relatively low. That included the firemen, the police, and all the sirens thereof. The emergency sirens and the panicky screams had all become minuscule noise compared to the almost deafening rushing waters that ruled the group's senses.

"What is it, mom? Why is everybody looking at the sky like that?" Pearl saw her lips moving, but could not hear a word of it over the overbearing rumble of the waters. She just stared at Kim with an inquisitive expression, as she really did want to hear her. But to Kim, she seemed disturbingly unresponsive.

Kim was afraid that her mother was not okay, and that she had no idea about how to help. *There's a lot more than a fire going on up there,* she thought to herself. She just sympathetically held her mother's hand as tightly as she could.

Nomad looked at Pearl, and he smiled to himself. He quickly pondered the universal reasoning behind her presence, thinking to himself. *Why is she the one to close the circle?* Pearl was the missing piece to an unknown puzzle, and Nomad recognized that.

But why? The thought persisted. He definitely had many questions for Pearl that he may never get around to finding the answer for. But his gut told him that he would indeed see her again.

He didn't feel a need to worry after any of them, and whether or not it was the last time they'd see each other. He just wasn't concerned with that.

Just as he had made a little bit of peace, Nomad was yanked from it. A gut-wrenching feeling overcame him, and he began to suffer a headache. He rubbed his temples, trying to alleviate some of his pain.

Beneath the lids, his eyes turned to bright emerald green. A few seconds later, he opened his natural, mismatching eyes. They were no longer emerald green, but he was in desperate need of a piece of paper to draw on.

He took a breath, then he walked over some yards to meet Pearl. He walked up and tried to verbally communicate,

"Please tell me you have a piece of paper I can draw on," he begged her. He had to play charades to get through, but his efforts were effective. Right away, Pearl thought of his colored pencil set and smiled.

She knew he had the pencils, so she knew he was probably looking for some paper when he appeared to be drawing in the air. She dug into the backpack, looking for something that Nomad could write on.

It was an insignificant journal entry by Ruby that she pulled out of the backpack for him. Seeing that he could use the blank side of the journal page, Nomad Artman began to draw. Without a full understanding of the event, he began drawing the sky just as he was seeing it right then.

Even in the struggle, Sammie wished well on everyone. Knowing that it had all been a wild chapter in a long story, she knew that she would see them all again. She had come to believe that the waters were the beginning of yet another journey in her existence, and she was no longer scared.

She was just ready to start the next chapter already. She looked over, staring at the frozen slainch, and she wondered if he would somehow go with them into the next realm. The thought was repulsive.

The reality was that she had no real answers. The group didn't have many answers at all. She just knew for sure that she wouldn't need all of the answers from her current chapter to help her get to the next one.

She may seek them, but she didn't need answers to move forward. She would forget them, and be reminded of them when it was time to remember. Sammie embodied the kind of peace only an odd gem could feel at such a time.

She might not be correct, but it was the very effective comfort that she had needed to embrace –from time to time. Because she needed something to keep her sane in the moment, she leaned on the belief that her business was simply unfinished. It was great enough for Sammie, and it was good enough for all of them.

All eyes from both sides of the parallel worlds were staring upward. Some bystanders were gaping at the outrageous fire that was burning through the Center's rooftop while the firefighters tried to tame it.

A new league to be was wholly captivated by the demanding, ill-tempered waves on standby to put the fire out. They blended in with the rest of the people, but they all knew that the fire was going to burn until the sky water broke its suspension.

They all kind of felt bad for the firefighters who were wearing themselves out for naught. There was no way to tell them that they should just let the roof burn. TJ then had a sudden thought, "Cup." He hollered out the name. Several people turned toward him to see why he was screaming so loudly.

TJ had forgotten that he could barely hear anything, but the water. He realized that his voice carried much louder than he had intended. He ran across the street, attempting to go in and find Detective Cup.

At the same time, Kai also remembered that Cup was possibly still searching the building for evidence, and he followed closely behind TJ. Unfortunately, they were met at the door.

Joy was running out with her hand over her mouth and nose, battling smoke inhalation. Kai pulled her some yards away from the exit, and checked on her.

"Are you okay?" he asked outright. TJ stood behind him, looking back with his eyes locked on Pearl. He was intrigued by the way she was staring at Joy from some yards away. Pearl started to walk over to get closer and see if it was truly Joy.

She confirmed that it was indeed the woman who had essentially helped her out of the Center the day before. She grew happy to see that Joy still kept the company of that same glowing, fuchsia butterfly. It was as if it had stayed with her, following her around the whole time.

"Get across the street, and stay away from this door. We have to go and find Michael Cup," Kai screamed at her. Joy's eyes were wide with fright, as she didn't understand why Kai was shouting at her. But she grabbed the front of his shirt and warned him,

"He didn't make it. None of the security guards did, from what I could see. I'm sorry, you can't go in," she yelled back at him. Kai and TJ couldn't hear her whatsoever. They were in a hurry to get to Detective Cup, so they just left her there. Still, she yelled after them.

"Oh god. What are you doing, Kai? Hey." Frenzied, she screamed out after them. Just as they were opening the door, three men came out. Two of them were carrying the third. TJ and Kai stepped back to let them through.

Kai could barely recognize Detective Cup, who was suffering gruesome fourth-degree burns all over his body. They got him to the street and laid him down as they called out for medics.

Kai already counted what he was seeing, as a failure at getting Cup out. Kai and TJ looked at each other with deep regret, then they hovered around Cup. As Michael was lying on the ground in horrible pain, Kai kneeled over him to speak,

"I am so sorry, I was coming to get you, I'm sorry," he shouted. The two men who came out with Cup looked at each other, confused about Kai's intensity.

"He can't hear you. An explosion took his hearing, and his ear," one of the men said to them, pointing to his own ear as he spoke. Although he was almost fully mute to their sense, they both looked down and saw that on the burnt side of Michael's face and head, his ear was gone. They looked over him in silence for a moment, but then Michael unexpectedly grabbed Kai's shirt.

He was nodding his head at him. He was struggling to form his words, but he managed to say them anyway. He uttered,

"I sent the videos of Canna to the police. All, all of it," he managed to say before becoming disgustingly wheezy. Kai, TJ, and the two men with them at Michael's side all looked at each other. The other two realized that neither Kai nor TJ could hear. So, one of them wrote Michael Cup's statement on a napkin from his pocket.

The young man from the H.R. department ended the statement with a question mark. He was totally unaware of the situation, and not sure if he'd heard Michael correctly.

When TJ read the napkin over Kai's shoulder, he was relieved. Kai was also glad, but they wanted Detective Cup to live. As they witnessed his suffering, they were saddened when they couldn't help.

Yards away from them, Nomad was growing frustrated at the image he was illustrating. His eyes moved up and down, between the water and his paper. Occasionally, he paused, upset that the drawing was not coming out correctly.

He sat with his legs folded, and the glowing box of colored pencils was next to him on the ground. He pushed through the obvious discouragement he was feeling. But every time he added a section, the sky changed again. He couldn't seem to keep up.

Each stroke of his pencil seemed to be moving in its own stubborn direction, and not as he intended. Nomad continued drawing anyway, even though he felt like he was messing up. He eventually gave in to the flow of the pencil, and not the imagery that he'd been trying to reproduce.

The sky exhibited several enormous waves that encompassed the rose-gold sun. In his drawing, there was a major difference that he couldn't seem to avoid. By the time he was done, Nomad was holding a picture of one huge sea-green wave curving itself around the rose-gold sun.

In his drawing, all the waves had conformed. It looked like they had all come together as one colossal wave, which was steering itself in one direction. A wave with no resistance in its path is what it was.

Yards from Nomad, the two men left Michael, TJ, and Kai. They went to flag down a medic themselves, as no one responded to their first call for help. They ran around the corner to an ambulance that had just parked and explained to the paramedics what was happening. Kai leaned over Cup, pleading,

"Will you hang in there for us? Please," he tried to coach Cup to fight through his pain. Cup somehow managed to form a slight smile, even though it hurt him severely to do so. The burn damage was gruesomely unimaginable, and it broke Kai's heart to witness it.

Pearl stood by Kim, and she grabbed the young girl's hand to offer what little comfort she had for her at the moment. She looked at Joy and the single butterfly that wouldn't leave her side just one more time before concluding that *everything was going to be fine*. She looked up, and the water had moved down even closer.

She looked over at Sammie who seemed to be all right, and not bothered by the crazy loud waters. It looked as though she had actually embraced its presence with some level of peace. But for Pearl, the volume of the rushing water became too overbearing for her to think.

They were all forced to focus on the single, gigantic wave that had formed while some of them were looking away. The smaller waves had all begun to flow as one, and they made one horrific body of water. Only two in the group had witnessed the formation of the new wave just moments before, Sammie and Nomad.

Sammie had been fixated on the water. She was shocked to see it still evolving. She finally looked away from it to keep an eye on the others. She looked over at Pearl and Kim.

They were standing side by side, braced for the worst. She looked around for her brothers. She spotted Kai and TJ, and she noticed the man who was lying under them. She wanted to know who he was, and what was happening.

She spun around, looking for Fowley. He was approaching Kai and TJ, to help them. She saw Ray standing alone, and he seemed to be very contemplative.

When she finally spotted Nomad, he was purely fascinated by the paper in his hand. Sammie wasn't aware that it was a drawing of the wave. She wondered, *what is he so mesmerized by over there?*

It sparked her curiosity, but she needed to help her siblings. She started to jog over to them, but she then halted herself when she remembered the zombie guard.

She trembled, mentally kicking herself for forgetting to keep an eye on him. "Oh shit," she muttered as she turned to see the frozen slainch again.

It was gone. It was no longer standing where TJ had frozen it. *Where did he go?* She thought to herself as she searched for it.

She was sorely afraid that she had lost him. The slainch had fully defrosted, and she lost her peace knowing that the mobile zombie wasn't in her sight. She stood there, pondering about where the slainch could be.

The few onlookers standing behind her began to call out to her, warning her. They screamed in fear for the temporarily deaf grandie. But Sammie couldn't hear them.

Only when she turned her head enough to sense their animated body language did she know that they were trying to get her attention. It was too late. As she turned around, the slainch tackled her to the ground and straddled over her.

Kim, Pearl, Leith, and Ray all rushed over and tried to pull the undead away from her. Sammie screamed and begged for her life. The slainch couldn't be budged. Neither Pearl nor Ray could move him.

No amount of super strength could separate a slainch from its maker after it has already clenched them. After a slainch has their maker in their grasp, the superhuman is made too weak to fight.

Sammie's gleaming amber irises ignited, while the slainch began to eat into her face and neck. Pearl and Ray saw Sammie's power slowly draining out of her eyes. Kim, and a couple of people in the distance, watched the zombie attack with unbelieving eyes.

"Help us. Please somebody help us," Pearl and Kim screamed out cries for help. People were running away, but nobody was running toward them. Ray ran over to get the other grandies.

Thirty seconds later, they all ran up and tried to snatch the slainch away from her. Even all of them together couldn't faze the zombie's grip, and no one knew why. No one knew what to do.

Kai spoke with exhaustion, and a golden gleam that passed over his irises, "Try the sand," he yelled at Pearl, pointing at her backpack. She grabbed out the sandwich bag with the sand and handed it to him.

But he wouldn't take it. He was covered in fire matter and didn't want to contaminate the sand in any way. He pointed his finger at Pearl yelling, "You do it." Pearl took a small amount of the purple sand onto her palm and kneeled down on the street, next to Sammie.

She blew the sand onto Sammie and the slainch. On contact, the undead guard let go of Sammie as he fell over onto the pavement, and he stayed there. Right after that, the world around them was once again motionless. Nothing below the sky wave moved.

Both the firefighters and the water spraying from their hoses were frozen in mid-action. The fire flames that were burning atop the Center stopped dancing. The people stopped in their tracks, everything did.

But the huge wave formation did not stop, the rolling sea-green wave was swirling itself in a big circle. Each of them knew the time was near. Pearl began to feel the pressure of saving Sammie, before it was too late.

Luckily, it didn't take long for the flesh in Sammie's face and neck to regenerate. Shocked, Pearl stood over her and witnessed the miraculous recovery. She knew the grandie was going to be okay.

"Whoa," she let out a huge sigh that eased her nerves. She looked over at the slainch, but the charred guard had already reverted back to his original, deceased state.

Fowley and TJ stood over her, awaiting her awakening and reveling in her recovery.

Purple sand can't bring back the dead, but it can prevent death? Pearl thought the possibility to herself as she realized how to rid a zombie.

Sammie was standing up a minute later, and her flesh had already completely healed. Without hesitation, she embraced Pearl with a huge hug and thanked her profusely.

"You've just saved my life. I owe you one," she pledged to Pearl. "Thank you," she spoke from a humble place.

"No. You don't owe me anything, Sammie," Pearl responded, glad to have her back to normal. It was then that she considered the fact about her. *Sammie is Lilli*, Pearl thought to herself, though it wasn't the right time to open that file.

The gems gave themselves a head start in getting away from the charred guard's dead body. As they began to walk away, Pearl remembered Kim. She turned to talk to the girl, but she was motionless.

"Kim, I forgot she's stuck," Pearl said to Sammie and Ray. They didn't want to be anywhere near the slainch.

Ray picked up the unmoving fourteen-year-old girl and carried her away from the guard's body.

Almost right away after Ray set her down, things started to move again. The abrupt change in energy when things resumed was something that Pearl knew she would never get used to. For the second time, the resumption scared the living daylights out of her.

People approaching that area stopped in their tracks when they saw the guard's dead body. A new commotion was stirred as a woman ran to fetch a medic.

She gradually became hysterical, as she tried to explain the burn victim she had just found to the paramedics. The guard was officially dead, for good.

There was no time left. There wasn't time to worry about it at all. They had no control over the matter, and Nomad seemed to have no control over his drawing.

Nomad was terribly agitated as he studied his picture. It didn't make any sense that the image could be so off. Something had hindered his hand from drawing what he saw, so he thought. He was hanging his head low, until he looked at the sky once more.

He looked up, and he wailed in disbelief. He slowly lifted his finished drawing up in the air against the sky, and the two were exactly identical. He exhaled in amazement because it appeared as though he'd actually nailed it.

Compelled to act, Nomad looked down at his watch and noted the date and time. It was 2:18 p.m. on June 21, 2018. Signing the date, time, and his name on the drawing seemed to be the seal that Nomad needed. A swift and heavy gust of wind forcefully blew the drawing out of his hand.

It flew upward as if the swirling wave was sucking the drawing in toward itself. Pearl saw it, and she knew it was over. She turned to Kim, who had been crying at some parts of the process, and said,

"Shh, don't worry. I will definitely remember you, eventually. I hope," she said as she smiled awkwardly at Kim. "Kim? I'm optimistic," she declared, as she marveled over the familiar name.

Kim stood there in her mother's embrace, choosing to look past the fact that her mother was loud and delusional. Pearl's chin rested atop Kim's thick, curly hair while she looked into the earsplitting wave, ready for it to do whatever it was meant to do. Leith watched the wave in fright.

The grandies, Nomad, Ray, and Pearl had become entranced, and they couldn't help but stare into the wave. Their hyperactive gleams blazed over their irises, and none of them could be moved. The last five seconds of the decatoure were completely soundless, and all things were again completely still.

The wave finally came crashing down and took them away. As they disappeared in the flood, the blazing fire at the Center was thoroughly extinguished, emitting a huge purple cloud of smoky steam that rose up from the Center's absent roof.

The people who were watching resumed motion and pointed at the purple cloud that seemed to form in the shape of a huge turtle. They all marveled at the odd omen.

While the water took the new gems away from there, it marked the extravagant ending to one existing storyline while initiating the beginning of another. Although the unknown story to come would be just as perplexing as the current, they all knew there was surely another story to come.

When the wave took them, Michael Cup marveled. Even in his painful and speechless state of being, he was completely amazed when he witnessed the grandies vanishing into thin air right in front of him. Unable to move his head, he had focused his left eye on the loud burst of steam.

When he saw it, he thought to himself, *Purple turtle?* The purple steam cloud entertained him in his last moment. After the steam dissipated, he saw that the furious flames were all extinguished.

Cup knew that he had just seen something that could not be registered by the average human eye. It was something about the way they had left Cup lying there on the pavement, surrounded by potential witnesses *who were too lost in the pandemonium to notice?* The thought shifted his mindset.

He then accepted that what he had just seen was a phenomenon that one normally couldn't observe, and still live. He then realized that he wasn't going to survive, that day. Detective Cup gave in to his magical mortality with a certain gladness about the job he had been led to do, within a mission so extraordinary.

He thought of his own children, and how much he would miss them. He mused over the two decades he had spent in his career, and he was content with his accomplishments. He thought fondly of Mari Hera and her contribution to finding the missing ones.

He was extremely happy to know that Canna was gone, and that Maquiller was going to be exposed. He had hoped that Maquiller would rot behind bars soon enough. Michael was feeling several different versions of peace, and he felt no need to fight.

It was the first time in his whole life that he didn't have to, or even want to. As a police officer, Cup had been shot three different times, hit by a car twice, and he had even been stabbed, multiple times. Cup was a tough man, and he was a survivor many times over.

Contrastingly, Cup was not always the good guy. In fact, Michael Cup had been no better than Ruby, Devan, or any other person in cohorts with power seekers. The only difference between him and the others is that Cup had both a change of heart, as well as a change of mind.

He was the only one who had expiated for what he had done, and he ran away from the path completely. He was supposed to have been the fifth snatcher during the Project H.E.A.D. recruitment, but he had turned his van around in mid transport to discreetly return the children to their neighborhoods.

He did immediately change his identity, and his life. From then on, he had begun to dedicate his time and money to investigating missing children.

Over time, it became an obsession. But Detective Cup was convinced that his obsession is what had been keeping him alive. He had eventually joined the police force with a specialty in missing persons, and things just fell into place as they did.

Whether he was appreciated, or hated, Cup never did let it change his humanitarian character toward the various communities he served. Cup had become a great person, considering who he once was. But he was also a tired man.

Oddly, the level of tiredness he felt in the moment surpassed the pain from the fourth-degree burns he suffered. He was confident that he had finally done enough.

He had found the missing children whom he had dedicated fifteen years of his career to, and he was willing with all his might that they may finally know their family's truth.

Cup had done all that he could possibly do, and he was glad enough about it to rest, at last. On June 21st, 2018 at 2:22 in the afternoon, Detective Michael Otis Cup left. He closed his eyes and took his last breath on earth, in Opal Firs.

*******End of Chapter*******

ODD GEMS Soaked by Suri R. Moon

Chapter 13

He's Gone

(June 22, 2018)

Fowley woke up abruptly, after sensing another presence in his room. "Who's there?" he called out. He blinked repeatedly as he sat up in his bed. There was a figure standing at his open bedroom doorway.

He trembled, as the dark figure slowly approached him. He reached over to his nightstand and turned his lamp on.

Once the light was cast, the tall, lanky, shadowy figure disappeared. Fowley was bewildered, and his heart was pounding. He regained his breath, then looked at the clock on his nightstand. It was 4:41 in the morning, and he had figured that he was just seeing things.

He debated whether he should wake up right then, or let his alarm do it at 5:30. It wasn't even a full extra hour to sleep, but he ultimately committed himself to enjoy every minute of it. He turned off the light.

As soon as he did, the shadowy figure became clearly visible, again. It hovered over his bedside.

Fowley hollered out, frantically. No longer moving, the dark figure dropped a piece of paper onto his bed.

The figure had been made visible by light that came from elsewhere in his condo. He had accidentally left the living room light on. The dark figure was made at the edge of the light in his living room where it met with the darkness in his bedroom.

As fear turned into curiosity. He boldly reached just past the dark figure to turn his lamp back on. When he did, the figure disappeared.

"What was that? What is that?" he asked himself as he eyeballed the paper, still a little dazed. He canceled his upcoming alarm because he was already becoming wide awake. He picked up the paper to read it.

It was a business card for a man from Virginia named Nate Cantelem. It included an email address, physical address, and two phone numbers.

Fowley had no idea who Nate Cantelem was, but he would soon find out. He first needed to call the others and tell them all about the startling escapade.

Thirty minutes later, Sammie, TJ, and Fowley met up in the back of Charles Dough's home. They bypassed the front door, as they normally would. Charles had a need for visitor discretion, even when it came to his family and friends.

They were chattering about the card that the tall, lanky, shadow figure had dropped off with Fowley. Sammie was studying the card when she asked him,

"You mean, you've never heard of this guy before?" She was just as stumped as he was.

"No. This never happens. None of it. Since when did this shit start happening? Shadows and what not?" Fowley asked. They all shrugged. Fowley grabbed the card from her, and he went up the five steps of Dough's back patio deck, behind TJ.

"Has anyone talked to Kai?" she asked them. They both shook their heads.

"He's not answering my calls. I accidentally left some info on Pearl in the stack of documents that we put in the car. He might be a little mad at me right now," Fowley divulged.

"Shit," TJ exclaimed. "It's not even six o'clock yet. Maybe he's still knocked out." Sammie shook her head as she shrugged,

"What can you do? But he still needs to answer," Sammie said with disappointment.

"Has anyone been watching the news?" They all looked at each other, assuming that at least one of them had turned on the news at some point. TJ responded,

"I'll pull it up on the phone after we finish here. Anyone talk to Pearl, or Nomad?" he asked, wondering if they were okay in light of everything. Fowley and Sammie shook their heads. "Leith, or Ray? And, where the hell did Goose go?" TJ probed, as he began to wonder.

"I'm curious about what the Center building looks like right now," Sammie shared with them. "I wonder if they've found the hidden floor. Room 321 was, um, messy," she added in a muddy tone.

Sammie was suddenly full of questions, and none of them had anything to do with suspended water, or oddly shaped clouds. None of them would know about those things, unless those forgotten things were re-learned.

None of them had knowledge of any first-realm happenings that had occurred. Yet, somehow, they still had plenty to talk about. To them, it was just another day in a horrible saga.

An online news-app notification chimed on her cell phone. Sammie searched her pockets for it as Fowley shook his head at her. She could never find her phone, quickly. But Sammie continued thinking out loud,

"We need to stop by Pearl's house, I think we should go when we leave here," she added as she unlocked her screen.

She started to read a news article she had just then received from her husband's sister on the phone. After reading the screen for thirty seconds or so, she paused in dismay.

She looked up at Fowley and TJ, who were waiting to hear what she was reading about. Her face was stress stricken, and she hazily stated,

"His body is gone," she spoke under her breath, clearly upset. TJ saw her lips move, but he couldn't hear her. Or, he just didn't want to. So, he probed for clarity.

"What did she say?" he asked Fowley, who also hadn't registered the statement. Sammie looked around the yard to ensure that no one else was near, then she stepped in a little closer to them to say,

"Al Canna's body is missing. It's not in the car," Fowley and TJ were taken aback.

"How is that even possible? Somebody came and moved his body?" TJ gathered. It made Fowley wonder,

"Who? Who moved the body?" he asked.

"Dammit. What if it was Goose?" Sammie shouted. Fowley found it hard to believe that Goose would turn the whole operation over just like that.

"I don't know about that," he confessed his doubt. But TJ made Sammie's point stronger when he highlighted one fact. He inquired to Fowley,

"But, where was Goose yesterday? Where is he right now? No one has seen him, so maybe he does know about it," he theorized.

"This is really happening right now, this is bullshit," TJ vented in his exhaustion as he turned to face the back door. Still speaking to them, he held,

"All right, we need those new IDs right now. Let's make this quick, then let's disappear." He knocked on the door.

There was no answer. After waiting for a reasonable time, he knocked again. He began wondering where Charles might be. As early as it was, he was sure that Charles wouldn't have gone far since their talk the day before.

He put his ear to the door, listening for movement. He quickly pulled his head away from the door, and his expression of horror frightened Sammie.

"What's wrong?" she whispered. TJ didn't respond.

He turned the knob to find that the door was unlocked. The house seemed quiet, but TJ walked briskly through it as if he knew exactly where he was heading. The two followed closely behind him, still wondering what he was doing.

"Are you crazy?" Sammie objected, though she stayed close.

"Yeah, what in the hell are you doing?" Fowley added his inquiry. TJ led them up the stairs to the second floor, and down the hallway that was being flooded by the bathroom door.

The three looked on at the water, and Sammie asked TJ, "You heard that? From the back door?" She was awkwardly impressed, and Fowley's jaw was dropped. He exclaimed to her, "Damn, I don't understand how he could've heard this from way out back."

Sammie said nothing. She shrugged at him, shaking her head. TJ didn't respond because he also didn't understand his own inclination to water, and he was focused.

The sink was closed with a drain plug, and cold running water had been overflowing from it for an extended period of time. TJ stretched one of the long sleeves of his shirt and used it to turn the running faucet off. Then he said,

"Careful not to touch anything," he said as he stepped back into the carpeted hallway. Every step they took was marshy, and their shoes sunk into the soggy fibers.

"I've seen enough movies to know that we're about to see another dead body, right now," Sammie warned the two.

"Don't be negative," Fowley griped as he began to check each room.

"Charles," TJ called out. "It's just us here," he said, hoping they weren't alarming anyone. "Are you here, man?" They moved the search party downstairs.

Once they were downstairs, nothing stood out in the open-space design that exposed almost every section on the floor. TJ stared at a closed door, hesitant to go open it. It was Dough's home office.

He swallowed a knot, then he walked toward it. Sammie and Fowley stayed behind him, and they all felt a sickening tension building up as they got closer to the door. TJ hesitated to turn the knob, and Fowley grew impatient.

He shoved TJ to the side exclaiming, "Just get it over with." Fowley turned the handle with a folded glove and cracked the door open. When it was ajar, they peeped inside and saw nothing out of the ordinary.

Fowley pushed the door to open it broadly, and there was someone sitting in Charles's office chair. A huge cloud of weed smoke rose in the air. They all sighed, relieved.

"Wow, you're starting very early these days, Charlie," TJ poked fun at him, laughing. They entered the office room, and Sammie shut the door behind them.

"Yeah, and you left your sink water running upstairs too," Fowley complained. "We thought something was wrong with you," he elaborated.

When the laughing and ranting died down, they looked at each other with revelation. They were making *all* of the noise. Charles had yet to say anything.

Just as they became quiet, the chair turned around. It was Beetie Smiles, a grandie who had stayed behind in Rhode Island. She was one of the other five blameless grandies, and Beetie had followed the footsteps of her adoptive father.

She was holding a tiny light-brown Yorkie puppy in her lap, and she nuzzled it with her hand. Fowley asked her without delay, "What are you doing here?" Beetie shook her head and said nothing. She just used her eyes to suggest they examine the closet next to Charles's office desk.

They approached the closet door slowly, as Beetie gently patted her burning joint on the desktop ashtray. She said to them,

"He didn't say he was expecting you today," she spoke with calm. TJ reached out to grab the handle, afraid of what he was about to find. Fowley swiftly shoved his hand down and away from the handle.

He stuffed a glove into TJ's palm. With the folded glove, TJ then opened the door. They instantaneously regretted beholding such a sickening sight.

Charles Dough was dead. His eyes were still open, barely. His dyed-green hair was soaked in his own blood. His intestines had poured out of his broken-open ribs, leaving the rest of his flaccid body disproportionately intact.

They all screamed. Fear and disgust quickly turned into anger and rage once they had digested the scene. "What did you do?" Sammie screamed as she spun around to confront Beetie, ready for a real fight.

Beetie was already gone, and a window was left open. Fowley ran to the opened window, trying to see which direction she went in.

"Oh my god. What did she do?" Sammie repeated, clearly disquieted. Fowley caught no sign of Beetie, as if she had vanished. He went to grab Sammie and TJ, so they could leave before getting trapped in another bad situation.

Sammie began to mellow out, as Fowley talked with her. Strangely, after Sammie was okay, Fowley noticed that TJ wasn't standing up. He was sitting on the floor with his back against the wall, and his frosty aqua eyes were gleaming, uninterrupted.

The two were scared for him. It was the first time that either of them had witnessed a hyperactive gleam, to their knowledge. Sammie and Fowley squatted down in front of him, and Sammie asked,

"What's the matter with him? What's happening to his eyes?" Sammie stared into his gleam, as she spoke.

"I don't know, I've never seen this before," Fowley replied. "Let's get him out of here," he told her. They wrapped TJ's arms around their necks and lifted him up. They took him far away from the scene where they had to leave behind their friend, and vital resource, Charles Dough.

****

~ 8:08 a.m. ~

When Pearl finally woke up, it was sudden. She'd heard some kind of movement just outside of her window, and it made her shudder out of her sleep.

As soon as she sat up, she caught an unclear glimpse of a man who swiftly ran past her bedroom window.

Her heart jumped at the element of surprise, and so did Pearl. She swiftly moved over to the window, hunched in her steps to stay low.

She widened her slightly open blinds to look out. There was no one there, from what she could see.

Just as she turned from the window, Kim walked into her bedroom. Kim's eyes were wide, and she seemed to have a lot to say. But she just said,

"You're awake," Kim's expression looked as if she had just witnessed childbirth for the first time. Pearl remembered her, but only from the day before. She saw that Kim was worried about something, but she was awkwardly relieved to see the girl who called her, "mama." She replied to Kim,

"Yeah, I am." She glanced at her bedroom window again. Then, she inquired, "Listen. You didn't happen to see anything strange this morning, did you? I think someone was just," she stopped herself, shaking her head.

Kim blankly looked at the window as Pearl shook off the inquiry, careful not to cause the girl to panic. But Kim still replied,

"No, nothing strange. But, I haven't been awake for very long. Maybe fifteen minutes," she guessed. Kim then hesitated a little, but she shifted her body language. Then, she expounded,

"Then again, there is something I need you to come see, mom." With her compact stun gun in hand, she motioned for Pearl to follow her into the living room, where the news was airing live on the TV.

Pearl followed Kim down the hall of her own home, which she was no longer familiar with. She marveled over the pictures of her and Kim together.

"So, I live here?" Pearl asked, eyeing her own home as if she were on some kind of a school field trip. Kim groaned when she realized that her mother wasn't any better than before, but she calmly responded,

"Yes. You do, mama," she said with sadness. "But, listen to what they're talking about," Pearl walked up to the TV monitor, and she stood right in front of it. She watched, and she listened to the anchorwoman's report,

"The Maquiller Research Center in Opal Firs has irreparable damage today after an uncontrollable fire that was set ablaze on its top floor, just yesterday. But, today federal officers have moved in on the Research Center's other locations, including its main headquarters in Rhode Island," she explained.

"Authorities have worked tirelessly to obtain the necessary warrants to search all four Center locations. A separate warrant to search the homes of the Center's head neuroscientist Leroi Maquiller and Opal Firs head practitioner, Al Canna, M.D. was also obtained, and that search is well underway, the reporter divulged.

"We must not forget the reports we've received here at KGEM about zombie sightings. Several people have come forward to support a statement that 'a zombie was attacking bystanders' just outside of the Center entrance," she stated, trying to keep her professional composure.

"You should know that police have not located any such beings. There were sixty-four injuries, and ten confirmed fatalities. There are six subjects who are missing, and seven missing employees, she listed.

"Furthermore, two mysteriously ghastly scenes have the public's full attention. Two separate bloodbath scenes with startling amounts of blood in plain view, both failed to offer any actual victim.

"The two gruesome scenes with no bodies to be found whatsoever have sparked new investigations of their own. It's been a weird week, she admitted live on the air.

"Authorities confirmed that the fire on Amethyst Drive, and the abandoned red car that was reported by a local landscaper yesterday afternoon, are indeed related. As we reported earlier, a sports sedan was found with an alarming amount of blood all over the back seat, and a similar ghastly scene was discovered in room 321 on a lower-level floor of the Center.

"Among the missing employees is the head of staff himself, Al Canna. With the ongoing searches in place, authorities believe that the Center's head doctor may be evading authorities. According to police, the abandoned red car in the reports belonged to Canna himself.

"They also found a substantial number of incriminating documents that suggest inhumane, and illegal, practices concerning some of the Center's head practitioners and their study subjects. More info to come later, she continued.

"In an effort to bring justice for all those involved, we are working hard to gather a better understanding of what the documents may imply. Those documents are being reviewed, right now as I speak. We will be keeping you updated with the story on those letters, a little later in the day," she announced as she began to wrap up the report.

When did that happen? Pearl screamed the words in her head. "Where is he? Where's the body?" she asked aloud.

Kim looked at her mom, shaking her head. She probed,

"Dr. Canna, right? I knew that's what they were talking about." She brought her mother up to speed on the reports. "They suspect foul play because of the amount of blood in the car, and the room. But they didn't have a body, so now they're testing samples of the blood from both scenes to see if it belongs to the same person -something like that, she informed Pearl.

"But, you saw the dead guy yourself, right?" Kim inquired, as she was trying to connect the dots as well.

"That's what I saw," Pearl said. She spoke faintly, contemplative about the situation. "Who moved the body?" she asked herself. Kim shook her head at her mother, still shocked in the revelation.

There was a loud knock at the door. Pearl and Kim looked at each other, in slight fright. They both were wondering who it could be.

Kim was about to go toward the door, but Pearl stopped her. She blocked Kim's pathway by extending her arm out, and she told her,

"I'll get it," she said quietly as she walked to the foyer. Before she opened the door, she asked, "Who is it?" A man's voice on the other side of the door answered her, saying,

"It's GP-EX. Global Postal? I have a special one-hour delivery for Pearl Lerell," he stated, in a professional tone. Pearl opened the door, and the GP-EX delivery man extended his arm to give Pearl a box as he spoke, "For Pearl Lerell? Signature is required, ma'am."

While Pearl answered the door, Kim remained watching the news. A breaking story changed the anchorman's topic. He reported,

"We've just received this. The body of a man that was discovered on Old Seaway Road early this morning has now been identified. The two girls who found the body said that 'he

appeared to be soaking wet, as if he had somehow drowned and washed up on the street,' he quoted.

"The body has been identified as Leith Nomea, a 41-year-old web developer, and local guitarist. There is no known next of kin, and police are asking for help, he announced.

"They are asking for those who knew Leith Nomea to please call their local station if they have any information about Leith's next of kin. We will stay updated with that info as well," he concluded.

By the time the reporter finished his segment, Kim's jaw had dropped. She immediately remembered Leith's story. She had to help him and his family, and she knew it.

She closed her eyes, contemplating on what she could do to help. Then, someone approached her from behind, and a hand in a black glove grabbed her over her mouth and muffled her scream.

Struggling with her aggressor, she was lifted off her feet and carried out of the glass patio door. It had been slid open while she was distracted by Leith's news story. In an instant, Kim was gone.

After signing for it, Pearl took the package from the delivery man, and she said, "Thank you." The young man went on his way as he said,

"My pleasure. Have yourself a good day," Pearl ripped the box open, anxious to see what it was. She turned around, facing the inside of her home while she pulled the object out of the protective cushion wrap.

It was the same amethyst wand that she was so mesmerized by at the bookstore. There was a little note put inside of the box with the wand.

It was from Pamelah at Emerald Books and Coffee. Pearl sighed because she thought it looked even more beautiful than the first time she had seen it.

The note read, *"Hi Pearl. I don't know why, but I feel like it belongs to you. Please have it. Sincerely, Pamelah."* Pearl was astounded, and she did feel connected to the wand.

She looked down at it in her palm with admiration as another man quietly walked up, and stood in the doorway. With her back to the door, she paid him no mind. Pearl was preoccupied with the wand.

Without looking back, she kicked the door shut as she gawked at her new possession. Inadvertently, she shut the door right in the man's face. Seconds later, there was another knock.

Startled, Pearl turned around exclaiming, "Who is it?" She then thought that maybe the GP-EX delivery man had forgotten something. She hopped back to the door and swung it open.

Expecting to see the GP-EX delivery man again, she was put off guard. The man who stood there now was emitting an eerie vibration, and his visage was grim.

The tall, older man didn't speak right away. He was wearing an expensive black suit, with a burgundy button-up shirt. His hair was dyed black, and something about his designer eyeglasses made him appear to be more psychotic than studious.

His eyes were hazel, but they were dark, nonetheless. Another man, in his twenties, stood behind him, and Pearl checked him out over the older man's shoulder. The tall man leaned in toward her and spoke,

"Where are my grandies?" he asked her calmly. Pearl was stuck, and she didn't know how to answer him. But she decided to start with the truth, and she replied,

"I don't know what that is, mister," she shook her head. But he didn't let up. He asked again, except a little bit slower,

"Where are my children, Pearl?" he spoke with great sternness in his deep voice. Pearl was becoming scared. But she repeated the truth,

"I don't know who your children are, sir. Who are you?" she exclaimed. But as soon as she asked, she was no longer puzzled. She was stunned to be presumably standing face to face with the notorious Leroi Maquiller. She took a few steps backward out of the foyer.

Maquiller turned and looked at the young man with barely a full nod of his head. The young man pulled something out of his pocket. Pearl saw that he was holding a palm full of shimmery silver sand. It was so bright and vibrant, to the point of illumination.

He held his palm up to his mouth, and the young man's eyes turned silver for a few seconds. Pearl saw it happen, and she gasped. *What is happening? This can't be real,* she thought to herself.

The young man took a deep breath, and he blew the silver sand off of his hand. The sand traveled into the house and throughout the open space.

It had grown into a small sandstorm that wrapped itself around Pearl in the shape of a tornado. She screamed for her dear life as she held her arms up, trying to cover her face.

The young man who accompanied Maquiller then stopped blowing his breath over the sand, and the tornado-shaped sand cluster returned to his hand. The spinning sand cloud reverted, and reduced itself back down to the sparkling silver handful in his palm, except with a hint of purple.

Both he and Maquiller were glad to see the sand's new color. The young man looked at Maquiller and announced, "I believe we've just found purple," he said with a lot of intrigue in his tone. Maquiller turned his face from him to look at Pearl, who had already run off to check on Kim.

"Kim, where are you?" she cried out as she ran back into the living room. When she entered the room, she saw that the sliding glass patio door had been left wide open. She ran over to it, standing in the doorway.

She was looking around the backyard, hoping to see her. "Kim," she screamed out for her again. She listened for a reply, and she heard a scream.

Without any hesitation, Pearl ran into the woods behind her house. Maquiller turned to the grandie whom he named Julius, and he commanded him, "Don't even go after her now," he ordered calmly, knowing Julius was capable. "The others will come here soon enough, trying to find her," he assured him.

Maquiller stood in front of the work desk in the living room. His eyes widened, and his jaw tightened, as he read each note that was stuck to the desk area.

Deep down, he was oddly impressed by some of the information that Mari Hera was able to obtain.

Even as he stood in her living room, his own home and businesses were being taken apart. He realized that he was in the home of a woman who could've single-handedly made that happen, based just on her sources alone. His hit list had grown by at least a dozen more names just then.

"Look what I found," Julius begged Leroi's attention. He was holding the black leather backpack in one hand, and the sandwich bag of purple sand in the other.

While Julius was eager to have possession of the Purple Opal sand, Maquiller was furious to learn that Pearl could produce it. The skill was wonderful, but his influence over its keeper was null. Pearl had made an impact on his grandies' behavior, so he thought, and that's really what made him angry.

Pearl found herself in the woods once again. Kim had stopped screaming, and was no longer guiding her direction. She slowed down, hoping that she would hear Kim again. But there was nothing.

There was no sign of her. Pearl held her temples, imagining that the worst had already happened to the girl whom she believed might be her daughter. "What happened to her?" she asked herself.

She ran farther down the trail, calling out for Kim, again. Out of breath, she checked over her shoulder for Julius. When she didn't see him, she checked the rest of her surroundings.

It was a mild summer morning, and the sunlight was leaking through the cracks of the trees. There was a tree that caught her attention. It was black, but it had a blue hue around its edges -from certain angles.

She continued circling, looking out for possibly injured Kim. She didn't see her, or anything that might suggest which direction Kim had traveled toward. About five minutes later, Pearl had completed a full circle and was back at the black-and-blue tree.

Something about it had changed. There was something on the ground at the tree's stump. A red backpack.

Pearl was not confused, she was sure that the backpack hadn't been there before, as the shade of rouge was too vivid to miss. Intrigued, Pearl walked toward it.

She stood over the red canvas backpack, noting that it was just like the one that the skater kid had the day before last. Unsure if she should pick it up, she searched around the trail again. Other than trees, there was no living thing in sight.

"So, where did you come from?" she queried the inanimate object with skepticism, still glancing over her shoulder for Julius. She looked down at it, wondering if it was going to explode if she touched it.

Her adrenaline had fully subsided, and her hand was beginning to hurt from being closed so tightly. At least, she was just then starting to feel it. She looked down, realizing that she was clenching something in her fist.

It was the amethyst wand. She had forgotten that she had it. It was all she had, and she couldn't go back for anything else.

She looked down the trail ahead, thinking about how it was just a matter of time before the police found the four corpses in the woods. There was also just a short time before the massacre in the empty office building would be exposed to the whole world. She knew that she needed to help Kim, and lay low -very low.

****

~ 8:45 a.m. ~

Nomad Artman awakened with his cheek on his drawing desk. The TV was still on, but the volume was turned down. He figured he had accidentally fallen asleep in his home office chair while watching the news.

There were sketches and drawings scattered all over his drawing station, as usual. But there was one drawing that just didn't fit in with the rest of them, and Nomad was not familiar with it -whatsoever.

The first thing Nomad saw once his eyes had cleared was the hand-drawn uncolored art piece that he had unaccountably completed at some point that morning. He stared at the pencil drawing on his desk with a blank face. He was waiting for something to click, and remind him where it came from.

He blankly studied the drawing, and he was silently disturbed. He was hazy as he gazed over the details of the artwork.

The drawing was done with regular pencil lead, and almost one hundred percent of the picture was shaded without the use of color. *That's not like me,* he thought to himself.

Whenever Nomad finished a piece, he had always signed his name, the date, and sometimes a piece title in the bottom right corner. He'd never signed an unfinished piece, but the seemingly partial work of art had his informal seal.

In the picture, only two objects were filled in with color, and those colors were significantly vibrant in contrast to the unfinished majority. The colorful objects were of no known significance to him, and the picture didn't make much sense.

One object was the amethyst wand that the woman in the picture held in her right hand. The other was a red backpack that rested up against the stump of a big dark tree.

In the drawing, a woman who resembled Pearl was standing on a trail in the forest, facing a black tree. *The Odd Tree* was the title that Nomad had absently chosen for the piece while unaware.

Slow to notice that he was still holding it, he dropped the purple pencil onto his work desk. He was struggling with the fact that he had illustrated a piece without knowing he was doing it. "This is nuts," he said, and he began to think that he might have been sleepwalking.

There was only one place to find information about *"sleepwalking,"* at least the way Nomad Artman defined it. He knew he would have to soon dig through his public storage unit for his *Odd Gems* comics, and he held to his belief that he may find what the Cr8 needed in them.

Meanwhile, he was stumped. He ran a hand through his hair, staggered.

How did I do this? When did I do it? He asked himself a long list of questions, only to frustrate himself further over his lack of any reasonable answer. He planned to call the Cr8 for Pearl's address.

He suddenly hopped up, running into his bathroom to brush his teeth. He washed his face in less than ten seconds. He ran into his room to swap shirts, trading one tee for the next.

He returned to the desk, folded up the drawing, and tucked it into his pocket. He dashed out the door, knowing exactly where to go first -to grab the comics. He figured he should then let Pearl be the first one to see what he had done, and hopefully make some good sense of it.

****

~ 3:30 p.m. / 6:30 p.m. (EST) ~

Kai was standing across the street from the yellow house holding his unfolded birth certificate. After traveling all morning and afternoon long, he was finally at Judy's home. It was much smaller than the home he grew up in, but it was much more welcoming.

Feeling jet lag, and hungry, Kai was finally at the place he had been in such a hurry to get to. He was in Alidamo, Rhode Island. He stood there long enough to wonder if he had only rushed to get there so that he could stand across the street, staring at the house like a creep.

When he detected movement, he saw a brunette woman working in a garden in the front yard. She seemed to be enjoying her craft from what he could see.

She stood up and tossed a handful of weeds into the wheel barrel that was parked next to her. Kai put the birth certificate away, as he wondered,

"Goodness gracious, is that my mother?" he asked himself, feeling nervous. He began to walk across the street toward her. As he approached her, he began to hear a tune that the woman in the yard was humming.

He recognized it, and he became ecstatic to finally know where he'd gotten the song from. He paused midway in the residential street, already convinced that he had just found a key person in his life. He was tense, and didn't know how to advance the situation.

He joined her in humming the tune, as he picked his steps back up. The woman, Judy, heard a second voice humming her song. She wasn't ready to turn around, so she just kept humming to confirm that the voice she heard was indeed carrying the same tune.

Standing six feet behind her, Kai hummed the tune with her -all the way to the last note. She wheezed, and snappily turned her body around to face him. He looked so different to her.

"Kid?" she asked him, hoping he'd answer. He asked with a scrunched grin,

"So, you and my father really did name me that?" But he laughed it off. With a smile, she nodded her head as she said,

"We had our reasons," she expounded, smiling like there was no doubt in her heart that the name was justified. "I knew you'd find us, she proclaimed.

"Would a hug be too much?" she asked, as her eyes filled with tears. Kai walked up to her, and he hugged his biological mother for the first time in twenty years.

"Not at all," he responded verbally delayed as he squeezed the short woman with brunette hair. "Is my father here, too?" he inquired. Judy's energy became lethargic, as her heart became heavy.

She quickly shifted her demeanor. She knew that Kai needed both her help and her honesty. She relaxed her tight facial expression some. "What name have you gone by?" she asked out of curiosity.

"Kai Paw, but I think Kid would be best for now," he stated, knowing he had new enemies to face somewhere out there. "In fact, this visit should be kinda short," he forewarned her.

She wondered what was happening, and if she could help. She pulled on his arm and walked him into the house. As she was opening the front door, she turned to him and said,

"Then we'd better make sure this visit counts, my Kid. There's a lot that you need to know about yourself, me, and your father," she said with a seriousness that Kai felt compelled to yield to. They entered the house, and as she was shutting the front door she said,

"I have a whole lot to tell you, and you're not going to believe me. So, I'll start with the things I think you may believe," she asserted. Her eyes gleamed with a gold-colored coating, and she showed Kai. He flinched when he saw it, exclaiming,

"How is that even possible? How did you do that?" he demanded to know, out of awe.

"You need to know one thing," Judy interjected, with her eyes returned to light brown. "We are at war. It's truly not your war, but you are now certainly fighting in it," she said, although he was still stunned by her eye trick. Kai replied,

"But, what was that? Why did your eyes change like that?" Kai asked in his new unknowing. Judy turned her chin at Kai, realizing that he wasn't familiar with the hyperactive gleam. She marveled,

"Good lord, this is interesting. You don't know anything about the hyperactive gleam? I'm sure you've witnessed it by now," she whispered as she studied him with intrigue. She continued, saying,

"You kids really do have everything you need to be all right, you'll see," she told him with confidence as she locked the door behind them. Near the kitchen, she opened a door to a staircase that went downstairs.

She led him into the basement of the home, and Judy turned the yellow incandescent lights on. They passed through the first area of the unfinished basement. They did the same at the next section, which was full of boxes and miscellaneous things.

After they had passed through the second section of the basement, they then stopped at a painting that was hanging on the wall. Kai was repulsed by it, and he wondered,

"Who painted that? A toddler?" he asked out of his harsh, but honest, reaction to the artwork. Judy nodded her head, but she looked somewhat embarrassed for him. After an extensive head nod with that expression on her face, Kai realized that he may have been the artist of the ugly painting.

"I painted that, didn't I?" he asked, mortified. She stopped nodding, then smirked at him. She used two hands to remove the canvas from the wall. Behind the painting, there was a built-in compartment with a plain metal plate covering it.

"You know, I can't believe you still remember that tune. That was certainly unexpected," she admitted as she gently laid the painting on top of a box. I had only hummed it to you, so you wouldn't even know the lyrics. That's so wonderful you remembered,"

"Trust me. I don't know how I remembered," he concurred, wondering how he was able to keep that one memory. Judy blurted her question,

"Who took you from us? Where have you been?" she asked as if she had been holding her questions in.

"Do you know Leroi Maquiller?" Kai asked her. Judy's nose flared. She then shouted,

"You mean the man who has been all over the news this morning? The neuroscientist?" she asked as she recalled all the news stories she'd seen that morning. "Haven't you seen the news?" she stacked her questions.

"No, I just wanted to see you, and my father. I need you to understand that I *am* the news, and I was there when the Center in Opal Firs, Washington caught fire yesterday. I was approached by Detective Michael Cup," he informed her. Judy sighed, and replied,

"Detective Cup found you? Oh, bless his heart. He's been working with us for a long, long time," she spoke fondly of the detective. "Well, where is he?" she probed. Kai dropped his head, as he told her,

"Sorry to have to tell you then, Detective Cup perished in the fire," Kai revealed, "He'd given me a copy of my birth certificate, just the day before."

Judy was saddened. She wished that the man were alive so that she could thank him for finding her son. She stood still in silence with her eyes closed for a moment, then she opened them.

The sudden hope in her eyes seemed awkwardly contingent upon her next question. "Do you still have the pink elephant?" she asked Kai the question with an anxious curiosity about her.

"What, you mean like a kid's stuffed animal or something?" he asked, clueless about her reference. She scrunched her face and said,

"Turn around, let me see the back of your neck," she ordered him, and she twirled her finger at him to make him spin. When he turned his back to her, she huffed in anger. She asked,

"What did they do to you? You had a birthmark. It was pinkish, and it was about an inch and a half wide. It was shaped just like an elephant. Someone removed it," she exclaimed.

"Here, I can show you," she suggested, and she temporarily abandoned the metal plate in the wall to grab a box with photos from the miscellaneous storage area. "I took pics of it often because it wasn't always shaped like an elephant, but by the time you were two," she spoke as she pulled out a photo album with pictures of Kai with her and her late husband.

Kai was amazed at all the pictures she'd taken. She confessed, "I know, I was very camera happy," she acknowledged as she flipped through the photo album. "See, there," she exclaimed as she stopped flipping, and she pointed to the pink elephant birthmark. Judy filled him in, saying,

"When you were really little, you'd sometimes come waddling into the room where he was, and your father would say, "There's a pink elephant in the room," she recalled, hoping to bring good humor. She paused, and sighed before she continued,

"Oh, I have boxes on boxes full of toys and blankets that belonged to you. Guess I was afraid that if I threw them away, then it was like I threw you away. So, it's all still here," she confided in him. She shook off her emotions and got back to the metal plate.

She stood in front of it as she explained, "I had always prayed you'd come here. Listen to me, Kid. I know that we don't have much time, she acknowledged.

"Only four hands could ever open this shelf. My two hands, and your two hands." She placed a hand on the metal plate, and it slid upward to open.

Inside there was just one thing. A book that was titled, *Odd Gems*. And it glowed gold around its edges. Kai was baffled.

"*Odd Gems*, the book? Wow, I've heard of the comic books, but not any textbook," he was completely amazed at its appearance. Judy stared at the precious book as she spoke to him, saying,

"It's everything that some people wish they could possess. It's the kind of knowledge that most people couldn't process. This textbook is what they were really after before the disappearances, I'm sure. We'd figured that it was because of what we are, that made them target us," she'd pieced together.

"They couldn't locate my textbook, so they targeted all of you kids. I'm so sorry," she testified to the kidnappings. "I know it was because of my DNA mutation," she clarified.

"And, now that you've told me that the guy from the news was the man behind it all, I need to know if he did anything to you.

"Did he take blood samples, or sample your DNA in other ways?" she asked with a serious visage. Kai was shocked,

"Where do I even begin?" he answered, knowing he had been pricked by a needle too many times to count. Judy's face expressed both horror and wonder, but she then purposely altered her demeanor to reflect a calmer attitude.

Kai knew that she was just trying to avoid getting him upset, so he went along with it, and asked, "Who do you mean by, 'all of you kids' when you say that?" he asked, thinking of all the other grandies.

"You're not alone out there, are you? There's more like you, right?" she probed. Kai answered,

"Yes, thirteen of us. Well, there were thirteen of us. Some are dead now, and the rest of us are scared," he admitted. Judy gasped before she interjected, telling him,

"Please don't tell me who has died. Not now. I'm not ready to know. I won't know what to tell their parents, and it could make things even worse if I know," she appealed with urgency, and she seemed to be entertaining multiple reasons for her request.

"Okay, I won't," Kai honored the request.

"Thank you," she replied as she shook her head, still sensing that something was not right about that number thirteen.

"No, how about eight? Thirteen isn't right," she asked with her brow raised.

"Well, eight of us definitely flock closer together, if that's what you mean?" he ignorantly explained to someone who knew much better than that. Judy sighed in slight skepticism before she stated,

"Well, you know that *'odd'* means strange, or weird. And, a *gem,* in this case, is exactly what you are. And, I know for a fact that there must never be more than eight gems of the odd kind alive at the same time. Gems? Sure. But, odd gems? No," she declared.

"Is this like the *Odd Gems* comic books?" he asked her, with anticipation. She turned her chin again, squinting her eyes a bit. She replied,

"What Odd Gems comic book?" she queried her long-lost son.

"There was an old comic book series with the title, I've heard of it from a friend," he informed her. Judy shook her head,

"I'd be careful with that one. Stick to the textbook from here on -for your own well-being, Kid," she advised him.

"Okay, I will. I don't even own any of the comics," he assured her, still clueless about the textbook's content.

"One day, that's not today, I will tell you more about me. But, it's about you and your friends right now."

"Well, they're more like siblings. Four brothers and three sisters," he boasted with a smile. Clearly, he was glad to have them in his life.

"Well, it's great to hear you weren't alone. That Leroi Maquiller is definitely going to get what he deserves," she declared as she stared ahead, in deep thought. She soon snapped out of it.

She flashed Kai an exhausted smile purely out of admiration as she began to inform him cautiously, "The book explains everything, but I can only hope that you are truly ready to know this much," she said.

"You do need to know it, nonetheless. But, it is sometimes dangerous knowledge to have. I hate to say it, but I know it killed your father," she confessed.

"My father died? What happened to him?" he asked. Kai was saddened by the news, and he wanted to know the story.

"If you're telling me correctly, then it would have been Maquiller's people," she answered.

"Oh my god," Kai said, as he thought to himself about the long history he had with Maquiller, and his research facility. Judy knew it was heavy for Kai to have to hear it, but she continued speaking,

"I was in an accident before I got pregnant with you. I was okay in a couple days' time, but they had insisted on running more tests to make sure my 'levels were good,' so they had said.

"Something in my blood tests must've thrown up red flags. I had begun to witness strangers who seemed to be following me, frequently," she recalled.

"And, I knew in my gut that they had figured out that I have the gem mutation. They recognized that I am a natural gem," she expounded.

"You're saying odd gems are real?" Kai asked, like a child listening to a bedtime story.

"Yes, as real as we will ever be. But, sometimes a person perishes for having too much knowledge, Kid. I tried to protect you from that," she educated him.

She sighed at the irony of her words, she then sustained, saying, "Your father died, but he did it to protect me. He was the only one who knew that I had one of the textbooks," she explained. Kai stopped her,

"Wait. *One* of the textbooks? There's more?" he asked.

"Of course, Kid," she explained. "One of you must possess silver?" she probed. Kai shook his head, no longer remembering its significance. She was surprised in his lack of knowledge.

"Well, another should control purple. Green, black, aquamarine, silver, and maybe even amber?" she could barely recall from the top of her head. "Anyway, I forget which color I'm missing, but there should be one more," she advised. Kai was stumped, still she continued,

"Well, I know you're gold because you are *my* seed. Anyway, there's a textbook, or a wand, somewhere out there for each gem color, and we have to keep them protected at all costs," she concluded.

Hereditarily, the Cr8 had always been superhuman beings. Leroi's process didn't make them odd gems. He had just activated the already unique, and formerly dormant, mutation in their DNA that did make them "odd."

He had caused them to become the very thing that their parents had once successfully kept them from becoming, burdened. Kai then understood that Maquiller's snatchers had abducted the children of those who had been hiding the *Odd Gems* text from his bloody hands.

Kai wondered after the woman whose eyes turned a gleaming gold, and he had gathered that she was a dangerous woman. He wondered if she was going to disclose how she did the trick with her eyes. Kai was amazed, and very ignorant about himself.

Judy could destroy anyone who set out to harm her, if need be. Judy could do it with her bare hands, or *whatever* she had in her hand at the time. But, possessing such capabilities, while living in this world, required perfect self-control.

Kai pulled up a chair. He sat down, and looked up at her with a thousand thoughts running through his mind. After a time of speechlessness, he vowed to her,

"Time is short for me and my siblings. Whatever you know, we're ready to learn."

Judy took the book off of the shelf, and she walked slowly toward him as the golden radiance beamed from its outer edges. "Now, you may take notes, but you may not take the book. It's *my* life that I must guard it with," she warned. Kai was enthralled by the vibrations he felt as she got closer to him with the book.

She brought it to him, and she gently placed the *golden gem's book* in the golden gem's hands. As soon as the skin of his palms touched the cover of the textbook, Kai blacked out.

(End of Odd Gems: Soaked)

About the Author:

Suri R. Moon was born in Virginia, and resides in Washington State. She has earned a B.A. in Journalism. She also enjoys writing non-fiction via articles, as she believes there is much to be learned from topic to topic. However, her favorite works are the ones guided by imagination. Or, in the case of *Odd Gems*, a very weird dream.

"Soaked" is first in Suri R. Moon's three-part series, *Odd Gems*. Moon's normal slasher aspect is lightened, as the story holds much psychological, and paranormal, weight. Moon's interest in horror guarantees an element or two of that genre in every tale. While being more inclined to write short stories, Moon wanted to introduce something fresh and outside of her norm. Hence, the *Odd Gems* Series.

Made in the USA
Middletown, DE
28 August 2022

72515204R00298